VOICE OF THE FIRE

ALAN MOORE

Top Shelf Productions

Voice of the Fire © 1996, 1997, 2021 Alan Moore.

Editor-in-Chief: Chris Staros.

Cover Design & Illustration: John Coulthart.

Published by Top Shelf Productions, an imprint of IDW Publishing, a division of Idea
and Design Works, LLC. Offices: Top Shelf Productions, c/o Idea & Design Works,
LLC, 2765 Truxtun Road, San Diego, CA 92106. Top Shelf Productions®, the Top Shelf
logo, Idea and Design Works®, and the IDW logo are registered trademarks of Idea and
Design Works, LLC. All Rights Reserved. With the exception of small excerpts of
artwork used for review purposes, none of the contents of this publication may be
reprinted without the permission of IDW Publishing. IDW Publishing does not read or
accept unsolicited submissions of ideas, stories, or artwork.

Originally published in Great Britain by Victor Gollancz in 1996.

Visit our online catalog at www.topshelfcomix.com.

ISBN 978-1-60309-507-5

Printed in Canada.

26 25 24 23 22   1 2 3 4 5

For Sylve and Ern
their fossil streets;
a coal-seam of the heart

CONTENTS

	page
Hob's Hog. 4000 BC	7
The Cremation Fields. 2500 BC	53
In the Drownings. Post AD 43	115
The Head of Diocletian. Post AD 290	125
November Saints. AD 1064	139
Limping to Jerusalem. Post AD 1100	155
Confessions of a Mask. AD 1607	177
Angel Language. AD 1618	193
Partners in Knitting. AD 1705	223
The Sun Looks Pale Upon the Wall. AD 1841	239
I Travel in Suspenders. AD 1931	253
Phipps' Fire Escape. AD 1995	277

HOB'S HOG

4000 BC

A-hind of hill, ways off to sun-set-down, is sky come like as fire, and walk I up in way of this, all hard of breath, where is grass colding on I's feet and wetting they.

There is not grass on high of hill. There is but dirt, all in a round, that hill is as like to a no-hair man, he's head. Stands I, and turn I's face to wind for sniff, and yet is no sniff come for far ways off. I's belly hurts, in middle of I. Belly-air come up in mouth, and lick of it is like to lick of no thing. Dry-up blood lump is come black on knee, and is with itch. Scratch I, where is yet more blood come.

In bove of I is many sky-beasts, big and grey. Slow is they move, as they is with no strong in they. May that they want for food, as I is want a-like. One of they is that empty in he's belly now, he's head it is come off and float a-way, and he is run more quick a-hind, as wants to catch of it. In low of sky is grass and woods go far ways off, where is I see an other hill, which after is there only little trees as grow world's edge a-bout.

Now looks I down, to grass in low of hill, and sees I pigs. Big pigs, and long, with one on other's back and shanking she, by look of they. It make a bone go up I's will to see. In of I's belly I is glean I may run down of hill to pigs, and hit a stone on one of they and make she not alive, for eat up all of she. That is I's gleaning. Now is doing of it.

From hill's-high there off dry dirt come I, through of cold grass and run down quick, that I is come on pigs when they is with no whiles for change to that I may not eat, as like to rat I one-whiles catch that change to little stones. Quick runs I down on pigs, that they is yet pigs while I catch with they. I's will is up, a bone in he, as shake this way and other in I's running, neath of belly. Quick runs I, but oh, I's feet fly up from wet of grass and falls I, oh, and falls I arse-ways down of hill.

Up quick, for catch of pigs. Fall make I slow, that they may come a-change, for I is sniff no pig at all. At this I's belly is with fright, for which runs I more quick, and looks to pigs as I is come more by of they, but oh. Oh, one, she is a-change, she's hind legs gone. All out-ways of she black face is turn in, and is now hole with darkness full. Runs I more quick that they is yet a bit of pig while I is catch with they, but oh, there is no move in they, and is they sniff with rot. They come more little pig as more tread is I make.

Now I is by they, and they is but logs of white-wood, lolling one on other. Eyes come wood-holes. Pig-foot come to branch-stub. Ah.

Set I on neath-more log, there flatting grass in low of hill, and make hot waters out I's face.

I's will is yet with bone. Rubs wet from eyes and stands I up off log to make of piss gainst she, as she may glean more good for keeping not as pig. Old will, now, bone go out of he, that he lie back down in he's skins, and I is like to this set back on log, where from I's piss-mark is grey water-smoke rise up.

Oh, many darks is come and go, and I is seeing not I's people, that is cast I off. They wants I not, and lone I sets up-on old log, and empty in I's belly.

Looks now bove of I. Sky, is he full with sky-beasts there, and all of one grey herd is they as runs from edge of world to edge of world. Dark is in little whiles come by, which-for I may see not I's long black spirit-shape, as follows in I's tread. All lone is I.

I's people is with not a want for I, and say as how I forage not yet eat of other's foragings. In of I's belly, I is hear I's mother making say, as while she is alive, how I is idle and not good that she is all whiles make to find of food for I. Says she, we's people like I not, and keep I with they while she is alive, which after no whiles more, and what does I say back to that, and like. And say I no thing back, and she is hit on head and legs of I, and make a noise. Ah, mother, there is not a bit of help for it. I is not with good gleanings in I's belly, like as others is.

Queer, now. One while I is with gleaning in of I, which after is no gleaning follow, where-by all is quiet in I. Yet other whiles I is with gleaning and an other is come by that is as like to it, which after many gleanings follow in a line, as with I's people walking neath of trees. They gleanings come that many and that quick as there is not a thing in tween of they. One gleaning comes an other, as with pigs and logs.

I glean of mother hit I's legs, yet now I is with glean as I is lie by she and all is good. Back of I's big head lie on dirt, where is a rub of grits and dusts. They prickle on I's head skin through I's babe-hair, no more as is on a berry. All in mouth of I is titty-milk as hang in strings bout of I's tongue, and there is not a thing in middle of I wants to run ways off, nor that is wanting of an other where.

I is in low of blanket-skins, by mother, warm in sniff of she, she's breath with sour-root in. She big, I little as one of they Urk-kine.

Now is other glean in of I, where-in is I come big, I's mother come more little now. We is in neath of trees. First bright is come and I is open eyes and see I's mother, set with back gainst of a white-wood tree. Is little bits of bright fall now there on she face through branches bove of we, and on she eyes, and move she not nor is she look from bright. Say I now, Mother, come a-rise, yet is she not make move, she's eyes full up with bits of bright. A fright is come in I.

Hold, Mother, say I now. Do not make queer with I. We's people is rise up and want for journey on. Rise, that we may not fall in hind of they. Rub now I's hand there on she leg for making quick of she. She is more cold as stones, and itchy-mites jump off she.

I is say more loud, rise up, and now take hold of she for pull and hit. There is no strong in hold of I, and down she fall. They bits of bright is move from out she eyes and hang on trees. She's head is lie in rain-hole, hair a-float.

I glean not how to help of she. Jump I on top she there and make to put I's will with-in of she, that he make she not cold, and make she for to move. She legs is hard, set one by other, knee on knee. There is not strong in I for open they, and is I's will stand not. I lie he soft gainst of she belly-hair, and push, and push. She's head in rain-hole move. She belly hair is cold, and sniff of she is other. Push and push.

A man is come now, of we's people, and he pulls I off from she. He says I is as shit and makes for hit of I, where is I little ways run off, in neath of trees. Now many people is they come a-bout I's mother. Pull they up she's head from rain-hole now and say, there is no warm in she, there is no breath in she, and like. Now is we's Gleaner-man come there, and by I's mother set, in feather belt that itch up arse of he, where is he all whiles scratch.

Say he, she is no more alive, and it is work as makes she come that way, by look. Say he, lie she to dirt, which after journeys we ways off.

Up says a rough-mouth woman now that if I's mother is no more alive, it is she's idle son as makes she like to this, that make she all whiles work and find for he. And many there is saying Aye, and she is right and like.

More loud say rough-mouth woman now how if I's mother is put down to dirt, it is not rough-mouth's hole for dig. Aye, is say man as pulls I off I's mother. Make boy dig she down to dirt, that he is work for she one while. Now Gleaner-man says Aye, and scratch at arse of he. Find boy, he say.

Make I to run. Ah, they is men, more long in leg as I, and I is that a-fright as runs at briar bush and falls there in. Out is they pull I, all a-scratch, for drag to feather-arse, as sets by mother. Down in wet she's head is lie. They bits of bright is crawl slow off from tree, cross grass and back in of she's eyes.

He scratch at arse and give I mother's axe-stone, that there is no strongness in I's hands for hold. Down is it fall, and Gleaner-man is hit I's face that blood come out from nose of I. Now take it up, say he, and dig she hole. That queer-sniff spirits is not come to she and in they's breath make sick of we. That rot-bird and rot-dog come not. That dirt is take dirt's due and is glean good of we, that he is not come hard low of we's feet. So Gleaner-man say now, and, licking nose-blood, digs I hard in dirt.

In low of grass is dirt cold, grey and soft as I may push all of one bit. Digs I a-bout of root and stone, and dig of I is slow. They sun-brights is come back on mother's face, off cheek of she and slow ways off in tween of grass and flowers. Lift I a stone, and neath of he is many worm. Dig I now sharp of mother's axe-stone tween of they, and of they many make more many yet. I blood I's fingers in I's digging. Blood on mother's stone, now. Blood in mother's hole.

I's people stand they bout of hole on one foot, now on other, wanting but that they is go ways off from here, that they is on with they's big round and walking edge of world a-bout from ice-while on to ice-while, finding prickle-rat, and pig, and chewing-root.

Sun walk high bove of we, with sky-beasts run a-fore of he, in fright that he may hot they all a-ways to no thing only sky. I dig, and Gleaner-man come vexed at slow of I and say hold now, and say as low of hole is good, and like, yet is I not but belly-low in hole. Say he, jump out and cast she down.

Out comes I, grey to knees with dirt, and look to she. No thing but white. No thing but bare, and quick is all go out from she. Take I one tread, at which an other follow. Grey like dirt she's hair. Make quick of it, say feather-arse, and come now, take she up, and like. Takes I an other tread, and this way come she by.

Stoop, for to take she's foot. She is more cold now, and no bright is on she. Lift I mother's legs, all white on top, and see that neath of she is dark, as full with blood. Pulls I, at which move she a little ways from rain-hole, dragging hair like water-grass in hind of she, and makes a fart. Like to this is we come by hole, I and I's mother. Cast she in, say feather-arse, and cover up of she.

I cast she in. There is not bigness in of hole for she. One leg stand up, in bove of edge, that I may not push down. I cover she, and grey I's hands in dirt, that dirt fall in she's eyes, in mouth, in belly-hole, and now she's face is go, and now she's arms and titties go, and now is she but one white foot stand out, which puts I dirt a-bout, and push it soft and grey to toes of she. Tread I down dirt, and feather-arse set mother's axe-stone by of hole, at other edge from where dirt rise bout of she's foot, like to a piss-mite's hill.

Say I, now she is put to dirt, and we may journey on for find of prickle-rat, and pig, and chewing-root. And now I's people look an other way, and is with quiet in they. And now at I, old feather-arse, he makes an eye. And shake he's head.

And sign for no.

All lone set I by mother's foot. I's people is not by I now, and far ways off is they, neath trees and cross of hill, and go, and come here back no more. Grey dirt on of I's hands and feet is dry, hard, as I may scratch off in little bits. Dirt that I push a-bout of mother's foot is like come hard, and bits fall off. I see she toes, and now in dirt as fall from they, I see a shape as like to no-toes. Mother.

Now an other gleaning is with I, in which a dark he come and I is set by mother's foot with not a where for journey to. All whiles is I with mother, and is not with want for go way from she now, and yet a hurt is in I's belly as say other like to this. Set I there whiles and glean not if to go nor keep here by.

Stand I, walk I ways off and back, now set, now more to stand and walk. Jump I on dirt, and hit I tree and tear of grass, and many things is say at mother's foot. Set I and move I not, and off in dark is noise of fire-tail dog in grass, and herd-dogs cross of hills. A-fright is I, and hurt in belly is come more. Make I a shit by tree, in tween of roots, and shit is like to water.

First bright come, and belly empty. Say I, foot, keep here by. I is go ways off for forage, after which come I here back with food for we. Now foot is quiet, as if for say that she is all whiles hearing like to this, yet no whiles sees it's doing. Walks I slow from she, and many trees off stop, and look I back, and there is foot. Lift arm of I and sign for all is good, and walk I on.

Trees come more little tween of they, and briar is come more. I follows path in bout of briar, where looks I back and sees not foot, but may I find she yet by sniffing shit of I, and I is not with fright. Walk on, through tree, and briar, and like.

As gleans I now, it is while I is come on blood-berries as first rain fall, hard like to many sky-beasts all a-piss. Quick stoop I neath of hole in berry-bush, and come there in, where is a briar-cave. There set I dry, and many of they blood-berries is eat. Out of I's cave is rain fall hard, yet in of he is quiet and little bright, and in I's belly is there good. Now rub I berry-blood off chin. Shut eyes, lick hand, and hear to rain.

Now is a while in which no gleanings come, which after all comes queer. I is no more in briar-cave. I is in neath of trees, and all is dark but where white-wood stands bright. How dark is come that quick I may not glean, nor how that is I come here by. All in a fright looks I a-bout, and see a shape as stands in tween of trees. It is I's mother. Lolls she with one hand to tree and looks to I. It is that good I tread more by of she, and seeing now she's leg, and one of they is come to bloody string, with not a thing low of she's turning-bone. Look I from stump to mother's face. She's look is vexed, as is she with no liking for I. Where is go I's foot, she say.

At this, makes I a fright-noise, big and loud as casts I up in sky and out from dark, and falls I back in briar-cave, where is yet light. All in a quick is this, that I may glean not way of it. Hear I not rain, as he is go ways off, and stands I up and stoop in neath of hole, and like to this come out from bush.

All wheres is wet, and many rain-hole is now set in dirt. Wet rise up sniff of dirt and grass, and sniff of they is good, and strong, and is not old.

I is sniff not I's shit. Rain, he is wet a-way I's shit and now I sniffs it not, I's shit that tree is where. That foot is where.

Runs I one way in bout of bush, now other, for that I may see where grass is flat, and like to this which path I come here by. Now see I as rain is fall hard, and all wheres flat down grass that path is not to find. In neath of trees runs I, and sniffs I no thing only grass. Now this way run, now that, by tree and briar, and make loud say to foot, and make loud say to mother. All a-bout, down ditch and up of rise with fur-grass thick on stones, and here falls I to dirt and glean not where of I.

No more is I see foot. Blood-berry bush is as like go, that I may find no more. In this way come I out there by, and walk in neath of many dark and bright, and all I's walking is without a where of they.

Walk I on open grass and little river is I jump. Through trees walk I, with dry-up skins of they all bout I's foot, and find a round of hut-fruit grow in grass, dark on they neath-edge as is good for eat. Whiles is go by and now find I no thing at all, and walk I on and find more no thing yet, and bright, and dark, and bright and dark.

Walk I where I may see not bove of grass, it is that high, and find I bird that is no more alive. I is that empty in I's belly as to eat of he, yet is he all with worm. Now sick is come out mouth of I, and make I shit down legs, and bright, and dark, and walk.

Through many ice-whiles now, I's people say, there is but little forage for to find, that whiles is hard for we as walk, and come they more hard yet. With ice-while after ice-while is there setting-people more, with many of we's walking-people come more little, that we is not many now. With one all lone as I, it is an empty belly and no help for it.

One whiles, I come on setting-people in I's walking, with they sharp-top huts of beast skin hung to branch, set high on hill. Huts is not many yet as finger on one hand of I. Sniffs I they's fire, and of they's fire-meats, which for in belly now I is with want.

Walks I up hill, and little ways up sees I man on top, and sees he I, with sick and blood on face, and shit on legs of I. Says he as how I look a-like with pig-arse, and what is I want of there, and like, and say of he is queer, with many sayings as I may not glean. An other man, more big in belly, come by now on top of hill, for look at I. In low of belly is he's will all little, more as like to babe's.

Now say I how I's mother is not more alive, and how I's people cast I out from they. Say I, I's wanting is but little food, that I is with a thing in belly of I.

Men look now one at an other, and now little-will, he stoop for take up casting-stick. Here is a thing say he, and say how is I like it in I's belly. Other man is take up stone, which cast he hard at I. Stone hit I's leg, and sharp of he tear skin low of I's knee, where is there blood. Make I a noise and is fall down, big hurt in leg of I. Man take he up an other stone, and say go off now, shit-arse, and say wants he not for sniff I more there by. Big belly man lift up he's stick, for cast at I.

Now stands I up, with hurt in leg, and make a queer-tread walk down hill, like to a sicking dog. In hind of I, man cast he's other stone, yet hit I not, with stone fall quiet to grass. Walks I quick as I may, and looks not back, and that is all of it, I's while with setting-kine.

On walk I slow, and dragging foot in hind of I. With come of dark is find I tree where titty-apples grow. They is yet hard, and little may I eat of they. Look I to hurt of leg and see as blood is dry with grey dirt and with shit, that blood come out no more, and that is good. Lie I by tree and shut of eyes that none may see I. Glean of no thing.

Bright come, more to walk. Leg is now good for step with, yet with prickling hurt in he. Walks on, and like, and now with high sun come I neath of white-woods on an open round, of grass all long and black, with trees a-bout. Stand out from grass is big old stone, as is with markings like to worms and net-mites scratch there on. Shut I now eyes, and come a-fright as I may not make breath.

I's people say as is no good in it, to make of markings. Markings take they shape from tree and dog and like, and make that they is tree, that they is dog, yet is they no thing only markings. If man look on they, he's gleanings is all come to queer, that he may glean not which is world and which is mark. I is hear say as many markings is that old as they is make by Urks and people of that kine in big ice-whiles. Now Urk-kine is no more in world, yet many say they little people is in low of hill, deep in they caves, and hide for catch of we a-bove. It is not good, to look on markings.

Shut of eye, takes I an other way in bout of open grass and stone. Falls I on root, and scratch of face in briar, yet opens up not eyes but now that stone is come far hind of I.

Out trees, and walking up of hill that is with sun like fire in hind, and see I pigs, and run now down and pigs is come to logs, and here now is I, set on they, with no more whiles for glean of.

Scratch I blood-lump on I's knee, and look I up in sky. A dark is come as I sit all a-glean, that I may not see sky-beasts now, yet may I see they's little eyes, bright there in high of dark. All cold is I, and lie in hind of log from wind. Shut eyes, that dark is come in I as she is come in world.

Now it is dark, and I is up on foot by logs and glean not how it is I come a-stand, with open eye. In little fright I is look bout, and now hear noise in hind of I, as one that walks in dry-up skin of trees. Turns I for see, and now I's fright is no more little.

There is shagfoal, stand in grass, not more as one man and an other long from I. She look at I, with eyes of she more bright as fire and big as like to tree stump. Make I piss down leg of I, that is come warm, now cold.

Bout of she shagfoal's feet in dark is little shapes a-move, and more not good for looking on is they as shagfoal. Black is they, and with no eyes at all, where glean I they is shagfoal-babes, all crawl and scratch in neath they mother. Tongues of they is long and white and like to worms, and wave they tongues all bout in fore of they, for lick and sniff of air. Make they no noise, and is I more with fright of they as she that stand in bove they.

Shagfoal look at I, and strong is go from I for move, that I is like to stone. Hard glean I now on shagfoals, that I's gleanings may make help for I. I's people say as shagfoals is they big and frighting dogs, which kine they is alive on world in big ice-while, as like to Urks, and now like Urk-kine is no more alive. Only they spirit-dogs walk now, up this world and down other, and where dirt come thin in tween of worlds, as with a cross-path and a river-bridge, shagfoal is come there by.

I glean, and there is not a help in all I's gleanings. There a-stand, more big as I, shagfoal look down with eyes like sun, as I may not make look away. In tween of big dark fore-foot belly crawl she babes, all lick and sniff, yet may I not look down from eyes of she, that come more big and yet more bright, as if all bout I is with fire. They come that bright I may not look, and shut now eyes, and may I see bright yet through eye-skins.

Now is all come queer.

I is no more a-stand, and is I down on dirt in hind of log, with bright of shagfoal see I yet through shut of eye. Now is I open they, slow, all a-fright.

Bright is no more from eye of shagfoal. Bright is bright of sun, that follow dark, and now look I and see as shagfoal is no more here bout, nor babes of she. Stands now, I's legs all wet with piss, and treads by where I see they spirit-beast. Stoop I for look. There is not foot-shape press in dirt, nor is an other sign of they.

I glean not what to make of it. I is not see of cross-path, nor of river-bridge, yet is they shagfoal come to I. Glean I on this, and now I's belly is make noise for say I is to walk more on, and find of food for he.

Walk I, and ways off turn, for looking back. See logs, and they is change to pigs now I is no more by of they. Top pig, he shank at she in neath, and look as he is with good whiles. Glean I if runs I back they is a-change, and come as logs for vex of I. Make I a spit, and turns, and walks I on.

Bove, through of tree-branch, is there sun, as follows I. Walk I through woods in way of other hill, as I is see from dirt-top rise where sees I pigs. From far-off, hill is look but little, yet is now come big, in by of he. Dirt neath I's tread is first rise slow, now more and more, and long whiles is I walk up hill by low of many tree. I's breath is hard, and leg of I is hurt as fire, and like to this come I by high of hill.

Here, thick of trees is stop, and come no more, which after is there only stump of they. Stump is that many, all ways off down hill, that sky is come more big where top of world is bare. Sets I now down on here this stump for look.

I is in bove of valley big, as go from here to world's edge. There by and there by is trees, yet more of stumps is they, as make a frighting open of it all. In valley low is river, with far off a bridge in cross of she by look, which is how shagfoal come these wheres a-bout. In tween of I and river is an other hill, more low, where is I look on that which I is no whiles see.

There is a making, there on hill, more big as I may glean. It is make all a-round, that is with rounds more little in, like to a dry worm lie on grass. They rounds is walls, and by of they is many dirt-hole dig, more low as hole I dig for mother and an other like. Glean I that dirt from out they holes is all push up for make of wall.

Round that is in of making more as others is with many beast there in, all white. Now wind is turn, and is I come in sniff of they, they's shit and like, and glean they is but aur-ox, yet is there more many of they as I's people sees from ice-while on to ice-while. There in middle of this in-more round is hut of wood, with ox all bout of it. Whiles is go by, and out from hut is come a man, all wrap in skins, for make a piss, which after is he go back in. May that he is set there in hut for keep of beasts.

Wall round of aur-ox is with many hole, for go of in and out, and holes is shut with stopping-woods, that beasts may journey not. In out-more round, in cross of wall from ox, is pigs. They is all many, and with fly-not birds as scratch a-bout by foot of they. I's belly make of noise, and is with hurt.

Cross wall from pigs is other round stand more out yet, but is with little where for move, in tween of it and pig-round. There is people walk a-bout, not many as they beasts, and stand for make of sayings, one at other, little there in low of I. Glean not I of a many people as may work a making like to this, it is that big.

A-cross and down of little hill, ways off from making, see I many sharp-top huts in by of river there. They is as many like to fingers put with toes of I, and many smokes is rise there by. Glean I that making is a work of setting-people, as for keep they beast, yet it is hard for glean that settings big like this is in of world.

It is not in I, how they come to work they's making by a river-bridge, where dirt in tween of worlds is thin, like as a babe may glean is make no good. Why, may it is that they glean not of shagfoal and they's like, for I is hear that setting-people may not glean more good as babes. I's people is with many a good saying for they setting-kine, as like to this. One say, how is he setting-man come by a mate, and other, he say back, why, he is wait for she to catch she horns in briar.

I is with hurt in leg, where other setting-men cast stone at I, and is not with a want for more of like. I see as I may walk by hill with making on, cross other side from sharp-top huts, and that way come by river-bridge that I may journey on.

Stands I, and walking down now hill, in tween of many stumps. They is all sharp at top, as valley she is like to mouth, and stump as like to tooth of she. I is not with a like in I for all this open, where they trees is put to axe. There is no good in it.

Come I now neath of little hill, which by hill come more big, and is I hear low noise of aur-ox now, from off on top he there. Hill is in way of sun-set-down from I, for which walks I an other way, as go to sun-rise-up. Dirt is come soft more now in low of valley, and as more low go I, more soft come he yet, that I may tread to knee of I, and walk is slow. They stump of trees is now not many as up hill, and is with rot in they, all black, mark with fur-grass and with snot-water full, where is there many stinger-mite.

Far hind of I is aur-ox make low say to mate. Pull foot out sucking-hole of wet and dirt, and walk I on. I may not see of river-bridge, as I is see from high, for is he come in hind of trees that stand all in a thick fore I, yet make I way for where I glean he set, a-cross of river.

Slow, through pipe-grass and through sucking-dirt. I's belly hurt. It is that empty all is queer with I, and I is all a-fright but that I's head float off, as like with sky-beast. Dirt suck on I's foot. Old dirt, he gleans I is not putting mother's foot to he and wants he's due, for there is one foot due he yet, and take he I's foot to make good for it. This gleaning puts I all to fright, that pulls I leg up high like to they walking-bird, and make I quick as may for trees, that set on dirt more dry.

By trees now. May I walk and suck not down in dirt, yet strong for walking is no more in I. They trees stand in a little thick, and glean I not a thing but go to bridge. Tread I in neath of trees, and loll with hand on they for stand, and fall more whiles as I is walk. I's leg is hurt with sick-fire. Falls I down. Stands up. Fall down. Stand up, and now is I through thick of trees, by other edge of they and looking out. I glean as I is come more good now, and is more with strong in I. Fall down.

I may not rise. Back flat to grass is I, head lolling gainst of tree root. Up in bove of I is no thing, only many branch of tree, where from all skins is fall. Look down, cross of I's belly, legs and feet and see I out from trees in way of river, where is noise of waters loud. No bridge see I. It is not where I glean. May it is that I find no way for bridge through thick of trees. Now shit-mites fly a-bout of blood-lump on I's knee, that is come black, and set they shit-mites on I's leg, where I is not with strong for hit they off.

Look I in way of river, where it is more good for look as leg of I. Tween river and here thick of trees see I a rise of dirt, with pipe-grass all about. On rise . . .

On rise is stand a thing all white, more high as one man and an other, where on top is hair fly out in wind, all black and long. It is a woman, all in white, yet is she frighting big, as is not in this world. Shut eyes, that she may see I not.

Now open eyes, but little, and I see she is not move. More open eye, for this is queer in look of it, and see that she is come a-change. She is not woman now.

Hut. She is hut, all hang a-bout with aur-ox skin and there by is she white. Sharp top is she, where from is hang a long of furs, all black that fly in wind. I glean not if is people in of hut, nor how it is they's hut set here all lone, ways off from other setting-kine and they's big making up on hill.

Look I now hard on hut, for is I not with other thing for looking on. All bout I, shit-mite make they little noise, which comes now more loud yet. Look I, and may see not a thing but grey, with shape of white where hut is stand, and now white is come grey, and grey come black, and black is he come no thing.

Noise. I's spit is with queer lick to he. Noise now of people, with one say at other. Big and old is one, from noise of he, and other little. Little one is say now aye, and say of thing I may hear not, and say of water. There is but a little bright through eye-skins of I now, and that is good.

Flowers, sniff I many flowers, as like it is not bare-while now, but flower-while. Up opens eyes, and sees I hut. One aur-ox skin that make of hut is now lift up, and out come one a-stoop, hair long and bright with belt of fur a-bout, and wrap in skins to knee. It is a girl, by look, and not more big as I. Sniff I, for sniff she's gill, and sniff I no thing only flowers, and see I flowers not, yet see I girl. I glean not if she is a flower that look as girl, nor girl that sniff as flower.

In tween she hands holds she a little shape, all grey. Walk she ways off from hut, and like ways off from I, down off from dirt rise and in way of river. Walks she tween of pipe-grass, yet is suck down not, as like she walks a path where dirt is dry. Now far ways is she, that I may not see she bove of grass, and sniff of flower is come more little now.

Now is thing move by hut, which look I back there to. White skin lift up, and out stoop now one that is big, bare but for belt and beast-fur wrap as cover will. It is a man. It is a frighting man.

He stand, for look here bout, yet look he not by I. He is more old a man as I is see, he's long hair white, with chin-hair like to this, and oh, he's face. He's face is mark with fire-black, where no thing only eyes of he is white. A little belt is bout he's head, up from where is come sticks with many sharp to they, that look he like to branch-horn ox. In of he's hands is one with flowers and other hand with sticks. Now look he more a-bout, and make a fart, and set he down in fore he's white-skin hut.

I may see not what he is do, but that he make a quickness of he's hands, and more whiles like to this. Smoke. Sniff I smoke. He is make fire, and now is put more sticks to it, for make more big. Take he up little stones as set there by and put they one on other, bout of fire, for make of fire-keep.

Back gainst of hut set he, and now take up a thing of wood and stone, not more long as I's hand, all flat and sharp. This hand-axe is he put to other stone there by, where scratch he fore and back, as if for make more sharp. Now lie I back, and hear to noise of this, and sun is come more low in sky.

In sniff of smoke now comes more sniff of flower, and lift I head for look to river. Girl is come here back with pipe-grass rise in neath she foot and wrap skins move all bout she knees. Tween of she hands is yet a little shape, all grey, and as she walks see I where little wet come out, and fall there on she arm. Glean I as she is hold a making like to little valley, that in river she make water-full. Slow walk she now up rise of dirt, where stick-head man is take she water for to set in bove of fire-keep.

Girl set by fire now on she knees, and is not move. Sun come more low, and as bright go from sky is bright of fire come more, that girl's black spirit-shape is long on hut in hind of she. More long yet spirit-shape of stick-head man, all black with dark sticks move like many worm on head. He take up flowers and cast they in of water, bove of fire, where from grey water-smoke is rise.

In bright of fire is see I now a low wall, make with dirt, as stand in back of hut. I is not hind-whiles look on this. May that it is for keep of beast, as like to big-more making up of hill, yet is I see but little of it, and glean not. Fire rise up high. Black spirit-shapes loll fore and back in cross of aur-ox skin.

A whiteness thick and soft like dust-ice is rise up from making bove of fire-keep, cross edge of he, where white is run down all for make of cat-noise now in fire. Wrap stick-head man a little fur bout of he's hands for make of they not hot. Take he from fire-keep making up, which is he now set down by he.

A little of thick whiteness out from making take he, one hand full and other like. Girl set she by on knees and is not move. Dark come in sky. Black spirits loll on hut. Now stick-head man put white on face of girl, yet move she not, and white is thick low of she eyes, and thick on mouth of she. In little bits it fall down on she titty-wrap.

Girl is not move. Black-face man now put hands all bout he there in dark, as if he look for find of thing, and now a big warm grey is come on I, and shut now eyes. Sniff smoke. Sniff flower and hear I more of scratching noise, as is scratch fore, and back, and fore.

And back.

Dark. Many little gleanings. Cold. Leg hurt with fire and oh. Oh, I. Dark. No thing. Leg hurt, oh. Oh Mother, I is not alive more ice-whiles as I's fingers. Dark. Dark, belly hurt and cold. Mother and I walk neath of trees, queer step and loll we one on other, for she is with but one leg, and with one leg a-like is I, we's stumps all bloody. Dark. Dark, cold, and no thing in I's belly. Flowers. Dark.

Bright. Sniff I . . . bright, through eye-skins. Sniff I flowers and . . . open. Open eyes and . . . flowers, and look I up at . . .

Look she down at I. Girl that is sniff of flower. Set she on knees by I, as lie with back to grass in thick of trees. Grey making is in tween she hands, as is she hold of river-water in. Long of she bright hair prickle on I's belly, and look we one at an other like to this, and glean I no thing for to say.

Eat this, she say, and say I no thing, only look. Now put she making to I's mouth, that wet from he comes warm on chin, on tongue, and it is milk, and milk she is that good. Eat I, and like whiles look at she, bove making's edge. How is it, now she say, as I is come here. Say of she is queer, with sayings come an other way a-bout, yet may I glean of what she say. I's mouth is full with milk, as I may no thing say to she, yet milk go down and is no more, and is she making take from mouth of I. How is it that I come by here, one more whiles is she say.

Make I of many sayings now, and all a-run. Say I of mother's foot, and of I's people go ways off. Say I of bird with rot-worm, and of setting-kine as is cast stone at I and tear I's leg. At this, girl make good mouth, and say that she is take rot from I's leg, and now I glean that leg hurt not, and is look down on he.

There is not blood-lump. Low of knee is shit and dirt all wet a-ways, and where I's leg is tear is tree-skin put, all soft and warm. Look I from leg to she and say, why, how is this now, and as like. Say she as she is find I here by with first bright, and see I's leg is hurt. She pull I more in thick of trees, for hide, and is she make good of I's leg whiles I glean not.

All this she say, and is she now with more that I may eat. Out from she wraps is take she dry-meat stick, which put she now in hand of I. Lift I up stick-meat to I's mouth, and chew of he is hard, yet lick is good. Say more of coming here, she say.

I is with dry-meat in I's mouth, that many of I's sayings is she make

I more whiles say, more good for glean. Say I of walk, and pigs as come to logs, and say I now of shagfoal. She is shake head fore and back, for sign that she is glean of they. Say I of how on valley is I come, and big hill-making see, which go I bout on other side and as like come here by.

Say she, is men on making see I, and say I back no, and say she this is good. How is this good, say I. Oh, say she now, they is rough men from river-setting come. If they is see I, they is like cast stone at I. Look I on leg, and glean a right in say of she.

Now look I by she, cross of pipe-grass where is hut on dirt rise stand, and river ways off, hind of hut. In river is there shapes a-move, which glean I is they flat-tail rat, all bout of making river-huts for they. How is it that she sniff of flowers, say I.

There is a way to it, she say, for take of flower's sniff and make there by a sniffing-water, as may put on skin and hair. Now look she off from I, in way of river. Say of she more little come.

Hob is want that she sniff as flowers, say she, that may he glean where is she go while he is see she not. Say she no more, and looks ways off. Now tear she up a little grass, and put it to she mouth. I is glean not of Hob, say I, and pull at dry-meat with I's tooth. Looks she not yet to I, but lift she hand and makes a finger now, in way of hut. That hut is Hob's, she say.

I is see Hob, say I. He is a black-face man with stick bout of he's head.

Turn she now all a-quick and look to I. How is it I see Hob, she say, and make of a queer eye. Back say I now of how I see she go for river-water, which is Hob set fire-keep by, where is a whiteness come. Say I of how I is see Hob put whiteness to she face, which after is I see no more.

Slow fall she, back to grass, with arm all loll in cross she eyes, for stop of bright. That white is sniffing water, say she, for to make she sniff as flower. Glean I that I is see how stick-head man is flower to water put, where is come white, as there is right in say of she.

Lie we on grass. In sky there bove of we is sky-beasts now run after sun, and not as other way a-bout. Catch they with he and eat he, where is sun no more and bright is go from sky. Grey is old river now, and pipe-grass like to this is grey. Say I, how is she finding food for I, and making good I's leg. Now set she up a little as she lie, loll on one arm and look to I. Bright hair is fall in eyes of she, where is she push it back.

She is all lone but Hob, say she. There is no one for she to say thing with, nor walk with in good whiles. Hob is he old, with dark in glean of he, where is he no more in good whiles, and is make little say. She is find milk for I and help for leg that I may say to she of many thing I see in world, and this way make good gleanings come in she while she is lone with Hob.

Soft is she face-skin, with but little scratch mark on she cheek. A mark-wing mite is fly all bout she hair, and set now mite on white fur belt, all wrap there bout she head. How is she come with Hob, say I, if he is dark, with no good whiles in he.

Make she a breath like soft wind now, and say as she is come from setting far ways off, and make to work for Hob. Hob is with big say bove of many setting people, for he is a . . .

Here make she a saying I glean not, and say now how is that, and say she back that it is like to Gleaner-man, yet with more queer to it.

Hob is no more with son to work for he at he's big makings, say she now, which is how she is make to come and work, and fire he's food, and find of wood and like. Make she a mouth that is not good with say of this. Come now low noise of aur-ox, high ways off, and pipe-grass bout of hut is grey and move as like to smoke in wind. Where is Hob now, say I.

Fore of first bright he is walk off, say she, for journey to they's setting-people down of river there. He is with many things for do, which after is he come back here.

At this a fright is come in I. Glean I of he's black face, he's sticks like horn of beast, and say how it is good I journey on, that he may find I not. Make I for stand now up, yet is there little strong in I.

Make girl a mouth more not good yet, and say she how I's leg is not with whiles for grow all strong, and how I is not with full belly yet, and she is right in this. Say she as I may hide where Hob is find I not, that only she is gleaning where of I. In hind of hut, she say, is there a making wall with dirt, for keep of pig. Hob is no more with pig, and making is stand empty for that I may hide there by. Glean I as this is making I is see by bright of fire.

There may I set, she say, while leg is come more good, and she is find of food for I. If Hob see as more food is go, why, she is say to he as food is take by rat.

This is a thing more queer as I may glean. Glean I now on it this way, and now that, yet is I glean it not a-right. How is this, say I now, that I is change to rat.

She make good mouth at this, and say I is not change to rat, but only is she saying this to Hob. I look to she. I is yet not with glean of that she say, and seeing this make she more good mouth yet. Why, say she now, is I not glean that one may say of thing while thing is not.

This is a gleaning as I no whiles hear, to say that thing is, which is not. It is more big a glean as I may hold in I all in one whiles. Look I at she with mouth of I hang open. Shake I's head, and sign for no.

She's good mouth come more wide at this, and say how it is good for she to find one like as I, that is all queer in glean and say of he. Come, say she now, as I is with not while for glean on this. Come cross of pipe-grass and by white-skin hut for hide in making there, she say.

Stand she, and taking of I's hand, and hand of she is little now, and warm. Come now, she say, and pull, and this way help I come a-stand. There is no strong in I, and put she arm bout of I's back, for help I walk. It is as like I walk low to I's face in flowers, for sniff of it.

Come we down slow off thick of trees, and now through pipe-grass walk, where is a path of dry tween wet and sucking-dirt. Path go by way of dirt-rise where is white-skin hut there stand, and now walk we up rise, she arm bout of I's back, and come by hut. We walks but little way, yet strong is go from I, legs all a-shake.

See from here by, hut is more big as I is glean, yet make for but one man and but one girl. For first whiles glean I how it is with Hob, with big say many people bove. Whiles is that good for he. May that whiles come as good for I. Girl pull she hand of I, and like to this is tread we bout of hut where come we pig-keep by.

Dirt walls of keep stand high to neck of I, with wall-hole shut by stopping-woods. Dirt low of pig-keep is all cover up with dry-grass, thick and warm, and where one wall is come by other, as in knee of they, is stand a little hut of branches make. I sniff but little pig here bout, for is I sniffing more of flower. Pull open she of stopping-woods, and in of pig-keep is we go.

Hob is not look here in, she say, now pig is here no more. Say she, if I is hide in dry-grass, she is go do work for Hob, which after come she back at dark with food for I. Put she now in I's hand an other dry-meat stick, for eat in tween of whiles, and now is open stopping-woods for go she out. I is with want that she may set more whiles with I. Forage I in I's gleaning for a thing as I may say at she and make she go a-ways more slow.

Say I, how is it she is say Hob is no more with son. Is son go off as pig go off, in keep of which is I now set.

At this is look she down, a dark come on she face. Hob's son is come no more here by, say she, and say as she is going now. Out wall-hole is she go, with shut of stopping-woods in hind she. Tread she bout of hut that I may look no more on she, yet sniff I she, like tree-flowers come a-fall.

Crawl I in little branch-hut now, and neath of dry-grass dig. Put dry-meat stick in mouth of I for chew, and in I's belly is there good. I's walk from thick of trees is make I come as with no strong, and is I lie now cheek to prickling grass, and suck on meat, and shut of eyes.

Now open they. All is come dark. A thing is in I's mouth. Why, it is stick-meat. End of he come soft like shit, and lick of meat thick on I's tongue. All prickling is I's cheek, and is I not glean where of I, yet glean I now of flower, and girl, of hut and pig-keep that stand by, and glean I's way of coming here.

There cross of pig-keep is stand white-skin hut, where by is I hear noise of man say many things, and noise of girl say back to he. Glean I that Hob is come here back from doings with they setting-kine.

Now all come quiet. Set I in dry-grass, making chew of meat, and whiles is go by like to this.

I is hear noise of stopping-woods move in they hole, and sniff I flowers, and why, it is that good. Girl is come pig-keep in, and cross to little hut where is I set. Make I to say of many things at she, yet is she put she's hand to mouth, and sign for make-not-noise. Now is she make quiet say, more like to noise as wind in pipe-grass make.

Say she, all little now, that she is come with food for I. Out wrap takes she now fire-meat and a chewing-thing I is not glean, all hard with out, yet soft with in of he. I takes it from she for to chew, and say I, how is this, all hard and soft.

Make she a cat-noise, as for say that I make more loud as I may. Say she that chewing-thing is make in fire with dusts from sun-grass take, as grow here by, with little waters put to they. Eat I, and it is good, and good is fire-meat now in mouth of I. Is ox, by lick of he. Set she on knees by I, and make not noise. Mouth empty now, and no thing may I glean for say at she but of Hob's son, and how he is no more here by.

Look she to I, and fly-rat make they's rounds through sky in bove of pig-keep there. Quiet whiles go by, and now with dark say she, ah, it is long in say of, and there is no good in it. Now is she quiet, as glean I she is say not more, yet is I not with right in this.

Say she that Hob is long whiles set by river here with son, where setting-people is come by that Hob may glean for they, and for they do of many thing. For all he's doings is they setting-people find of skins, and food, and many thing for Hob, as is he's due.

Of all that is for Hob to do, she say, one doing is more big as others is. Say she that there is many settings, cross of world from water to big water, and all settings is with stick-head man as like to Hob. They stick-head man is come all in one where, for glean and say one at an other, after which is they all say of a big doing, as they glean in tween of they. Set I an other way a-bout in grass, for hear of this is good.

Say she as stick-men's gleaning is for make of path, more big as path is yet, which path go from big water's edge, in way where warm wind come, and run to where of many trees, as cold wind come there by. Path is to run by way of hill and high-where, and by valley's edge.

This is a far more long as I may glean, for I is no whiles see big waters. Only is I hear of they. How is it good for make big path, say I to she, as set in dark and make of idle with she hair. Say she as path he is for come and go of many people, that men of one setting may to other setting journey, far ways off, and take of stones and hides with they, for which is they take back of other setting's wraps and makings as they due. In like to this, all settings come with things they is not hind-whiles glean, and good whiles come to all of they as set a-long this path.

Why, if path like to this is make, she say, more good whiles yet is come by setting here as come by settings other where, for here is river-bridge, where journey-men is with no other way for go, but that they come here by, and many good thing come here by with they.

Turn I now belly on, with dry-grass prickle on I's will. Lies I with arse and legs in little hut of branch, I's head and arms with out. Turn head, for look to sky, where sky-beasts is all shut they eyes, for no bright is I see. Glean I on path, as girl is say all bout, yet full of it I is not glean. Say I to girl, how is path make if not that many foot is tread there by. Yet how may people walk a-long this path if they is gleaning not of way.

Now say of she come queer, and hard for glean. Say she, there is a way that man may yet glean path if path he is that long as go all world a-bout, and way of it is this, she say. In all they many settings is they stick-head men make of a saying, queer and long, that say of many things. It say of setting where is stick-head man, and say of hills and ways where is he's setting by, that people come from other wheres may find a way to he. Now all of many sayings by they many stick-head men is set they in a line, for make of one long saying more big yet, that say of way from warm-wind water's edge to cold-wind where is many trees.

Why, how is this, say I. If saying is that long, a man may glean it not all in one while. Ah, she is saying now, that is where queerness come. They stick-head man make they's long saying in a way as man may hear it one while and now one while more, which after is he all whiles of they saying glean. The say of it is make with noises, one like to an other, that it is with say-shape as no other like, more good for keep in gleaning of.

Here is she say no more, yet is she set more up and take in breath to she. Now make she, soft, a noise that is with sayings in, yet is more good as I is hind-whiles hear but from they bird, and say of she is like to this.

Oh, how now may I find a mate, he journey-boy is say
Up valley edge, in dark of tree, by dirt-worm hill and all
And lie with she while is I not yet put to dirt all grey
Up valley edge, in dark of tree
By dirt-worm hill and river's knee

And there is lie they, he and she, in neath of grass and all.

It puts a cold in of I's belly but for hear of she. Now is she quiet, and say no more, but may I hear she's saying yet, for it make round and round like sick-wing bird here in of I. Up valley edge, in dark of tree . . .

Now come big noise from white-skin hut, in cross of pig-keep there, and it is Hob. Loud say he, where is girl, and is it girl makes noise in hind he's hut, and like to this. Girl jump she up and say, all low, as she is go ways off that Hob he is not come for find of she and find he I a-like. She make to walk through dry-grass off, she sniff of flower all bout she like to wrap. Hold, say I low, for fright that Hob may hear. Say I, she is not say of Hob's son, nor how is he go ways off, as I is want for glean.

Say of this thing is long, say she, more big as may be say all in one while. At first light Hob he is go off, where is she come here back that I is hearing more, and of Hob's son. Now stoop she down, and now is lick I's cheek.

Stand she, and turn, and she is go a-way quick like to branch-horn ox, through wall-hole, bout of pig-keep, off in dark and see no more. She flower-sniff is take by wind, as wind is want that no one sniff it, only he. In neath I's belly, will of I is with a bone, where by is dry-grass prickle sharp. She's spit come cold there on I's cheek.

Low sayings come from white-skin hut, as man to girl and girl say back to man, and now is quiet. Sniff of she flower is all go way, that sniff I more of pig that hind-whiles is here by. Sniff rot of tree with stump all come snot-water full, and sniff slow river, moving far ways off. Turn I now fore-side up, with back to dry-grass, looking up to sky. There is no thing in sky but dark.

Glean I on how it is that one may say of thing, yet thing is not, and more, on all a man may do with gleanings like to this, they is that big. Glean I on how a long queer saying may is like to path, as man may journey world all bout. Girl, she is put that many queer big gleanings in I's belly as there is no quiet in I. Turns I this way and that on dry-grass, and now is I want for make a piss.

I may not piss by white-skin hut, where Hob may sniff of I. Crawls I from making all of branch, for stand and cross of pig-keep. Out by hole in wall, and now is I tread quiet in fore of hut, where is a little hill of branch and briar, as girl and Hob is forage many fire-woods for to put here by. Go I now bout of stick hill, and by edge of dirt-rise is I come.

There in sky bove of I is sky-beasts all pull back, one from they other, and in hind of they is moon. By bright of she is I see pipe-grass stand all sharp and white, that may I see where grass is tread all flat, as like to path that girl go river by, for water find. Come I now down off rise, and come a dry path by where is not sucking-dirt that I may walk.

I's leg hurt not, as is come strong in he, and looks I down for see of it. Tree-skin as girl put low of knee is yet there by, hold to I's leg with dirt-and-water. This is good, and walks I on, and this way come where slow and dark of river move in tween of trees, where like go I. I is not glean as I may walk this far for piss, yet is it good for walk and not in pig-keep lie.

Come I now long of river and through trees, where now ways off in fore of I is I see river-bridge as I is see from valley edge. It is that big, all make with trees, and glean I now how stand there many stumps here by. Bridge is he lie on top of many river-huts, as flat-tail rat is make, and noise of river is come big in low of he. On other edge, in cross of river, see I path as go ways off, all bright in white of moon.

There is a want in I. There is a want for walk I cross of bridge, by moon-white path from valley go and come here back no more. I's mother is not make I for to set by huts with stick-head man and flower-sniff girl and queerness like to this. I is one of they walking-kine, and is for walking make. I is with want to rise up out this low, where is all wet and sniff with rot. A setting by of river, where is shagfoal walk. There is no good in it.

Yet glean I now of many things. If I is walk all lone and is not find of thing for eat, I is make belly-empty, like to whiles I is not yet come here by white-skin hut. I glean on girl, with ox-fur belt hold back she long bright hair, and sniff of flower all bout and many good things she is say. Glean I now on Hob's son, as I is with a want for hearing of, and look I now on bridge and white path cross of he, and hear to loud of river, falling there in dark.

Make I now piss in gainst of tree, and turn, and back ways go by river's edge, and pipe-grass through, up dirt-rise and all bout of white-skin hut, where come I pig-keep by. Crawl branch hut in and neath of dry-grass. Make now shut of eyes, that all of world is go from I.

Flowers. First bright. Girl is say, come, Hob is go he off to setting down of river. Come, set up, and like to this. She take I by I's rat-tail hair and make a little pull. Come now, she say, and say she is with food for I. Now open eyes, and sets I up.

Ah, it is good that I is not go cross of bridge by dark, and see of she no more. Set she by I with bright of sun on she, she's skin more white as aur-ox belt that wrap all bout she hair. In one hand is she hold of chewing-thing that is of sun-grass make, while other hand of she it is with titty-apples in.

They titty-apple is that soft and good for eat, with wet of they run down I's chin. Make she good mouth at this, and say as she is find of other thing for I, yet not as I may eat. Now looks I, and by she is I see wraps. Is leg-wraps, belly-wraps and wraps of dry-skin make for foot. How is she come by wraps, say I, and in I's saying spit of titty-apple that is fall on hand of she, a little bit. Now lift she hand, and make a tongue and licks it off, and all this while is look at I. A prickling is come in I's will.

Wraps is they wraps of Hob's son, she is say, and say no more to this, and look by river, bright in sun, where is she make all little of she eyes. Say I, how is it son of Hob go off and take he not he's wraps.

Look she to river more. Say she, he is not want of wraps where he is go.

Now stand she up, and turn to I. Say she, come, put they wraps on that we may walk by of river's edge. Stand I, and make as she is say, where put I wraps bout of I's legs, I's belly and I's back, and now on foot of I, and rub of wraps is queer.

From pig-keep go we by of hut, where hill of fire-branch is in fore, as stand more big as I. Off rise and pipe-grass through by river's edge, where is I hind-whiles come for piss. There walk we water by. Say I that she is say to I of stick-head men and of they big path-saying, yet is she not say how Hob's son is all one with this, nor how is he go off.

Say she, if I is set with she in neath of trees by river's edge, there is she saying all to I. And now is we find tree, and set we here on grass, she with she foot hang down and toes of she in water, where is make bright rings.

She is now say of stick-head men, and of they saying-path. Path is a making more queer and more big as making hind-whiles is in world, more big as stand-round-stones that people say is make there on big open, far in way of sun-rise-up. Say she, for make this saying-path they stick-head men is want a strongness and a queer of glean that is not hind-whiles in of they. A strongness that is come from other world, in neath of dirt, where is they spirit walk.

Hob and he's stick-head kine is take this strong from spirit world, say girl, and spirits is as like take of they due from stick-head men. Now is she quiet. How is they spirit taking of they due, say I.

Say she how spirits take that which they stick-head men is more with want of as an other thing in world, as may that is. This thing is put to axe by stick-head men and make no more alive, that it is take by spirits down to other world. As due for this is spirits put a strongness in of stick-head man, and queerness in he gleanings that he may make saying-path a-right.

And how with Hob, say I, and with this thing he want more as an other thing in world, which spirits make he put to axe. Take she now foot from river, white and cold, with little eyes of wet stand out there on. It is he's son, she say. It is he's son.

A-cross of water rise up many flat-mouth birds, all in they noise, and fly ways off in bove of wet and water, way of valley edge. A tree-skin worm fall on I's foot, one of they fur-back kine. I takes he up in tween I's finger now, and pull, that he is come in bits, where make I idle with he long whiles like to this, and lick he from I's hand. Girl turn from river now, for look at I. Is walking-people put they sons to axe, she say.

No, say I. Nor is beast nor bird, but if they is with sick in glean of they. I is not hind-whiles hear a thing as frighting nor as queer to this. Why, put of babes to axe is more not good as that I is not glean. More say I like to this, and say, is Hob not with a like for son, that he may do of this with he.

That is not it, say girl. That is not it at all. Hob is he more with liking and with want in he for son as is in man for mate. As is in fire for dry-wood tree. He is not want to make he son no more alive.

Say I, why, Hob may say he no to this, and say he is not put he son to axe, for he is with big say bove many people.

People want of path, say she. People is want of skins and meats, and of good whiles as path make come here by. They setting-kine is long whiles find for Hob he food and wraps and like to this, and now is want he make of path for they, as is they due. If he is not put son to axe and make a-right of path, he is with big say bove of they no more. If he is not do right by they, why, they is like for make he and he son go off from here. Cast out, and make to forage, where may is they come no more alive.

How is Hob's son glean on this thing, say I. Move she now neck of she and arms, for sign that glean she not. Say she if Hob's son glean this way nor that, yet is no good in it for he. If he is run ways off from setting is he not with thing for eat, that he is not long whiles alive. If runs he not is Hob put he to axe. Hob's son he may do one thing, and may do an other, yet not one nor other is make good for he.

Put up she arms, for make long of she back. She little titties push a shape of they gainst of she belly-wrap. Now is she stand and saying to I, come, that we may walk more far long river's edge. Out put she hand, for pull I up to stand, and hand is wet with hot of she.

Walk we by river now, and no thing say, but tread low to we knees through hill of dry-up tree-skin, and with tread we cast they all bout. Come we through neath of trees, where see we bridge ways off. Bridge is more big by bright of sun as I is see by dark, and say I like of this to girl. Stop she, and turn for look to I.

Say she, how is I see of bridge by dark, and say I back how I is come here by for piss, which after go I back to pig-keep there. She looked at I, as if she glean on this, and now is make good mouth. Come, is she say, that we may stand on river-bridge.

Walk we all long of path, and river-bridge is come more big as come we more he by, that I glean not how many of they trees is fall for make of he. At here-by edge of bridge is black old woods rise up to he, for cross of bridge is make more high as river's edge. Girl now is lie she belly down on rise of bridge, nose push to black woods for to look in tween of they. She wraps is make good shape bout of she arse that glean is come in I for lift they up and look on she, but ah, there is no doing of it. Come, say she, for look here by, in tween of logs.

Lie I now by she, down on bridge, and look where she is say, through of black woods to dark in neath of they. For little whiles is I see no thing, only dark, yet now I's seeing come more good, and see I shape all thin and white, as lie dark in, and moving not. I may not glean if it is a man nor woman, yet see I as they come all to bone and dry-up skin, and no thing more. They is with hole-through wraps all bout, yet is no hair on they bone head, as is it tear from they. They hole-eyes is make as for look on we, and set in low of head bone is they teeth all make good mouth at I.

Is woman, girl is say. Woman in put alive here by, that may she spirit keep by bridge and make bridge good, that fall he not, and that he is not come a-fire. Now girl is stand and say no more, and walk up rise and on of bridge, where follows I a-hind. As she is walk is she make now an other saying, queer and like to bird, yet not as saying of they valley edge and dark of trees and like. This saying now is with more quick in say of it, and hear of it is good, and like to this . . .

Lie she there in neath of wood,
and bone is she, and bone is she
Lie she there, I's woman good,
and by of river go we.

Walk we cross of bridge, and tread from round of log to round of log, all slow, that we is falling not with snot-grass as is grow there on, and come we middle by, where is one edge not more far off as other. Now old wind is strong, and river make that loud in neath of we as one may not hear other say. Girl say a thing as I hear not, and say I, how is that, and, say more loud, and like to this. Now bove of river noise is she say, look now. Look to other edge, and with she's finger make a sign at where she is with want I look.

There cross of water see I now of many setting-men, at find of beast. They is with casting-stick in hand, and drag of branch-horn ox in hind of they. I is a-fright, for is I glean as girl is say they may cast stone at I, they is that rough. This say I to she now, and make for run off bridge, but say she hold. Say she as they is glean of she, and is not hurt of I while is she by. Look, say she now, they men is make of sign at we.

Make sign at they, say she, and sign for all is good.

They far off men is lift they hand, where lifts I hand as like. Girl is not move. Say she as it is good, that see they I with she. How is this good, say I, and say she back as men is seeing now that she is glean of I, that is they no more cast at I of stones. Way off on other edge is men walk bout of trees, where is we no more see of they. Come now, say girl, that we may go there back by white-skin hut while Hob is not yet come from setting river down, where is he go.

Slow is we tread on wet woods, walking back. Down rise from bridge we come, and is I glean now on bone woman lie in dark low of we's foot, on all that she is glean, in of she thin and empty head.

Long path, through trees at river's edge, a-cross of pipe-grass and as like to this is come we pig-keep by. Sun is in high of sky, from which, now-after, is he only fall. Black spirit-shape of I is come all little and a-fright, that he is hide in neath I's foot.

A-loll on dirt wall, girl say is she now go and make work for Hob. Scratch at she neck, as if with itch, and say how she may come not pig-keep by at dark, for Hob is want of she with many things. She is come see I while all dark is go and bright is come here back. Say she, I is with chewing-thing of sun-grass make, that I is not come belly-empty tween of whiles.

Say I back aye, and, she is right, and like to this, yet is I with a dark in say of I, that she may glean I is with liking not that she is long whiles go from I. Ah. It is as she is hear not of dark, there in I's say. Turn she from I for walk in way of wall-hole and of stopping-woods, where is she stop and turn here back. Make she a good mouth now at I.

Say she that wraps is good on I. Say she as wraps is make of I more good for look on. Now through wall-hole, where by shut she stopping-woods, and go ways off is she, no more for see, but as I is make shut of eyes, where may I yet she good mouth see, in glean of I.

In low of dry-grass lie I branch-hut by, and takes now leg-wraps off from I, for look to knee. Tree-skin as girl is put on leg is come more dry, and dirt-and-water hold of he to leg is come dry like to this. Take tree-skin tween of finger now, and lift of he way up from leg, which low of is there soft skin all a-grow, and tear in leg of I is all but go.

Now puts I wraps back there in bout of leg. Say she as I is look more good in they, and glean I there is right in this, yet rub of wraps is queer to I. From fore of white-skin hut is I hear girl go this way and now that, for do of things I may not see, yet sniff of flower is all bout. Hand in of wrap now scratch I soft skin growing low of knee, as makes to itch. Chews I on sun-grass thing, while many gleanings come to I.

Glean I as leg is no more now with hurt, and how as I may journey on. If I is set more long whiles pig-keep by, why, Hob, he may not help but find I, and it is more good here from go I ways off. Yet now I glean as I may forage little if all lone I walk, and like to this come belly-empty. Glean I now on girl, on little of she feet, and thin of turning-bones and leg low of she wrap. Glean I on hair of she, all bright and wrap a-bout with aur-ox white. I is with want in I for pull this wrap from she that bright is all fall down bout of she arms, and glean I now that for to go here off is see of she no more.

In of I's belly is I's gleanings all come vexed, and fall they now to hit and bite one at an other, like to cats. There is no quiet in I. Hear I a noise in by of hut, as of man say to girl, and glean as Hob is come here back. There is no like in I for Hob, and all I's gleanings glean a-like in this, that they come quiet in of I's belly, where by is they lie and all glean dark on Hob.

Chew I on soft and grey of sun-grass thing and sun come low in sky. I's spirit-shape, no more a-fright, is loll he's long black head in cross of keep, and put he's ear by aur-ox skin, as if for hear more good of sayings there.

Cross river, see I sun is hurt as come he by of sun-set-down. Glean I they sky-beasts is all catch and tear at he, for blood of he is fall on they, that all of sky is come as blood. Hard is I hear, for hear hurt-noise of sun, yet is he more far off as may make noise.

I is not long whiles move, that hurt is come in bones of I, which for crawls I from branch-hut now to stand. Fore-ways and back walk I, for make more good in leg, and look now out, cross wall of pig-keep and cross world as like.

Ways off is see I Hob, and stoop in hind of wall that he may see I not. Put eyes in bove of wall-top now for make of little look. He is cross pipe-grass by to thick of trees, in other way from river. Edge of world in hind of he is all as come to smoke and blood. Hob stands, with bright of it to back of he that he is come all black, like to a spirit-shape. Sticks bout he head is like to thin black hands, for scratch at sky and catch of all he's gleanings, that they is not fly ways off.

Stoops he, now stands for walk, and now comes more to stoop. I glean as he is forage wood, for is I see now branches neath he's arm. May that they is for hill of branch as stand in fore of aur-ox hut. Walks he as like to one that is with doing to he's gleanings and with gleaning to he's doings, which is saying as I's mother all whiles make, yet not of I. Stoops he now there, now other where, and many of they branch in neath he's arm is come more many yet.

Turns he now bout, that one edge of he's frighting face is all with bright, and sun blood wet on branch-horns of he. Glean I Hob is not of dirt, as is I and I's walking-people, born of dirt and live by dirt and put to dirt and all. He is of fire. Fire's black bout of he's eyes. Fire's blood on of he's horns.

Makes he for come here back by through of pipe-grass, which for stoops I now more low in hind of wall, and crawl on knee like as a pig to little hut of branch, yet go not in. I is pull dry-grass bove of I for make a warm, and look to sky, where sun-blood is dry up and come all black, as with I's knee.

There is a path, off out in dark, all of queer sayings make. It go from edge of world to edge of world, and many sons is come to axe for make of it. May as it is they bones is set in neath of path, as bone of women set in bridges neath. A path of bones, all bout of world, that bones is make a top for world in low of we, where is they shagfoal tread through dark, with little Urks set on they backs as scratch of boy-meat off from bones that hang in bove of they.

This world is come that big and dark all bout of I, and pig-keep wall is look as far ways off. I is with belly-want for girl, that she is lie here by of I, like to I's mother yet more good for sniff. This world is make I little, that with fright I may not move nor do a thing. Shut eyes, and sky is go, and world is go, yet dark go not, and keep here by. There is not way for stop of dark.

Now is an other queer-while come. I is hear noise, and glean it is I's mother, making one-foot walk through trees for find of I, and open eyes for look to she, yet I see she not. There is but pig-keep, quiet in dark, and noise is come from hind of wall where in is wood-stop hole. Stands I, for walk to wall in bright of moon, which is come high in sky while glean I not. By wall, and look I now in cross of he.

All bout of dirt-rise, pipe-grass is come white and sharp as like to ice in moon. Low to he's belly walk in grass is Hob, and by of he is walk a boy. Like moon and pipe-grass is they white, and all is white, and see I now as face of Hob is no more black but where black is rub dark in eye-holes of he, as he may not wet a-ways.

Boy walk by Hob, and hair on head of he is black and all a-stump. See I as he is not with hair of chin nor face, where glean I that he is not old as I. Out pipe-grass now, they white shape tread up rise to little thick of trees, and Hob is walk with hand in hand of boy. Moon is make bright on of they back and of they arse, which white is go now in of trees and is come all to bits in black of branches there, where is I see no more.

Long whiles is I at no thing look, and now set back in dry-grass down. Glean I that boy is son of Hob. Glean I of mother, loll on tree and saying where is go I's foot. It is a queer of dark. Dark makes as we may see they spirit-dogs, and people that is come no more alive. Dry-grass is warm. Dark press on eye-skins now, as I is not with strong in I for hold they up. And warm. And dark.

Cold now in feet, and cold in hands. Make for to open eyes, yet is they all hold shut with eye-snot, which now scratch I off, more good for open they. A bright is come, yet is he come all grey. They sky-beasts is that many for to make of but one beast, that big as is it hang all cross of sky. Old wind is hard, and make a dog-noise bove of pig-keep here.

Now sniff I fish-meat, make in fire. Now sniff I apples. Sniff I flowers.

Come, say she, here is food. Where is it I is want for go this bright, she say.

Eat I of apple and of fish, while is she set by I, all quiet on knee. Stands I, for make a piss. Old wind is with that big a strong in he as make sniff of I's pissing go ways off, that may I piss on pig-keep wall with not a fright that Hob may find of I. I's will is big, yet come more little as they water is go out from he. Turns I, and see as girl is look on will of I, and makes good mouth for see of he.

This bright is we go up of valley edge, she say, in bove of beast-keep making high on hill. There from, say she, we may see of they river setting, and all many things.

Hide I now will in of I's belly-wraps. Aye, say I, this is good, and like, yet is a hot come in I's face. Stand she, for walk by wood-stop hole. Wind is pull at she long bright hair, that she is pull down aur-ox wrap more hard a-bout. It look that good, all fly in wind. Come now, she say. Come up of valley edge.

In tween of pipe-grass and through thick of trees, and now down with they wet and sucking-dirt, where is they stumps all black with rot. Girl walks a path in fore of I, that she is tread not down in sucking-holes, nor I as follows she, and like to this is come we up big hill as go by way of valley edge. Bout of we is they stumps, and open sky in bove of we. By way of sun-set-down is hill with making on, where sniff I ox and pig, and hear they's noise, for wind is come from they in way of I.

As I and girl is walk up hill, wind is make many dry-up tree-skins run at we, all cross of grass. Edge bove of edge they come, right quick, that they is like to many little beast as run in fore of tree-fire.

Up now and up more come we, and look, and see that we is come in bove of hill with making on, where go we more up yet. In making is they aur-ox set all down, with pigs lie by of dirt-wall, for to hide from wind. Follows I girl, and no thing say, for make of breath is hard and wind is take all say ways off from we. Walk up and up, in way of tree-line, rise all black in bove we there, by valley edge. Girl walk in fore of I, and wind is rub she sniff of flower now in I's face.

By tree-line stop and set we down on stump, and long whiles is we hard of breath as we may not make say. Looks I at making, set on hill in low we there, where herd-keep man, all little, come from hut of wood that is in middle stand of making's in-more round. Walks he in tween of aur-ox, cross of round, and come through wood-stop hole by round where is they pig and fly-not bird. In hands of he is holding a making, which it may is full with sun-grass dust, and throw he dust to fly-not birds, that may they eat. Now is he go there back in wood-hut by, and see of he no more.

Turn I to girl, as set I by on stump. How old is Hob, say I.

Look she to I, and look she now ways off, for pull at ox-skin bout she wind-fly hair. Say she, Hob is more old as she, and I, and as an other like to I. He is more old as man that she is hear of. Say I back how it is queer, and is not good that man may keep long whiles alive as like to this. This say I with a dark, as she may glean that I is not with like for Hob. I is with want as she is come with liking not for Hob, that is she with more liking come for I. Yet is she only make good mouth, and look now valley cross, and no thing say.

Say I, I is see Hob and son of he, by bright of moon.

Is turn she quick to I, and look she hard, and say of she is quiet and little. How is this, she say.

Say I of all that I is see, and say she no thing back at I. Say I, it as like they queer-whiles that I shagfoal see, and mother see. It is a seeing that is come by dark and shut-of-eyes. At this is she shake head, now fore, now back, and sign that there is right in say of I.

Say she that in they dark whiles, as we is shut eyes, there by is go we to an other world, where shagfoal is, and where is people as is come no more alive, and many queerness like to this. Say she, it is this other world as makes more queerness yet in say of Hob and son.

Why, how is this, say I. How is a saying queer as this come more queer yet. Girl look to I, and make she good mouth not. Make she no mouth at all. Look she at I, yet see of she is far ways off.

Say she, they setting-kine is make Hob put he son to axe, and if Hob is not do this, is Hob and he's son cast out, and come no more alive. Yet is Hob not with want for put of son to axe. He glean and glean on this, yet is there no thing he may do, but one.

Say I, how is this one thing he may do.

Say she as this is where a queerness comes. Say she, Hob is put boy to axe, that he is come no more alive. Yet none may say if is boy put to axe in this world, nor if is boy put to axe in other world there by. No man but Hob may glean now which it is, say she, this world nor other. This is thing like as I may not glean. Look I to she, and no thing say.

Now say she, if Hob is put boy to axe in other world, why, boy is yet alive this world here by. And if Hob is put boy to axe in this world, is boy yet alive in other world, where is I see of he and Hob by bright of moon, as is I say to she.

This is more hard a thing for glean as I is hear. No thing say I, but look to far ways off, where setting is by river stand. They setting-folk is all to do of many thing, by look of they. Bright skins is hang they up on huts, and many fires is all a-smoke, where bout is people make a quick-tread walk, all in a round, this way and that. Glean I as is good whiles for they, yet how of it I is not glean.

Girl stand now up off stump and walk she, slow, in little rounds for make of idle, hit at dry-up tree-skins with she foot that they is fly all bout. She little rounds come more big yet, as take she far and more far off from I, that she is come by trees-edge, rise in hind of we. Glean I as she is turn, and come here back by I, but oh. Oh, she is walk in neath of big dark tree, and go where I may see she not. All lone is I, with stump of tree all bout, in low of frighting open sky.

Quick stand I up, and run for tree in way where I is see she go. Loud say I, come here back, and where is go she, and as like to this, yet no thing is she say and come I now in tween they high, dark woods and stop for look all bout. All wheres is tree, with more tree stand in hind of they, and many dark path come there by. Make I to hear noise of she little tread on tree-skin, yet is all a-quiet, as no noise is she make.

Sniff I now flower, through trees in fore of I, where tread I soft in way of sniff, and come where tree is fall to rot and sniff of flower no more. But, ah. Wind make of sniff come more here by, and more with strong, all long of path to sun-set-down of I. I is not put yet one foot nor an other on this path but is I hear she make of saying, as from far ways off.

Oh how now may I find a mate,
he journey-boy is say . . .

Sniff come more strong, where runs I quick on path, with foot make loud through dry-up tree-skins neath of they. In bove of this is hear I say of she, all little float through high of woods.

Up valley edge, through dark of tree,
by dirt worm hill and all . . .

Come I by briar bush, where turn for follow sniff. It is like run and catch of beast for eat, and glean of this is queer and good in belly, and I's blood come quick in I. They tree-skins fly all bout where foot is fall as like to many dry-up birds.

And lie with she while I is not
yet put to dirt all grey . . .

Now sniff of flower is all where, and a bone is come in of I's will, that is he rub all rough on belly-wrap. Noise of she say is come more loud, as that she is not far ways off. Up valley edge, in dark of tree . . .

See I a bright of sun in fore of I, where from is sniff and say come more strong yet, and run I this way by. By dirt-worm hill and river's knee . . .

There is an open in of trees, all bright with sun, where come she voice, where come she sniff of flower, that glean I is not far a-hind. And there is lie they, he and she . . .

Out through of dark high woods tread I, all quick, and come a stop in open, where is trees all bout stand in a round. I's breath is hard, and he is loud, yet all but this comes quiet. Girl is not here, yet sniff of flower is here, and I is glean not how she . . .

Look I down. All bout I's foot and cross of open round is flower, is many blood-eye flower all bright and low to knee, as is I walk in blood. There is not noise. There is not girl. She is all change to flower.

Noise. Fright. Quick tread I back, and oh, and many skins of blood-eye flower fly up like as to many mark-wing mite, and girl set up from where she hide in tween of they, and make good noise at I.

Walk I through flower by where she set, yet making noise at I with hand to mouth of she and belly all a-shake. It is that good, for see of she, yet is she put a fright in I that I may find she not, where is I vexed. Say I, she is not good that she is hide and make I run, as if she want that I is look as babe, and like to this. More is I say, and more vexed is I come, that all I's sayings is with spit.

Put she a hand now on I's will, through fur of wrap, and hold she fur all bout he hard, where is I's sayings come a-stop.

Set down, she say, and pull on will that I is now come set by she in blood-eye flowers down. I's legs is shake, for bone is go from they and is now up I's will. It is as if I's gleanings is go down from out I's belly, that they is all hold now tween she finger there.

I's belly-wraps is make of little hut. She is with want for see I's will, and pull she wrap-furs back from off he, like with man as pull back skin off beast as he is catch and run to dirt. I's will is stand in cold air of this open tree-round, dark and hot, and now is wrap she finger bout of he, and fingers is they more cold yet, but this is good. She hand go up, now down, which-in I's will-skin is go like to this, and oh, it is a rub that soft, and is she fingers come now warm.

Puts I now hand in neath she wraps, that I may put I's finger up she gill, but is she shut legs hard and catch I's hand in tween of they, all soft and strong and wet with hot. No, say she, and say if I is not take I's hand ways off she gill, nor is she rub I more.

I do as she is say, yet say now may I suck she titties, and she say back no, and that no man may put a hand to she. Say she as may I only lie in blood-eye flowers back, while she is do good thing there on I's will. Back down I lie, that blood-eye flower come high like queer bright trees bout of I's head, from low where is I see they. Lift I head, for see of that as girl is do.

She is make stoop, and loll she head that long bright hair of she is hang like tree-strings there all bout I's will. Now in she hand is catch she up a long thick of she hair, for wrap in finger of she bout hot bone of I. Oh, she is rub I with she hair, all up and down, all quick and hard that is it pull and like to hurt she head, yet make she not a noise but only rub and rub, and rub of it is good, and glean of it is more good yet, she hair that soft and bright with sun and strong of it move up I's bone, slow like to hut-back worm, from arse, through thick of will to sharp where is it prickle good, and now is come a little round of belly-milk on he, as like to eyes of rain that come on grass while is first bright, and is she rub more quick, more hard, and I is glean as that it is not rub of hair in hand, but rub of hair all bout she gill, and oh, and glean of this is go quick down I's belly, up I's will and oh, and girl is hold more hard that is with hurt but hurt is good, and more hard yet, for stop I's belly-milk, but it is now, and now, and now, a string of milk fall on she cheek, in hair, and wet on aur-ox skin bout of she head, and more, and more, on legs of I and down she fingers, wet on grass and white in bloody eye of flowers and oh, and Mother. Mother.

Quiet. In bove we's open in of trees a many of black birds is fly all one, this way and other way with wind, that high as they is come more little yet as mites. Girl rub she hand on grass, for rub off belly-milk. Now sign she with one finger for to look, and sees I where I's milk is hang like to a little string-bridge tween of blood-eye flowers, ways off. It go more far as is I glean, that I and she is make good noise at this.

More quiet now. Far ways off on wind is come noise of they setting-people, making of good whiles all bout they fires. Is noise of many say, and is big hitting noise as make with hitting-skin put bove of round-wood, and is noise as of a man make mouth-wind with a pipe of hole-through bone. Is noise of babes and dogs. Now wind is come an other way, and noise is go. Say girl as we is go now down, and back by hut of Hob, that he go not there back and find she is not by. Say she as I may put I's will back in of belly-wrap, and make good mouth at this.

Stand she, where stand I now as like, but is I's legs yet all a-shake and not with strong in they. Come, is she say, and take I's hand in she's and walk we through of flowers like to this, and through of trees, and down bare hill of stumps. All this while I is I glean of no thing but she hand, we's fingers catch all up in tween of other. I is with more good in of I's belly as in other whiles I is alive. Down hill, by way of sucking-dirt and stinger-mites, with rot in stump and rot in air. Flower-sniff on girl is make they stinger-mite come by of we, that I is all whiles hit they off.

Up rise with little thick of trees, now down in pipe-grass and like this to hut and pig-keep by. Long whiles is we up hill, that sun is go by high of sky, and come more low. A cold is come, that pull I now more hard all bout I wraps of Hob's son, as is not alive nor with a want of they. Girl open stopping-woods and say for I to go now in of keep, that is she find more food for I while Hob is not yet come here back.

This is I do, and set on dry-grass down with glean of many thing in I. Girl is go off, for forage now in white-skin hut and find of thing for eat. I glean as how she is shut legs, that I may rub not gill, nor titties like to this, and how she say no man may put of hand to she.

Now is I glean an all of it.

By dark, is she in hut all lone but Hob. He is more big, and make she do of thing. He is put will in she, and shanking she. No. No, it is more not good as I is with want for glean. May he is make she rub he's bone with hair of she, as like to I, and glean of this it is more not good yet. Hob is want she is shank with no man only he, and is put fright in she, where is she make I not put hand to she. A vex is come now on I. Why, it is as if she is not she's, but is she Hob's.

I glean on how it is not good for she, that she is keeping all whiles by a man that dark and queer in glean of he, like as to Hob. He is more old as trees, and is put son to axe in this world, that in only other world is Hob now see of he. In other world, where Urk-kine is on shagfoal set, in neath he cave-top all of boy-bone make, where Hob is make he son to go, as spirits is in due put Hob with gleanings that he may he's queer path-saying make. It is not good as is no say for it. I is make girl to keep here by no more. I is make she and I to go ways off, and walk, and journey on, and not to set. It is not right that people set. There is no good in it.

By white-skin hut cross pig-keep hear I girl, as is she looking yet for food. Glean I on how it is, if we is run ways off, but she and I. Glean I as I is make not good of forage while is I all lone, yet girl she is more good in glean of she as I, and may she forage many things for we, as is I's mother do. This gleaning is that good. We may walk cross bone-woman bridge, and cross of world there by, I and she flower-sniff girl. Come whiles as she is not by Hob and is no more with fright of he, where is I make that she put off she wraps, and open of she legs up far as is they like to go.

In of I's wraps, old will is make but little prickle, as not yet with strong for stand.

Now flowers, and girl is come from hut by wall of pig-keep bout, and through of wood-stop hole. She is with bird-meat and with sun-grass thing. Set she now on she knee, and is put food to lie in dry-grass, as that I may see of it.

I is not look at food, but is say out all quick they things that is I glean. Say I as is not good for she to keep by Hob, and how may I and she go off and far ways by, but we all lone, and forage good that is we want for no thing. Take I of she hand, and hold now hard of it, and say

I that I glean she is not with a like for all whiles find of wood for Hob, nor put he meat to fire. Say I, she is not with good whiles by Hob, that she is want for I to keep here by and make good whiles she with, as she is say to I. She is now quiet, but shake she head fore-back, for sign that this is right.

Say I, if she is come ways off and journey world all bout with I, that all whiles is good whiles with we. Make I of many sayings like to this, and come as I may glean not more for say, and now is all come quiet and whiles go by, and no thing is she say. Oh no. Glean I that say of I, it is not good. She is not come with I. She is make I go off all lone, for see of she no more. I's belly is he full with fright, it is that quiet in pig-keep now.

Look she to I. Make she good mouth.

Aye, she is say now. Aye.

This is more good as I may glean. Say she that we may journey off by dark, while first bright is not yet a-come. Say she, if we is want for walking far, how it is good to make we's belly full for do of it. She is come back while first bright is not yet here by, with thing for eat more many and more good as I is see. We is make belly full, which after is we journey far way off, but I and she.

She say, she is now go, as Hob is he but little whiles comes back. Say she as I is one more dark in pig-keep lie, where after whiles is lie with she. Stoop she, and lick I's cheek, and lick I's mouth. Back is I lick she face, where lick of belly-milk is strong, dry on she cheek. Stand she, and make good mouth. While first bright is not yet, she say, and is out wall-hole, shut of woods and go.

Sun is come low in sky, and is I eat of bird-meat down to bone. Hob is come back here by, and is I hear low say of girl and he in hut. Hob say thing, where girl make good noise back at he, and this is good, for glean I girl is want that Hob he is with like for she, that may he glean not she is make for go ways off, and come he by no more.

Make I good mouth at this. It is that good, as girl may say a thing to Hob while thing is not. If she is gleaning good as this, like is she glean good where to forage food and find for I. Through pipe-grass, cross of river, sun is come that big and low that hot of he is make world's edge to smoke. River is still that through it may I look on darking sky of other world in neath of waters there, where other bird is fly, as make no noise.

Now bird-meat is all go, and sun all go as like from sky. Now is there only dark, and chew on bone.

There is no see, that hear is come more strong. Of rat in dry-grass cross of keep. Of river that say quick-lick, quick-lick, quick-lick, way in dark. Now come a far noise like to setting-people as is walk they river by. They is all make good noise, and loud that I may hear at all, they is that far. High and a-ways is mouth-wind come in pipe of bone, and is there noise of hitting-skins, and is they make of queer say, as like girl is make to I. Wind go, now come, that I may hear not all they's say, yet one say is I hear.

Make a fire and make it hot,
and bone is he, and bone is he
Path is long, yet is we not,
and by of valley go we . . .

There is more to this, yet is they setting-people go far down of river, in way of they many huts that I may not more hear they say, nor of they hitting-skins, nor of they bone-hole pipes. Off river down, they setting's many fire is make in sky a little blood-bright come, up on high hang of dark. Puts I now one hand and an other in I's belly-wraps, for cover up I's will and make warm of I's hands, and shut of eyes. There is no thing at all . . .

. . . but dark.

And flowers.

Open eyes. I's face is cold. A grey is come in dark by other way of river-setting, as like many whiles is go they by. Sniff flowers, and hear quiet-say of girl from out of pig-keep, by of wood-stop holes which open stands.

It is not yet first bright, she say, and she is here with many food. Come out, she say, that may we eat, where after journey we a-ways.

Now is I glean on all that we is say for do, and is with good-fright in I's belly. Walk of world with girl. With girl find food, and lie with girl. Ah, good whiles come as that I may not glean. Quick now, she say. Quick now.

Stand I, and cross of keep for come by open stopping-woods. Glean I as it is good she is find wraps for I, it is that cold, with bare-while coming slow a-change to ice-while. Eyes is come more good for see in dark, where is I now see girl. She is set on she knees, with out of keep. In fore of she set apples, chewing-thing and meat of many kine. Sniff I of food, and sniff of flower, and is with want as I is all whiles sniff of they. Is I with want as girl is by I all whiles as is I alive, and is not go off like I's people. Like I's mother. Look she deep in eyes of I. Come out, she say. Come out.

Through now of stop-wood hole tread I, and out from keep. I is but one tread and an other off from she. Make I good mouth, yet make she no mouth back but only look in eyes. Now holds I out an arm, and glean not if it is for take of food, nor take up of she long bright hair for rub.

Hand on I's back.

Arm bout I's neck. Man-sniff. Hot skin. Strong in he's arm on neck, he's belly to I back. May I not make of breath. May I not make of say. Fright. Fright and sniff of man, of he's hot will. Feet is no more on dirt. Girl deep is look in eyes. Big arm hurt hard and stop I's breath, oh Mother, and now is a thing come bright and quick and make a little cold on neck of I, where is big warm now come.

Glean I man is he cast warm water down I's belly for to make I wet, yet is glean not a how of it. Move I this way, now that, but oh, there is no help, and more warm wet fall yet now on I's belly and is strong all slow go out from I. Arm move from neath of chin that I may take of breath, and arm is come now low I's back and low I's arse for lift of I. Lie now in strong of arms. Look up, and eyes all white look down on I, yet there is not a face. Is only black and dark. Now low of eyes is come an other white, and it is teeth, and Hob is make good mouth.

Oh, he is find we. He is glean we make for journey off. Turns head and look to girl, that I may say for she to run, yet is a bad lick come in of I's mouth that I may no thing say, and only spit. Girl look to I, yet is she not make face of fright, nor make to run. She make no move, she make no face at all. Now Hob is walk, with I in arm of he. Strong is all go from I as like I is with sick. I may not make a-ways. Girl stand for follow quiet by Hob and I. Sniff flower. Sniff man. Sniff blood.

Make I hot waters out from eyes, and make for say as I is do all thing for Hob if is he hurt I not. I is go off. I is not see of girl. All this make I for say, but mouth is full and may I say of no thing. Hob is take I bout of pig-keep, fore of white-skin hut, where is there bright as of a little fire, and see I now he's black face and he's horns of wood, and see he is with blood on he. As like is I. Oh no.

Now is he lie I down, as like to babe, on prickling thing in fore of aur-ox hut. Come many sharp in back and legs, where is I glean he put I on of branch hill, as I see he make. Now take he hand from I. Lie I on branch-hill with no thing for hold I, and makes I for move ways off, yet may move I not. There is not strong. There is not strong in I. May move I no thing, only hand for rub of neck.

There is a hole in neck of I, where by is wet come out, where by is blood come out, that is not stop. Hob. Hob is put of hand-axe to I's neck while that I is not glean. Oh, all I's blood come out on belly, neck, and branch hill neath of I. Sniff I not flowers. Sniff I of no thing only blood.

Hob is walk off from branch hill and of I, and come he by of little fire in fore of hut, where is he stoop. He spirit-shape rise high and black on white of aur-ox skin, and is he take up stick from fire, which stick is come with fire as like. Now Hob is turn for come back way of I, he's fire-stick hold in hand that make white wets of bright move on he belly, on he arms and edge of he black cheek.

Look I to girl, and glean not how she is not make of help for I. Stands she ways off from where is I on branch-hill lie, and take she aur-ox wrap now from she hair, and is not look on I. Wrap-skin is fall, a little white in dark. Girl turn she head in way of bright, and see I she is wear of wrap for hide of not-good mark there on she head. In bove she eyes there is a frighting tear. There is not blood, but skin lift up at edge, all long in neath she line of hair.

Now is I's arms and legs come all a-shake, as I may not make stop of they. Arse is make noise, where is shit come on legs of I. I is not want for girl to see of this. I is not want for look to she. Turns I head, all slow, and look now up. Hob is come back here by, and is stand bove of

I. White eyes. White teeth in low of empty black where is no face, and branch-horns rise there by.

All good, he say to I, and put he's fire-stick now of branch-hill in. From woods in neath of I is come a noise like many mites all making little say of, quick, and hit, and set, and like to this. Now noise of mite is come as noise of rat, and rat say scratch, and rat say stick-it-black, and like. Sniff blood. Sniff smoke. Oh, now. Oh, where is girl.

Girl is she stand and take of wraps from off she titties. Thick is wraps, yet titties is that little now. White there in bright of fire, they is as like to titties not at all. Rat-noise is come as cat-noise now, and is a warm neath I and in of branch-hill. Where is many smokes rise there all bout.

Warm is come hot, on back of legs, and hot is come to hurt, where for is I make move of legs, but no where may they go as is not like with hot. I is now sniff of hair a-fire, and it is wraps of I, where make I noise, loud noise and full with hurt, yet is I's say come thick and wet. Blood in I's mouth. Blood on I's chin.

I is not want for come no more alive by fire, as like to this. It is not right. It is more hurt as I may hold. Fire on I's back, fire neath of head, and little grits of bright is rise all bout in way of dark sky bove we all. I may not make of breath. Girl is take off she belly wraps and wraps from off she legs, it is that hot. All bare is she. In tween she legs is . . .

Put she hand to head, where frighting tear of skin is low of hair, and finger is she put to skin-edge by, where pull she now and . . .

Smoke and blood in mouth. Bright hair is fall in dark with head-skin fall there by. She will, more big as I's, that is I sniff not for they flowers. I is not with a breath for make of noise. Girl is come change. Girl is come change to boy, as rat is come like stones and pig to logs. It is this change that is in things. It is this frighting change as is make all of world not right. Smoke rise and fall like to grey river bout of I, and hurt come big as sky. No breath, and see of I is come all dark.

In dark is queer and many things, with many little seeings hang in smoke. See I of fire-hair men as may make fire to run as blood from stones. See I a where as man skin is fall black from sky. See I a path, from water to big water long, where is brights go now fore and back, more quick, more many as they fish. See I a making as like to a head-bone, big, and black, and all of fire. In of it's mouth is set a man with fire come out he hair and all with hurt. See I now women hold to log, with fire all bout they foot. Look we, one at an other, from we fires. There is not hurt now. Only is there smoke.

In hind of smoke see I now dogs with eyes like tree-stumps big. Lift I now hand, for hit they off from I, and hand is all with fire. Skin is rise up in little rounds and is make cat-noise, neath of he all black. Through smoke is I see Hob. Boy is set by of he, fire bright on stumps of he dark hair. Hob is find little rounds of grey-dirt, push all flat, and is with stick in hand for make of mark on they. It is not good, for make of mark.

Fire is in hair, and this way come in of I's head, and of I's belly, that a gleaning is come in of I with fire. It is not glean of I, but glean of fire, full of queer sayings as no tongue may make. Phror. Becadom, sissirishic and huwf. Hob is set more by I, for hear. Make he a mark in grey of dirt with stick, and now an other, cross of it.

Opens I mouth, for make noise in I's hurt, and say of fire is come through I, and rise, and rise, with grits of bright, in neath of old black sky.

THE CREMATION FIELDS
2500 BC

Floating downstream, away from me, it's like a big white hand, dragging its fingers through frog-coloured water, tufts of black hair growing there between them.

'Do you go as far south as Bridge-in-Valley? We may walk together there for safety,' says she.

She is travelling to her father, who is dying, and she tells me that he is a cunning-man who comes one Summer long ago up track from Bridge-in-Valley, past the Great North Woods, far as the land's edge, where the cold grey sea begins. He makes his children on a woman there, both boy and girl. Takes boy away with him and leaves the girl behind. All the long Winters pass. She does not see her father. He does not see her. Now he is dying.

'Bridge-in-Valley?' comes back my reply. 'Yes, that is in my way. There is a short path by the river we may take, if you walk after me.'

About her neck, she wears blue fancy-beads.

Now it is almost out of sight, no bigger than a clot of spawn that slides away across the river's smooth green belly, swollen with the rain. It tangles in a willow's trailing scalp, moves on and leaves me taking off my wraps between the rushes, whispering like willage girls.

'How do you like my fancy-beads?' says she, and tells me how up track and past the Great North Woods the men make ore-fires on the shore. The sea-grass dries in long black strips upon the slippy rocks, then burns within a furnace hole of sand, above of which another chamber lies. Here is the ore, and smelted copper runs as quick as blood down sand-cuts into casting troughs. The juices of the burning grass are mixed with sand that turns to one smooth lump about the fire. The copper makes it blue, and young girls chip it into beads.

`Now, where is this short path?' she says.

`Not far,' comes my reply. `Not far.'

Lifting my elbows up above my head to pull away this stained old shirt, the wetness on my hands runs down my arms, as quick as smelted copper, in between my breasts. Washing it off, crouched at the river's edge, brown clouds uncurl into the slopping green about my waist.

`Your father does not know you, leaves you as a baby with your mother and does not come back. Why does he send for you now he is dying?'

Here she turns her head towards me, setting all her beads to chime, and tells me that her father, as a cunning-man, has many hides of land and wealth besides. It may be that her brother, lost to her from birth, is dead; or that he quarrels with the old, sick man. It may be that her father, with no son to share his wealth, is thinking that it should be passed to her.

About us, rain is sizzling on the leaves. We near the river's edge.

Drying myself with dead leaves, splintering, crackling, stuck in flakes upon the wet and duck-bumped skin. Amidst the black-stained tangle of my rags, a prickling glint of bronze that snags the eye.

Reach down. My fingers, closing on the wooden hand-hold, turn a cold, flat metal tooth against the light.

And wipe it with sharp rushes, blade on blade.

`Oh no,' says she. `Oh no, don't. Don't do that.'

`What is your name?'

`Usin! My name is Usin. Oh, let go. Let go and don't do any more.'

`What is the old man's name?'

`What do you want with him? You cannot make me say!'

The ear. The thumb. Birds scatter up from reeds to sky in flapping, blind alarm.

`Olun! Olun, that is my father's name. Oh. Oh, these things you do. Oh, that it comes like this with me.'

`Hush. That is all. Be quiet now.'

Later, stripping off its clothes and dragging it. The dull, deep splash, and my surprise to find the rain no longer falling. Everything is born to die. There are no spirit-women in the trees. There are no gods below the dirt.

They look so pretty, blue on my brown throat as puddles on a path. Her boots alone are not a fit for me but must be folded in my bag, heavy enough without them. Why, it tips me over on one side to carry it, making my way back through the sting-weeds and the dog-flower up towards the track.

Barefoot, then, south to Bridge-in-Valley. Nothing here to look at but the way before me, at my poor cold feet upon it, such as is my usual view of things. Mud, thick as ox-cream, quickly paints me yellow to my knees.

Wading through ash, among the highland mountains as a child. The grey fields all about, the oxen lumbering breast deep through dust. A darkness is upon the world, where is day come and brings no light. The sun is rare and strange. Vein-coloured skies at close of day. Piercing in blanket cloud, green shafts illuminate the skeletons of trees, spines split and ribs snapped off, bleached, twisting from the powder-dunes.

Our crops are buried. Nothing grows, and pale, slow clouds rise at our every step. Ash streaked in copper hair, the children's faces white with it, its bitterness in all our food. Our animals go blind, their eyes like blood, the sighted centre part become a dull grey caul, as with a skin of fat upon raw meat.

We leave our homes, our settlements, a great crowd near as many as when people gather in to raise the stones. Beyond the woods, they say, there lies an old straight track to guide us, now there are no stars. Amongst the cinders, blind birds peck and scream. We travel south, some of us walking still.

The track is wider, coming up by way of valley's edge. How many dead men's feet does it demand to make it so? It is a fury and misery to think of being one day in my grave and yet this track still here. Its deep ruts, older than our great-fathers. Its flood pools, all the frightening straightness of its line, still here. Still here.

It rises steep before me, firm beneath my tread, and yet the walking's hard. Sharp pebbles cut my feet, the mud upon them drying to a sun-split hide. Shifting my bag from one hand to other, muttering, telling myself to leave the track atop this hill and walk upon soft grass about the rim, so as to come down upon Bridge-in-Valley from the east.

The day's light starts to wane, and soon the ditches by the track are speckled brilliant green with fire maggots. Song of bats. Call of a night-eyed bird. My footfalls, slapping in the dusk.

Somewhere downstream it rushes through the dark ahead of me, not swollen yet, but without colour. Snails upon its thighs. Face down, unblinking, sees the river-bottom slipping by below, each stone, each minnow-bitten weed. Cracked shells, and clever, branching lines that unseen currents leave upon the slow, smooth bed. The dead eyes, missing nothing.

East, along the rim. Between my toes cool grass, wet grass, and finally, below me, fires in the valley dark. A ring of sullen lights, too few to be a willage. What, then? Setting down my bag and straddling a toppled log, my eyes fix on the fire lights until they come more clear.

The view is of a hilltop, further down the valley's eastern slope. A circle given shape by low and broken walls of dirt is risen there, another much alike but smaller set within, and inside that a smaller circle yet. This centre ring is dark, a hole. The fires, a handfull only, burn within the greater round beyond, some of them little more than embers, almost gone.

The brightest has a gathering of people stood about it. Trapped beneath their heels, stretched shadows shy back from the flames, yet do not jump or dance. What are they burning there, so still by night?

My rest upon this log gives me new strength, and once more taking up my bag seems less a task. Stand up. Walk downhill in amongst black stumps where all the trees are burned away. Below the ring-topped hill, downwind of it, come women's voices, calling, tangled with the smoke.

No. No, not calling, but a lower noise that has less sense to it.

At foot of hill, the ground becomes a bog, yet there's a raised path running south across the valley floor to where the night above the treeline glows dull red, a cooling metal that betrays the willage fires below. A long walk, from the look of it, but that will give me time to think of all there is to do, and say, and be.

Usin. The sound of it is plain and easy in the saying. Usin, Olun's daughter. Name like an abandoned shell, a husk. The living creature once concealed within is gone. The name lies empty, hollow and disused. It waits for hermit crabs to crawl inside and try it on.

Usin. Deserted name. Mine now.

Ahead, the path crawls through the weeds into the willage, there to die. Along its length the signs and droppings of this place are strewn, lit one side red by its approaching fires: a broken basin, grey and pricked with spots; a mitten; blunted flints; a little man-in-kind made out of chicken bones.

The settlement is big, half bounded by a ring of blackthorn, heaped into a wall. Its roundhouse squats there at the centre, hulking giant, a necklace made from torches strung about its shoulders, dark above the huts that sprawl against its smoking flanks like sucking-pups.

Stopping to make a piss some way yet from the willage's north gate, it is my luck to note while crouching in mid flow a torso garden set beside my path. Fixed through, and hung from stakes. No limbs nor head. No doubt they are the last remains of cheats and thieves hung out in warning, heavy flags of meat. It is a common practice now, along the track.

There are as many stakes as legs upon a dog, and all but one have women on. No. No, the one this end may be another man, seen closer to. As eaten by the weather and the wild swine as they are, it's hard to know. This one has bright red hair about his sex, and this the needle-picture of a snake marked on one breast, her other gone.

Wiping my gill with grass, and pulling Usin's breeks up high about my waist, there's not a thing to do but journey on, towards the walls of thorn, sharp black against the fires contained within. A frightful nest, filled not with eggs but embers, smouldering in the night.

Bridge-in-the-Valley. Stupid name. There's valley all about yet not a bridge in sight. My wager is the willeins in this settlement don't call it by that name at all. My wager is they call their place `The Willage', as do all the other dull-wits in their dull-wit settlements along the track. `Why, life be good here in the Willage, be it not old girl?' `Aye, may it be, but it is better in a place up north they call the Willage, where my mother has her people.' `Well, the Willage is a good place if you're wanting oxen, but if you want pigs you're better going to the Willage.' `We must let my brother settle this. He does not live in either place, but in a settlement down south. It has a queer and outland sounding name that's gone from my recall, and yet it may be `Willage', come to think.' `You do not hear of many names like that!'

Across the sea and by the world's end, where the black men are, there's settlements with different names in different tongues, and all of them mean willage. There are willages upon the moon, those rings of huts that may be seen when it is full.

My names are better, made up from the spites and griefs these stale and stinking little pest holes put upon me in my travellings: Beast-Bugger Down and Little Midden. Squint-Eyed-in-the-Bog. Shank Sister Hill and Fat Arse Fields.

Bridge-in-the-Valley? No. This place is worth a better calling. Fool-'Em-in-the-Fen, with luck.

Or Murder-in-the-Mud.

There is a watch-hut by the northmost gate, set up against the wall of thorn. Inside, a tall youth birth-marked red from eye to chin sits plucking birds beside an older man, his father, or, as it may be, his grand-sire. Torch lit, crouched in feathers to their boot tops.

Now, close up, the old man's hands come into sight. They tremble, shake with age or palsy, knuckles on the one wrapped fast about the pale pink carcass, fingers on the other picking in the down about its neck. Both hands are black to some way past the wrist, not dark with dirt or sun scorched like the traders come from other lands but black, an old deep stain that fades to blue along its edge, as with a dyer's hands.

A dried-up cone is crushed to sudden splinters under my bare foot. They both look up. Young cherry-cheek puts down his half-bald fowl and fumbles, reaching round to find his spear. He speaks as if to put me in my place, his voice half-broken and the pitch of it betraying him so that he squeaks where he is wanting to be stern. He does not meet my eye, but lets his glance fall to my neck where torch fire sparkles blue upon the fancy-beads.

'What are you wanting in the Willage?'

There. The Willage. Why, my wager is already won.

'My name is Usin, Olun's daughter, come here from the North to see my father, who is sick. Who'll take me to him?'

Fiery-face turns round towards the older gateman sat beside him, black hands shivering like a corpse-bird's wing. A look is passed between them and a fear come into me: Olun, the cunning-man, already dead and buried, goods and all, below the flowers. His secrets rattling useless in his skull, else passed on to his son. The death-bed whisper, 'Is my daughter here?' Too late. My schemes are all too late.

The elder watchman spits a yellow curd into the feathers at his feet.

'Olun's the Hob-man here, for many years.'

He spits again. His jerking, shadow-coloured hands are trying to point between the huddled dwellings at his back.

'This night he's set down-willage at the roundhouse making say, although we fear he has not many sayings left in him. We may walk down that way together, if you like. Are you all right to pluck these birds alone, Coll?'

This is said in way of master juice-jowels, who looks put about and sulky-eyed. He grunts his answer, so to sound more like a man.

'Aye. What with all the while you take to pull a feather, shaking like a broke-back dog, it's just as quick to do it on my own. Get off and let me be.'

The elder gateman stands and, spitting once more in the feathers, steps outside the hut. He takes my arm between his spasming fingers and now guides me down a path between the huts towards a looming round of posts, bark stripped away and white wood naked, thatched with reed above. Damp torches hiss, a knot of snakes beneath the eaves. A baby wails, behind us in the willage night.

'Olun is known to me, both boy and man these many years,' says he. 'You are not make like him, nor like young Garn.'

The brother's name is Garn.

'No. It's my mother's side that shows in me.' This seems to put him at his rest, and he sets one black hand to quiver at my shoulder, steering me through drawn-back veils of rush into the smoke and stink.

The roundhouse. Many people, some too old or young to talk, are sprawled on mats of reed, with flame-shapes slithering on their knobbled backs and freckled shoulders in a fog of sweat, and breath, and half-cured hide. Up in the shadows of the under-roof a shroud of smoke is spread out carefully upon the air. It trembles with each movement in the hall below, folding and fraying and unravelling.

Towards the round's far side, across a sprawl of hairy limbs and tallow-light, there sits a monstrous woman, sunk in furs, grey ropes of hair hung to her thighs. A fierce white scar runs through one eye and down across the nose. The other, from a socket swathed with fat, gleams like a bead pressed into dough. About her puffed out bullfrog neck, an ornament of gold. The Queen.

To either side, behind her, stands a man . . . no. Stands the same man. How is this? My gaze stops first with one and then the other. Back and forth, again and yet again. There's not a fingernail of difference in between them. Shaven skull and brow and jaw, standing with their long arms folded, fixed blue eyes, snake-lipped.

Each smiles upon a different side. Why does this frighten me?

'That is Queen Mag,' the old, black-fisted man is whispering, behind my shoulder. 'Those on either side of her are Bern and Buri, though there's none but they know which is which. They are her rough-boys. Let them well alone.'

'What are they?' My voice, hushed as the gateman's own. My eyes are moving back and forth between the awful look-akins and may not glance away.

'A monster birth, but do not say it while they are in hearing. It is said their father puts his seed into their mother while she leans against an oak that's lightning-split. When they are born, most of us say they must be put to knife, but Mag says no. She takes a pleasure in their oddity and rears them for her own. They put a scare up people's arses now they're grown, and Mag takes pleasure in that also.'

Both of them turn their sand-grey skulls as one and look across the room at me. They have one smile, each wearing half of it. A knowledge comes within me now that makes me look away from them: these are the ones that tend the torso garden. They clip back the limbs and gather up the fallen heads.

Dropping my gaze, it falls upon a ruined figure, resting there upon a pallet made of sticks before the seated queen. The figure speaks, a dry voice lower than the drone of bees, within my ears since entering this hall yet only come to notice now. A man. Once fat, he has a sickness eating him within. It sinks his eyes and dries his lips to figs, shrunk back to show the all but empty gums.

Where all but he are clad in robes, he lies there naked save a fine, strange cloak of blackbird quills beneath him, spread upon the bier. His will is long and skinny, bald about the root. A band of antler-twigs is tied, the bare points circling his brow, skin hanging from his bones in folds, and all of it has marks upon. The wasted body swarms with needle-pictures. Every thumbnail's width of him from head to heel is pretty with tattoo.

'That's Olun,' comes the stale breath by my ear.

A cold blue line that severs him in twain from balls to brow. A red wheel, drawn above his heart with many smaller rings about. Crosses and arrow points, loop within loop on belly and on breast. The pale green patchwork of his thighs.

An eye may find no sense within the curls and turns, no image of a snake nor of a bear, as favoured by the northern men. Shaped after nothing one may see within this world, it is a madness, wild in its device, and speaks that which we may not know. Star-scalped. The likeness of a womb upon one palm.

The words he speaks are small and dry like beetle husks, spat out as if he does not like their taste.

'The leaves fall dead at news of Winter.'

(The leaves. Fall. Dead. At news. Of Winter. Every word, he stops to catch his breath.)

'Now is the sleep of lizards. Now the shortening of the days. The crops is in. The shed is full. Now must we offer thanks.'

Some men are nodding in the crowd. A little boy is led out by his father to make water up against the hut wall, then led back again, picking across the mat of tangled legs. Olun is speaking, sockets staring up into a still, flat veil, the net of smoke cast floating just below the roof.

'Once, long ago, there is a cunning-man who may make say with all the gods below the dirt. They tell him that he must give up an offering and thank the soil for being good, and full with fruit.

'What must be offered up?' the Hob-man says.

'Your son,' the gods say back.

'On hearing this he falls to weeping, begging them to spare his child, but they are stern and bid him do the thing they say, for he must show he has more love for them than for his only flesh. And so it is. He binds his son and leads him by the river's edge, where is a fire built up.'

(The river's. Edge. Where is. A fire. Built up.)

'He sets his son upon the wood. The fire's made ready and the dagger honed.

'Then speak the gods below the dirt and say that it is good for him to keep his faith and love his gods more than his only flesh. 'We are so pleased,' they say, 'that we do spare your child. See, yonder is a pig caught in the mud. Take down your son from off the fire, and let us change the pig into a boy that you may slaughter in his place.'

'And this is done. The pig-boy burns, the child is spared, and from that time we offer up a pig-boy to the fire upon the night.

'When next the light is come we have one day to stack the wood.

'We have one day to stalk the pig.

'We have one night to please the gods.'

He sighs. 'The gods are good.' The crowd are muttering a muddy echo to his words, one voice chopped up with morsels lodged in many throats. One day to stack, one day to stalk, one night to please the gods. The gods are good. It seems these mutterings are a sign that Olun makes his say no more this night, for people stand and make to leave. They flow about us like a scum-tide, draining through the door and out into the night, coughing and laughing. Only scattered huddles stay to whisper in the hall.

Black fingers, shuddering, rest upon my spine and push me from behind to urge me on.

'Go to your father,' says the gateman.

Father dies of bee stings while we're passing through the Great North Woods, all wading belly high through hollows deep with wet and shaggy grass. Above us, where the tree's high branches make a web of twigs against the light, a bird is singing, clear and all alone within the stifling afternoon.

My father cries out, jerks his foot up now to clutch its underside, then topples backwards with a moan, is swallowed in the grass. We reach him, mother and myself, but now he's twitching, making noises in his throat, the sweat a bright and sudden gloss upon his nose, upon his brow. He wheezes first, then rattles. Both his eyes are open, dull and seeing nothing. One hand clutches at the grass beneath him now and then, but all in all there's little here for me to look at and nothing to do. Leaving my mother kneeling there beside him, it comes upon my fancy to retrace his last steps through the laked grass.

In the flattened patch where he first grabs his foot and cries out lies a half-pulped bee, a smear of dangerous colour wiped across the print mark of his heel. Somewhere close in the grass my mother starts to low. Taste of my fingers, sour like metal, crammed into my mouth to stop the laughter.

Still the bird is singing. From its perch up in the high woods there it may look down and see me, see my mother and my father and the bee, though separate as we are amongst the grass we may not see each other. As in one flat picture it observes us, with the all of father's death caught fast there in the bird's jet eye.

The hag-queen wheezes something to her look-akins. They raise their great moon heads and watch me make my way towards the old man on his bed of sticks and feathers set below them there. Don't meet their eye. Don't seem afraid. The pack-dirt floor, arse-warm beneath my slow, unwilling feet.

A woman crouches by the pallet, gathering the Hob-man's cloak of blackbird quills about his starved and naked shoulders, folding it to cover up the senseless decorations pricked upon his ribs, his sunken breast.

She's big, this woman; man-boned at the hip and plain to look upon. Hair bound up all one lump atop her head, the colour of a baby's turd, held with a spike of wood. Red cheeks. A flat face, long about the jaw and nothing clever in her she-ox eyes.

She's past her child time, yet too young to be the old man's mate. Another daughter, then? No. No, one son, one daughter, that is all they say to me, the girl and gateman both. What then? His sister, or his sister's child? A slave? About her thick grey neck a piece of thin bronze, scratched with tear-shaped marks and hung on string twists in the tallow-light.

Now, at my drawing near she turns to look at me, a flat and stupid look that has no spark in it. Pay her no heed. The old man's lying wrapped within his feather cloak, so that he looks like to some terrible black bird that has an old man's head and feet. His eyes are closed as if the making of his say tires all the life from him. Him. Talk to him, the old man. He's the one.

` Father?'

My voice. It must sound more akin to hers, the girl who met with me upon the track. He may recall the way her mother speaks to him so long ago and know me as one come from other parts. Think. Try to think back how the girl speaks, there upon the river's edge. ` Do you go as far south as Bridge-in-Valley?' ` Do you like my fancy-beads?' Her voice, more in the nose than in the gizzard like my own. Yes. Yes, that's it. Now, call to him once more, but in the way the girl is speaking in my thoughts. And louder.

` Father?'

Sunk in sockets deep and crumble-edged as earth-bear holes, his dye-stained lids creep back across the wet and yellowed balls below. One eye is green and black, like water in a stump. The other eye is white. Blind white.

He lies there, staring up at me, and slowly frowns. The markings crumple on his brow. Some of the needle-painted lines are spread about their edges with the ageing of his skin, become a faded smear of dirty blue, yet in their centre they are sharp. It is as if he has the markings made again from year to year, gouged deeper still to keep them clear and new. His green eye squints at me, his white at nothing. By his bed, the great slow woman squats to watch us, no more life within her face than is within a stone.

`Father, it's Usin.' Trying to talk down through my nose, not from the throat.

`It's Usin. It's your daughter.'

Your daughter trails her eel-chewed toes through river-bottom sand and dances off towards the sea. Her hair floats out and has the look of weed, more comely when it's drowned.

She's far beyond this place by now, tripping her slow dance through the night. Its steps are clumsy, rousing no man with the movement of her flesh, nor ever may again. Only the current holds her, fast against its stinking breast.

He stares at me. The long, unblinking silence holds and holds, and only now he speaks.

`Hurna? Back to my hut now.'

Not to me. Although he stares the while into my eyes he does not speak to me but to the hulking, silent woman looking on. Her name is Hurna, then. Out of her crouch she rises, wearily unfolds her largeness, all without a word. She turns her back upon the bed of sticks then stoops to grasp the poles that thrust out from its head. She lifts. The smallest grunt escapes her, less from effort than her need to mark a task completed.

Having lifted up the old man to a tilt, not steep enough to tip him from his bed, she drags the litter off towards the roundhouse door, whereby the man with dyed and shaking hands still waits and watches us. The pallet leaves a pair of grooves behind it, scratched upon black dirt, and still the old man holds my eye even as he is dragged away, bound in his blackbird shroud.

` Well? Are you coming, daughter?'

There! He speaks. He speaks to me and calls me daughter.

` Coming, father. Does your woman need my help in dragging you?'

He makes a creaking sound. It comes to me that he is laughing.

` Hurna? She is not my woman. All she does is wipe my arse and feed me, drag me here and there, and in return it is for me to suffer through her thoughts upon the spirit world and all her foolish gods.'

Her. Foolish. Gods. The words burst out between the shallow breaths. The woman pulls the litter, slow and even; does not seem to hear the Hob-man make complaint against her. Follow, walking in between the scratch-lines scored upon the dirt behind. Deep in my throat there is the smell of tallow smoke and feathers.

One last glance behind: the monster boys are sitting on the furs to each side of their bloated queen. One, Bern or Buri, nuzzles with his head to kiss her underneath the arm. The other has his hand beneath her wraps. Look quick away. Out through the veil of reeds we step into star-frosted air. The palsied gateman with the blackened hands watches me pass, but does not speak or follow.

Outside, it seems that Olun and his tow-horse woman do not wait for me, but drag away into the twists of path foot-worn between the crowding huts, asleep and sunk in dark. They make me run to fall in step with them, walking beside of Olun's bier and talking to him once my breath is caught again. About us, shiftings, mumbles in the thatch-topped dwellings, bodies settling for the night into their rags and straw.

The old man turns his head, looks up towards me from his bed of sticks that bumps along here by my side.

` How well are things,' he says, ` now that here is my daughter come. What is the many of the nights you spend upon the track?'

This is an answer that the dead girl does not give me, at the river's edge, one of the things it slips my thoughts to ask her. Too late now to cut away her other thumb. My wits must save me and my wits alone.

`More days than are within my reckoning,' is my reply, then, quickly, moving on: `All of those nights, sleep passes by and does not take me with her, so great is my fright to hear that you are sick.'

The old man smiles, lips crawling back from off the few and yellowed teeth. The skull is restless, eager for that day soon come when it may shed the dried meat and the sun-cured hide, emerge from Olun's head wearing a grin of victory at conquering the flesh. These teeth, poked through the shrivelled gums, are but the heralds of its coming. Up above his smile, the old man slides his ice-white blinded eye towards me, sidewise there between its greying lids. It seems to stare at me.

`Do you think that your scheming is not known to me?' he says, the smile grown wider still, and in my stomach something heavy flops and moves and makes my arse pull in all tight. He knows. The old man knows about my plan, the borrowed beads, the dead thing in the river. What is there for me to say or do but make to run and hide myself?

He speaks again, and holds me with his smile, his dead-snake eye. `You think to win my favour with your words, is that not it?' He laughs to see me, staring like a throttled cat towards him in my fear and wonderment. `You think to have the old man's treasure when the old man's dead. There is a little of your mother in you yet,' and here he laughs again, and shuts his eyes and laughs so much the laughter turns to coughing, wet and deep.

He does not know. He thinks me sly and greedy, but he thinks me his. Thank all the gods, though none in truth there be.

My answer is come easily to me, with just the ring of feeling hurt yet touched with shame that such a girl might have: `How can you mock your daughter so, that walks the great long way to be beside you? How is it you say she does not care for you? Why, there's a notion in me to walk back again, so little is my want for such a father or what wealth he has.'

At this the coughing stops. His look is worried now, less sure he has the hold of me.

`No. You must stay, and pay my tongue no mind. It is an old man's jest and nothing more. You are my only flesh, and you must stay with me until my end.'

His live eye searches mine, afraid that he may drive me off from him with all his taunting. He has need of me, and is not certain of my need for him: the game is mine. My voice is sniffy and uncaring in reply, to make him squirm more fast upon the hook.

'Oh yes? Your only flesh, you say? What of my brother Garn? You favoured him above me once before. Why not make him your comfort now and leave me in my northland home, if you can think so little of me?'

Here he looks away, and for a while he does not speak. There's silence save the drag and rattle of his bed across the soil and stones; the noisy breathing of the woman as she trudges onwards, pulling him between the huts.

'Garn is no son of mine.' His words are hard, like unto flint. He stares up at the stars and does not look at me.

My best course is to hold my silence, wait 'til he says more of this. The huts crawl by. The woman pants like some great dog, and now he speaks again.

'It is our custom, passing teachings to the boy, as it is our custom to seek mates among the further lands so that it gives a strongness to the blood. That is why Garn is taken far away and you are left beside the great cold sea. It is our custom, to pass teachings to a boy, but Garn . . .'

He stops and hawks, spits something dark into the dark about us.

'Garn will not take up the task, and sets a face against his duty. Says he's not a cunning-man and makes work as a metal-monger, which he thinks a craft more fitted to our time. He says he does not care to know the old and secret ways. We cannot talk save that we quarrel, so we do not talk at all.

'Why, even when he knows the sickness is upon me and my living all but done, he does not bend, nor put aside his hammer-stones and molds. There's none but you to take my learnings 'fore my breath is gone, girl. None but you.'

His eyes are pitiful, cast up at me as with an ailing beast. When men are weak, my heart's made harder yet, but there is only care within my voice, hushed so as not to wake the sleepers in the reed-topped mounds about.

'What is your illness, father? Is it in your wind, that you have not the breath to speak?'

His bed bumps heavy, dragged across a sudden hollow in the dirt. He grunts, discomfited, and then he sighs.

'This willage is too much a part of me. Its sicknesses are mine. If there are beetles in the grain down at the southfields, then it gnaws my vitals here.' His hand, a brittle crab, moves low across his belly.

'And if the old rounds up on Beasthill fall to ruin and neglect, then in my back the bones grow weak as yellow stone and crumble where one scrapes upon the other.'

Now he lifts his fingers, gestures to the useless clotted eye, like curdled milk. 'This happens when the dye-well in the meadows west of here runs dry. Or else a tunnel in the under-willage floods, a cave subsides and leaves me pissing blood from one moon to the next. They burn the trees from off the great east ridge to level it atop, and now my will no longer stands. The hairs fall out and make it like a babe's.'

Ahead, set some way off from all the other huts, a pile of shadow hunches in our path, to where the woman Hurna trudges, drags the old man in her wake who drags me like-ways with his words.

'The people are the worst of it. When Jebba Broken-Tooth takes mad and kills his woman and their child, then is there seeping from my ear. Or, if the brothers Manyhorse are feuding my teeth have a cold burn. And now all the doers of wrong that we get here, the cut-bags and the cheats, the tap-and-takes all living in stilt-settles by the drownings. They give me the lice.'

He grins, and shows his lonely teeth, that ache with all the angry words that pass between the brothers Manyhorse, whoever they may be.

'One time, it pleases me to pick a fat one out and split it with my thumb. The next day, word is come of how some bucket-belly fenland cheater gets caught in amongst his stilt logs when they fall, so that they crush him near to one piece and another.'

Here he laughs again, the creaking of a dead bird's wing, and here we reach a halt, the woman ceasing in her haul before the heaped up dark that is the old man's hut. She shoves aside the stop-woods on their swing of rope, wherefrom a dull red light pours out, as from a torture hole, and as she drags the old man in he's laughing still and makes a pinching motion at me, thumb and finger. Black nails bite together.

There in Little Midden once a girl not much more than a babby tells me how she may not find her mother in the market crowd, as if it's given up to me to do her mother's minding for her. From a black man in a robe whose colour is outside my power to name, she fetches me a bright new dagger and a silver piece in trade.

Upon Shank Sister Hill a millman gives me a half a pig for near as many bags of dirt as there are fingers on one hand, with but a finger's depth of grain spread out atop each bag to mask the soil beneath.

In Dullard's Way they curse me still for trading dried out dog-stool wrapped in bark as proof against the pox.

An elder man of Reekditch gives me half a skin of mash to have me in the mouth, then falls asleep to wake with treasure bag and gizzard cut the both.

In Fat Arse Fields, the opened mound by night, my shoulders racked by all the shovelling, a rag held to my nose. The rotted fingers swell beneath the rings, which must be twisted off. The softened flesh rucks up about the joint, sloughs off completely as the ring's pulled clear.

In Sickly that big fat girl and her half a loaf of bread . . .

The old man clicks his beetle-coloured nails and mums the splitting of a tick.

Inside, the great bellhut's a lung stitched out of rush and hide on ribs of wood, filled with the breath of souring piss and damp that marks the old, though spiced with rarer scents. Big, yet made small by all the clutter stacked within, fantastic cliffs of dog-skin masks and god-faced shields, of rattles, feathered bones and claybaked men-in-kind. Strange birds, dead yet unrotten, stiff and staring, caged in woven wood. A snarl of pickled rats all knotted at the tail and nailed to bark. A cured and varnished heart. Rocks finger-marked by monsters, cooking bowls and spools of stitching gut and more and more in hazard-footed screehills to the roof's dark underhang.

There are but shoulder-narrow passages left clear between the listing scarps of muddled tool and fetish-stick, between the dust-dry garlands and the eelskin robes. Is this like something seen before, in a forgotten baby dream of mine?

A fist of amber with a horrid little sea-fright caught inside, its body flat with tufts of bloodworms growing from the back of it, raised up on many pin-stiff legs, and from one end a bulb where is a face that makes me jerk away. A bowl that may be seen through, and an unborn baby girl, curled up, her blind head chalked to white then painted brightly, like a whore.

Somewhere towards the centre of this queer-mazed round an ember pit throws up a sulking light. Like beads of melted ore it prickles red upon the rubbled ornaments; is caught in painted sailsheets, shadowbacked; cut into smoking slats of pink and greening dark upon the sharpness of their edge. Slabbed black falls on the passageways amongst the useless things, slashed here and there by shafts of bloody forge-light spilling from the heaped-up side-paths of those corners where one channel forks into another.

Saving when they drag through such a chimney-shaft of sudden warfire brightness, nothing may be seen of Olun on his bed of sticks. Following them with ears alone: the pallet's rasp across the scored black dirt, the woman's foot-thud muffled, drumming through it, tickling beneath the bareness of my heel. Now losing them about a bend and hurrying to catch them up, come round the turn in time to see the old man's needle-harrowed face bleed sudden red and bright from out the dark as it drags through a stripe of light. The stripe grows wide. We are stepping out into the ember-lighted round of open space there centring this puzzle-track of piling casks, dream tumbles, rary bits.

Her flat face gleamed with sweat, the woman, Hurna, sets the old man and his pallet down to rest beside the sunken fire, then lumbers off without a word for wood to bring back to the flame. Lost in a moment, great bear footfalls stumbling off into the maze of relic toys.

The old man's tired, so sends me off to sleep in one far corner hung with hides and set apart. He tells me not to pay it mind if he and Hurna set and talk about the embers for a time. It's plain he does not wish me to keep company with them, and so my bed is made from furs, the fireside's light shut out about me by the hangings.

Soon, there's the sound of Hurna coming back with wood, the clatter as she throws it down. They talk then, low, the first time that she speaks within my hearing. Why, she sounds more flat and stupid than she looks, which is a thing to say.

It is my hope that they may talk of shanking, or of something good to listen on, but no. She drears about a god that swallows us, which does not sound the god for me. She says once we are swallowed up then we may be born new amongst the gods. As what? A turd that bobs there in their golden midden-hole? Things may be born then swallowed, though it may not be the other way about, not in my reckoning.

Once in a while the old man's voice breaks in and crackles something sharp with scorn, withdraws again to let the woman's answer drag away and on and on into the night. She pulls their talk along, a pallet weighed with blunt and heavy words.

Below my fur and naked save my fancy-beads, my eyes are shut but not my ears. Her words float through me. Essence. Spirit-ore. The hobbles of the flesh. Change. Be transformed, refigured in the passion, passion, passion ash . . .

The ashfields. Me a little girl. This snow is dry, warm grey, its smoothed and rounded flanks just right for stepping in, a powder finer than the stone-ground corn, as cool and slippery as water on my foot that now sinks in, and in, expecting ground, and deeper, there's no firmness underneath the ash to stop me falling . . .

Start awake. The furs piled up about my neck. The hangings, pink lit on the other side and still the woman's voice beyond them. Sweat all up my back and silky wet between the breasts. These furs make me too hot. Take out my arms and shoulders from beneath. That's better. Cooler. Turn and roll upon my other side. The beaded hoop of wire now digs into my shoulder that it must be pushed away. There. Now the all of me feels good, so slack and tired that it escapes my thoughts just where my leg rests, or my hand. All one soft piece, that does not know the different bits of me.

The woman's words, smooth of all meaning now, are only sounds, grey pebbles sleek and wet that tumble slow through nothing, here inside my eyelids: Beasthill. Heartring. Urned with queens. The cheated worm. Bones milled and raked. And when you. And when all of us. When we. When we are sparkborn . . .

In my dark, the colour flukes play blue, no, red, and run to make a ring. It cobwebs out, it cobwebs out and at the centre comes a melt, deep winter green and, glimmering, breaks apart, the ripples, river, river's edge, and here she comes, the girl, her throat all open but she does not pay it mind, and she is smiling, pleased to meet with me.

'Come up the river bank a little way,' she's saying now. 'There is a big black dog up there who says he knows of you.'

She turns and walks, leading ahead. Where is the river gone to? There are bushes at each side and piles of clutter stood amongst them, heaping mounts of queer and clever things that are well known to me, although their names are not now in my thoughts. The girl is calling up ahead, along the passageway.

Trying to catch up next to her but something's tangling my feet and makes me slow. Her voice goes further off from me. She's talking now to someone, yet her words are flat and have no spirit in. That must be how it is, the talk between the dead. Push on. Push deeper after her. It's darker now. Is that her calling me? It's darker now . . .

Light. Morning light. What place is this to find myself awake?

Olun. The old man's hut. The father of the girl. The girl beside the river's edge.

Ah yes.

Yet half asleep, still furry in my thoughts and muttering to myself while pulling on her clothes, my clothes, then crawling out into the centre round of Olun's hut. Deserted. Fire pit cold and dead. The greying, liver-coloured ranks of oddment that surround me robbed of all their midnight glamour by a sun that's strained in dusted spindles through the chinked rush roof above.

They have a stillness and an old hush in them now, these chines of bauble and remain. The narrow paths ravining through them are less mazed as seen by pearl of morning, making it a simple thing to find my way out, stumbling and mumbling to day. Squinting against this bright; the world smears in my lashes.

'Usin? Usin!'

He says it yet again before it comes upon me that this is my name. Turn about. The old man lies before me on his raft of twigs, wrapped not in feathers now but in a robe of many dog-pelts, whole, so that black snouts show here and there above the slashed vent of a mouth, below the lidded fastening holes.

Beside him food is spread in bowls of polished bronze. A hot fish, gaping. Clouded with alarm and great unhappiness its steamed eyes fix upon me. Near to this a dish not bigger than a thumb-cup, filled with bitter cherry mash. Crust-hided haunches of grey bread to dip. A skin of goatwarm milk to wash it down.

'Hurna and myself, we eat at dawn. She's off to worship with her people now and is not coming back this side of noon. Now you may eat.'

He signifies towards the food, a spasm of his patterned hand.

He watches me crouch cross-kneed, take the dagger from my pouch and score his fish along its back, about its tail, the gill-line of its throat, grey vapour bleeding up from where the black skin splits, peels back beneath my edge. Thumb out the spine. Ease up the hairbone prongs of rib from smoking whitemeat slots. Now lift the brittle centipede of backbone out with face and arsefins all, to set aside. Prick out a slat of flesh, raised smouldering and pushed between my lips on daggerpoint, which gives me cause to think of how that point is last employed.

My chewing takes some whiles, my swallow hardly less. Out from beneath a dishrim, flaring bronze, the fern-tailed skeleton is staring, girl-eyed, there beside my plate. Chew, swallow, take some more, but this time with my fingers. Olun watches me, and when he sees my mouth's too full to make an interruption without choking me, he speaks.

'While Hurna is not here we may walk up the river path a way, as may be to the bridge and back. If you're to have my leavings, it's as well you have a cunning of the land and all its lie.'

It comes to me that he says 'We may walk', when it is only me who's fit to do as much. He means for me to drag him, in that ox-legged woman's stead, and me so little built! The flakes of creature in my mouth and mention of his leavings: these are all that stop me calling him the lazy, crafty gill clot that he is.

He does not speak again throughout the fish, the bread or sweet, dirt-gritted milk, and yet from while to while he opens up his mouth as if to do so, though he makes not any sound at all. It's only now it comes to me that these are gasps he makes to take his breath.

The cherry stew's too sharp for me, left barely tasted. Afterwards, upon my bending low to wrap his dog-coat tighter in before his pallet's taken up and dragged, he lifts one hand and gently wipes away the goatmilk beaded on my underlip, a taste of stale and smoke-cured finger-end. He smiles, eyes creasing in the web-skinned sockets. Three small fish-marks drawn bright red upon one lid are lost within the sudden fissured deeps.

No sire or dam of mine has need to make me drag them all this way. The father lowered bee-stung to his grave up in the hollows of the Great North Woods, he does not ask for me to drag him, stinking, all about the land. Nor is my mother carried when she sickens, whoring in the mine camps east of here, the both of us together now that father's dead, and when her cough starts putting off my customers there's nothing more to do than leave her. ' You rest here. It does not take me long to find some firewoods and come back. Rest, Mother. Rest and wait for me,' and morning finds me in another place, down track, alone.

The both of them are dead and gone now, neither are they carried there.

My grip is sore about the litter's poles, hands wealed and callusing, and we are barely out the willage, barely out the skein of knotted dust tracks where the children laugh and fight between the bustling huts, their thin brown shapes that tumble in and out of view like spirits through the pot-haze, stew clouds watery and dismal to the nose, a fever fog that damps the cheek.

Though he is dragged behind upon his pallet in my wake it feels as if the old man's pushing me, goading me on beyond the hut-rings to the settlement's north gate. We cross paths with the birth-marked boy who plays the guard on my arrival. Walking with a short, soft-fatted girl whose speckled shoulders pale to milk beneath her blood-gold hair, he does not look at me.

The watch-hut by the gate is empty as we scrape between the shored up brackens to the field beyond. The empty watch-hut troubles me, but once we're through the gate its reason's plain: the withered man with dye-blacked hands is stood outside, turned face towards the barrier of thorn, a corded will limp in his rattling hands. On watch alone he steps outside the gate to make a piss, but from the look of it he stands and nothing comes.

As we pass by him, me in front, the old man dredging there behind, he glances up, sees Olun, and calls out.

'You have a daughter, then. That's new.'

'Aye,' Olun croaks, replying. 'Aye, that's new.' Thus we pass on and take the path beside the river, yellow dirt trod bald between the scrubs of grass. Bronzed leaves pile against trees that stand like widows, shoulders bare and bent with grief, heads hung and grey hair catching in the riverskin where currents braid to silver, split on twig ends. Looking up from frozen, trudging feet and back across my shoulder, see the soot-gloved gateman leaning, still with face towards the thorn and waiting for the dam to break.

We scrape and clatter on beside the river, counter to its flow. The twig-bed crackles, drawn along the hard-worn path behind me, like a brushfire at my back from which a voice comes now, the old man's, crackling also.

'If you're ...' A breath. 'To follow me ...' Another. By these constant, desperate suckings-down of air his talk is broken, sudden eddies in its flow.

'If you're to follow me, then you must know my path. If you're to be the cunning one when I am gone, why, then you have my leavings, but it must be that you have my learnings also.'

Listening to him speak, it comes to me that though he may be old he has his wits about him. You can hear it in the way he fits his words one to another, clear despite the interrupting breath. My mother, younger far than he, says only 'Cack' and 'Wet' and 'Where's he gone?' those last few moons. This Olun is no fool, and so he has my ear.

The fire voice sputters on, above the litter's cracklings. `My way of learning is my path, still trodden in my thoughts, although my walks in this world are no more.'

He does not need tell that to me, me with my palms all blistered and my shoulders sore from dragging him.

He draws his frantic, drowning breath and then goes on. `This track of knowing's beaten through wild overgrowths of thought by long moons of repeating, yet means nothing if it has no counter in this world, the world wherein we walk and die.'

He leaves the walking up to me and, in return, the dying's left to him.

`My path of thoughts is therefore drawn from all the paths about me in the truth of life. These territories that we span are as like spanned within, where there are monuments of notion, chasms, peaks and streams for night-thoughts there to spawn. If you would know my path and follow in its way, then know the land about, both track and willage, in its bridge and in its drownings. Know the outcast rat-shacks, relic stones and gill-halls. Mark each path above and know the underpath below, its secret way from vault to treasure hole.'

My peace is held, all the long while he talks. This word of treasure, though, must not slip by, and bids me to break in.

`What underpath is this, and how is it for me to walk, if all its ways be secret?'

He is sniffy, waving me away with his reply.

`We have our Urken-tracks beneath the soil. Only the Hob or Hob-wife know their ways, that pass from hand to cunning hand across the ages. Many treasures of our craft are there, but this is yours to know when you are ready, filled with knowings of the plainer tracks above that are an equal to your calling. On that day, it may well be that you go down and walk the candled leagues yourself, where these old feet of mine once tread the wormslopes and the chilly rock, that only tread there in my dog-dreams now. Before that day you must tread all the paths above, and know the stories set along their way.'

This troubles me. It seems the old man has it in his thoughts for me to drag him all through up and down along these paths he talks about, which does not please me, not at all. As for the stories set along their way, the ones that hang there in the torso garden are already known to me, and it's not my desire to hear of any more. It strikes me, since we do not pass in sight of those staked carrion, my path of last night gone must lie some way east of this river-walk, which pleases me right well. Trudge on, the leaves all kicking up about my feet.

Now Olun calls for me to stop a while, and bids me look away now from the river to the east, where rises up a hill with white smoke twisting out in ribbons from its top. It is the hill by which my way is made down to the bog-struck valley floor upon my coming here, its crest-fires burning still by day. Far off, across the fields, the little people stood about the blazes on that peak may yet be seen. Their chanting, faint and distant, comes to us with each new shift of wind, one voice of note more strident than the rest, that carries further.

'That is Hurna,' says the old man, cackling the while and spraying spit across his pup-faced wrap. He offers up no further word, but bids me heft the poles and carry on. Our shadows shrivel up beneath the climbing sun. The whiles pass by.

Ahead and to my right a meadow swamp of rushes fans away, a hollow of blanched spears that has a crop of solid land knobbed up from out its middle like an island in a lake of reed, and there upon it stands a mound of wood, as for a fire. There are some children playing near it, boys who crouch about another of their kind, who lies upon his back. They jab, and fondle him, and make loud cries.

As we tread nearer, passing them, it comes to me that this is not a child that lies between them but a boy-in-kind, whose empty rags they stuff and poke with straw to lend him form.

'They're readying the pig-boy in the Hobfield, then,' says Olun, but it's better that my breath is put to hauling him, and not to asking him the where of every mad-head thing that he may say. Trudge on. The leaves burst up like birds, and on, and on, and only now, my back nigh broke and fingers fit to fall away, is there a sighting of the bridge, there at the far end of this river track, all passage-walled with peeling birch trees, ashen silver in the light. Almost. We're almost there.

The old man tells me all his secrets just before he dies, and lets me journey down into the tunnelways beneath the settlement, where there are silver bowls and wristlets made of gold. By still of night, this hoard is carried off down track a way, to where my new home waits for me. My new wealth's traded in for land, for oxen and fine wraps and pretty slaves, that all those passing by my hut may see its grandness and its herded grounds and say, `How fine a woman must live there.'

My food is nothing save the rarest fish and the most tender pieces cut from infant beasts. Tall, painted warriors are set to guard my days; the strongest service me by night, and every moon my willeins offer up their thanks and bags of grain to me. Their children dance between the rose-twined pillars of my stilted chair.

This is their bridge, then. Big black logs that smooth together down across the ages make the curve of it, that rises gently up away from us towards its hump, above the foams and churning deeps below. For all my care in hauling him and litter both across the bump-topped woods, the old man grunts and clicks his tongue and makes complaint to me each time his bones are jarred.

Here, on its near-end slope, the blackened span has chinks between the timbers. It seems there is a little pit dug underneath this south side of the bridge. My eyes squint, peering, but whatever once may be to see inside the hole is long since gone. There's only pale flecked dirt, lit bright where sunlight's wrung between the roof logs over which we make our way now, passing on.

`Stop here,' says Olun as we reach the middle of the bridge, and bids me set him down and sit beside his litter on the wetworn logs, the waters roaring under us. The cold strikes up my arse. We do not talk of much. He makes remark upon my fancy-beads, blue sparks hung on their copper strand about my throat, and asks me how they're made.

It startles me, the ease with which this stolen tale comes tumbling from my lips: the sand fires, seaweed banked, seen through the shore fogs, burning. Men with puckered, flame-scarred hands who tip the ore and curse if it should splash, the reek of singeing beard, a scorching in the lungs and, afterwards, the glazed sands all about the furnace hole made hard, shot through with bitter juice of kelp and bladderwrack and coppered blue. My words pour, effortless, and conjure tangle-headed beachgirls, skirts damped dark about the hem by surf, that pick for skybeads in the fire-struck dunes, as if these sights are ever known to me.

The old man nods and smiles and gazes off downriver where the stone-green waters bend away amongst the western nettle wastes. A bark-boat breasts the current there, two men whose shoulders roil and wheel about their paddle blades, a glittered spray each time these cut the frothing swell. They lean into a turning masked with trees, are gone.

Off on my right a man calls to another, leading me to turn my head and look about. Up by the bridge's farmost end there's someone crouched to squint into the belled and ringing hollow underneath its arch, where fray-edged water-shadows shoal to form a ghost bridge, top-side down below the blurring torrent.

Now the figure stands, a grey, pot-bellied man, and calls again to some few fellows who are sitting sharing bread just up slope from the river's edge. They call back to the man beside the bridge and seem to laugh at him. He speaks again and makes a sign towards the hidden shallows of the underspan. One of the feasters passes on his bread and stands, runs stumble-footed down the bank to join the other by the bridge, where both now stoop to peer. More shouts. Another man trips down the slope to stand with them, and yet one more.

It is some game they play to put aside for now their slog amongst the ditches and fields, which is no great concern to me. My gaze turns back upon the old man, hound-clad on his bier. Side-edged to me, his skull is round and beaked, a grey shaved bird. The eye that's nearest me stares into nothingness, its socket pool froze white in Olun's winter. On his leather cheek, a patchen stole of coloured scars.

He asks about my beads: It may be that he waits for me to ask of his tattoos.

' These markings that you have are of a style that is not known to me. It seems they have not rhyme, nor a device.'

He turns his corpse-bird skull that he may see me with his good eye, sucking in the air to speak. His breath, warm game that's hung too long, blasts stale against my face and makes me flinch away.

' Oh, they have a device, girl, and a rhyme. Don't you think otherwise. They are my crow designs.'

His crow designs? The worm-blue mottle of his shoulder, bowlined red from nipple back across to spine? His firmament skull, scribbled jowl, fern-cornered lips? There's nothing here that's of a like to crow or bird of any kind. What is his meaning?

Lifting up my gaze from out this skin maze, back to meet his own and further question him, it seems that he forgets me. Staring past my shoulder to the bridge's northern end, only his dead eye lights on mine, looks through and out the other side, which makes me shiver with a notion of not being here. It's plain that he is looking hard at something off behind me. Glance about, to see it for myself.

The men stand in the shallows, wading thigh deep as they gang about beneath the bridge. They reach with sticks to hook out something lodged there; yell like boys, excited, to each other as they poke and splash and heave: Go careful. Here, watch out. It's coming. Here it comes . . .

Big. Grey and bobbing, water meat. The young men crowd about. A gas-blown calf that's taken by the flood, or . . .?

A sudden thought's come into me. The young men grasp the creature fast beneath its arms and draw a silver furrow to the bank, where it is hauled up streaming, flopped out bare and heavy on the grass that we may see it properly.

Oh no.

Boiled fish her breasts. Weed-tongued and staring. Why is she not half-way out to sea by now, couched to her ribs in silt or strangled in the crabnets, sopping, lying still amongst a sprawl of severed hands that writhe and gesture yet? How is it, dead, she has the wit to stop here at the place she seeks while she's yet quick and warm? How may the dead have destinations? Trickling mouth. Leech ridden, phlegm-black jewels that cling upon her instep there.

They do not know her, do they? Nor the old man. She is not come here before. Weir-carrion, that's all she is. A poor thing river-born and fish-mouthed at the throat, done in, but no one's daughter. Usin. That is my name now, and hers is washed away with all her blood and colour. Rotted tide-fruit, bare and nameless, floundered in the stripes of scum that mark the water's highest reach, she is not anyone's concern. The bedstream's ripple-sands are copied, soaked in replica upon her logged and runnelled skin. Cave-nosed, and one cheek holed by sticklebacks.

The old man bids me lift him, pull his stick-wrought bed across the causewayed trunks to where the willeins gather, down beside its farmost end. Legs bristled to the wading line with jewels of wet, the down ringed into hooks and coils, they stand as still as heel-stones all about the stiller yet.

Hearing the racket of the litter drawing near across the wood, the men look up, make frowns at me yet wipe them off when they see who it is dragged here behind me. Olun lifts his head from off the bier and cranes to overlook them, standing closed about the corpse. The bubble-gutted man who sees the body first below the bridge touches one finger to his brow and mutters, `Good luck to the Hob,' then looks away from Olun, staring at the grass as if afraid. The other men do likewise. What is there to fear about this painted bag of sticks? And yet they shuffle there below us on the river bank and wait for him to speak.

`This morning there is bleeding in my stool, which tells of trouble at the bridge, and brings me here.'

The men look to each other, scared and marvelstruck that this event is known to Olun long before they think to peer beneath the shadowed arch. The laughter chokes and bubbles in my nose: if all his tribe are shit-wits such as these, it is no wonder Olun's thought the cunning-man. This very morn he lets me drag him leagues, yet makes no mention of this omen given from his bowel, the crook-tongued little fiend. It comes to me he lives by gulling lackards, and in truth we are one kind. Why, he might nearly be my father, all things said.

The man so fat he looks with child now waves one hand towards the throat-cut woman at his feet.

`Well, here's the reason to your sign. We find her underneath the bridge, brought up against the beaver dams.'

By all the markings, there's the why of it! There's why she is not by now danced half-way to Hotland in the undertow or pecked clean on a reef of crusted salt: the bridge is built upon the backs of beaver dams! The fat man falls again to silence, waits once more for Olun to give voice, his fellows hulking restless by his side.

Now Olun does a queer and frightening thing. He shuts one gaudy lid across his sighted eye, so that the white-yolked blind one seems to stare upon the spraddling girl meat, cold amongst the weeds.

` Her throat is cut. Her ear is gone, and like to this her thumb.'

It's plain the old man notes these things before he shuts his one good eye, yet still it makes a weird to see him take her measure with his deadsight only. Mummery and nothing more, yet no less hackling for that.

` She's thrown into the river last of all, for it is only reason that her gullet's slit before. Alike to this, the torture of the ear and thumb may not come after she is dead, so must be suffered first of all. She is not cut for sport, for why then stop with but one ear, one thumb? These cruelties are with purpose, and with purpose served are followed swiftly by the kill. Somewhere up river, not a day since gone.'

No, it is not the slowness of his tribe alone that makes him seem more cunning. Here is clever. Here is clever deep enough to drown in. Looking down, it takes my notice that the woman's neck is banded by a stain, mould-green. It is not there when she's thrown to the river, save it's hidden 'neath the blood since sluiced away.

` See that she is not moved. We go to tell the roundhouse what is here.'

With this, he bids me lug him back across the river, juddering down the bridge's southern slope, and now along the balded turf that ribbons by the waterside. Back past the marsh-pond white with rush, its island with a firewood crown whereby the unhaired boys bask naked, belly down on sun-cooked rock. Atop his pyre their rag-child sits, his straw head tipped upon one side, regarding us as we pass on, though yet without a face. The same leaves rise, a dry gold splash about my heel.

The silence holds 'til we are near to half-way home, whereon my question may no longer go unasked.

` What happens now, about that poor killed woman?' Lightly spoken, this, and sounding free of care.

His voice comes back above the creak and crackle of his bier, a whisper from the blaze.

` Oh, nothing much to speak. The river brings us matters like to this from while to while. All nature of occurrences take place amongst the passes north, their remnants fetched up here: unwanted newborns, oxen with too many eyes, or the encumbering old. Saving for if they have the mark of plague we put them to the earth within a day, with flowers offered in the stead of goods. That is the custom here . . .'

He pauses. On the east wind comes a wail, as from far off. Before me, turning to look, stretch the sodden fields and then the hill, its summit wound about with smokes. The tiny figures fling their arms up, keening in the distance.

` Although there are some who wish it otherwise,' the cunning-man concludes, and we go on from there to come at last upon the bracken-fortressed settlement. There Olun tells the gateman, with his bat hands flapping black, about the murdered woman by the bridge, and bids him pass along the story.

` Good luck to the Hob,' say all the willeins as we groove the dirt between them, dragging back to Olun's dwelling. ` Good luck to the Hob.'

It comes upon me now that they are speaking to the both of us.

No. No, not me. To be a Hob-wife is no lot for me, the tiresome learning of each chant, a hut you may not move within for all the tokens sinister. To know each duty and each ceremony, dressing in a robe of faces. No.

Nor is the thought of wasting moons while learning all the old man's mummery a pleasing one. There is no saying how long it may be before he dies. It's up to me to find some quicker way of worming out his secrets.

Here's a thing: though he casts off his son and has no love for him, it may be that the son has knowledge of the father's ways. Aye. Aye, that's neatly thought, that it may be as well to pay a visit to my brother Garn before the shadows grow much longer. He may tell me of the tunnels that his father walks in dog-dreams.

What are dog-dreams?

After a while, big Hurna lumbers back to Olun's hut from her devotions on the hill, her slab face flushed with blood, all bright after her sing-song in the smoke. The old man tells her she is lazy, and that he has need for her to caulk his sores. 'They're bad today,' he grumbles. 'It's a long job that you have.'

She nods, without complaint, and pulls him from the sun and through the cram of charm that bounds his hut. Let here alone, it seems that now may be a while as good as any for to visit with the Hob-man's son. Hurna is talking deep inside the hut, still trying to persuade the old man to her faith while she attends his weals. Scraps of their converse drift out past the swing-woods hung to one side in the doorway there.

'The world is made in fire, which is thereby superior, and ends in fire as all the prophets say. The grave-soil may bring pests and blights to rack the living, and yet we who choose the bright track into dream-while leave no miseries behind. All that is pure within us rises, save our residue. We that proclaim this creed . . .' and on and on, her voice flat as the murmur of a hive. It is a marvel how these godly bodies manage it, to be at once both mad and dull. Let me steal off, between the dozing huts and leave them prattling, away into the noon.

There are no spirit-women in the trees, there are no gods below the dirt, else that they be as daft as Hurna. People all are born with no more why to it than some poor sagging fieldgirl shows her arse off in the high weeds, and there's scarcely better reason in the dying of us neither. Where is there a god that strikes us down with venom from a trampled bee? Who puts us in this place then floods the crop that there is not enough to feed us with; drops ashes from the sky and strikes our cattle blind? If it be gods, they have queer sport.

And yet in every willage there are fat-faced little men and sickly girls who scourge themselves and fast to please some spirit-bear, or else a tree they fancy speaks with them. How can the gods demand starved ribs and lash-striped backs above the sufferings that they already fashion for us? If we in this world are cruel by harsh necessity, how much more wicked are the gods who want for nothing yet torment us to the death? Such things there may not be.

It is not gods that welcome us beyond the grave, but only worms. Small children shriek and dart between the willage huts, where men smoke fish above low fires and women flint away the last few bloodied snots of meat from off the wool-stripped hides. Their mothers chew the skin to make it soft. The squeal and bark of chatter everywhere. Amongst the cauldron steam a dog limps by, the mouldered pelvis of another fast between its jaws. With eyes like bile it watches me walk on.

A gaunt man milling grain upon a flat-stone tells me Garn has made his forge upon the valley's eastern edge, above the Beasthill. This is all the worse for me, that my bare feet must walk again this morning's great long round, but there is nothing for it, and the day is warm.

Outside the settlement's north gate, a lard of men is settled thick about the bowl-rim of a fresh-dug pit, wherein an earth-bear's set against a brace of dogs. One of the hounds is near to gutted, sundered by the earth-bear's shovel paw. It drags its hind legs in the bloodied dirt and whines, its purples bulging through the belly's rent.

The other dog is stronger and starved mad, to see its eyes. It snaps and lunges, scores a stroke of pink across the white stripe of its adversary's brow, which trickles down until the earth-bear is made blind in its own juice. The men about the hole crowd in and laugh, so that a quiver ripples through their soft, grey-spidered tits. They cheer. They fiddle with their balls and do not know it. In the pit, now hidden from me by a wall of wart-hung backs, the earth-bear screams in triumph, else in agony.

Continuing along my path that winds out from the willage gates across the marsh, the torso orchard comes upon me in the bluing flesh even before it comes upon me in my thoughts.

They seem like giant, severed heads, sex-mouthed and nipple-eyed, each with a plume of meat-flies trailing in the breeze. Ant freckles moving, out the corner of my eye. Don't look. Walk on, and stop my nose against the maggot sweetness in the air.

Across the dampland hulks the bare-flanked pile they call the Beasthill, with the fires about its top extinguished now, its silver crown of smoke dispersed, all wailing stilled. Above this, on the valley's eastern slope, a yarn of grey twists up alone through paling sky from out the coppermonger's forge.

This is the last age of the world, for we are come as far now as we may along our path from what is natural. We herd and pen the beast that's born to roam. In huts we cling like snailshells to the fenland that it is in our great-fathers' way to stride across and then pass by. We cook the blood from out the earth and let it scab to crowns and daggers; pound our straight track through the crooked fields and trade with black-skins. Soon, the oceans rise and take us. Soon, the crashing of the stars.

Across the reaches, lush and puddle-sored; the beds of quaking sphagnum moss; midge thunderheads above a stream as dull as tin. The massive wildsheep grazing on the lower slopes regard me from a distance, watch me circle warily about them and continue to the valley's brim, up track beside the Beasthill's northmost face.

Above the hill now, looking back. The dirt-walls ringed atop it, seen by daylight, plainly once hold beasts within them, yet are given to another purpose now. Amongst the banked up rounds huge flowers of soot are seared into the dirt, the shadow petals flared about a grey and crumbling heart, still warm. There are no people to be seen, and so my climb continues up to where the trees are burned away to stumps along the torn sky's ragged edge. Tooth-coloured smoke is ravelling from the forge in tatters, brief and dirty flags to guide me there.

It stands alone, Garn's lonely den, amongst the ugly, char-topped stumps; all roof, with walls so low they hardly can be seen beneath the ghost-green cone of rush. The forge is drystone built and caulked with mud. Neck high, it stands outside the hut and by it swelters Garn. It must be he, his eyes so like the cunning-man's, and yet how different in his frame.

Bare to the middle with an apron hung about below. Fat, yet the fat is hard, slabbed thick in bands about his red and glistening arms, his oak-wide breast that does without a neck but rounds directly to a bull-ox head. His features seem too small, all crowded in between that spread of babe-smooth cheek, beneath the damp and sweeping blankness of his brow.

In one hock fist he grasps a clefted pole that holds the metal to be worked above the coals until it colours like the dawning sun. At this he lifts it, ginger in his movements, to the beating block where, with a hammer-stone, he pounds its clear and heartlit otherworldly length to fine leaf all along one edge. The heft and clang, the heft and clang, a sudden wash of sparks along with every beat, the sound made visible, that rings out bright and then showers dull to earth.

And now the blade is quenched, thrust in an old bark trough, moss powdered, where the water coughs but once to swallow it, then gasps up steam to further bead the coppermonger's jowl. Making my way towards him in amongst the fire-felled woods the fierceness of his purpose hushes me and yet he glances up and squints to make me out against the sunlight at my back. His chin is rounded, like a crab-apple that bobs half sunken in the billowing flesh. A salted pearl drips from it, then another, and he lifts one hand to throw a half-mask of cool dark across his eyes.

`What do you want?' His voice is marvelous soft to come from such a furnace-brute who snorts and clamours in the spark-blown fumes.

`Are you named Garn?'

He lowers now his hand and turns back to his forge.

`Aye, that's my name. What do you want?' He works a bellows made from horse lung, bringing back the coals to heat.

`My name is Usin. Usin Olun's daughter.'

Here, the bellows catch their breath, are slowly lowered from their task so that the embers cool and film across with mothdust. Now the great head turns once more towards me, eyes grown narrow with suspicion. Ill at ease, he wipes the back of one great paw across his lips and leaves a smear of black from beak to chin. The silence holds a while, there in the cinder-grove, and now the sooted corners of his babe-plump mouth begin to turn up, ruefully.

`It's you he sends for, is it, when he mayn't send for me? He wants to dump his load of carcasses and painted picture-barks and that on you now, does he? Well, good luck to him.'

He twists his face into a sneer, turning away from me, and furiously works his bellows. `Good luck to the Hob,' he adds across his shoulder, whereupon he spits a gob of bitterness to sizzle in the glowering coals.

`Is that all you've to say now to your sister?' My words stumble slightly to betray my courage, faltering. He makes me frightened with his size and his ferocity.

`My sister?' He does not look round, but squeezing his contraption made of mare's lights all the harder, fans the embers to their noon.

'The old man claims me as no son of his, and for my part he is no Da of mine, so how then may you be my sister? All that you are after is the old man's treasure, else why are you come here all this way? It's not as if you care for him, who does not wish to see you all the while since you're a babe.'

The brightness of the coals now paints his arms and brow. The bellows cease, and here he wades a few slow paces to a stump nearby, where lie the rawcast lengths of ore, all cold and rough. He does not look at me the while, but speaks, his mouthings full of grudge.

'If you desire his wealth so much, then have it. It is tainted stuff, all full of fevers and queer notions. Much good may it bring you. Just leave me alone to do my work. It is enough that all my growing up is done there in that curse-draped warren that he calls a hut, so don't you bring me any more of it. It's bad stuff, that is, all that crawling underground and talking with the dead. Just give me my clean ore and let me be.'

He chooses now a blemished, ugly rod that's coloured like the leaves about our feet, returning with it to his forge.

My path of questioning is clear. 'What's this of crawling underground? Do you, with your own eyes, see Olun do these things?'

Garn now takes up his handling-pole again, to wedge the ingot in its cleft. He turns his head to glare at me, a sulking youth for all his flesh, then looks away. With his split wand he thrusts the ore-strip deep within the furnace mouth and holds it there.

'What, see him go down holes or into hollows? Are you mad? To see those secret runs is not allowed save you're a cunning-man. That's where their treasure's kept, you know, and all the bones of Hob and Hob-wife gone.'

He smiles about at me, and has a knowing look, his voice grown low as that between one plotter and another one alike.

'But here's the trick: you may not know a little of his secret, lest you know the all of it. To know, like him, each weed-lost path and passage, and the name of every field. To know, as he knows, whence the floods are coming, and where cattle-grabbers make their sly approach or have their hide-aways. To have each tree; each rock; lanes that you do not walk for years, all held within your thoughts at every moment by some rare craft that no common man may fathom. Every well and fisher bank. Each tomb and buried lode.'

This last one puzzles me. Amongst the coals, Garn's bar is turned the colour now of old blood, now of fresh.

`How is it bad to have such knowledge? Why, with you a metal-monger, surely it is all the better that you have a cunning of the lodes and seams?'

He shakes his head. `If all his wisdom's mine then metal-mongering's my craft no more. If all his thoughts are my thoughts also, why, then he is me and me a Hob-man just like him, left having no thoughts of my own. These thoughts, they are not even his, nor yet his father's nor his great-sire's. They are old as hills, these notions in him that shape every deed of his and word. It is as if the old man and the old men come before him are all one, one self, one way of seeing, single and undying through all time. It is not natural.

`My way of seeing's not the same as his, nor is it to be put aside that his old way endures. My forge, my fire, my knowledge of the favouring heats and tempers, these are things to fit the world that we have now. His dowsing and his chanting have no use to me, they give me bad dreams still, and make me set myself apart from him and all his works. This hill's the place for me. It has a feel about it that is right for furnaces, and fire sits well here.'

Now the metal in the forge is near too bright to look upon. He lifts it out with cloven pole and takes it to the beating block.

`But surely, you need not come all the way up here to get away from one old man who may not walk? Why not take somewhere in the willage, nearer to your trade?'

Garn stands with hammer raised, about to start once more the sparrow-scattering din, but pauses, lifts his head to stare at me with eyes so filled with scorn and loathing that it makes me take steps back away from him.

`Live in the willage? Ha! And how may Olun be escaped within the willage? Are you listening to me not at all?'

He speaks between bared teeth, a hiss much sharper than the quenching-trough: `He is the willage.'

And with this he turns away. The hammer lifts and falls. Its deafening chime dismisses me, driving me from that charcoal glade, back to the path that twists beside the Beasthill, down towards the valley floor. Descending, in the far south-west the settlement may yet be seen, long shadow fingering the fields. Late afternoon.

Behind me, going down, the hammering grows faint. Above the distant huts, a pall of smoke.

Unease. It gnaws in me and yet its name may not be said, nor where it comes from, like a low horn sounding in my heart, a cold that rimes my bladder. Is there something going wrong here?

Beasthill, fen and torsos. Finally, the willage gates come into sight, but all thereby is clamour and commotion. Smoke hangs everywhere, that wreathes the sinking sun and drowns the settlement in smoulder-light; great choking banks that seem more made of noise than vapour, cloaking the lament of ghosts, the yowl of unseen babes. My pace grows faster, running now towards the wall of tangled thorn and fume.

The young man with the birth-stained face leans from his gatehouse when he hears me call to him.

'What's happening here? Is . . .' Now the smoke bites in my throat and makes me cough, unable to speak more.

The tears gleam on his mottled cheek, though born of grief or from a smut-stung eye is not for me to know.

'A fire, amongst the eastern barns. It's out now. No one's killed, but there's as many huts as claws upon an owl's leg put to ash.'

Making my way between the coiling drifts, the veils flapped open by a breeze to show me now a woman crouched to wipe her soot-blind infant's face, or now a pair of men that stand beside a guttering ruin, making sour jokes with one another.

'You see how our Dad gets out all right, then?'

'Aye, and me half set to grab his lazy arse and drag him back.'

The veil drifts back. They laugh, and do not see me pass them by.

Beyond the settlement's south reach sets Olun's hut, untouched by fire nor troubled much by smoke by reason of a south-west wind.

This same draught brings me now a noise that quickens once again my pace. Olun is squealing louder than the great black swine who run before the deadgod's hunt. Reaching the hut and making now my way inside, it echoes from the avalanche of hex and foe-skin drums, a shrill that guides me through the morbid huddles to the centre round.

Naked upon his bracken bed he writhes and weeps, with Hurna knelt beside him, meat-faced as she dabs wet rags about his breast, half lighted by the fire pit.

Stepping nearer, crouching now to have a closer look at him, it's clear he has a monstrous burn below one shrivelled nipple. Weeping blisters udder from the scorched and gritted flesh amongst the tattooed shell-curls, hoops and signs. He squeals again, then sinks to fever-talk.

Shifting my gaze to Hurna now, who meets it with her own, the stolid eyes as flat as nail heads.

` How is Olun burned? The blazing in the willage does not come as far as here.'

She shrugs her ploughboy shoulders, grunting her reply. ` It's when the fire starts, over in the eastern huts, before they bring us news of it. Your father yells and bids me look to see, and there it is upon his chest, this awful burn.'

She wrings a little smirk from out between her rind-thin lips. ` You ask me, it's a sign for him to change his faith.'

The old man screams again.

If fire burns a willage, may its welts be raised on one who thinks he is a willage? Does the smoke gust from his lungs and from the settling's narrow paths alike? A blaze for curing fish runs out of hand and half a league away a breast yet blisters in its heat? No. Such things may not be, unless the footsteps of our days are echoed in his veins; unless it is the piss of dogs on distant stumps that yellows now his tooth. Do our skies darken if he shuts his eye, our banks burst if he wets his litter in the night? That sour-meat breeze that wafts amongst our huts, is that his breath? And does the dead girl bob downstream through his intestine, so that blood clouds up from where her corpse-nails dredge the sponge-soft bed, brought up at last against the log-dam of his fundament?

No. No, it must be that the old man burns himself, unless this Hurna sears his breast for sport. It's one way or the other, for a place it not a person, nor is there a sympathy 'twixt flesh and field.

We die. The track endures.

The shifts, the crumbles and collapses barely heard within the dulling coals are all that mark the passing whiles in Olun's hut. That, and the gradual fading of the old man's plaint, the slowing of his pained contortions into but a twitch; a shudder now and then.

His moans come softer: no less urgent, yet they sound as if they hail from further off, the old man wandering lost away from us, his cries for help grown faint as he recedes down dusk-paths woven through the queer and complicated willage of his dreams. Naked upon the bed of wefted twig he stills; he sleeps.

Sat there to either side of him within our cone of ember-light, big Hurna and myself do not have much to say. We share a bowl of curds with crusts torn from a thigh of bread to make our sops. From the surrounding steeps of curio, dead birds observe us as we dip and slop and wipe our chins. Their eyes unsettle me, filled with bleak knowledge of demise.

On finishing her bread and curds, Hurna sits silent for a while, a strange look on her face until she looses a great belch that rumbles on and on like toads in chorus. Seeming much more settled after this, she's quick to start with talk about her faith while making out she wants to talk of mine.

'You hold with all this, do you?' Here she gestures to the teetering stalagmites of dross that stand about us, leaning in like bullies. My reply is but to shrug, which she takes as encouragement; agreement with her side of things.

'No? Well, you do not look the sort for it, and there's no blaming you for that. Dirty old notions, that is all they are, and it's a lucky thing that most good people in these whiles are come to know a better way.'

'Oh? And what way is that?' My question's asked with little interest, and yet she seizes on it like a hare-lipped man upon a compliment.

'My way. My people's way. We do not hold with gods who dwell below the earth and there receive the dead. Why earth is but the lowest of the spirits, having wood and water, air and fire all above it in their import. Earth is that which we must raise ourselves above, not put ourselves below! Young Garn, he sees that well enough, but Olun does not listen.'

Here she tilts her head towards the old man, twitching on his bier and naked save his lines and whorls, his crow designs.

`Your father clings to his old ways and pays no heed to reason. Even when we tell him that when he is dead he may rest in the heartring there on Beasthill, urned with queens, he does not seem to care.'

Her stupid little eyes grow sly.

`If you talk with him, if you tell him that our way is best he may abide by what you say where he will not pay mind to me or Garn.'

It angers me that she is making plots against the old man in this way. That's mine to do.

My words are sharp. `It makes no difference to me where a man's put when he's dead, nor woman. Bury them there where they fall, or . . .' Checking myself sharply, on the brink of saying `Throw them in the river', my quick wits come to my rescue just in time: `. . . or leave them hung out for the birds. It may be that this is a thing of great concern to you and Olun, but it is not any great concern of mine. Now, all this talk is tiring me. My bed is soft, my father's sleeping peacefully, it seems, and it is time to make my rest. A quiet night to you.'

Leaving her squatting fish-jawed by the bier, making my way through decorated hangings to my screened-in bed: there is a deep, still well of fur and comfort waiting for me; waiting for my bones that tire with all the walking of the day. Upon removing everything except the copper ring where hang my fancy-beads, the hides close over me like warm, dark waters. Sinking. Sinking deeper in the swirling black.

A big dog turns, its great eyes empty save a white like lightning, fierce and flameless brightness that may burn away the world. Harsh brilliance pouring from its mouth now, as it splays the rawness of its jaw, and lunges . . .

Scream and sunlight both awaken me, so muddled in my rousing thoughts that sound and shining seem to be all of one part. The scream is mine, cut off as realization comes upon me.

How is morning here so quick? It seems no sooner do my eyelids close than these rude rays are come to prise them open, stuck with sand and lashes though they may be. A food smell finds me now shucking off my night-skins; pulling on my clothes. The dream that woke me up in such a fright is gone, for all my efforts to recall it in my thoughts. Ah, well.

My stomach growls and bids me rise to trace the skein of cooking-scent that's threaded in between the dumps of lore and curse and keepsake. What great feast does Olun set for me this morning? My hand shoves back door-woods on their creaking rope to let me step without and view my meal.

The dead girl's at my feet, stretched out and belly up there in the dust before the hut. A cloudy-eyed and gazing accusation, face expressionless yet there's a black smile just below her chin, above the slime-green stains that stranglemark her throat. Blue-white. A subtle shine, a mooniness about the skin. Her back teeth, clenched together, bared to vision by the fish-hole in her cheek.

There on the corpse's far side, facing me, the hag-queen's rough-boys, Bern and Buri, crouch upon their glittering haunches like to one man with his shadow given flesh, both naked save for will-sheaths made from hollowed catfish that start bulge-eyed with the horror of their plight, the ugly ribboned mouths agape, exposing yellowed spikes of fang. They stare at me, the mould-cast bullies and their catfish all.

Glancing in panic from the shaven rough-boys to the dead girl sprawled between us and then back again, my eye alights on Olun, resting with his dream-daubed and loose-larded frame propped by one tattooed elbow on the bed of sticks, that's drawn up right beside his murdered child. Though better than last night, he yet looks sick with weakness, worse by far than he has seemed of late. Upon his breast a dressing made of rag and plastered mud is tied to stem the weeping of a burn that scorns all sense, and dog-skin robes are draped across his lower half. Some way beyond him there is Hurna, looking put-on as she stirs a mess of fish and meal above a stuttering fire.

Craning his thick-strung neck to peer up at me now with ill-matched eyes, the old man speaks: `Why do you scream? We hear it right out here.'

The thudding of my heart stops me from making sense of what he says, and so prevents an answer. All that's in my power to do is goggle at the picture-hided witch-man and his river-raddled daughter both.

'What is she doing here?' This is the best that may be squeezed out past my lips, set tight and bloodless as a rein upon the terror welling in me.

Olun looks down at the cold, still girl beside him with surprise, as if he but this moment notices she's there, then he looks back at me.

'Her? It's our custom to inspect the unknown dead for marks of plague or other signs before they're put to rest. This is accomplished at the roundhouse in the usual way of things, but being sickened by my burn it is not in me to be moved that far, so Bern and Buri bring her here. Sit down and watch. Remember that upon my death, these duties pass to you, with many more beside.'

What is for me to do but kneel as he directs me? Both the rough-boys bare their sundered smile at me as Olun turns once more to his inspection of the girl. My smile is faltering in reply.

Closing his good eye, Olun now regards the dead thing with his blind and frosted orb alone. One brittle, painted claw creeps out to crawl across her belly, cold as polished stone. It kneads and probes her flaccid breasts, then scuttles further, past the stripe of green about her neck, to linger at the caked lips of the gash below her jaw. One finger traces this along its length and then moves up to rootle through the hole gnawed in her cheek, and to caress the tube-shot scab of red where once her ear is joined. A shudder passes through me when he speaks, although it is not cold considering the season.

'She is pulled from out the river one day since. She is perhaps another day afloat before she's found, and so is killed not far up river north of here. Her throat is opened by a dagger or a short-blade knife, both sharp and hard enough to cut through bone, as in her thumb.'

Though they may see me staring hard away from them, the brothers Bern and Buri now both speak to me in turn, and force me to look up.

'It seems to me she dies the day that you arrive.' These words are spoken by the brother on the left. His voice is slow and drawling, filled with strange amusement, though he does not smile or crease his eyes as he squats there regarding me across the slaughtered woman.

`From the north. Arrive here from the north, the same as her.'

This is the other brother speaking, though in voice and manner they are both alike as in their looks. What do they wish for me to say?

The left-most brother speaks again. `Do you hear anything of robbers in the passes while you are upon the track?'

Half-drowning in my fright of what they may suspect, this notion is a welcome raft to clutch at.

`Robbers? Why, you may be sure of it! The travellers that meet with me these last few days upon the track all talk of nothing else. A great fierce band of men, they say, though speaking for myself it seems the cut-bags do not show themselves to me. My way here is without event.'

Both brothers purse their lips at once and then nod thoughtfully.

`A band of robbers?' says the one upon the right. `It may be so. Such things are known to us. You're lucky that you do not meet with them yourself.'

`Aye,' adds the brother on the left, `considering that you must be not much more than a league or so away when she is murdered. Very lucky.'

All of us nod gravely here, acknowledging my fortune, and let Olun carry on with his investigation.

Still with nothing but his blind eye visible the old man shifts his hand back down the woman's drift-meat belly to explore the curl-ferned mount there at her fork. His knowing fingers sort amongs the coils and ringlets, moving them aside to better see the cold white hillock whence this overgrowth is sprung.

`There are no bruises.' Here, the old man clucks his tongue in disappointment and a sudden chill falls over me: he does not move aside the hair to look before he shuts his sighted eye. How may he know a bruise is there or not by touch alone? The hand moves further down now. Fingers struggling like blind-worms crowd in, eager for admission to her rigor-narrowed aperture, and yet without avail. The frail and painted hand withdraws. The witch-man speaks.

`Her gill-caul is unbroken.'

Here the rough-boys both look up at Olun with the same frown drawing tight their shaven brows.

`She is not shanked by force, then?' Buri says, or Bern.

`There's queer now,' Bern comes back, or Buri. `She's a comely girl and if she's to be robbed and killed then why not shank her first?'

He does not need to add `That's what we'd do,' for it is in his eyes. Instead, his frown grows deep and, after thinking for a little while, he ventures now his next remark. `Does she have pox?'

The old man shakes his head so that the stars designed thereon swoop wildly from their course.

`No pox. No mark of plague. She's safe to bury.' Here he turns his face to me, and shows me all the pain and fatal weakness graven in its lines. The old man's nearer to his death than is my guess before today, and he does not yet tell me of his tunnels or his treasure holes.

`Usin?' he says now. `We are finished here. You may as well go take your feast with Hurna while we ready this poor child for burial.'

Though Hurna is not any favoured company of mine, it does not grieve me much to do as Olun says, so great is my relief to be away from these same-seeming brothers and the corpse they peck about so thoroughly. It's bittering scent is all about me, walking from the hut to where the dour, god-muddled woman crouches by her fire and shapes the fish-meal into flat grey cakes.

She passes one to me that's like a half-formed animal, so horrible it is squashed flat beneath a rock at birth. We do not speak, still thoughtful of the words that pass between us this last night. The dead girl's smell is everywhere about my hair and clothing, and my appetite is poor. Each mouthful of the fish-meal cake takes me that long to chew it is not in me for to finish more than half of it.

Shifting my gaze from Hurna to the group before the hut. It seems the bully brothers are employed in rolling up the corpse within a drab, soil-coloured sail of cloth, the old man looking on as he rests there beside them on his bier. About to wind the shroud about her head, one of the rough-boys points towards the stripe of bright stump-water green that's ringed below her open throat. He mutters something to his brother, then to the old man, who nods and makes reply, too far away for me to hear a word. The brothers shrug, and now continue in their dressing of the dead.

Beside me, Hurna gives a sudden snort as if to mark contempt.

'He need not hope for me to drag him to his filthy rite. That's up to you, girl. It may serve you well: you're sure to pay more heed of how the dead are put to rest if you must make the long walk to their grave yourself.'

She laughs and makes her tits shake. Overhead a single crow looks down in passing and calls once, as if alerting us to the approach of something that may not be seen save from that soaring vantage. Clouds mass on the west horizon. In the willage, children chase a painted pig between the huts, now cheering, now complaining as the frightened creature veers this way and that, a gaudy smear of colour streaked amongst the barns and horse-yards, squeaking. What hope may there be for anything so shrill and bright? No hope. No hope at all.

There is a fearfulness that gathers weight and form within my belly day by day, grown restless and uneasy as a cold grey baby turning in my womb. You must be gone from here, part of me tells myself, before another dawn is come to find a dead girl placed before your door. Leave with the wolf light when there's nothing save the birds awake; steal off between the snoring huts and never more return. It is not safe here. There are shadows that loom big behind each happenstance, each chance remark, and more is meant than what is said. Move on. Take up the track again and put these whispering huddles at your back.

And now another part of me replies: You cannot leave, it says, and throw away the only chance for ease and wealth that you may ever happen on, not when the stink of it's so close. Think of the tunnels that may snake, gold flooded, here beneath you as you sit; the wells of treasure deep enough to draw from all your days. Are you a child, to start at dreams born of bad curds you eat before your bed? To mewl when there are creakings in the dark? These night fears must not cheat you of the old man's leavings, that are yours by right. Stay. Stay and bide your time, and come at last to wear a coloured gown and dine on fat.

But what of her, the dead girl? If they find you out . . .

Don't pay that any heed. There's not a thing to forge a link in twixt of you and she. Why, even now the rough-boys, like as berries on a missel-sprig, prepare a bier on which she may be hauled to burial. She is not long above the ground, and when the soil is fallen on her face, then you may put her from your thoughts.

But if his dead eye truly looks upon a world we may not see . . .

All that is nothing save for mummery. Put it aside and think instead of Olun's gold.

But . . .

Oh, be silent, both of you. There is a fishbone lodged between my teeth, and over by his hut the old man calls for me to drag him to the grave fields. Coming, father. Coming.

For a change, the journey is not far. We walk south from the settlement, with Bern and Buri carrying the cold and naked bride upon her hasty bed, while me and Olun scrape along behind. Above us, dead leaves rustle in great muttering crowds upon each yearning bough.

The grave site sets upon a weed-cleared rise that's higher than the puddled boglands soaking all about. The women from the willage are already gathered there as we arrive. They glance up, silent, narrow-eyed, kneeling so to surround a place where all the turf is skinned away, the earthmeat there below scooped out and heaped up to one side as if with taint, a man-deep wound revealed. They crouch about the grave and braid a ring of flower-heads between their many hands.

The women part to let the shaven brothers and their lifeless burden move between them, making high steps, queer and delicate so as not to disturb the floral braid. Once by the graveside, Bern and Buri set the bier upon the grass, one of them clambering down into the pit to take the body from the other who now lifts it up, his fingers clenching in the curls beneath her arms. She's lowered thus into the gravemouth, eyes still open, staring at us 'til she sinks from sight in awkward jerks, each lurch and start accompanied by grunts from Bern and Buri. Settling her upon the gravebed now the bully boy climbs up to join his brother by its edge. Crows wheel above, charred flakes of noise that scatter and re-form against an empty sky.

The ceremony is a dull thing with no rise or fall of feeling, no relief, made flatter yet by this wan, uneventful morning light: the gravewords called in Olun's failing snake-skin rasp, each phrase cast up but briefly on the shores of speech then dragged back by the undertow of straining and collapsing breath; the women, chanting their response learned long and hard above the holes of mothers, husbands, sons, now lavished on a stranger; Bern and Buri, taking up an earth-axe, one apiece, before the chanting's over, standing shift-foot with impatience to refill the hole and be away back to their queen, their suckling place.

The call and echo of the bone-chant dies away, replaced by other rhythms. Bern and Buri, each in turn, now stamp an earth-axe deep within the hill of soil discarded by the gravemouth, scooping up the dirt upon their blades to shower in the dead girl's eyes. The grit-edged chop and bite, the rattling lift and fling, again and yet again. Her body lies unmoving in this sharp, dry rain like some abandoned settlement back in the highland north from which all life is fled, silent and still beneath the steady fall of ash and mud that covers now her wrinkled tracks and bristling gorse, her sinks and outcrops all erased. The breasts and face alone remain. Now nothing but her jaw; her chin. She's gone.

The grave is filled. The women chant again, and Olun scatters dog teeth on the damp, untrodden mound. The petals of the braided flowers begin to curl and darken. Everyone goes home, with Bern and Buri striding off in step across the fields, the women trailing after them all in one long unravelling knot. We bump and judder in their wake, but soon they are too far away to hail, leaving me and Olun to our own company.

`Why do you scatter dog teeth on her grave?'

My question is put forward more to break the dismal silence of the marshes than from any great desire to know its answer, yet the old man answers anyway.

`That spirit-dogs may keep her safe, and guide her through the underpaths into the willage of the dead.' He seems about to venture more, but now a dreadful coughing falls upon him and he may not speak.

`There's none save you and dead men, then, as know these underpaths?' This is my next inquiry, offered once his hawking dies away.

`That's true enough. It seems you must have one or both feet planted in the underworld to know its windings.' Here he laughs, a brittle noise that's thick with mucous, very like the crushing of a snail.

'Except old Tunny. He knows every turning of the path, but all the knowing's in his fingers. None of it is in his head. He . . .'

Here the cunning-man breaks off, as if he thinks it better not to tell me more. At least, that's how it seems to me. A moment passes, then another. There is still no voice come from behind my shoulder where the old man drags, there at my rear. Turning about, the reason for his quiet is plain: his eyes start out like painted eggs. Beneath the crazing net of signs that mark his flesh the skin is turned a slow and ghostly blue.

Not now! Not now before he's told me everything! Dropping the bier to run, my screams alert the settlement before my feet can bear me halfway there. Out from their huts they waddle, slow at first then faster as they see who calls and understand what must be happening. They hurry in a line towards me through the long grey meadow-grass, wiping their hands upon their coats or hitching up their leggings as they run.

He's still alive when we get back to him, some of the blueness faded now, his bird-breast settled back into a lurching rise and fall. He tries to speak as one great oxen-shouldered man scoops Olun from the pallet up into his arms to carry like a babe. His lips move, crinkling their coloured scars, but no words come. Across the field he's borne amidst the buzz and whisper of the willagers that crowd about him in a wavering swarm, towards the far hives of the settlement, already humming and alive with rumour and lament.

Beneath the soil she lies, her yawn packed full with earth, a dry and bitter lace of root-hair snagged between her teeth. She comes here for her father's leavings, closer to them now than all my cleverness brings me, with secret paths of gold coiled all about her while she sleeps and stinks and falls apart. Jewelled gravel lodging in between her toes, and chewed by silver worms there in the wasted treasure houses of the dead; the dead, alone of all the world in that they have no greeds to satisfy, no fears to salve or needs they must placate. Their sockets brim with wealth more splendid than their living eyes may ever know, and it concerns them not at all. My body, warm and anxious, moves to cruder drums.

Outside, beyond the cluttering strangeness of the old man's hut, noon comes and goes, marked by the squeals of panic drowned in children's laughter as the painted pig is killed, off near the roundhouse by the sound of it.

Olun is dying. Sprawled there facing me across the burned-out ember pit he does not seem to breathe at all, but only sigh from while to while, his blinkless eyes fixed on me, blind and sighted both. He sinks into his death and grows remote, unanswering for all my urgent query and demand.

`Please, Father. There's so little time and you must give me all your learnings. Teach me. Tell me how to be a cunning one like you before death draws a curtain in between us.'

Olun smiles, a dreadful splitting of the picture-bark that is his face, and tries to speak.

`The curtain . . .' Here he coughs, breaks off, recovers, starts again. `The curtain's torn. There is a way we may speak with the dead and have their learnings. Patience, daughter. Patience.'

Patience? What is all my toiling; dragging; all my listening to his dull mumbles if not patience?

`How, then? How then may your learnings come to me if you are dead? Please, Father. Why not tell me now, while there is time?'

Again the smile, the decorated bark peeled back. `A test. A final test. If you're to be the cunning one then you must learn to hear the voice of those that bear the name before you. Come now, daughter, do not look afraid. It's not so hard to know the teachings of the dead, for those whose wits are quick and have the eyes to see.'

My mouth falls open here to make complaint, yet Olun lifts one trembling hand to still my protest ere it's born.

`Let's talk no more of this, for there's another matter: something you must give to me while there's yet breath within my mouth. Something of yours, to be my comfort in the tomb.'

What's this? He makes no hurry passing on my leavings, yet he asks a gift of me? My tongue grows tart, as if with bile. `You say that we may talk when you are dead. What need is there for comfort more than this?'

He shakes his constellation-spattered head. `No. Though my voice may hail you from beyond the grave, it does not work the other way about. You may not speak with me, though there's a way for me to speak with you. My need is for some token, some possession of my daughter's for to hold beside me in the dark and make me less alone. It is our custom here. What of those beads about your throat?'

My best chance seems to lie in pleasing this old fool, so that he may relent and tell me all he knows. Making no answer save a shrug, my hands reach up behind my neck to fumble with the knot of copper wire that holds the threaded beads in place. My fingers wage a brief, blind struggle and the hoop of hard blue sparks lifts free, held out towards the old man on his bier.

He does not take the beads, nor look at them. Instead, his gaze still rests with me, seems fixed upon my chin or shoulders just as if the loop of fancy-beads still dangles there. At last, his eyes fall to the gift that's held out in my hand. Reaching, he takes it from me, holds it to his face and then begins to weep.

'My daughter. Oh, my daughter . . .' More tears fall, his words slurred to a moan, an idiot snuffling. It fills me with unease to see this softness in his manner, he who holds a frightened willage in his thrall. To think it brings such grief upon him, just to part with me. How does this world endure, if all its sages are so weak?

He lifts his head and stares once more into my eyes and there is something fierce within his look. Perhaps he feels an anger with himself, to bawl thus like a babe before his child. He speaks to me, his voice grown flat and cold. 'Send Hurna to me now. It is my wish to speak to her alone.'

There's nothing for it but to do his bidding. Picking over hurdles made from gaudy wands and caps adorned with fishbone, my way's made from in the hut to where the dough-faced woman sits and tends her cooking fires outside. She seems surprised at being summoned thus and, after gawping for a while in disbelief, she hurries through the wood-stopped door to be by Olun's side.

Sat tired and disappointed in the dust with back against the bare-stripped wooden walls my vision lights upon the view between the willage huts. Off by the roundhouse men with knives of copper flay the face from off the carcass of a coloured pig. My eyes close, shutting out a world that swiftly moves beyond my understanding. Lurid shapes transmogrify and melt against a scab-thick dark.

The rounded woods still press into my back, the hard-stamped earth against my spine. Off in the mottled dark behind my eyelids there are distant calls and coughs and creakings, willage sounds that penetrate my doze, serve as reminders that the world is yet about me. Half-dreams come. Thoughts blossom into pictures, then dissolve.

Garn hammers bees upon his anvil until black and yellow pulp drools down its side. He stands knee deep in ash that rises slowly in a warm grey flow-tide, covering his thighs, his belly, everything except his head, which has the features of a pig, and now the women of the settlement are come across the risen powder-flats to knot a ring of bright blue flowers about its throat. Their stems leave stains of vivid green against the swells of fat and now an understanding comes upon me that Garn's body is no longer underneath the ash: the head is severed, and the flesh torso hangs nearby, transfixed upon a spar of wood. The bulging skin is painted everywhere with images of birds.

Off from the willage in another world a cry is come, at which the birds rise up in flapping blind alarm and take me with them high above the riverside where, looking down, we see one woman cut another's throat, drag off her clothes and throw her to the sluggish waters. Rising higher now, until the people are not visible and all we know are fields and hills; the clustered pale green dots of distant huts. These sights, though strange and thrilling, are yet known to me from somewhere long ago, but where, and when? My body rises up and up until the acrid scent of wet-furred dog awakens me.

My eyes are open now upon an afternoon grown longer since they close, yet still the sour hound-perfume lingers. Are there dogs about? A half-remembered dream rolls over, flash of black-scaled underbelly just below the surface of my thoughts that resubmerges and is gone, unrecognized. Rising up stiffly to my feet it seems to me the spoor is come from Olun's hut and therefore make my way inside where it grows stronger, thick enough to sting the eyes. How great a dog is this to have a stench so fierce?

Shouldering through the lurid piles and trick-tracks of impediment, the rain-dog smell becomes more overwhelming with my every step towards the centre round, its stinking heart.

There are no dogs.

The fire pit, kindled now, casts up a dance of red across the curves and crannies of the old man's hut. Across it, Hurna sits and faces me, arms hooped about her drawn up knees and head cocked to one side. There comes the spat and hiss of green-wood from the embers, but all else is silence in the junk-ringed clearing. Something in the noise-shape of the hut is wrong. There is a part removed; some sound no longer there. Listening for a moment, the omission's plain: it is the rhythm of his breath.

The witch-man lies upon his bier, bathed in the ghosts of flame that shift and tilt the shadow, setting his tattoos to writhe though he is still as stone. Each staring wet and blind to where the fire pit's smoke is hauled in ragged twists out through the chimney-hole, his eyes achieve a final match, both fogged and frosted now. His breast becalmed, the hands that rest upon it knot and petrify about my hoop of fancy-beads that glitter violet in the coal-light. Piss, his final offering, soaks through the pup-skin robe whereon he lies, from which the scent of dog steams thick and clinging in the fireside heat.

Tell me your secrets now, old man, the way you promise. Peel apart your death-gummed lips and speak to me.

'It happens when you send me in to talk with him,' says Hurna. She is calm and smiling, squatted in the hearth-light next to Olun's corpse. 'We make our converse but a little while, and then he dies. But do not worry . . .' Here she notes the anguish in my eyes, mistakes it for compassion. 'Olun dies a rightly death. His spirit treads upon the bright path now, and best of all he leaves no drudgery for you. His funeral matters are in hand and there are no great tasks you must perform. All things are well.'

All things are well? Gods curse this stupid woman blind! How may all things be well if Olun dies before the secret of his wealth is shared with me? How may she sit and smile and look content when all my schemes are falling down to dust? Beneath my feet the golden tunnels fall away, recede beyond recall. What may be done to bring them back?

A thought comes to me: dragging Olun back towards the village from the dead girl's funeral, and asking if there is no man alive save he that knows the underpath, the trackways of the dead. The old man's laughter, like the splintering of snail husks; his reply that bubbles thick with tar from out amongst the whorl-marked shards: 'Except old Tunny. He knows every turning of the path, but all the knowing's in his fingers. None of it is in his head.'

'Who's Tunny?'

Hurna looks towards me, startled first then puzzled by my outburst, for she may not see how Tunny is connected with my father's death. She frowns, and when she speaks her words are slow, filled with a gentleness that makes me furious. It is as if she's talking to a babe.

'Tunny's the gateman here, the old one with the shaking hands, but you have other things to think of now. It is the upset of your father's death that muddles up your thoughts. Why don't you rest, and leave the readying of Olun's wake to me? You need your time to mourn, and . . .'

Turning from her, stumbling through the hulks and hinders to the dusking air outside.

Her cries of consolation follow me: 'Don't run. You're just upset, but there's no need. He's in a better place. He's on the bright path now. . .'

A strange excitement hangs upon the settlement as twilight falls and objects lose their shape and edge to merge within the falling light. From every hut the people are emerging, laughing, chattering and firing torches, one from off the other, flares of yellow in the settling grey. In whispering groups they drift towards the northern gate, a great slow swarm of amber lights that travels in the same direction as myself. They watch me dart among them, running hard towards the watch-hut with the sweat of desperation on my brow and yet they do not pay me any heed, caught up in some excitement of their own.

The ancient gateman with the black and trembling hands is nowhere to be seen and it appears his post is empty and unmanned until a muffled grunting causes me to peer inside. At my back the torch-lit throng moves through the willage gates and out along the river path, a thread of floating lights.

Inside the watch-hut, by the wall, the red-haired girl with freckled shoulders sits beside the birth-marked youth whose name, it comes to me, is Coll. They have their breeks let down about their ankles and their lips locked hard enough to bruise. Each holds the other's sex.

'Where's Tunny?'

Startled fingers suddenly withdraw from in between the loved one's thighs to cup between their own. Their lips part, shackled only by a silver chain of spit.

`Shank off! He isn't here. Shank off and leave us be!' The boy's spoiled face becomes so red that all its markings are consumed and lost within the flush of blood.

My question, though, is urgent and may not be put aside. `Where is he, then? Come, tell me quick and you are rid of me.'

`He's gone to watch the pig-night in the Hobfields. That's where everybody goes tonight, and more's the pity you're not gone there too.' Here, breaking off, he makes another face and grins to show the stains upon his teeth. `Unless you care to stay, that is, and try a bit of this yourself?'

My wad of spittle breaks against his cheek. Cursing, he clambers to his feet and starts towards me, hobbled by his breeks and far too slow. Only his cries of rage pursue me out beyond the blackthorn walls and through a dark alive with shrieks, calls, trailing flames.

The pig-night. Fires and dolls and painted swine and flickering processions, blazing spills of rush that move along the river's edge reflected in its depths like burning fish. A smell, a thrilling taint upon the air and fever in the children's faces. Pig-night. Every year these passions and these lights, sparked in their fathers and great-sires alike, and back and back to when the Urken leap and gabble in the autumn smokes. This night is not a single time but is as many as the stars, a string of nights drawn through the ages on an awl of ritual and hung with old fires in the stead of beads.

Blanched rushes, pale and craven, bow in quivering supplication to the wind, a landlocked pool of them where from the middle bulges forth a skull of brain-grey flint and crumbled yellow stone that wears a crown of burning wood. Of all the willeins crowded in the Hobfield, but a few have room to stand upon this outcrop, faces red and sweat-bright, backs in shadow as they gang about the pyre. The rest are forced to perch about the sodden meadow's edge upon the harder, risen ground while children scamper back and forth along the narrow spines of path that join this human wheel-rim with its blazing hub.

Fat Mag, the hag-queen, has her place atop the knoll, with Bern and Buri flanking her. The brothers' voices carry on the breeze across the reed-bog, seeming louder and more guttural than when they speak with me. They are both drunk on mash, and one of them now fumbles with his will-sheath then makes water on the fire. A copper stream pours from the drawn-back eel lips of his sheath, whose eyes look on, appalled. His brother and the hag-queen laugh and clap. Old Tunny does not seem to be amongst those on the knoll.

Atop the pyre, amongst the ribboned smoke and flame a figure sits. It is the queer and faceless boy-in-kind that me and Olun see the children making when we drag past here towards the bridge. Making my way about the meadow's rim to see if Tunny is amongst the crowd that gathers there, the straw-stuffed body is concealed from me by rising veils of fire and fume, which now the breeze draws back . . .

It is no boy-in-kind that roasts upon sputtering woods. It is a child. It has a face that seems to turn towards me, eyes alive with pain and fear and lips that move to shape themselves about unknown and terrifying words. Its snout . . .

No. Not a boy. A pig. A pig that has the body of a boy. It is the figure made of rag and straw save now it wears a face flayed from the gaudy hog that's killed this afternoon. It is the settling of the wood that makes it seem to tip and lean at me; heat-rippled air that brings the stilled squeal of its mouth to life. A prickling cold trails spider legs against my nape and then is gone. Push on. Push on between the jostling strangers, tiny furnaces alight in every eye.

Strung out along the raised-up half-moon of the rim the crowd congeals to separate clots of people, no more than a handful in each straggling knot. They drink; they laugh; they hold their smallest children up to see the fire across the ghostly lake of rush. Some have withdrawn into the overgrowth nearby for making sex, touched by the wild scent of this night as were the birth-stained gateboy and his copper-headed girl. From out between the sting-weeds drift their little cries of grateful pain, their hot and frightened breath. Above, the beady, lecher stars look down and know a jealous wish for skin.

Ahead of me a cooking fire is built upon the Hobfield's edge, a smaller brother to the central blaze. Above it, spit from arse to gizzard, turns the carcass of a pig whose face is skinned away, over and over in a great slow roll as if its hissing flesh recalls old wallows in cool mud. Along one flank the meat's already pared down to the bone, white ribs bared in a grin through pink and sizzling gums.

Not far beyond this, Tunny stands apart, a gaunt and rangy thing with skull tipped backwards savouring the smell of fire; of roasting pig; a sniff of gill borne from the weeds behind him. By his side, forgotten, hang the stained and shivering hands. He turns his head at my approach and recognizes me.

`Ah. Well. Your father's dead then, is he?' Awkward in his speech, he is not used to consolation.

`Aye, my father's dead. He speaks of you before he dies. He says you may have things to tell me.'

`Oh? What things might they be, then?' Old Tunny looks confused, the dye-dipped fingers grown more restless by his side.

`The underpaths that lead beneath the willage. Olun says you have a knowledge of them, you alone in all the world save he.'

Across the beds of sickly reed blow smoke and laughter from the fire-topped knoll where burns the pig-boy. Tunny frowns and shakes his head. `What underpaths? That's cunning talk is that, and does not mean a thing to me. Why, Olun barely has a hail or fare-you-well for me since my affliction forces me to quit my calling and take on a lowly gateman's lot.'

His eyes grow distant, damp with memory. My gaze shifts down from them towards the palsied, black extremities. Within my thoughts, a dark thing crawls towards the light.

`Before you are their gateman, are you . . .?'

`Their tattooist. Yes.'

`And it is you that marks my father with his crow designs?'

He gives a braying laugh that seems too big for such a pinched and narrow chest. Off on the knoll there's nothing left now of the pig-boy save a charring mound that puffs and bursts and shrivels in amongst the roaring tongues of light.

' His crow designs? If that is what he calls them, why, then yes that is my work, although they do not look like crows to me. They have no sense in them at all and yet he makes me copy them so careful from his painted barks, as if no other half-wit scrawl may do as well. When we are done he burns the picture barks and makes a proper thing of it, you mark my word. Each year he comes to me and has them traced afresh to keep 'em bold, but then my hands get bad and Olun comes no more, nor anyone. Who does their tattoos now is not for me to know.' He pauses, wrinkles up his nose and squints in the direction of my neck. ` Who does that one about your throat? It must be someone in the willage, for it is not there when you are first arrived.'

What is he speaking of? My hand flies up unbidden to inspect the soft skin there below my jaw. There is no scar that may be felt, no raised-up lip of fresh tattoo. This flutter-fingered fool is either addled or else blind, and there is much for me to think of without paying further notice to some lack-wit gateman's mutterings. Still squinting at my neck he lets me clasp his shuddering hand and thank him for his help, then watches me turn from him, walking off into the firelit crowd along the meadow-bank.

The dark thing in my thoughts crawls closer still. Old Tunny's fingers know the underpath, though there's no knowing in his head. Old Tunny's the tattooist. He scores Olun's marks, his blackened fingers moving, year on year, along those mad and weaving tracks, the old man's crow designs that do not look like crows, yet now is all come plain. They are not images of crows at all.

They're what crows see.

The river from above become a line, a crooked thread of blue. The patchworked fields all hemmed with bramble, huts made small as finger-rings and forests shrunk to fat green slugs, all crinkle-edged and veined with paths. That is the means by which the old man knows each track and by-way. There's the reason Olun feels the willage is too much a part of him: the all of it is etched upon his hide. Its hills, its ponds. Its underpaths. Its vaults and treasure holes. That's how he means to speak with me when he is in his grave.

My shovings and my squeezings now return me to the riverside that wanders back towards the willage. Casting one last look towards the knoll it strikes me that the hag-queen sits alone before the pyre, with Bern and Buri gone elsewhere. My eyes sift through the ragged crowd about the Hobfield's rim and finally alight upon the monstrous brothers, standing by the spit on which the painted pig is roast. Old Tunny stands beside the pair, looking afraid and talking with them. Now he lifts one hand and gestures to his gullet. Both the brothers nod. They stare as one across the flickering yellow reed-field, peering through the smoke towards the river path and me, although they may not see me this far from the fire.

Turning away from them, my hurried footsteps bear me off into the lapping dark, back to the willage and the old man's precious, cold remains. Even if Hurna is already settling him within his grave, it is no obstacle for one as skilled in resurrection as myself. My feet are tingling as they pound along the riverbank, warm with the feel of all my gold that's hoarded there beneath them.

Is there something on my neck?

Inside of me, the dark thing slowly drags towards the light. There's something missing here, some knowledge that's not yet disclosed. A picture comes of Hurna, squatting there by Olun's body, smiling through the coal-glow of the inner hut. What does she have to be so pleased about? Atop the Beasthill to my left are dancing lights, wherefrom a distant hollow keening rises bare into the night.

'He's in a better place,' she says.

'He's on the bright path now.'

The understanding, when it comes upon me, tears a scream from out my throat.

Forget the willage. There is nothing there for me now. Run. Run up the Beasthill. It is not too late. My tears may be misplaced, to make so much out of a word, a look. Keep running, up and up.

Besides, what reason may there be for Olun to consent to such a thing? He has no love for Hurna or her gods, and says time after time that he wants me to have his learnings and his leavings when he's dead. He has no cause to change his mind . . .

. . . but then there is the way he looks at me after he takes my fancy-beads. His eyes and voice grow cold and then he asks to speak with Hurna as if . . . No. Forget it. It is nothing. In my side, a pain. My gasping breath, so much like Olun's.

Stopping half-way up to rest and looking back a pair of torch-lights may be seen, that move along the river path towards the Beasthill's lower slopes. They seem to come from the direction of the Hobfields, following my own route here. A group of revellers, perhaps, all overfed and drunk with mash, that make for Beasthill so to ask some god's forgiveness of their gluttony before returning home. The lamp-fires glide along the riverbank, their pace matched perfectly as if the bearers walk in step. They start to mount the Beasthill. Run. Run on.

Across the flattened summit stretch the rings of broken wall, one set inside the other, ancient banks of earth heaped up by men yet now reclaimed by grass that looks like slivered metal underneath the stars. Away towards the hilltop's further side, beyond the smallest and most central ring, a crowd of women are convened, all wailing.

They are standing in a ring about the fire.

Shouting and screaming, bidding them to stop, my frantic, hurtling form careers across the stretch of grass and dark between us, dodging through the crumbling gaps that separate the turf-capped walls and leaping puddles wide as baby ponds to come at last amongst them, sobbing, half collapsing there at Hurna's feet who stands beside the pyre.

She smiles down fondly. Off across the field two torches breast the hill and start to move towards us. Bern and Buri. Hurna's voice is hearty and forgiving, brimming over with dull-witted sisterly affection.

'We are pleased that you at last decide to share our ceremony. And your father. He is pleased as well.'

She looks up here towards the towering centre of the blaze, much higher than the pig-night fire.

He sits erect upon his burning throne, shrunk to a hideous charcoal infant by the flames. His blackened sockets stare as if to scry the smoke for messages, for intimations of reprieve. Behind these gaping orbits soft grey tendrils smoulder from a soot of brain. Across his breast, held in a death-grip, cindered fingers clench upon his daughter's fancy-beads. His skin flakes off to rise as great slow moths of ash into the firmament, above the heat where they grow cool and fall to lazy spirals of descent, raining about me.

Bern and Buri stand behind me now, patient and silent as they wait for me to turn and face them. From the sky a frail black fragment, tumbling as in a dream, drifts down to settle on my arm. Upon it, barely visible against its black, the faintest silver tracery of lines may yet be seen: a gentle curve that is perhaps a stream or else some buried lane, the clustered spider-marks that may be trees viewed from above.

It breaks against my wrist and falls to dust, caught by the wind to scatter over the cremation fields.

IN THE DROWNINGS
POST AD 43

The plaiting of the rushes and the cutting of the stilts. A hollow beak that spits out darts; its making and its use. The method of these things is like a voice inside that endlessly repeats its dull instructions. It's been in me for so long that I no longer hear it. When I do, it soothes me in that I need think of nothing save this grey, unending list and thus at last may fall asleep with it upon my lips: *The plaiting of the rushes and the cutting of the stilts. A hollow beak that spits out darts, its making and its use.*

Before I wade upstream towards the shallows, I look back at Salka and our children playing. Water beaded on her breast, she turns and holds me with her black-eyed gaze too long before she looks away and dips her face once more beneath the river's skin. The young ones splash and circle; build an argument between themselves but then abandon it in favour of some better, louder disagreement.

This looking back whenever I set out and leave my family behind, as if to gather all my loved ones up into my eyes and hold them there, it has become a habit with me lately. Still it gnaws me, this concern that one day I might glance away and, when I look back, find them gone. It seems that I cannot be rid of it and so I stare until their shapes are lost against the rippling glare that dances on the water. Turning, I make away against the current, strong and boiling where it clefts against my thigh.

I had a different wife once, and another family. We did not live here in the Drownings but some way off to the west, up in a great round hill camp high above a burning-ground. One morning I awoke and ventured out between the bubbling breakfast-pots to hunt and fish, and that was all of it. I cannot now recall if I had any kind word for my wife on setting out that day, only that I became ill-tempered when I found the broken draw-string of my boot unfixed, and thought ill of her laziness. I may have said some little thing, some words, I can't remember. Knotting up the string as best I could for want of thread and needle, I tied up my boot and limped into the dawn and that was all of it.

I kissed my little girl farewell, but could not find my son to kiss. She had just eaten curds. Her breath was hot and sweet upon my cheek, and that was all of it.

As I walked on all hung about with nets and spears amongst the rousing huts, I saw my mother some way off, upon the settlement's far side. I called to her, but she was old and did not hear me. That was all of it.

I stopped to talk with Jemmer Pickey's wife, and while we spoke I had some thoughts of her without her skirts and skins, although I knew there would be nothing come of this. I said goodbye, then carried on my way.

Near by the main gate, in amongst the old, grassed over stones of Garnsmith's Forge I saw our willage Hobman standing lost in thought, the yellow antlers drooping, tied about his lowered brow. All in a ring about his feet were many markings, sketched in meagre soil there with his mistle-rod. He muttered to himself, twisting the grey snarls of his beard between stained fingertips, and seemed more ill at ease than I had ever seen him. Of a sudden he looked up and saw me as I passed. He made to speak, then seemed to think the better of it. I have often wondered what he meant to say.

I passed him by and went out from the camp, making my way down hill and past that lower peak where lie the burning grounds. I'd heard that there were walls there once, great rounds set one inside the other. These were long since worn away, but from the camp-hill's upper slope the rings could yet be seen; a certain darkening of the grass best looked upon by afternoon. Off to the west, down where the riversiders had their settlement, thin ropes of smoke were strung between still sky and distant fires, and when I'd come too low upon the hill to hear the willage noises at my back, there was a silence, stretched across the world unto the further trees. I walked down into this, with looping bindweed strangles tearing round my feet as I descended. That was all of it.

As I stilt through the water now, less deep here than a forearm's length, the trees stoop in above me and the river is in shadow. With no sun to dazzle from the water's face the depths beneath become more plain, so that the fish who move there may be seen. I stop, and am become as still as stones. My wooden legs are two trees rooted in the streambed, whereupon the water folds itself then folds itself again. Beneath its surface I regard my stilts that seem now crooked, bent with age, although I know that this is but some water-trick. I move my sodden cloak of rush aside, and lift my spear, and wait.

When I lived in the hill camp it took more than half a day to reach the Drownings. Horses will not ride there for the ground is treacherous and filled with bogs and pools whereby the midge-flies cloud about, a small and angry weather. Many men have died there. Minnows navigate between their teeth.

I reached my favourite hunting-place at close of afternoon, the twilight raising up like dust before a herd of coming stars. First I collected sticks and sods to build my hide, where I would sleep, more like a swollen grave than like a hut. I laboured next in failing light to gather rushes, that I might have work within my oil-lit hide to keep me busy after dark had settled on the fens.

The horse-hair wick, coiled like a worm in curdled fat, refused to burn until I'd wasted half a bag of tinder and come near to wearing smooth my newest flint. I sat cross-ankled in the shivering light and plaited rushes on into the grey approaches of the dawn. The gown I made was long and green, shaped like a mash-skin that's turned right-side-down, sealed at the top save for a slit to see through and a hole wherein to fix the hollow beak. I slept for but a small while and was up before first light to cut young saplings for my stilts and find a piece of wood that I might scrape the caulk from out to make my blowing-pipe.

My work was finished as the sun completed its ascent through chilly morning air, only to slump at last exhausted and commence its fall. I took a rolled-up rag from out my sack and opened it to choose one of the iron slivers pinned in rows along the unrolled strip, a tuft of dirty ram's-wool fastened at their dullest ends. Selecting one, I placed it in between my teeth, point outermost, and crawled head-first into my gown of reed, the bored-through wooden beak clasped tight inside my hand. I struggled for a moment to adjust the hood that I might see, then dragged the stilts inside the gown, to bind with strips of ox-hide to my legs.

The wooden beak was in my mouth, one end protruding through the helmet's hole, the dart already nestled in its bore. Swelled up with spit, the woollen flight stopped up the hole. Its bitter strands stuck to my tongue and teased inside my mouth so that I had some difficulty in dislodging them without the blow-dart falling from its pipe.

At last, my mummery complete, I lifted up my short-spear and tried carefully to stand upon my fresh-cut legs, using a lonely tree trunk as support until I'd found my feet. With this assured, I delicately picked my way, a giant green bird, toward the current's ragged edge whereby I dipped one wooden toe within, unmindful of the water's chill.

With great slow steps that left the river's surface undisturbed, I waded in amongst the witless fish and unsuspecting water-fowl, whence I commenced to hunt.

Standing a-straddle of the shallows now a fat bass moves between my feet to nibble pale grey weed. My fingers tighten on the spear-shaft then relax as it thinks better of its meal. It whips its tail as for a face-slap and is gone.

Sometimes I dwell on how the fish and ducks regard all this. Unseen, I stalk amongst them and they think me one of them. They are too dull to understand that I am of a higher kind and that I mean them ill, and so they disappear, uncomprehending, one by one. They watch the great green bird stride there between them, yet forge no connection with their missing kin. They are made blind by that which they expect to see.

There may be beasts more subtle yet than we, strolling amongst us at their leisure, picking, choosing, bagging now a woman, now a man, and none shall ever know where they have gone, so sparse and scattered are the crimes; so few and far between, save when these subtle monsters feel the need to feast and glut themselves.

Another fish, this time a roach, moves nuzzling between my planted struts. This time I do not wait, but drive the spear down hard. I almost miss and pierce its side instead, lifting it thrashing on my shaft into the sunlight, beads of river-water falling all about it in a mortal dew.

I hunted all that day and yet another day besides, curled in my hide by dark, and at the close of it were many fowl within my sack and many poles of fish, and when another morning came I set out for my home. The air was good and clear that day, as air that follows from a storm, and yet no storm had passed. The blue sky coloured all the pools and puddles of the fen, and vast white clouds passed overhead, piled up into fantastic shapes for which I had not names. My bag was full. The sun was warm upon my back. I sang the only words I could remember of the Old Track Song, about the journey-boy and how he found his bride, and frightened herons off a pond the singing was that bad. It was the last time I was happy.

Now I sit upon the bank and let my wooden legs trail in the current while I eat the fish. When first I came to live for good out in the Drownings, I would cook my food before I ate, but now it seems a nuisance. No one else here cooks their food. I split along the creature's belly with my nail and feel an odd content at just how large a piece of skin I can peel off in one attempt. (Here, partly flayed, it startles me by flipping once, but then is still.)

About to pull my beak aside and eat, a movement on the south horizon draws my eyes. Red flags. Red, tiny flags that drift apart then draw together as they flap towards me from across the distant fields. I squint, then draw my legs from out the water so as best to stand. I leave my beak in place.

Not flags. Not flags, but capes, red capes upon the backs of riding men. A hand-full by my reckoning. No more.

I know them. Men of Roma, come from lands beyond the sea. Some of the young men in the willage where I lived before said that these Romans had a will to take the land from us, but all this is a puzzle far beyond my figuring, for land is not a thing that one can take, and nor is it a thing that can belong, and so I leave such quarrels to the younger men.

They are much closer now, and have dismounted, leading on the horses by their reins, picking their way between the mudholes and the bright laked silver of the pools. One of them bears a staff crowned with a strange device of gold: there is a snake, a fat man standing, then a mouth wide open with the tongue lolled out, and finally a fat man walking. Metal helmets. Skirts like women. Metal plates across their tits.

Their horses see me first, and shy. While trying to rein in their rearing steeds, the men whirl all about to seek the cause of this disturbance. All in green against the tufted river-bank, at first they cannot see me.

I've no quarrel with them. I call out hello, and now they turn and look at me. My voice is sore, unpractised in the speech of men, and from their faces it is plain my greeting sounded terrible and was beyond their understanding. One amongst them starts to babble, high pitched, in their curious tongue. I take another step towards them, rearing high upon my wooden legs, and try again.

The horses scream and bolt. The men run after them. I watch their red cloaks flap away across the fens. The more I call for them to stop and have no fear, the faster do their horses flee, the faster do they follow in pursuit. What must I sound like, after all this time?

They're gone, and so I sit back down there at the water's edge to eat my fish. I think of how they'll tell their friends they saw a bird much bigger than a man, all green, that stalked the marshes on its monstrous legs and uttered dreadful cries. Around a mouth-full of cold fish I start to laugh so that the grease spills out into my beard; onto my feathers made of rush.

After a while the laughter stops, because it sounds bad in this place alone. I eat the fish down to its skeleton.

That day, when I walked home towards my hill camp, I was thinking of my wife, my first wife. It's a strange thing, but her name was Salka too. I'd known her since we both were small and played at chase-and-kiss out in the Hobfields, which they say is haunted by a murdered boy. Once I told Salka that I'd seen him, standing on the mound there with his throat all cut, his hair all burned. She knew I'd made it up, and yet she made as if she thought it true, and clung to me and let me feel her gilly there inside her breeks.

The hill came into sight, with supper-fires that smouldered on its crest, so that my weary step grew quick to think of being home. I had not had the chance to tell my son goodbye before I left, and thought that I might play with him along the evening paths while Salka cooked the fattest of the fish for us, wrapping our hut about with its delicious stink.

I was halfway uphill towards the camp before I realized that there was no noise.

I throw the slick white fishbones from me, down into the river where they bob for but a moment then submerge. I fancy that I see them swim away beneath the water, and I entertain a river where naught save the skeletons of fishes glide and dart and comb the currents with their naked ribs. I stand and make to wade downstream, back to my family. I feel the sorrow gathering about me, and I want to be with them.

I walked into the village with my poles across my shoulder and a sack of meat and feathers in my hand. The supper-fires were burning low and somewhere off between the huts I fancied that a dog was barking, though I now remember that the smell of dog was everywhere. It may have been the smell that made me think I heard the noise.

Just past the open gate the relic stones of Garnsmith's Forge drew my attention. In their centre, where the moss grew brightest green, was now an ugly scorch of black. It looked as though a monstrous red-hot cooking bowl had been set down, dropped in relief by sweating men with blistered hands.

No sound came from the beast-pens of the inner camp to drown my hesitating step which, although light, was deafening amongst the gaping huts. Halfway along the centre street, there in the dust, I found a set of ochred antlers trailing broken strings. I did not dare to pick them up. I gazed at them a moment, then passed on.

A meal half-eaten. Corn querns, smooth and new, left stacked against a wall. The black flies on a haunch of lamb; their small, vile murmurings as loud as men. The curtain of a jakes not long since used hung open, dried leaves in a hand-full there untouched beside the reeking hole. From the untended, dwindling fires great gouts of smoke would roll across the trackways where I walked, so that these things were briefly glimpsed, then gone, as in a dream. The hole in Jemmer Pickey's roof he'd sworn to mend since winter last. An old man's sun-hat floating in a puddle. Washerwomen's rocks, still cowled with long-dry clothing. Here a solitary footprint. There a pool of sick.

Outside our hut, my boy had failed to clear away a game that he had lately taken to, involving little men-in-kind I'd carved for him from pebbles. Set as for a hunt, he had them spread across the open door and ringed about some animal he'd fashioned out of sticks. I thought perhaps it was a wolf. Stepping across this small, abandoned slaughter, I decided that he must be scolded, though not hard, for leaving all his nonsense strewn so carelessly about.

The hut was dark. My little girl was sitting in the shadows on its furthest side. I spoke some words that I cannot recall to her and, stepping forward, saw that she was nothing but a pile of furs that for a moment in the dark had seemed to hold her shape, sat there with knees drawn up, her head tipped back the way she sometimes held it. Only fur. The hut was empty. For a moment all I did was stand there in the gloom; the silence. Nothing happened. I went back outside, stepping across my son's abandoned game with care, so that he should not find it spoiled when he returned.

Across the silent willage to the west the sun was drowning in a purple cloud. I cupped my hands around my mouth and yelled hello. I heard it echo on the empty beast-pen's curving wall and then, after a moment, called again. The yawning huts did not reply. Their quiet seemed uneasy, just as if there were some awful news they could not bring themselves to share with me. I called again, while dusk fell all about.

After a while, I sat down in the middle of the man-shaped stones set in a ring outside our door. I picked one up and looked at it. No bigger than my thumb, it bulged at top and bottom, narrow in the middle that it might suggest a neck. I'd scratched the likeness of a face there on the smaller, upper bulge. I'd meant to make him smile but, turning it to catch the failing light, could see that I'd been clumsy with my awl, so that it seemed as if he were instead forever shouting something with great urgency, forever beyond hearing.

As I touched the stone I took a fancy that it was still warm from my son's hand and raised it to my nose that I might smell him on it. Reason left me then. I put the pebble in my mouth and I began to weep.

Crane-legged, I step downstream now, careful not to let the current rush me on too fast. Above the sourness of the ram's wool on my tongue it is as if I taste that pebble yet. I hurry on, that I might be beside my newest wife and young before I am quite overcome by memory.

I sat there in the ring of pebbles all that night. Sometimes I wept and moaned. Sometimes I sang a little of the journey-boy. With dawn, I stood and walked back through the empty willage. All the fires were down to cold grey dust, and for a while I played a sorry game where I imagined everyone was but asleep, about to rouse and stretch and stagger cursing, joking, out into the waking day, but no one came.

I went back through the gates and next walked once and once again about the outside of the camp. There were no footprints there, nor any flattened weeds as where a tribe of many families had fled downhill, or where as many foemen had crept up. Save for the ash-scarred turf in Garnsmith's Forge, a burn no more than half a man in width, there was no sign of fire, and neither was there any mark of wolves or, saving for the vomit in the street, of sudden plague.

I stumbled to the bottom of the hill and circled all about its base, then walked back up. Making my way back through the silence to my family's hut, I crawled inside to sit. I saw, with rising anger, that my wife had left her cast-off clothing thrown about the floor, a lazy habit on behalf of which I'd often scolded her. Cursing her slothful ways beneath my breath, I crawled about upon my knees and gathered up the scattered rags.

Her breeches smelled of her. I raised them to my lips and kissed them; sank my face deep into them where it was stale, and rank, and good. My will grew stiff beneath my breeks, so that I reached to pull it free then rubbed my hand upon it, wildly back and forth. The milk splashed through my fingers, fell in beads upon a mat of grass our daughter made. No sooner had the spasm passed than I began to weep once more, my seed grown thick and cold upon my palm.

After the tears, there came a sudden and enormous dread, so that I could not breathe. I ran out from the hut. I ran out from the willage and away downhill, my limp will flapping as I ran and slipped and stumbled. When I reached the bottom I dare not look back, for there was something terrible about those mute and clustered rooftops, that dead skyline. I ran on, sobbing and gasping, on across the fields, a groundfog blur of seeding dandelions about my feet, and did not stop until I reached the riversider's settlement a little after noon.

I raved at them, and asked if a great many people had passed by this way of late; if there had been some dire catastrophe; if there had been an omen in the stars. They stared, and called their children back inside 'til I'd passed on. I shouted at the closing doors and told them that the people from the hill camp were all gone, but if they understood me, they did not believe. When I would not be quiet, a big man with a hare-lip grabbed me by my arm and dragged me to the outskirts, where he cast me in the dirt and said that I should go and not return, his gruff words smearing on his palate's cleft.

I had nowhere to go, save for the Drownings.

I reclaimed my spot beside the river just as darkness fell. My hide was still intact where I had left it, with the robe of rushes rolled inside. Upon my belly, I crawled in and pulled my bird-cloak up to cover me, and there I slept, all of that night and all the next day as one dead beneath the swollen, pregnant grave that was my hide. There never was a time when I was more alone.

I've lived here in the Drownings ever since, and in that time have found another family, another Salka, and I am alone no more, nor maddened with bewilderment and grief.

I see them now, ahead of me, sat resting on the bank down where the river curves; lengthen my step that I may be upon them sooner, striding through the eddies, stalking down the shallow and cascading steps where slippery mosses drift like banners in the flow. I have not taken off my stilts for many moons, and there are sores upon my water-wrinkled legs.

Salka lifts up her head to watch as I approach, alerted by my splashing. Soon, the little ones are looking also as I rush towards them, teetering, precarious and eager for their consolation, falling forward more than running now. I lift my arms as if in an embrace that's big enough to span the distance yet between us, feathered rushes hanging in loose, flapping folds below, like great green wings. I call out to them through the warped flute of my beak. I tell them that I love them. Tell them that I'll never go away.

My voice is cracked and hideous. It startles them. As one, amidst a mighty beating, they rise up into the darkening sky and, in a moment, they are gone from sight.

THE HEAD OF DIOCLETIAN
POST AD 290

My teeth hurt.

Standing here beyond the margins of the village there is only night; the hollow yawning of November wind across cold, furrowed earth; a dark that swallows utterly, so that I cannot tell where darkness ends and I begin. The tin-sharp soreness in my gums is all I have to tell me where I am, and I am almost glad of it out here amongst the black fields, where the damp wind cuts my cheek.

I have been staring at this void so long my eyes are watering, unable to distinguish between sky and landscape; near and far. Worse yet, this is the second night I have subjected my complaining lungs to this ordeal, this vigil out here in the miserable chill before the winter comes. All for the sake of some half-witted local yarn, the fancy of a farmer's boy with eyes so close together he seemed bred out of a pig.

Still, for all that, he answered when I spoke to him. He did not make pretence at inability to comprehend my tongue, or simply spit and turn away as have the other villagers, though all he said was antic mysteries, fantastical accounts of walking spirits: on a hill, not far from here and up past the cremation fields, there is an ancient camp, hundreds of years of grass and weed above its ditches and its ramps. A settlement, he said. Score upon score of people who one night, according to the tale, were quite devoured by giant dogs with neither hair nor drop of blood to mark that they were ever there. As is the custom with such histories, the place has ever since been shunned, afflicted by ill reputation. There are spectres, naturally. On certain nights the fiery eyes of monstrous hounds may yet be seen atop the hill, their awful gaze enough to light the sky. I'm watching for them now, but there is nothing.

Off behind me in the village, distant voices, quarrelling at first, then laughing. Foul and careless oaths. The hateful braying of their women, coarse, insinuating. Is it me? Stood here, out in the bluster and the tarry dark for no more reason than the village fool sees light upon a hill-top? Is it me, the source of all their scorn, their noisy ribaldry? My teeth are screaming. Soon. A moment more then I'll give up the night, make for the tavern; bed; my bad, louse-worried dreams.

Robbed of my range and bearings by the dark, the sudden flare of low cloud lit from underneath seems closer than it should, before my face rather than off across the fields. Its shadows lurch and flicker, make as if to leap towards me so that I step back unnerved and almost fall before my tired eyes have the measure of it.

Lights. Up there beyond the burning grounds where they reduce their dead to ash and cinder. Lights upon the hill, not cast by dogs unless they walk upon two legs.

I have them.

No. No, better not to think such things, that fate is not provoked: there might be other reasons, commonplaces that will quite explain these glowerings. Tomorrow, with the light, I may ride up that way and judge things for myself. Why, here I am as good as ordering the crosses built before a single shard of evidence is in my hands. I can imagine Quintus Claudius there in Londinium, his office at the treasury, how he would cluck his tongue with disapproval.

'First the tests,' he'd say, 'the scales, and the coticula of basenite. If there are further proofs required, employ the furnace and a white-hot shovel. Then, and only then, announce the guilty and bring out the nails.'

Above the tumulus the grey lights shift and writhe. At last I turn away to trudge and trip across the rutted earth, back through the long, unbroken dark towards the settlement, the listing wooden alleyways with tiny, crooked windows squinting.

I have been here for some several weeks now, and the tavern is no longer plunged in hostile silence when I enter. For the most part they ignore me as I pick my way across the straw-tossed floor between the pools of vomit and the copulations, making for the stairs. Tonight at least, they've better entertainments, with a buck's night celebration in full throe.

The groom, a youth of thirteen years or so, is climbing drunkenly to stand upon a stool that lists and tilts, abetted by his friends and uncles. All around the tavern's lower room the hulking, copper-headed creatures whoop and clap their hands together in a fearful unison, a rhythm that grows faster as the young man wobbles there upon his stool and beams, befuddled, down upon his audience.

Now they throw a rope across one of the black and sticky-looking beams, with one end fashioned in a noose. A horrid intrigue seizes me and at the bottom of the stairway leading to my room I pause and turn to watch. Jeering and sputtering, their faces pink and bright with perspiration, they are settling the loop of rope about the bridegroom's throat, yet still that foolish grin across his face. One of the brutes, a great fat creature with his skull shaved bare save for a top-knot, presses something that I cannot see into the young man's hand, then turns towards the audience, his tattooed belly glistening as he stills the pounding handclaps with a string of slurred vulgarities. He belches, and is met with waves of laughter. In the bridegroom's hand, I see it now, a short bronze knife. With his other hand he waves happily down to a dark-haired girl at the front of the pressing crowd, barely aware of where he is through the clouds in his eyes.

The fat man kicks the stool away.

The rope jerks taut against the dangling, kicking weight and now the clapping starts again, its mounting pace set off against the slower, burdened creakings of the beam. How can it be that I am witness to such things? The young man twisting there between the floor and ceiling smiles no longer, and his eyes bulge terribly. His thin legs, swimming, tread air. From out of the crowd now, as one man, a kind of grunting is commenced, as that of animals in rut.

The nature of the game is now made clear to me as suddenly the strangling boy remembers that he holds a knife there in his hand. Reaching above his head, his darkening face suffused with horrid concentration, he begins his desperate sawing at the rope. Clenched in his trembling fist, the short blade plunges back and forth, this motion echoing grotesquely that of solitary pleasure. Quite as if responding to the lurid and familiar movements of the hand, although remote, a bulge is raised that strains against the young man's britches, and the dark girl points to this and laughs. From broken, scattered comments overheard amidst the din I understand that if the youth survives this game the dark girl shall be his, a final whore before he's wed.

The young man twirls, and jigs, and rasps the knife's edge back and forth against the rope, face purpling, and fearful throttled noise leaking from him now. If Rome falls, all will be as this. All of the world.

Unable to bear more, I turn away and stumble up the stairs, the tread worn thin there at the centre and the worm-shot risers dusted green with age.

Safe in my room beneath the low-slung eaves, the door pushed shut behind me, from below there comes the muffled thud of body hitting floor with cheering in its wake, so that, despite myself, I am relieved. I dare say that his windpipe will be crushed and bruised, and he'll be helped home in no state to claim the proffered prize for his ordeal. No doubt the same friends who encouraged him to mount the stool will see that any favours paid for in advance do not go wasted.

In the corner, stained grey bedding. Morbid spiders curled about themselves, translucent, hang from rafters in dust-coloured shrouds of their own making. The girl who used this room before me moved into a chamber downstairs at the rear when I arrived, but every day I find some piece of her: a chipped shell comb, the scraps of clothing halfway through their journey into rags, blue beads strung on a hair of rusted wire. Sometimes I smell her ghost upon the blankets and the boards.

When I came to Londinium a half-year since, I thought it hunched and squalid, breeding ugly humours, pestilences in amongst the jetties and the narrow yards, pooled urine yellowing there where the cobbles dip. The locals, hulking Trinovante fishermen or shifty Cantiaci traders, had a pleasing insularity, despite their sullenness. They kept amongst their own kind and made little fuss, yet fresh from home I thought the city Hades; they its fiends and chimaera. One of a team of treasury investigators sent from Rome at the request of Quintus Claudius, I spent my weeks there with my fellows quaffing vinegary wine, awaiting our assignments complaining each new inconvenience, each fresh indignity.

I work one thumb and forefinger inside my mouth and gently test the teeth to see how many move, loose in the blue and shrunken gums. I fear that it is all of them, and wish that I were in Londinium again, for it would seem a paradise now in my eyes.

Sent here into the middle-lands two months since with reports of forgery, I was a child with nothing to prepare me for this place, these Coritani, reeling drunk through short and bloody lives they take for granted; for their unconsidered, unrelenting violence; for the coloured scars, the curls of ink that craze their brows and backs, as terrible and queer as painted dogs. When I arrived here, I was yet so delicate of sensibility that I might blanch to hear some lurid passage from a drama told in verse, and now I watch them hang their young for sport, and scarcely think of it.

I light the lamp and sit upon the crumpled bedding to remove my army-issue boots. Downstairs, a woman starts to hiss and snort, as rhythmic as a bath-house pump, thus signalling that someone has received the hanged boy's prize. The women here discomfit me. They are so big and filthy, smell so foul, yet not an hour goes by save that I think of them, the red hair lacquered by their perspiration coiling into tiny sickles underneath their arms, their cow's-milk haunches swinging under prickly skirts. I have not had a woman for a year, not since the dyer's eldest daughter back in Rome. How long before I take a whore? Their flat white faces, and their speckled breasts. I must not think of it.

Naked now in the chill November room, I pull on the night-shirt I have taken, folded, from my army bag, that has the stencilled crest. There's few signs of the Empire to be seen out here, a scattering of villas where retired generals struggle to afford their mistresses. Some small way north beyond this settlement one Marcus Julius, a veteran of the Emperor Aurelian's campaign against the Gallic Empire, still maintains a modest farm. I was told to visit should I find myself close by. It was excruciating. On discovering I was not long from Rome, he seemed capable of making only one enquiry: `Well? How fare the Blues?' I told him I took little interest in the chariot races, whereupon his disposition to me cooled, so that I left not much thereafter.

I fancy it was him who let the cog-name by which I am known be bandied back and forth amongst the village folk, so that they do not call me Caius Sextus now but taunt me with `Romilius': `Hello there, Little Roman! How d'you like this woman on my arm? I'll bring a stool that you may kiss on her above the waist!' All of them hate me, all the women, all the men, though to be just, it is not without cause. They know why I am here, and further know the punishment for forgery. How shall they be the friend of one who's come to see them crucified?

I burrow deep into my bed, such as it is. Downstairs, the woman barks this people's word for copulation, over and again. If Rome should fall . . .

Put that aside. The day will never come while we are still producing Emperors of Diocletian's mettle, men of scale who, single-handed, vindicate their times. Those bold reforms to stem the plots and murderous feuds that threaten our stability, dividing up his office so that Maximian is become Augustus in the West with Diocletian as Augustus in the East. The weavers and the brewers carp, complain that he has fixed the price of rugs or beer, and yet inflation is contained. Our currency is strong. Without that strength the wilderness would have us all.

And yet my teeth hurt. Mine and all my fellows' teeth alike. Why, on the boat across there were some ten of us, investigators to the man, all with the same blue and receded gums, the headaches and the lethargies, the lapsing concentration, lapsing memory. One of the youngest said he felt as if already dead and crumbling away, stupid with maggots, though for my part it is not so bad. It's just the teeth. No one can fix this ailment with a name, nor yet determine any cause. We speak about it as `the sickness', if we speak of it at all.

Perhaps we are so much a part of Rome that we grow sick as she does; some peculiar bond, some sympathy of flesh and land. The bangled, ragged kings are at our gates and we appease them, grant them settlements and territories in the lands surrounding Rome until it is as if the vagrant tribes sit patient all about a sumptuous table at some beggars' feast, with Rome the centre-piece. They sit politely for the moment, but their stomachs growl. If they commenced to dine the world should all be gone. The dark that gusts above the chill fields at the village edge would swallow us entire; the bright towns guttering, extinguished, all across the globe.

Sprawled on my side beneath the coverings, I notice that the quality of lamplight in my room has changed, and glancing up I realize with a dull uncertainty that all along the girl who had this room before me has been sitting there against the furthest wall, cross-legged, watching silently. She stands and walks without a sound across the cracked, uneven boards towards a doorway set behind my bed. Rising to follow her, I notice as she passes through the door that it is inlaid all about the frame with black and tarnished coins. I wonder that I never noticed it before.

Beyond the door I follow her by tallow-light through winding passageways between great piles of nameless oddities. She rounds a bend ahead and, as the half-light catches on her features, I begin to feel disturbed. They are more small and pinched than I recall, so that she seems a different girl. I would not know her save she wears her necklace of blue beads, the wire that threads them burnished to a brazen sheen.

Now we are at the centre of the labyrinth, where painted skins are hung. About a low red fire peculiar figures gather in a ring, and wait, and do not speak. There is a boy that I at first mistake for the young man I saw hanged, but this one's younger, still a child, and on his throat the wounding mark is not a rope-burn but an ugly gash. Beside him sits a beggar, barely conscious, vomit matted in his beard and mumbling to himself. A crone with one foot gone. A black-faced man with twigs tied in his hair. An awful stork-limbed creature, half as tall again as any man, stands agitated, shifting now from one foot to the other, shoulders hunched beneath the ceiling, coughing now and then. The girl and I step up and join the circle; gaze like them into the dying coals. Outside, there is a fearful barking, growing closer by the moment, and I feel a monstrous loss, a crushing sadness unlike any I have felt in life, and I am weeping. Next to me, the boy whose throat is slashed steps close and takes my hand. He makes great show of giving me a pebble that's been carved into the likeness of a tiny man. I put it in my mouth. The sound of dogs is deafening.

I wake up with the mare's-tail grey of morning in my room.

There's something rattling in my mouth.

A sudden terror grips me and I spit it out, afraid that it will be the pebble-figure from my dream, its scribbled eyes and gaping maw, but no. It is a tooth. My tongue-tip probes the bloody socket left behind with childish satisfaction, and I roll the ivory pellet in my palm, letting the pallid daylight rinse away the after-flavour of my dream. I think about last night, the bale-fires dancing there atop the hill, recalling my resolve to ride that way and make inspection with the morn, and then I dress and go downstairs.

Breaking my fast with cheese and fruit and bread, the only foods on offer safe to eat, I walk down to the stables where I choose my horse; a tan, steam-snouted thing with eyes more civilized than any else I have seen in this place. Leading her out between the water-troughs I notice several men that loiter near the stable-entrance, watching me. One of them is the fat man with the top-knot, he who thrust the knife into the hung boy's hand. The other men I do not recognize, but all their eyes are on me as I mount and trot towards the gates, not looking right nor left, attempting to display more unconcern than I can truly muster in my heart. They watch me go. Some difference in my bearing has alerted them. They know I'm close to something.

I ride near the river's edge much of the way, then branch towards the looming hill; follow along the beaten path meandering up by the cremation fields. Halfway towards the summit, I look back, the fields a pauper's blanket made from scraps displayed beneath me. Further up the road that passes near the bottom of the hill I spy the low sheds of the Christian colony, established there upon a swelling mount beyond the bridge's further side. I almost feel a pang of kinship for the wretched, ranting lunatics, subjected as they are to all the same suspicion and mistrust the villagers afford to me.

The cultists own one of the only two mills in the settlement, the other being managed by a drunkard with an idle son who lets the business fall to disrepair. The Christians, irritating with their sombre dirges and their palsied testifying, are yet shrewd in matters that pertain to commerce. Finding their reward in faith alone, the converts work the mill unwaged, all singing while they slave, and as they toil the major trade within the village falls to them and so the coffers grow. Soon, it is rumoured, they will buy the other mill. Increasingly dependent on these jabbering fanatics, so the village grows uneasy while its children wander off, next seen garbed all in black and crooning at their millwheel.

If I find no solid evidence that will connect a culprit to the forgeries, I might fare worse than to attribute authorship to these religious outcasts. There's no doubt that it would be a popular decision with the villagers, absolving me from blame or, more alarming yet, reprisals. Better still, the Emperor is presently inclined against the sect and of a humour that would welcome persecutions. Though a dozen forgers crucified might earn for me a favourable report, a Christian plot against the treasury, against the very heart of Rome, might earn me a promotion. We shall see.

I turn the horse about and move on up the path, coming at last upon the summit, where a splendid quiet and desolation reigns. Save for a general indentation, nothing can be seen that marks the fated hill-camp's site, whatever contours that may yet remain all smothered by the heaping weeds. Here I dismount and leave my tethered steed to slobber on the grass while I regard the flat expanse more closely.

After a moment's scrutiny the rounded outline of the camp is made discernible, part fringed by briar. The rill of risen turf that measures the perimeter is broken at one point, perhaps denoting where a gate once stood. I walk across towards it and, on my approach, notice a smaller ring of time-worn stones set just inside the gap; perhaps a remnant kiln or oven of some kind.

Save that there are warm ashes at its centre.

Although the fire is dead, these cinders are its voice: it speaks to me. Someone has set a blaze atop this hill, and on more nights than one if what I'm told is true. Too big to simply roast a fowl or warm the hands by, this is fire with purpose, and that purpose would seem clandestine. Why else choose this remote spot, shunned by all your superstitious kinsmen? Why else choose the crack of night to be about your labours unless they are secret; works which, if discovered, would ensure that you were pinned out in the sun to dry?

For purposes of forgery, a quiet and isolated spot whose vantage will allow intruders to be noticed half a league away's preferable. A haunted hill is quite ideal. The fire would be required to heat the unmarked metal blanks and make them soft, following which they would be set upon an anvil where is raised the obverse imprint of a coin. A punch, cylindrical in shape, is placed above the weighed blank disc, and in the punch is a reverse impression of the same silver Denarius. The punch is beaten with a hammer and in this way are the fresh-forged coins stamped out.

I drop down to my knees and carefully begin to comb the dew-drenched grass, working out in a spiral from about the remnants of the fire. If they were beating out the coins by lamplight, hurriedly, and if my luck is with me . . .

After one half of an hour I find it, fallen there between a brace of grey and spectral dandelions. I lift it up between my thumb and finger, turning it against the light. The head of Diocletian gazes unforgiving, out across the buried camp.

A bird shrills from the briar hedge. I flip the coin about and note without surprise a fault there in the reverse. Simply, it is that belonging to a different coin; a different year, perhaps the reign of Severus. Mismatchings such as this are commonplace, for though an anvil with an obverse die might last for sixteen thousand punchings, only half as many would be made before the punch wore out, so that another was required. If the correct reverse could not be found, a different one was used on the assumption few would notice.

But this Little Roman notices. He doesn't miss a thing.

My trophy safely fastened in a hip pouch, I remount my horse for an uneasy stumble down the hill towards the river-track, where my excitement at my find quite overcomes me and I gallop all the way back to the settlement. The crew about the stout, top-knotted man mark my return and read my agitation. There are decorations hung about the streets in preparation for some senseless festival. A small boy dressed up as a girl walks at the head of a procession with a pig upon a leash, but in my haste to get indoors and race upstairs I fail to register this vision until I am in my room, pulling a set of scales from out the army bag.

There are three proofs for silver, any one sufficient to establish forgery. The first employs the use of the coticula, a touchstone made of basenite or lydian. When it is rubbed on silver or on gold, from the markings an expert may read the metal's purity down to the closest scruple. I have seen this done, always by older men, but do not have such confidence about my own abilities.

The second proof requires a furnace, with an iron fire shovel heated white, the metal to be tested heaped thereon. At such heats, purest silver will glow white, while an inferior grade will glow dull red, and black will signal worthlessness. The test is not infallible. The shovel may be drenched first in men's urine, and will then provide a different indication.

On the whole, for coins, the proof by weight is still the best, and easiest. Assembling the scales, I take the forged Denarius from out my pouch and set it down beside another coin, a newly struck one given to me at the mint there in Londinium, to serve as a comparison.

Each coin, if genuine, should weigh one-sixth part of an ounce. Adulterated metal would not weigh so much, having less heavy silver in the blend. This test is a formality, yet one which Quintus Claudius specifically requires, and so I set the coins, both true and false, one in each bronze pan of the scales, to weigh them one against the other. Then I watch.

The false coin sinks. The true coin rises.

Frowning, I remove both coins and test the scales before replacing them, taking especial care to see which coin is in which pan.

The false coin sinks. The true coin rises.

How is this? How can this be? The coin found at the camp can be no other than a forgery with its two sides mismatched, and yet . . .

(Upon the stairs up from the tavern to my room there comes a muffled sound: one of the dogs that haunts the inn. Engrossed in mystery, it barely registers.)

I take the scales apart and reassemble them. I set the coins back in their separate pans. The false coin sinks. The true coin rises. Are the laws of nature now reversed, that such things may occur? How may a wren outweigh a horse? How may a coin plucked from a forger's den outweigh one fresh struck from the mint itself, unless . . .

The forgery. Unless the forgery were purer, had the purest metal, purest silver, purer than the mint. But no, that cannot be. No point in forging money purer than the Empire standard, not unless . . .

Unless it is not that the forged coin is more purely struck, but rather that the true coin is found lacking. This cannot be so. I saw it, freshly minted. Held it, yet warm, closed within my hand. It is as pure as any coin in Rome.

(Outside my chamber now, a closer scuffling. Something nears, and still I cannot take my eyes from those of Diocletian, argent and severe.)

Unless. Unless we cut the coins.

The blood is scalding, simmering in my cheek that I should entertain such blasphemy. It is grotesque and flies against all reason to suppose the Empire capable of such adulteration, to the point that ounce for ounce a worthless forgery might hold more value. Why, if that were so, if all the wealth of Rome were but a gilt concealing poverty, then Rome itself would be the forgery, a sham, as good as fallen with no rampart save for promissory notes to keep the tick-scarred hordes at bay. It is monstrosity itself, this thought. It is a night-start. It is stark, and bottomless.

And it is true.

It crashes in, the fearful certainty, and breaks me. Let me die, or better yet have died before this cold, weighed fact could murder me, before I knew that we were poor and all was ruin. Though my cheeks are simmering yet, the eyes boil over, tears that sting like vinegar. Behind me now the door is opening. I hear a shuffle as of many feet, and know it is the village men, that they have come to kill me, but I cannot look at them for shame: for them to witness me, to witness Rome like this.

At last I lift my head. They stand hulked in the door with muscled cudgels in their fists, the grey man with his paunch and top-knot to the fore. Stone-faced, expressionless, they watch me, watch the little Roman as he sobs above his scales, and if they feel disgust at this display it is not sharper than my own. They pass a glance between them, and the grey man shrugs. They're going to kill me now. Kneeling upon the floor, I close my eyes and I await the blow. A final silence falls.

Then, many footsteps, moving off downstairs, an avalanche of wood and leather. Doors slam somewhere far below. I open up my eyes. The men are gone.

They saw it in my face. They saw me as a man already slain, not worth the killing. Rome is dead. Rome is dead. Rome is dead, and where shall I go now? Not home. Home is a stage façade of paper, peeling, faded by a sun of cheap pyrites. I cannot go home, and who, who else will have me?

I crouch staring at the coins, one false, one falser yet, until the light begins to fail and they are both become pale blurs there in the gloom, no longer to be told apart, a shadow fallen on that noble brow.

The room fills up with murk. I cannot bear the darkness here, that drinks all definition, and I rise and stumble as one in a dream, first down the stairs, then, dazed, into the street. The celebrations are already under way, streets heavy with the stench of ruffian life. They piss in doorways, swing oars at each other's heads, and laugh, and kneel in their own sick. They fornicate against the alley walls like prisoners. They fart and shout and they are all that is, and all that will be. Slow, I shuffle out amongst the great lewd push of them. A jug of ale is pressed into my hand. With rotten smiles they grip my arm, and kiss my tear-tracked cheek, and draw me in.

NOVEMBER SAINTS
AD 1064

With age, the act of waking has become a great confusion. I no longer know upon which decade of this life my eyes will open: lame and frost-burned by the old church gate or in my convent cell here, morning's first sick blueness on the wall; blue of the dead.

My cot is hard, that I may feel the bones that are inside me, restless and impatient to get out. Not long, they think. She's old. Not long. Beneath the rough dusk sheet a chill aches in my bad leg's starving marrow and I know it is November. Last night, on All Hallow's Eve, I dreamed I was a man.

Rain-blind, he rode the fierce night through upon a fever-horse towards Northampton here, though in my dream I thought of it as Ham Town and I know not why. The drizzle stung my face and cold draughts rattled in my ears, and as I rode it seemed that all the terrors of November were upon me, rude jaws snapping at the steaming fetlocks of my horse so that I wept in fright, and when I woke I did not know at first what year it was, and placed a hand upon my leathered sex for fear that I should find instead his instrument, mea culpa, mea culpa, Blessed Virgin forgive me.

Creaking inside my chest I rise from off my cot, the sour sheet flung aside, my burlap habit pulled on in a single, shivering movement; coarse folds, grey against grey dawn. I finish dressing in the half-light and I limp the damp stone passages to Matins where I offer up all thanks to God that I may limp at all and dwell instead upon the passion of Our Lord. I work the days, I count the beads and say the names.

When they are mindful of my halten foot they set me to a task where I may not walk far, as when I tend the gardens here at Abingdon. My bone fists tug amongst the weeds and often will my thoughts turn now to Ivalde, when he kept the graves and gardens in the old church and I lay against its gate-post, begging. Sometimes he would talk with me, his idiot talk that had no reason since a cart-horse kicked his head while he was but a mite. Now I recall his pale green eyes, his Norse-red hair. He was not more than sixteen winters old, without a jot of harm in him.

'Alfgiva,' he would say to me, 'one day I shall set out and make a pilgrimage to Rome, all for the honour of the Drotinum. What do you think of that?' Drotinum was a word by which he meant St Peter, blessed be his name. The word means 'Lord'. He would go on and on with Rome and all the places he would go and I would lie against the gate-post with its bare stones digging in my back and, may the Lord forgive me, I would hate him. Hate him for the things that he might live to see while I saw nothing but that grey stone post; the same great wheel of tree and field that spun about it every day, the slow and shallow river downhill from that church, the bridge of blackened timber that had surely spanned it since the world was small.

He'd know the smell of foreign ports and cities all of gold, and I would lie and count the figures and the faces, raised up from the stone, that capered in the church's eaves, and I would wonder, as I did each day, about the figures and the faces on the far side of the church, that I had never seen although they were so near. For these reasons would I hate him, may the Lord forgive me. In the winters I would freeze and in the summers did not have the strength to brush the flies from off my face or bosom.

Ivalde never went to Rome. A humour came upon his lungs the day that he and noble Bruning lifted up the flagstones of the church to dig the worm-laced earth beneath and I was with them there. His chest was never better from that day, and he was put below the ground before the month was done. I took my vows not long thereafter, in the year of Our Lord one thousand and fifty. It is fourteen years now since I last saw Ivalde's face, or heard his senseless talk. May God have mercy on our souls, both his and mine.

I did not hate him all the time, except when I was bitter, which was often, but upon my fair days I would talk with him, and laugh, and wish him well upon his voyages. I never once saw Bruning laugh with him or heard him say a kind word to the boy, though Bruning was the parish priest and was responsible for Ivalde's keep while Ivalde tended to the carrot crop and kept the graves. Nor, for that matter, did the noble Bruning ever throw a coin to me for all his wealth; for all he passed me every day there ragged by his gate. Still, that is in the past and Brunigus himself is dead these four years gone. I am the last alive who stood there in that church and saw: Alfgiva, who lay broken in its shadow all her life, then fled to see its light unearthed, there near the crossroads, by the river-bridge.

November grows long in its icicle tooth and I scrub the worn flags till the wet and the shine on them cast by the rare shafts of sunlight would blind you. I pray and I count off the beads. On the twentieth day of this month is the feast of the Blessed St Edmund, and we are shown pictures depicting his passion that we then may know him more nearly. We see him first scourged and then shot through with arrows, his faith yet unshaken, his God unrenounced. At the last is the head of him struck from his shoulders to roll at his feet, where a beast on all fours stands to guard it. The Reverend Mother would have it the beast is a wolf, though its image looks more like a dog, and yet monstrously big is it made so that I grow afraid of this picture and think of it even when it is no longer in sight. We can none of us know, what it is that walks under the ground.

So the days pass. A woman of Glassthorpehill over the Nobottle Woods is possessed of a spirit, and vomits up animal beings like little white frogs. This is told me by Sister Eadgyth, though I did not wait in her company long enough that I might come to know more. She endures constipations that make her breath foul, and her humour alike, but she is a good Christian and hard at her work.

I did not walk at all, from the time of my birth to my thirtieth year, when I lived in the yard by the chalk-merchant's house that was over the way from the church. In a lean-to of sail-cloth and old, painted boards I abided alone, for my father had taken his leave while I was yet unborn and my mother had gone to the colic before I was ten. With the rise of the sun every morn I would crawl from my shack like a beetle and drag my weight over the stones of the lane to my place at the gate by my elbows, where until this day is the skin dead and worn, without feeling, and may be pinched up in grey folds that are like to dried clay.

On the boards of my lean-to were pictures of angels, but half unmade; drawn with an unpractised fist. It was sometimes my fancy that they were the work of my father and left incomplete by his leave-taking, although I knew them more likely the mark of a stranger's hand, someone long dead, or passed over the river from Spelhoe to

Cleyley. I had these boards turned with the pictures faced inward and, laid by my candle at night, I'd imagine the clumsy embrace of their arms without hands, these omitted for want of pictorial skill. I would think myself fanned by their unfinished wings.

Now the near-winter skies have a burnished and argent light to them, hung over the convent at Abingdon here in the far fields north-east of the old church where so long I lay. As the feast of St Edmund approaches, so too does my sleep grow more fitful and restless; fraught with the most wretched of dreams, where I ride through the hurricane night as a man with my thoughts in a bitter confusion and enemies hot at my heel or, worse yet, I will wake and cry out in despair at the death of my brother, though brother in truth I have none, nor have I ever wanted for such.

On the day of the feast I awake with such words in my mouth as to frighten the wits from my poor sister Aethelflaed, there in her cell next to mine. With the voice of a bear I am growling of murder: ` In Hel's Town was my brother Edmund flayed first from his neck to his loins, whence he wept and complained, lying spread as if garbed in a blood-shirt that Ingwar's men folded back, shewing the red, stinking harp there beneath.'

I console Sister Aethelflaed, calming her, even though truly I am more afraid for myself. I have such thoughts inside me that make me ashamed before God; other voices and lives speaking in me, not only in dreams but throughout the day's labours. I sit by the well in the yard with my better leg folded beneath me and busy myself with the washing of smocks, when I find myself thinking how foolish was my brother Edmund to hold with his faith through the earlier torturings, only to shriek out its renunciation in his mortal pain as he begged them for death.

Now my hands become still in the well's freezing waters, the fingers grown numb that the smock I am rinsing falls from them and floats in a thin scum of November leaves. I am thinking that should I be captured then gladly will I offer praise unto Wotan, for all his one eye and the pale shyte of ravens encrusting his shoulders, if he will deliver me from this demise; this blood-eagle, that it may not unfold its bloody-ribbed wings and make naked my heart . . .

I may not say how long I am sitting there until I come to myself, and rise up with a cry at the horrors that visited with me while I sat in reverie. Shaking and pale, with my bad leg dragged useless behind me, I go to the Reverend Mother and tell her that I am afflicted by dreams such as may be the work of an incubus, asking permission that I might be scourged for to rid me of these noxious thoughts. Here she voices concern with respect to my frailty and age, bidding me reconsider and suffer some penance less strict and exacting. I tell her of my imprecations, alone in my cell; all the rosaries said but unanswered. I beg that she let me be scourged, that the flail drive away what the beads cannot halt, lest my immortal soul should itself be imperilled. At last she consents, with the penance to be undertaken the following day, that I might yet have time to more fully consider the rigorous path I have chosen with all of my heart to pursue. I must not shrink from this, for I fear for my faith in the face of these infidel visions and flukes of the night; Blessed Virgin forgive me, deliver me.

Later, alone in my cell with the candle-sketched devils of shadow that leap and cavort on its walls when I move, I am thinking of Ivalde, so many years dead now. He came and he sat by me there at the gate where I lay on a cold morning just before spring. In his slow, simple-minded inflection he told me of how he'd set forth on his pilgrimage that very day. He was going, he told me, to Rome, although Bruning had scolded and railed at him, saying that God and the Blessed St Peter had better to do than pay heed to a half-witted garden-boy.

Though I'd no liking for Bruning, it suited me on that particular day to agree with him and thus give vent to my spite, for I had not slept well and was weary of Ivalde and all of his unceasing chatter of Rome. `You should listen to Bruning,' I told him. `It's only the rich and the holy like him as should think themselves worthy of going to Rome! Why, you're nothing but only a simpleton. You may be sure that St Peter would care not a bit more for you than he would a poor cripple like me.' He looked hurt at my words, like a baby, and fell to a stutter while making attempts at professing his faith in the Drotinum. I turned away from him then, and would speak no more to him till he went away, seeming woeful and filled up with puzzlement.

Inside my heart I was sure that this fresh talk of pilgrimage would come to nothing; that on the next morn I'd see Ivalde stooped, tending his crops with his idle dreams yet again put to one side, as had often-times happened before, but it was not to be. He had gone, Bruning said, in the night; on a wagon that made for the coast in the hope that he would find a ship whereupon he might then work his passage to Normandy, thereafter Rome.

Ivalde's leaving threw good Bruning into a temper so fierce as to last for some days, and it seemed to me that the priest knew a great scorn for poor Ivalde's presumptions. No doubt Bruning felt that if anyone were to petition St Peter then he, Bruning, should be by right and by rank at the head of the line. I would see that stout priest red of face, cursing under his breath as he stooped to pull weeds from between parsnip rows in the untended garden, and knew it was Ivalde he cursed. So the days turned to weeks and not until the feast of the Passion was Ivalde returned to us.

That afternoon I was sat by the gate with the grey cloud hung heavy and low, fit to snag on the church's low spire, and a sad, sagging heat in the air. All my clothing was damped in this miserable warmth so that I was for ever unpeeling my skirt where it stuck to the tops of my legs. I did not notice Ivalde until he had breasted the hump of the river-bridge, downhill and over the crossroads from where I sat ragged and slumped by the gate. Even then, when I noted the strange, shambling figure's approach, I at first did not know it for Ivalde, so changed was the boy in the wake of his travels. Not till he had come by the crossroads and I saw the red of his hair did I know who it was, and confess a mean gladness to see that he could not have visited Rome.

As he walked up the hill with that shuffling gait that he had not been marked with before there was something about him that I cannot easily fit into words, as if here were a picture that I knew of old and had seen many times in the past, though I cannot think where: this wan fool with the yellowing darts of grass caught in his hair, stumbling over the bridge to the crossroads like one fresh returned from a battle; a look in his eyes as if he knows not where he must be, only that he must be there. He walked up the lane with the sky blinding white at his back, and I thought 'This has happened before', and I watched him come near, at once strange and familiar in aspect like one of the queer painted figures that grace a cartomancer's deck.

'I have come back, Alfgiva,' he said when he neared me. His voice sounded hollow, with none of the life it once had. All the nonsense was gone from him now, though I cared little more for the faraway oddness it left in its stead. He stood by me, and yet did not suffer himself to kneel down by my side when he spoke, nor did he look towards me but all the while stared at the church, and his face was without any feeling at all; without even a blink in his eye.

With my neck all craned back like a bird I spoke up to him as he stood dark there with bright silver sky overhead. `Ivalde? Where have you been? You did not go to Rome?'

He glanced down at me then, and a cloudiness came in his eyes as if he did not know me. The small birds fell quiet in the yew and what afternoon shadows there were seemed to pause in their crawl to the east, and at length Ivalde spoke with his voice small and wondering, almost as if he recounted the tale of another boy, someone he'd met long ago and remembered but dimly.

`Not Rome. I did not go to Rome. Thrice I boarded the boat, but he came to me so that I fell in a fit, and he told me that I must return.' His eyes drifted away from me, back to the church, and I tugged at the leg of his breeks as I spoke to him.

`Who sent you back? Is it Bruning you speak of? He's been at this church since you left.' Slowly, and without looking away from the church as he did so, Ivalde shook his great copper head so that sharp stalks of grass were dislodged from his hair. I followed their fall with my eyes to his feet, which I saw with alarm to be bloody, the boots hung in rags.

`No. Not Bruning. The Drotinum. He sent me back. Him or one of his angels.' Ivalde looked once more to me and I could see that his green eyes were brimming with tears. `Oh, Alfgiva,' he said. `Oh Alfgiva, whatever has happened to me?'

As his face grew first pink and then crumpled itself as he wept, I could but stare at him. Quite unable to answer his question, I ventured now one of my own: `Ivalde, what are you saying, the Drotinum sent you back here? You do not mean St Peter?'

He started to nod, then instead deigned to shake his head violently, eyes clenched and streaming. `I don't know. It looked like an angel, with folded green wings and it stood twice as tall as a man. It said I should come back.' Here he opened his eyes and he stared at me fiercely. 'Alfgiva, it spoke down a flute, and it walked through the wall upon great spindled legs like a bird.' He looked back at the church, and I saw he was shaking. 'The room was too small to contain it, and yet it stood tall and the ceiling was melted like smoke so that I might look up through it to where the Drotinum stood there above me, with eyes full of care.' He fell silent. A pennant of black cloud was slowly unrolled, hung up over the church with its shadow fell on to the garden and graves, the turfed humps of them, pregnant with skeletons.

This was not Ivalde, his nonsense of old to be lightly waved off, for I saw that a change was in him, and I shivered and knew I believed what he said, though I did not feel glad. For a moment I sat with him, sharing his silence, but could not long keep from my questions and asked if this angel, this Drotinum had come to Ivalde on more times than one. He looked full of such misery then as he nodded, I knew that if Ivalde had ever in innocence craved for a sign from above, then he'd surely repented and now wished his visions behind him.

'The first time it came to me, I did not see it, but felt as I walked up the boards to the ship as if something more big than a horse were stood blocking my path, and my face and my fingers would creep if I made but to take a step forward. At this, I grew frightened and would not set foot on the boat so that it sailed without me and left me to wait on another ship bound for the Normandy coast. I grew vexed with myself as I waited and, cursing myself for a coward, I vowed I would board the next vessel to dock.'

Seeming now to regain his composure, he gazed at the church. Squatting over its door, carved in stone, was the token of Lust with her legs set apart and the cold, mossy lips of her sex gaping wide, her six fellows beside her with three to each side.

Ivalde's face seemed to slacken and settle. The vague fogs of distance were risen afresh in his eyes as he spoke. 'When it came, it was due to set sail with the dawn, and I said I would sleep until then in some fisherman's sheds I had found on the edge of the sand, up above the sharp grass. I awoke in the night with my feet tangled up in the slippery fish-nets, to find that the angel was standing above me. Its sorry green feathers were dripping with wet and though I dare not look I was filled with a queer understanding that smaller things, hairless and blind, struggled down by the stumps of its awful thin legs. It had eyes like an unhappy man, but it spoke through a beak like a flute, and it told me that I must return. I woke up with the piss on my legs and dare not leave the hut the next day till I knew that my ship had put forth.'

'The third time I boarded the ship and was sent below, that was the time that I spoke of before, when it came through the wall while I sat there awake and instructed me, so that I ran from the ship in my fear and so too did I run from that town on the coast. I have run, and when I ran no more then I walked, till I came here. I came by the brow of the hill to the west of the town. It was there that I saw him again, and less time ago than it would take for a candle to burn half its length.'

From the doors of the church, as if birthed from the chill cunt that gaped in the stonework above him, fat Bruning came striding out over the wet grass, through which trailed the hem of his dark robings so that he seemed more to glide, without feet. He was shouting at Ivalde, his mouthings too angry to forge any sense from, yet Ivalde ignored his approach and continued to speak with me, gazing above Bruning's head to the tower of the church.

'It was waiting when I reached the crest of the hill and could see the town spread out before me. It stood far away from me this time, alone in a scorched patch of grass, off across a great ring where the trees had been cleared. Tall and green, I mistook it at first for a sapling and then was struck still as stone, cold with a terrible fear when it waved to me. Though it was too far away to be heard, and I cannot recall any sound being made, yet it seemed that I heard its flute voice just as if it were stood by my shoulder. It said the remains of a friend unto God were hid under the church, and that I must tell Bruning. I hurried on. When I looked back all I saw were two saplings, their trunks close together and like unto legs.'

Puffing mightily, Bruning himself was upon us now, bullying Ivalde and jeering at him for his failure in visiting Rome. 'So the Lord did not see fit to favour your pilgrimage after all? What did I say! You have come crawling back in hope, vain hope I say, that I may yet have saved you some task. Well . . .' Here, Bruning trailed off, made uncomfortable both by Ivalde's remote unconcern and by his silence. A look of uncertainty clouded the face of the priest, and it was in that moment as if he first knew himself outdone; could tell by some mere thread of meaning, some clew in the garden-boy's stance that Ivalde had passed nearer the world of the spirit than Bruning himself ever had.

When the priest had grown silent and shaken then Ivalde related the tale of his travels to Bruning as he had revealed them to me, and so coming at last to the spectre's instruction to dig neath the floor of the church, where a friend unto God would be found.

Bruning stared at the lad while he spoke, but did not once break in with a jibe or remark, and when Ivalde had finished the priest was grown pale, and could not seem to speak for a while. When he did, there was nothing of rancour nor superiority that might be read in his voice, which was faint and unsteady. 'Come, Ivalde,' he whispered. 'I'll find for us spades.'

They set off up the path to the door of the church, leaving me quite forgotten behind, though I called them. I watched them a while, and then made up my mind I would follow them, though it were further than I was accustomed to crawl. With my cold elbows soaked by the dew I dragged over the grass, my eyes fixed on the door and the crater-eyed vice that crouched leering above it. I feel to this day the dank slither of grass on my belly, the ache in my arms as I felt it then. It was the last time that I ever crawled.

Sister Aethelflaed snores in the next cell to mine and my candle is guttering. Now I recall that tomorrow I am to be scourged and a fear wells in me that I swiftly fight down; turn instead my attention to prayers, supplications that I may for once be spared terrible dreams in the hours before light comes again. With my rough sheets drawn fast all about my cold back I turn on to my side with my ear flat against the hard wood of my cot. The patch under my cheek, where the timber is dulled and made soft by the dribblings of hundreds of women, asleep . . .

I am leading my horse down a hill in the dark with the wild cries of Ingwar's men over the crest far behind me, too far to make out what they say. Near the base of the hill is a treacherous mire where my steed loses footings and sinks to its haunches, eyes mad-white and rolling and all the time whinnying fearfully. I grow afraid that the enemies gaining upon me will hear it and so in my panic abandon it, making off over the fields, my feet heavy, gigantic with mud. Viking curses hang brutish and blunt on the night in my wake. The blanched rushes rear up in the moonlight before me, and there from their midst looms a great mound of earth like the skull of an ice giant, long dead, toppled face first in river-weeds. At my back, closer now, rough men are calling a word that grows gradually clearer, becoming a name, and waist-deep in the rushes I know that the name is my own. As their heavy fur boots tread the reeds flat behind me I know who I am, and this cold recognition has shocked me from out of my sleep to the dark of my cell with the dream-name still thick on my tongue.

Ragener. Blessed Ragener, brother of Edmund and murdered like Edmund before by the North-man invaders when he would not honour their gods. Sainted Ragener, wearing like Edmund the crown of the martyrs, his feast day a single day after the feast that's afforded his brother. How could I, of all men and women that live, have forgotten?

I lie in the blackness alone with the blind hammer-beat of my blood, feel the spray smashed up over the sheer cliffs of blasphemy cold on my brow. In our lessons we're taught how the brother saints would not submit to the Viking usurpers, nor would they renounce the true God, and for this were they scourged and then shot through with arrows, beheaded at last but with souls yet intact. In my dream, things work differently. Edmund is dead with his lungs all but torn from his breast, his last agonized words a denial of God while his brother flees terrified into the night where he plans his conversion to Wotan that Ragener may thus avoid all the torments that Edmund has suffered. I cannot believe that these dreams come from God that so contravene all that is taught by his ministers. Wondering, ill at ease as to the source of my dreams if not God, I lie wide awake here in my cell until morning is come on this twenty-first day of November, the feast day of Blessed St Ragener, when I shall at last be scourged of these visions that now are so hateful to me.

Having noted the lack of my presence at Matins, the Reverend Mother is brought to my cell where I ask that I might be excused all my duties that day, so to better prepare for the scourging that I must endure when the evening is come. Here the Reverend Mother expresses again both her doubts with regard to the ordeal itself and her estimates as to my chance of surviving the flail, with my late years and lameness considered. At last, having seen my conviction, the Reverend

Mother agrees I may stay in my cell the day long, that I may come to peace with myself and with God.

I sit there on my cot, one knee drawn to my breast, with the hours drifting by through a dulled gauze yet fraught with uneasiness. When at last Sister Eadgyth is sent to my cell that I may thus be brought to the scourge, I discover my good leg has fallen asleep while immobile these hours, so that Sister Eadgyth must carry me clung on her arm to the place of my punishment, head close to mine with her midden-breath full on my cheek. Thus unable to walk, I cannot but recall when my legs failed me last, as I slithered on elbows and belly across the cold stone of the portal and into the nave of the church where both Ivalde and Bruning were already stripped of their shirts, prising up the great flags of the floor with their spades, the flat slabs levered up on one edge then allowed to fall back, thus exposing the dark plot of bloodworm-crazed earth underneath.

As Eadgyth half lifts and half drags me the length of the passageway, I am unable to say where I am, or what year it might be; am as nameless as one freshly woken. I crawl through the nave of the church to where Bruning and Ivalde are digging, great shovels of earth flung up careless and high to come rattling down on the flags where I drag my weight over the dirt to the edge of their hole. Now, face down in the earth, I am Ragener, weeping and pleading as strong Viking hands seize me hard underneath my arms, wrenching me upward to stumble beside them towards the pale mound hulking up from the rushes. Their hands are become those of Sister Eadgyth, now helping me into the little stone room where the leather-backed horse made from wood is prepared and the Reverend Mother is waiting.

Her voice sounds so far away. Sister Eadgyth is stripping me bare to my waist and arranging me face down the length of the horse with my flat nipples tightening, pressed to the chill of the hide, and the cold in my chest is like that when I lay on the floor of the church, with my fingers hooked over the edge of the flags that now bordered the hole where both Ivalde and Bruning were digging, with Bruning stood there on the slabs to one side of the pit mopping sweat from his pendulous bosom, while Ivalde, the ribs showing through at his sides, stood waist deep with the earth raining up from the blade of his shovel. I'd only just pulled myself up to the edge to peer down when the dirt-floor collapsed beneath Ivalde to wide yawning dark and the rattle of loose soil below.

Showers of dirt trickle down from the bare knoll to fall in the rushes encircling its base. Ingwar's brigands are hauling me up to the flat rock on top of the mound, where they laugh at my tears and pathetic attempts to befriend them while dragging the clothes from my body, and when I am naked they laugh at my manhood and throw me down hard on my face with one of the men kneeling before me and pinning me down by my forearms. I gaze at him with the blood gumming my eyes. It has leaked from my scalp where they cuffed me, and through it his face is more terrible than I had e'er hoped to see in this life, with the plaited beard dyed into stripes of all colours and maddening drugs on his breath in this year of Our Lord Christ eight hundred and seventy.

Stood at the top of the leather horse holding my wrists, Sister Eadgyth breathes rancid and hot in my face and the year is one thousand and sixty-four. Somewhere behind me the Reverend Mother is raising the flail of raw hide past her shoulder. For what seems an unending while I can hear the uncured thongs as they whistle down through the chamber's cold air and a blind, searing pain rips from shoulders and back to engulf my whole being in terrible light.

In the Lord's year one thousand and fifty Ivalde screams to Bruning for help as his legs churn through waterfall dirt in attempting to run up the sides of the hole while its floor falls away into dark down below. The fat priest lurches forward to pull the boy clear as I lie peering over the rim of the pit, flagstones chilling my belly. Beneath me, I see that the base of the hole has collapsed into caverns or tunnels existing below. For a moment it seems that I make out the indistinct bulk of the tomb that is later revealed to be hidden therein and containing the bones of the martyred St Ragener, brother of Edmund. At most, squinting into the black, I perceive its vague outline for only a moment before my attention is called to the sense of another large shape in the darkness beneath me, this one with a sound that suggests a huge, shuffling motion. I have but an instant to marvel before the uncanny thing happens. Good Bruning, when he has recovered, will later describe what we saw as the Holy Ghost made manifest in its terrible radiance, but I am flat on my face with my head hung out over the mouth of the pit and I see. When it opens its monstrous eyes I am staring straight into them. Smothering brilliance is everywhere. Off in the empty white nothingness Bruning makes sounds like a woman.

I scream as the first of the Viking men plunges his hardness inside me, but after the third I sob only a little and then to myself at the thought of my life and this terrible end. As the last of the men takes his weapon from in me I'm turned on my back, whereupon I start pleading again and profess my allegiance to Wotan. The sound of my terrified voice is a curse in my ears until one of my captors brings silence by raping my mouth to the jeers of his fellows. I try to take in the immensity of what is happening to me. The smallest amongst my tormentors now brings out a knife, and before he has touched it to me I am screaming.

The scourge cuts my back and I writhe. Sister Eadgyth holds tight to my wrists while away in the distance the Reverend Mother is praying and there is a high noise that goes on and on.

Bruning screams, Ivalde screams and the white light is everywhere. Something of hideous size flutters over my head as I lie on the floor of the church. Later on, when the light has gone and I go back to find Bruning and Ivalde both sat by the wall staring blank into space with the floor gaping open before them, the fat priest will claim that the wings brushing over my neck are the wings of the Heavenly Spirit; the dew that it scatters to fall in my hair he will call holy water, yet why is it slippery and thick like the seed of a man, or the slime of old rivers? And why is the Heavenly Spirit not manifest here as a bird but a terrible fluttering fan of pale green luminescence that trembles and whirls in the dazzle of white, scarcely solid, so that parts of it will appear to pass through other parts without harm, or to slice through the great wooden pillars supporting the church just as if they were air? There's a terrible clattering, clattering. Blinded and frantic with terror, I leap to my feet and run out from the church. Not until I am halfway down hill and approaching the crossroads do I understand what I've done.

In eight hundred and seventy they have cut open my chest. I had not believed any plight suffered by man could be equal in horror to this, that is happening now, in this moment, to me. They reach into the cavity, seizing the ribs to pull upwards and out, and I pass beyond pain. I am straddling a carpenter's horse in a cold room and know that I am an old woman. My back hangs in ribbons. I call out to Wotan for succour and at this the woman who flogs me flogs harder. I lie on a smouldering pyre with my throat cut, and cook, in a great skull of iron or bound to a post, and I rot as the head of a traitor hung high on the gates of this town. I am child. I am murderer, poet and saint. I am Ragener. I am Alfgiva, and gone beyond hurt to a flagellant rapture that only the martyrs may know, coming bloody to Paradise, hands burned to stumps or all bristling with arrows, our breasts rendered open whence spills the great light of our hearts.

I am lifted above, with the noise of the world a great roar in my ears, and if I am in Heaven then where come there so many fires?

LIMPING TO JERUSALEM
POST AD 1100

Hard as new steel the sun cuts from a lard of cloud, although its light seems wearied by the effort. I am old, yet is this ceaseless and exhausting world here still. My piles nag, saddle-chafed, wherefor upon this showery morning I am filled with a choleric bile and have twice cuffed my squire. As we descend the street of Jews into the reek and clamour of the horse-fayre he falls back to ride behind me that I may not see the poison in his look.

Ahead, my dogs run on amongst the market traders and their fly-chewed nags. With pink jaws wet and frilled like cunny, here and there they chop and snap upon an ankle or a fetlock, for the sport of it. The crowd fall back that I may pass, blunt-headed gets of Saxony with spittle on their chins, although the girls are often fair. The scuffle of my charger's hoof is loud upon the hard-packed dirt, the fayre now fallen into quiet as whispers from a comely woman's skirt may hush an ale room. Now they touch their scabby brows at me as I ride by, and look up fearfully. Were I not halt and aged I would bed their wives and daughters both before them ere I took their heads . . .

I must not think of heads.

My squire and I pass on. The crowd is knit once more together in our wake and falls again to chattering and barter, with our passage through its midst a wound soon healed. Before and to the left of me the crumbling church looms heavy in its sandstone walls of dirty gold, named for Saint Peter, by whose intercession were the relics of Saint Ragener here found, or so the tale is told. A half-mad nun of Abingdon, dead twenty years or more, spoke of an angel or a holy bird within the church that healed her crippled legs.

That may be very well for her, yet I am lame and filled with aches, and know her vision to be but the ravings that are come upon a woman when her monthly bloods have ceased. Since the Crusade, I am made out of sorts with God. A ray falls out from Heaven now to strike the church so that its gaping windows seem to fill with brightness, yet I know the light is false, surrendered soon to squall.

This island rain: I am already wet inside my jerkin from the shower endured whilst hunting, early-on this day. The dampness hereabouts has raised a leather in my cheek that was not always there, but my complaints are weak, and lack conviction. Did there ever come a morning out there in those Holy deserts when I did not wake to find my belly black with flies, the sweat boiled out of me and pooled between my dugs, and pray to know again this sickly northern light, this drizzle in my eyes? The sun here throws us only scraps, already having squandered its great bounty on the distant Heathen, stood amongst his hills of sand.

The church is fell behind, and on our right hand here Chalk-monger Lane winds up towards the castle's higher grounds as we descend upon the cross-roads at the bridge, whereby its gated yard stands opened out. We clatter in between the great brick gateposts and across the flags. Yard-boys, who not a moment since were no doubt cursing me as every harlot's son, run out all smiles to take my bridle, crying, `See! It is Lord Simon. He is home.'

My eyes, without volition it would seem, climb up to where Maud's chamber window over-looks the courtyard. No one there. Dismounted, with a yard-lad either side of me, I hang one arm across each of their necks, and with my weight supported thus am steered towards the great door, one leg dragged behind, scraped through the silvering of puddles as I go. Once, in a rage, Maud said that she would lie upon her cot and weep to hear that sound, that scraping, for it meant I was returned. Helped up the three broad steps, I am inside the castle. In my bag a brace of ducks are stiffening, cooling in their thickened blood. Black eyes that stare, unblinking, into blackness.

In the fastness of my chamber are the wretched, muddied garments pulled from me, whereafter I am dried and dressed to take my meal: cold mutton, warm bread and sour beers. Maud does not eat with me. The clatter of my knife and dish fall on a ringing silence.

Sucking lukewarm gravy from my moustache I can feel her pacing in the upper rooms and in my mind's eye see her, all her bitterness made plain within her bearing. Now she crosses to the window seat, her head tipped down to gouge her breastbone with a small, sharp chin; her arms crossed tight below her budding teats; white, brittle fingers clasping either elbow. She is tall-built, twenty-nine years old and awkward in her gait. She does not laugh, nor yet make pleasant talk, but only sulks and scowls. It sometimes seems to me that it would be as well if I were married not to her but to her mother after all. Ah well. That's done with now.

A knot of muttonflesh has worked into the socket of the sole back tooth, half-crumbled, that is left within my lower jaw, which morsel now my tongue makes secret, complicated motions to unseat. Maud, naked. Some fifteen years since. I had seated her upon my knee one night, our wedding not long past, pinched by her shoulders that she might not draw away. I tried to make her play with my old man but she made faces and vowed by the Holy Virgin she would not. When I released her upper arm that I might take her by the wrist and force her to comply she struggled free and jumped from off my lap to cower amongst the hanging drapes.

If I had only beaten her on that occasion more severely, she would surely have enjoyed a sweeter disposition to me since. If I had taken off my belt to her and thrashed her skinny rump until it bled. If I had seized her hair or twisted on her tit until she howled. The anger makes my chest thud, answered by a hopeless twitch from the forgotten beast that nests below my paunch. It is not well to stir my temper in this way, lest I should bring an illness on myself, and as the mutton-pellet holds its own against my questing tongue I turn my thoughts to gentler affairs.

The church that I am building on the rise up by the sheep-track rests half-done, the pagan relic there before pulled down that we may use its substance for our own construction. Some of its bricks are carved with monstrous and obscene antiquities, much like the gape-cunt hag of stone that squats above the portico of old St Peter's. These we shall discard, save where necessity and shortage of materials should otherwise dictate. Already we are forced by circumstances to retain a pillar inlaid with a barbarous, serpentine device, some leering Teuton devil-wyrm coiled down the column's length. I should be anxious that this remnant not offend, were the good people not offended more by my proposal for the church itself.

`Lord Simon, can it be you jest?' they say. They say, `Lord Simon, reconsider your design lest it prove an affront to God himself.' They say, `But my Lord Simon, what of the tradition in such things?' (This same tradition being cruciform; it hardly need be said.) They carp and make complaint for all the world as if I had raised up a monument to Moloch or a tabernacle made for Jews. They mutter and they cross themselves and lay each stone with such grave faces, just as if they fear but that they wall up their immortal souls.

Round. All I ask is that they build it in a round, as was the Temple raised by Solomon there in Jerusalem so builded. Round, without a corner where the Devil may find purchase or concealment. Round, that God should likewise know no hiding place. If He is there, then He must show Himself. If He is there . . .

The fringe of beard was fine and silvery. Its eyelids were stitched shut; the nose collapsed into a hole. It smelled of peppers, hot and dry. In its expression, something foreign and unreadable, there at the corner of the mouth where it had come unsewn, the small brown teeth revealed . . .

I close my eyes and push my dish away. I lift my hand up to my face and cannot help but groan at what is in me, at the weight of it. The servants look toward me, mute and frightened, then toward each other. Gathering up my half-completed dish, my half-drained cup, they whisk away to tremble in the distant kitchens, hurried footsteps quick and soft as rain across the empty, echoing hall, then gone.

The brief screech of my chair, pushed back now from the table so that I may rise, is hateful and alone in this giant room. I call aloud for John, my squire, who comes after too long a time and helps me to my chamber, on which tedious and protracted journey do I scold him thus: ' Why are you come so late upon my call? Do you suppose that I have grown new legs and so may dance back to my rooms without your aid?'

Staggering with his shoulder pressed beneath the hollow of my arm, he glares down at the flags and mutters all his ' No, Lord Simon's and his ' God Forbid's, telling me that he'd been at stool when first I called to him, whereon I make remark that should he suffer me to wait henceforth then I shall have him whipped until he shits his breeches.

At these words a sense of that which is before-seen comes to me. Was I manhandled lame along these corridors before with thoughts of flogging hot upon my brow? I know a far-off, singing dizzyness: Saracen voices droning to their Devil-God across the dunes. I have stood from my meal too quickly, that is all. Dismissing John upon the threshold of my chamber I shut fast the door and make my heavy path towards the bed, using a chair-back as support along the way.

The room is cold, but I am warmed by beers as I surrender to the bedding. Here I may digest, and be alone without a thought of Maud to trouble me, her rooms being upon the castle's furthest side. Though the November air be chill, it's as nothing to the empty, bone-deep cold that falls on desert when the day is done, and resting here I am content. Above me, in the ceiling's timbers, fissured lines and whorls call to my mind a map of ancient and unconquered territories . . .

Good Pope Urban did as Peter, called the Hermit, had entreated him: he called on us to take the Cross; to join with his Crusade and rid the Holy Land of its Mohammedan oppressor. Though the early expeditions of both Peter and one Walter, called the Penniless, were cut to pieces by the Turks, we were not to be stayed. Thus, in the ninety-and-sixth year of this Millennium we set our sails for Constantinople and not a one of us thought other than that he would reach again his home a richer man.

Great God, but the immensity of that cruel Heathen sky. It made men mad. While on our way to join with Robert, Duke of Normandy, in setting Antioch to siege, we came across a fellow broiled as black as any Saracen who yet sang out loud hymns in noble French as he paced there in circles 'midst the bare, slow-shifting hills. Alone without his comrades for who knows how many days or weeks, he'd patiently dug out a long and looping trench, deep as a man's waist, that stretched back across the dunes as far as we might view. He cursed us when we broke a small part of its sides down as we led our mounts across. Upon his brown-seared chest the rags of Flanders hung, their bright green fading yellow in the shadeless desert light.

When we had ridden on a little way and left him raving far behind us, I glanced back and with a queer surprise saw that his endless trench, when looked at from afar, did not snake back and forwards without meaning, as it seemed to when close by. Viewed from a distance, it became a line of monstrous script reeled out across the dunes, scrawled in a giant and uneven hand. In many places words and letters had been wiped away by shifting sand, so that it came to me that this poor soul must spend his days in pacing up and down along the message's drear length, digging anew its strokes and flourishes, hymns spilling from his parched black lips the while. The only words that I could read were `Dieu' and one that may have been `humilité', spelled out across a violet-shadowed slope's soft flank. His message, and of this I have not any doubt, was meant for the Almighty, who alone resides at such a height as to review the text entire. We left him crouched upon the bridges of an `m', frantically scrabbling to wipe away the hoof-prints where our steeds had damaged his calligraphy.

And so we ventured on, and sacked the smaller towns that lay along our route to Antioch. There is a sound that plunder makes; a hundred smaller noises all confused in one: a wailing baby, dusty thunder of collapsing stone and whine of injured dogs. Horse panic. Lost and trembling query of escaping goats with women weeping from their guts; men from their noses. Gruff cries, unintelligible, sunken to a language only made for war. The mortal chime of blade, the howl of buggered children, all one voice that spits and crackles in the moment's smoke-black throat. I hear it now.

We set their shrines to torch. We took their lives, their wives, their horses, silks and jewels and some of us took more besides. One of my captains wore a belt hung round with Heathen tongues until we chided him about the stench of it. They were great black things, bigger than you might suppose, and no two quite alike. These barbarisms were not strange to us while we were in that place, though I have thought upon them since and know now that such actions lack all dignity. Still, others took far greater strides along that route than we. Some leagues from Murzak we rode for a way beside a company of knights from Italy who dined upon the flesh of slain Mohammedans, saying that since their foemen had not Christian souls they were more like to beasts and could thus be devoured without a breach of covenant. It was quite plain they were made lunatic by eating Heathen brains, and I could not but wonder how they'd fare on their return to Christian lands. As it occurred, returning through those territories back from Murzak at a later date we came upon their heads, daintily set there in an inward-facing ring between the shimmering drifts, scraps of their azure tunics tied about their eyes, blindfolding the already blind for cultish reasons that we could not guess.

I longed with all my heart to see Jerusalem, that city of the scriptures that the pagan Emperor Julian of Rome sought in his vanity to build anew and was struck down by God ere the foundations could be laid. A whirlwind and upheavals fraught with gouts of flame erased his works, in which some see a proof of the Divinity's displeasure. (My round church at least has its foundations set in place, whatever may befall it hence.) I longed to walk amongst those hills, and see that ancient heart of piling stones from where the Holy verses sprang, but what I saw instead! Better my head were settled blindfold in that dismal ring of Roman cannibals, my blood congealed like egg-yolk in my beard.

I must not think of heads.

Somewhere below my bed, below my chamber floor, the castle is alive with catcalls, footsteps, and recriminations; grand and cold and echoing, and built to last a thousand years. I can recall when only Waltheof's Baronial hall stood here, all wood and thatch that swarmed with fleas, before the King decided that a knight of Normandy might overlook these districts better than a Saxon Earl.

Poor Waltheof. I met him once or twice and he was likeable, though quite without intelligence. As a reward for his collaboration in the Conquest did William the Bastard first give Waltheof the Earldom of North Hamtun, then a traitor's grave when he had tired of him. Such calumnies and grave accusals did they heap upon his head that by the end the old man came himself to think his treasons actual. Had he conspired against the King? It seemed to him this must be so, for had his own wife Judith not thus testified? That William, being old and filled with panics, might seek merely to consolidate his own position by arraying fellow countrymen about him in the Baronies would seem a notion quite beyond the grasp of Waltheof. Nor did he grasp that Judith, being William's niece, would testify in any way her Royal uncle might require. Led weeping to the block, he even called aloud for Judith to forgive him, whereupon at least the treacherous whore summoned the grace to wince and look away for shame. She was her uncle's creature, quick to do as he might bid on all occasions.

All occasions save for one.

The light outside my turret window is grown wan with the progression of the afternoon. I doze, made drowsy by the beers, and when I wake to find the windows filling with November's early dark I have a memory of nonsense, drifted through my thoughts while reason slept: out in the wastes of Palestine, caught in some mapless region quite devoid of landmark, I am come upon a human foot that sticks up from the sand. With much delight it comes to me that buried here is my true leg, the lame and hateful thing that I have dragged about with me these years being a mere impersonation of the same. Eager to walk as once I did, I kneel and start to scoop away the dust about the ankle and the calf, when of a sudden I am made aware of someone watching me.

I look up, not without a start, and see a woman crawling on her belly with a horrid speed across the lazy dunes to where I crouch beside the jutting foot. Dressed in the black robes of a nun and crippled in some manner I may not discern, she drags herself towards me down the baking slopes, and now I hear her calling to me imprecations, bitter curses, telling me the leg is hers and warning me to leave it be. I grow afraid of both her furious spite and beetle-like velocity as she propels her black-draped carcass down the hillock in a pittering hail of grit. Wrenching now frantically upon the ankle that protrudes, I here attempt to haul the leg up out the sand and make away with it before the nun has reached me, but it will not budge. Within the ghastly instant that is prior to waking, I become aware that there is something underneath the desert floor that pulls against me, something hidden and yet hideously strong that yanks upon the leg as if to draw it under from below, at which I wake to wet palms and the clanging of my anvil heart, here in this darkening turret.

I am so afraid. I am afraid of being dead, I am afraid of being nothing, and that great unease that I have kept so long at bay is made companion to me now. I see the life of me, the life of all of us, our wars and copulations, all our movement and philosophy and conscience, and there is no floor beneath it, and it stands on naught. Beyond my window, early stars emerge into a firmament with purpose fled.

After a time, I call to John, at which he answers with such haste that I half fancy he has sat betimes without my chamber door for fear of being absent when I summon him. Raised up now on the bed and pulling on my breeks I bid him fetch the Lady Maud to me and, after his removal and the lighting of a candelabra, kneel beside the bed to make my water in a chamber-jug. The stream is thick and brownish and with melancholy I observe my prick to be yet chancred and inflamed: one more amongst the relics brought back from the Holy Land.

I never saw Jerusalem. It had become quite plain that by the time we came to Antioch the greater part of all the fighting (and the pillage) would be done, and so we were content to take a more meandering route that brought us upon towns and Heathen settlements both less defended and less likely to already be picked clean. I took a native woman up from one of these to carry on my travels, and for some nights had great sport with it, though on the ninth such night she killed herself. The women of this like were plentiful. Once, when such things became the fashion with us for a while, I tried a boy, though never liked it, for the smell of Heathen boys is not a pleasing one. In time, such pleasures anyway were overcome by heat; a carnal lassitude; a deadening of ambition in the flesh.

We had veered far, come almost into Egypt when we chanced upon the knights in red and white. All of that week our travel had been hard and filled with queer occurrence, as when five days sooner we had seen the ground beneath our largest and most deeply-laden wagon crack apart, so that the whole front end of it plunged down into the sudden cave that yawned beneath. We clambered down through rising veils of dust to look upon the damage, where we found an ancient buried tomb or bone-room stretched about us in a stale dark, whereupon the sun's harsh, brilliant shafts now fell after a wait of centuries. It had almost a chapel feel, its huge descending pillars fashioned not with mortar but with light. Piled all about were skulls, some of them crushed like morbid eggs beneath the iron wheels of our fallen cart, sharp flakes of yellowed shell upon the whiter sands. It took the most part of a day to raise the wagon up from out its pit, and by the close of it we all were coughing fearfully and spat great quids of jelly. Some time later, in the lower ranks, a fellow named Patrice swore that he'd watched a bright and quivering city hanging in the dawn, all of its frightening weight suspended high above the further dunes. There were more instances akin to this in those last days before we happened on the stranger knights.

We saw their lights at dusk, when the distinctions between sky and sand were lost and we had not ourselves made camp. Fearful lest we had come upon the enemy, we broke procession to a hush in which the scuttling of sand-rats and the night-call of green beetles might be heard. Borne on those serpent winds that rake the wilderness we heard their singing, lusty, full and French, and were relieved, at which we hailed them and were so made welcome by their fires.

The leader of their company, which numbered eight or nine, was one I had known distantly before, called Godefroi, come from Saint-Omer. He seemed pleased enough to meet with me, and thus it was we sat and talked together while my comrades clattered and made oaths in darkness as the Nobles' tents were raised, there in the endless gloom beyond the firelight's reach. I marvelled that Saint-Omer had a skin of wine perched on his lap, since nothing in the manner of strong drink had passed my lips for near to half a year, whereon he kindly offered some to me. It quickly warmed me, and a little more engendered in my ears a low and pleasant singing that dispelled the vile, incessant whisper of the desert insects, thought by Saracens to be the howl of Pandaemonium itself.

Above, great constellations wheeled to which our bonfire sparks ascended in their tiny mimicry. I quizzed my host upon the curious device that he and his companions wore, with rose-red cross arrayed upon a field of white, whence he confided that they were a fledgling order, not yet fully birthed, and yet complacent of their greater destiny. I liked him, for he did not seem to boast, but only spoke of his designs dismissively, as though they were already made accomplished. Although younger by some years than I, it seemed to me he had a wisdom and firm certainty about him that bespoke an older man, and so I listened on, entranced and not a little giddy from the wine.

After a time, another of Saint-Omer's order came to join us where we sat, this being one called Hugues, of Payens. While younger still than Godefroi, his zeal toward the fledgling brotherhood surpassed that of his elder, though in this it may be that he had partaken of more wine. Brazen where Saint-Omer had been restrained, he spoke of all the wealth and influence that would be theirs once time had run its course; a fortune that might span the world in its effect. At this I gently chided him, and said if words were wealth then he should be alike to Croesus, asking whence he fancied that these riches might appear.

Drawing offence from this, he turned at once more arrogant and curled his lip into a sneer of such lop-sidedness I knew him to be in his cups. He hinted, though obscurely, at a certain secret guarded by his order, before which the Pope himself might soon be brought to kneel. Here, Saint-Omer did lay a counselling hand upon his fellow's arm and whispered something past my hearing, after which the pair excused themselves by virtue of their weariness, and soon retired. I sat below a thin-pared Heathen moon until the embers palled and gave play in my thoughts to all that they had said, their hints and wild assertions, being in the last resolved to press them further on the morrow. Had this resolution been forgot in sleep, as are so many nobler urges, then might I have come upon my dotage and my death a happy man.

The sudden yet half-hearted tapping on my chamber door now rouses me from out my arid reveries, and when I bid the one who knocks to enter, there is Maud, with young John fidgeting and shifting in discomfort by her side until he is dismissed, closing the door behind him as he goes.

She stands composed there in the creeping silence, gazing on me without kindness, nor with fellow feeling. Next she stares down at my chamber-jug and makes a face, so that I hide it back beneath my bed before I turn once more to face her.

'I would have you sit.' I gesture here towards the chair, halfway 'twixt bed and door to aid my passage to and fro across the room.

'As my Lord wishes.' Now she brushes off the seat before she sits, as if to rid it of contaminations. In this manner is she wont to craft all of her words and deeds into some subtle, ill-concealed rebuke. As if her cunny does not reek. As if her shit were made from gold.

'How fares my son?'

The look she gives me in reply, blank and unfathoming, is in truth all of the reply I might require: she neither knows, nor cares to know. The child is in the charge of nurses, somewhere in the castle's eastern mass. His mother took against the child from birth and will not see him, hating as she does the man who got him on her and the manner of that getting.

Now she glances to the side and speaks, indifferently. 'The young Lord Simon, I am told, has been afflicted with the grippe, yet otherwise fares well, if it should please my Lord.'

Her eyes, hoar-frosted with disdain, cast insolently back and forth across such few effects as I have gathered in my chambers here: a casket with four angels of Mohammedan attire in gold relief upon its lid; a Merlin stuffed with shavings and a Tartar's finger on a fine, bright chain. With every piece, with every look, she judges me.

After the death of Waltheof, William the Bastard was concerned that I should take up Waltheof's position here. More than position: it was meant that I should take Waltheof's widow, Judith, as my wife, so that my claim to all his lands was given strength. Now, she was William's niece and had until that time obeyed her uncle's every charge, and yet at this she balked. Judith, who with false witness had her husband parted from his head for no more reason than it was the Bastard's will. Judith, who knew should she refuse her Liege that all her land and titles should be forfeit. Judith, who would sooner copulate with goats than lose her uncle's favour.

Judith would not marry me.

She said it was because I had a halten foot, and yet in this I know she lied. What is it that they see in me, these women?

Maud is watching me from where she sits. She waits for me to speak, or to dismiss her. I do neither one. In these brief years since when she was delivered of our son her youthful bloom has gone. The teeth she lost from the fatigues of motherhood have stripped the vestiges of plumpness from her face that made it comely. More and more I see now Judith's chin and Judith's nose, the mother's hard, sharp features mirrored in her child.

When William said that Maud should be my bride in Judith's stead, still she did not relent, though it should spare her daughter's maidenhead, and all of Maud's wet-cheeked entreaties could not shake her from her grim resolve. Why did she fear me so, to offer up her daughter's hairless little cat upon my altar in place of her own?

The silence in this chamber is no longer to be borne, and so I turn instead to talking of my church, its glorious chancel windows; the unique arrangements of its nave.

`The nave is to be in a round, Maud. There! What do you think of that?'

She stares, with Judith's eyes.

`I'm sure it is no matter what thoughts I may have, my Lord. I am not witting of such things.'

Knowing a criticism to be hid within these bland assurances, my ire begins to rise, and I press further on this selfsame tack.

`If I have asked, you may be sure it matters. If you be in truth unwitting of such business, why, then I shall be amused to hear your witless thoughts. Now put off your delays and answer plainly: what are your opinions of a church built in a round?'

She shifts upon her chair, and I am pleased to see she is discomfited. Become less certain in her insolence she does not meet my eye, and in her speech I fancy that I hear a trembling, absent hitherto.

`There are some who might say, my Lord, that it was a configuration not hospitable to Christian worship.' Here she swallows and pretends to lose herself in study of the Heathen angels raised upon my casket's lid. Turned to the side there is still beauty in her face. It comes to me that were I yet equipped to plough her she would not raise such a fury in me, at which thought the fury doubles.

`Do you think I care a fart what some might say? The counsel I am seeking is your own, and I shall have of it for all your damned evasions! Let the ignorant hold that my works do not well suit their low-born Christianity, still shall I hear what you would say in this!'

Brief silence from her now that is much like the rolling of a drum, in that it has the same air of anticipation.

`My Lord, you force me to admit I must agree with those that say these things.'

I rise up from the bed where I am sat and, clinging to its foot-boards lurch towards her so that she shrinks back.

`What do you know? What do you know of Christianity, of its antiquities? Come! You shall come with me to view my church this instant, that I may instruct you to a proper sensibility!'

She starts at this.

`My Lord, it is too dark. I cannot venture out with you this night, when it is sure to rain.'

I take a further step towards her, one hand gripped yet on the foot-boards of my bed and hear the thunder crashing in my heart.

'By God, were we made sure of Armageddon on this e'en, yet would I see you do my will in this! Get up!'

Now she is weeping, furious because she knows that she may not gainsay me. Wet-ringed eyes spit venom, and without much thought of it I find that I am rubbing with the hard heel of my palm against my loins, the old thing in me come awake to find such passion in her. When she speaks her voice is rough and hateful, like a cockatrice. I know that she would strike me if she dared.

'I will not! Drag yourself through storms to gloat on your misshapen relic if you will, but I'll not come with you!'

Risking my balance I let go the bed and topple forward, catching at her chair-back with my hands so that I come to rest propped over her, gripping the chair on each side of her arms, my face pressed not a hand's width from her own. Speaking, I see the white froth of my spittle fleck against her hollowed cheek where she has turned her face away, eyes wrinkled tight.

'Then I shall drag you by the hair, or have men do it for me! Shall I make you bare and thrash you? Shall I?'

Defeated now, she shakes her head; takes small hiccuping breaths, gulped deep into that narrow chest, snail-path of snot upon her upper lip. I let the silence simmer for a moment, wherein nothing save my breathing may be heard, then, lifting up to stand beside her with one hand still on the back-piece of her chair, I call to John.

When he appears, his pallor and timidity are such that he must surely have been listening, beyond the chamber door. He glances to the Lady Maud, who turns her face away from him so that her discomposure might not be in evidence, and then he looks to me.

'My Lord?'

I bid him summon men at arms and next deliver Lady Maud and I to horse, saying that we are wont to visit church and would that he make company with us and with our mounted yeomen. He seems puzzled and afraid, and gives a glance of silent question to the Lady Maud, who will not look at him, and so he bows and makes away, and all is done according with my will.

At length, we quit the castle by its bridge-side gate, with Maud still weeping as she rides beside me, while John and the men at arms stare straight ahead, affecting not to notice this. The rain that stripes the dark is thin and spiteful, does not quite remove a scent of distant woodsmoke lingering upon the air, and when I ask as to the source of this, my squire reminds me that this is the night the villeins light the bel-fires that they drive their cattle in between to make them proof against disease. As we ascend from cross-roads up to horse-fayre I can see the sky a hellish red behind St Peter's crumbled spire, that marks where such a fire has been assembled on the green towards that church's rear. Much merry-making can be heard come from this quarter as we ride our horses by and on towards the street of Jews.

Upon the threshold of those teeming Semite hovels we break left and so begin our weary and prolonged ascent of that steep path that runs from the horse marketplace, up to the outskirts of the boroughs and the sheep-track just beyond, where is my church in its inchoate state.

The reek of fire is everywhere upon the wind, so that I cannot but recall the smell of older fires, in older darknesses. The fire where I first sat and talked with Saint-Omer; the fire we built our camp about that next night, after riding with Saint-Omer's strange-garbed company a day. Sat there about the burning brushwood's hurried and imprudent blaze, I quizzed him further on the claims that he and young Hugues had made when last we spoke. The foresaid Master Payens was not present on this new occasion, having gone with several of his fellows to a spot remote from where we camped, for purpose of some service or observances peculiar to their order.

Crouched beside me, face made brazen by the flames, Saint-Omer made again his boast that with his order he should rise until they were made rich beyond the dreams of Avarice, with influence to beggar Alexander's. Urging me to join my cause with theirs, he promised all who stood beside them at the outset should come into greatness and reward, when they at last laid claim to their inheritance.

`As you shall see, my Lord of Saint-Liz, though our rise may be assured, there are yet certain preparations to be made that would assist us greatly when we come at last to power. Our form of worship, as an instance, makes requirement that we gather in a circle, such as is not easily accomplished in the common style of church. We shall therefore need churches raised across the world according to our own design, these fashioned after Solomon's great temple in Jerusalem.'

He paused here with significance, as if to make me plainly understand the offer he extended: should I aid his venture by the building of a novel church then would I be repaid a hundredfold when his new order's hour was come about. I shook my head in heavy protest.

'By my faith, Lord Godefroi, I should need more than air and promises e'er I was made enthusiastic for such ventures. Though I doubt not your intentions, how is this great wealth of which you speak to be achieved? Whence is this awful power to come?'

He turned towards me, half his face in flame, the rest in darkness, and he smiled. 'Why, from His Holiness the Pope. I have no doubt Rome's coffers will prove adequate to our demands.'

Seeing the speechless, blank discomfiture with which I greeted this announcement, he pressed on, while in the deserts all about us devils sang through insect throats.

'It is as my Lord of Payens said when too filled with wine to be discreet: we have a mystery in us. We have secret hid within our order not a few would soonest were not made instead a revelation. But to say more, I must have your pledge of silence. Further to this, I must have assurance that if this great knowledge is made plain to you, and having seen yourself the means by which we shall make good our boasts, then shall you build for us the place of worship that I have described.'

I thought upon this for a time, and at last gave assent, reasoning that if Saint-Omer did not make good his promise that I should be satisfied by that which was revealed, then I should likewise not be bound to carry out his last conditions. Having sworn an oath of silence, I enquired when I might be at last made privy to the great concerns of which he hinted.

'Why, upon this very Sabbath night, should you desire.'

I frowned here, having lost all notion out amongst those timeless sands of month, or week, or day. Was it in truth the Sabbath?

Saint-Omer continued in his speech without regard for my confusions. 'Even now, the young Lord of Payens and all my fellow knights are gathered at a place not far from here, where they make preparation and await my coming that their service may be thus commenced. If you would go there in my company, then all that I have said shall have its proof.'

Decided thus, we rose up from the halo of the fireside and excused ourselves before commencing on our trudge across the dunes to where Saint-Omer said his comrades were retired. My leg was not so bad then as it has become of late, yet still I hung upon Saint-Omer's arm as we went wading through the dust, the same encumbering dust that slows my legs in ghastly dreams of flight I've lately suffered.

Overhead, the quantity of stars was frightful; that vast multitude of ancient silver eyes that saw so many generations come to dust, and never blinked, much less allowed a tear, and as we laboured through the cooling drifts I asked Saint-Omer when his order would attain the station they foresaw.

'Five years,' he answered, adding, 'if not five, then ten,' as if it were the merest afterthought. Since then I have learned, with some bitterness, that if not ten, then fifteen would suffice; or if not fifteen, why, then twenty. As I climbed those showering, sliding mounds with Godefroi Saint-Omer on that distant night, I was as if lulled by the beetle-choirs, and did not think to ask of such eventualities.

Besides, we were by then come high atop a ridge, the slopes of which fell down before us to an even plain, where there were lights; a ring of candle-flames that stuttered in the darkness, with another ring alike, save smaller, set there at its centre. In the circled track between these fiery boundaries, pale figures moved in slow procession, from where came an oceanic murmuring that was resolved into a mournful plain-chant as we stumbled further down the hill towards the candles and the circling, singing knights. The inner round of flame was set about a flat stone called to service as a makeshift altar. Something rested there upon it I could not make out, beyond the squinting stars of brightness dancing on the wicks that hemmed it round. We lurched downhill towards the glow, Saint-Omer and myself, and as we went the air about was filled with hideous, hurtling blossom: monstrous desert insects headed for their brilliant, brief extinction in the candle-flames. Heedless, with Saint-Omer leading me on, I could but follow their example. Mournful voices lifted up and we went down, and we went down . . .

The rain that beats now hard against my cheek is like the fluttering insect carcasses that beat against it then. Beneath our party's hoofs the green and fibred smears of horses' shit give way to hard black jewels of dung, whereby it is made plain that we have reached the sheep-track, where the matted, tick-infested herds are brought from Wales. Maud stops her weeping for a time as we descend, although her cheeks are wet, but this may be the rain.

A blackness that appears more present and more solid rises now atop a hillock to our right, against the paler dark behind. It is my half-made church, its eight great piers reared up towards the churned miasma of the heavens. Signalling to John and to the solemn men at arms, I reach across and take the bridle of Maud's horse, reining us both outside the low stone wall that binds the church-land's lowest edge. It looms above us, incomplete and yet suggestive of its final gravity, as we are aided by our yeomen to dismount and climb the wet grass slope towards it. From the shadow comes a dreadful bleating and the scattering of bone-shod feet, so that Maud cries out in alarm, but it is nothing, only sheep that graze the pasture here and crop the weeds about the church.

I take Maud's arm in such a grip she winces, hanging on her to support myself as I step nearer to the ring of piers that soar up massively into the starless dark towards their rounded, many-scalloped capitals. Between the eight great columns now the yawning chasm of the open crypt comes into view, where rough stone steps lead down into the rain-stirred mud, and though she shrinks away I draw Maud to the very edge, so that we stand between the piers, on which I lean and find support.

Now Maud renews her weeping, and as I look back to where my squire and men at arms stand at some small remove behind, I see that they are also disconcerted, whether by the hulking church or by my manner I know not. I shout, that I am heard above the bluster of the wind and sizzle of the rain, gesturing to the oblong-cut foundations and half-built walls of the chancellery that lie upon the far side of the gaping vault.

'There! Do you see? That shall be the Martyrium, that represents the Passion of our Lord, whereas these vaults, once closed, shall signify the cave wherein he lay, there at Gethsemane. Come! Come down to them with me. I shall show you . . .'

Here, and with a throttled cry, Maud breaks away from me and runs back from the crater's pillared rim to where John and the men at arms stand dumb-struck, pausing there to turn and stare at me, her eyes wide and afraid, her pointed chin now quivering like a compass needle fixed upon my North. I rail at her and at the men who stand there idly by yet make no move to drag her back to me.

'What? Are you made afraid by this mere shell, this mere anatomy that is not yet a church? How much more frightened should you be to see its spire! If you will not come with me to the vaults, then damn you, for I go alone!'

I half expect at this that John might move to my assistance, but he merely stands beside his Lady Maud and gazes at me in a trance of fear alike to hers. Cursing them both I turn and, gripping on those stones that jut out from the vault's completed walls, I make my slow way down the moss-slicked stairs. With one leg dragging, I descend into the mystery.

Back in the desert we came down upon those circling knights, Saint-Omer and myself, that we could hear their song more plainly as they trudged in their great ring above an altar rimmed with candles. In their tuneless moanings now and then I heard the blessed name of Jesu, so that I became assured there was no Devilry attendant on their ritual. We stepped across the outer ring of candles, and at our approach the chanting knights fell back to let us pass on to the inner ring of lights, and to that altar which they guarded.

Nearing to it, Saint-Omer stooped low to whisper in my ear, his words plain even though we were amidst the chanting of his brothers. 'Do you see, My Lord of Saint-Liz? Do you see the face of our Baphomet; of our praised one before whom the nations of the earth shall surely bow? Look closer.'

There, beyond the winking flames . . .

I stand now in the slime made by the rain here in the lidless vault of my unfinished church. Above me, peering from between the columns, are the faces of my yeomen and the Lady Maud, who have with trembling step come to the edge, that they might view me better in my ravings.

Though the fierce rain pools within the sockets of mine eyes I lift my face towards them as I bellow. 'Here! Here is the cave in which

Christ slept, while up above me in the nave's great round shall be the symbol of his resurrection . . .'

Of his resurrection. Standing with Saint-Omer there beside me I leaned forward, squinting so that I may see beyond the ring of lighted candle-stems to what sat there upon the rough stone altar in their midst. Ringing about us in their vests of ghostly white with bloody cross upon the breast of each, the knights were singing, Jesu, Jesu . . .

Clinging to the crypt's dank walls for purchase, I begin to hobble round the great stone ring, hauling my lame foot through the deep brown puddles, shouting as I go. `You think, alike with fools, that this is blasphemy, this Holy circularity? Why, if you knew what I had seen . . .'

It lay upon the altar, and its skin was black and shrivelled up with age. Those hairs that yet clinged to the scalp or chin were long and silver, glistening in the light of star and candle.

`There,' came Saint-Omer's breath beside my ear. `There. Do you see?'

The eyes had been stitched tight, and there remained a strange, unreadable expression in the corner of the mouth, there where the lips had sagged and come unsewn. It was a head, but whose I might not guess, that was expected to reduce all Popes and Potentates to merest servitude.

`There,' said Saint-Omer. `Do you see?'

I splash on in my lumbering circuit of the vault, and yet the words I shout have no more sense in them than there is in the spit and crackle of a villein's bel-fire. I am weeping, stumbling, roaring, while from up above the frozen masks of Maud and John and all the startled yeomen hang there, staring down at me, my judges.

`I am old and almost in my grave, and still they make no move! They have no care for me! They will achieve their kingdom only after I am gone, so that there shall be no reward for me, not here, nor yet in any other life! If you knew what I know . . .'

I knew whose was the head. It came to me with such a force and certainty I stumbled back, as if the sands beneath my feet might of a sudden open up and plunge me straight to Hell.

`There,' said Saint-Omer. `Do you see?'

I slip, and fall down cursing in the mud. Still neither men nor

Maud make any move to aid me. I am weeping as I drag myself upon my knees about the crypt, hanging upon the stones that jut from the uneven brick to pull me half erect.

I gazed in mortal terror at the head, whose features seemed to jerk and twitch their shadows in the candle-light. Then it was all a lie, all the Crusades and Christenings alike. The central stone on which faith rests was pulled away from me, and in its stead was left this hateful relic, mummified and black, that seemed to fix me with its catgut-threaded stare; that seemed to twist the untied corner of its mouth into an awful smile. I shall be dead, and nothing shall be left of me but worm and bone. I shall be wiped away, be absent in the endless and insensate dark where no thought comes. I shall not rise into the nave of rebirth, echoing with angel voices, and no more shall any of us, for the Heavens are become an empty place and dead men do not rise, nor push back stones. Our souls know no ascent, nor have they final destination.

Laughing, weeping, with my dead foot dragged behind, I circle, circle round, forever round beneath an empty sky that neither man nor martyr ever rose toward, nor ever saw the flame of man relit when once his spark had gone, nor ever knew of any resurrection.

CONFESSIONS OF A MASK
AD 1607

It disappoints me to recount that lately I have found myself again afflicted with identity and so beset by a great pestilence of thoughts. Arid, inconsequential things, they rattle uselessly within the parchment seed-pod of this smirking mask I am become. Worse, they provoke a fearful itching at the rear interior of my cranium where, I fear, yet clings some withered clot of mind; grey husk of brittle sponge, wrung dry, crusted upon the inner shell like relic snots discovered on the pages of old books.

I find if I contrive to let my skull tilt back and forth, as in a breeze, the iron point of my spike will scrape against the irritation and thus bring some measure of relief, though this does not dispel the main source of my aggravation, to whit, that I am myself at all with the capacity for thought or for sensation when I fancied (fancying nothing) that I was, at measure, done with such bleak chores.

When did I last know anything? Without sight, I may not determine how much time I've whiled away in dangling here and stinking since I last came to myself. If memory does not play me false, that was in Summer, when this bone cathedral's dome rang to a monk's drone of green-bellied flies; the munch of grubs where once dreams shimmered. Summer last or Summer before that I cannot tell. As I recall, I had hung here but several months, which made it by my reckoning the year Sixteen Hundred and Six, three years into the reign of Good King James, may the Almighty rot his eyes (a skill which the Almighty has deployed with great success upon diverse occasions, to which I myself may testify).

Upon the creased corpse-paper of my brow the wind is damp with Autumn; brings a hush among the bluebottles. October, then? November? But which year? In truth, I scarcely care, longing to have away with dates and know eternity. I fancied that I had it, that last time. I fancied I was gone. Instead, mere sleep; a further crumbling of my worm-drilled wits, only to wake again, too bored for horror now.

I wonder, is my father yet alive? Poor Tom, as mad as I; almost as hampered in his movements, cloistered there through law on his estate by virtue of his faith, the queer, three-sided hunting lodge he built in which he meant to signify the Trinity, whereby to taunt his captors. Shrouded in a language all my father's own, occult and mystical, I fear this taunt sailed high above his gaolers' heads and altogether missed its mark.

Three floors. Three sides. Three windows made from triangles of glass on every side, on every floor. Great numbers, threes and nines, set in the brick, that signified I know not what, though I recall that once my father made great effort to explain their meaning to me.

'They are dates, young Francis. Dates as reckoned from our true beginnings on this Earth, and Eden's founding.' As he talked, his great grey head rocked forward, nodding to make emphasis; the last exhausted peckings of a lame and ancient bird.

My father's calculations hinged upon a calendar suggested by a certain Bishop (I do not recall his name) who had established to his personal satisfaction the specific date on which the world commenced. To my chagrin, I must confess this most important anniversary is also fled from recollection, one more memory eaten by the meatflies. I remember, though, that the Creation was accomplished on a Monday.

Thus far, while by no means sane in any ordinary sense, my father's motives in the building of the lodge were at least still within my comprehension: he desired to raise up a triangular affront to all good sense, and in this fashion to commemorate the Holy Trinity in whose name he had suffered his incarceration. Further to this, he desired to date his edifice from that primordial Monday morn when the Almighty condescended to allow the Light.

However, this was not the limit of my father's odd preoccupations. In addition to the massive numbers set out in relief upon his lodge, were also letters, most of them pertaining to quaint word-games played upon the family name, this being Tresham, which abbreviates to 'Tres', that is to say, to three, which brings us neatly back to Father, Son and their celestial pigeon.

(If I am allowed to venture an aside, and in some modest measure a rebuke, I must say that in all the months that I have waited to attain to the celestial realm, I have not once been visited by this aforesaid blessed fowl, although I wear a skullcap of his cousins' dung.)

I'd stand within the arching door of Rushton Hall, watching my father while in turn he overlooked the building of his folly, there across the fields. He would strut back and forth and all the while call out encouragements to those who laboured on the lodge: ' Pray, Cully, further to the right! Be sure to take your measurements in threes, sir, if you love me! Make the inclinations at the corner nice and not splayed out like whores' legs!'

Here within Northampton is a church made in a round, raised to these blasphemous proportions at the time of the Crusades against the Saracen. According to conjecture, it is built this curious way that Satan may not find a nook wherein to hide himself. What of my father's lodge, then? Surely he had fiends in every corner, devils on all sides, that drove him on through pride, through bitterness and into lunacy? What drives us all, that we engage ourselves in such catastrophes? Surely it was not the Almighty's voice that guided him to such a sorry end, but rather that voice issued from the furnace, from the fire's mouth, trailing spittles of white ore?

For all my loyal protestations that I shared my father's creed since his conversion, still I found it difficult to countenance a God that would award Sir Thomas Tresham for his faith with house arrest and then direct him to pass his remaining days in the construction of a great stone wedge of cheese. (I make complaint here only for my father's treatment at the hands of the Almighty. Note that I do not debate the Justice meted out to me, which I would say is fair, up to a point. That point, it must be said, is thrust uncomfortably up my ragged windpipe, whence it juts, not without pain, into my cobwebbed cerebellum. That aside, I must congratulate the Lord upon his widely mentioned lenience.)

The round church and my father's three-faced lodge, these huge and simple solid forms set patiently upon the shire's map; carefully, painstakingly arranged like children's building-blocks across long centuries by slow, half-witted gods, too few pieces in place as yet to guess their final scheme, if scheme there be. Sometimes, as thoughts drift in the muddy, half-awake plane that alone remains to me, I know a sense of vast, momentous tumblers falling, somewhere far away; of an eventual unlocking there at Time's rim, though of what I may not guess. If scheme there be, my present state tends to suggest that I am not considered vital in its outcome.

I decorate the North gate of the town. Though lacking eyes I yet observe they have not moved me while I slept and dreamt my sweet and silent dream of being dead. Moreover, it is plain that they have not replaced the watchmen billeted within the gate-house, John and Gilbert, whom I recognize both by their voices and by the distinct and separate perfumes of their water, which they make almost in ritual unison against the gate-house wall each morn when they arise.

It is like this: first Gilbert wakes with the full weight of last night's ale upon his bladder and begins to cough, these hawkings low and gruff, much like his voice. Next, John is woken by his fellow watchman's barking and begins his own, though in a somewhat higher register, being, it seems to me, the younger of the two. Meanwhile to this, Gilbert has leapt up from his cot, pulled on his trousers and his boots and stumbled out to piss. The sound of this seems to go on for ever and, as such sounds often do, provokes in John an awful sympathy so that he hurries out to join his fellow; adds his meagre stream to the tremendous gushings of the dam already breached. At the conclusion of their sprinklings, both men next break wind, first Gilbert and then John, the pitch again reflecting their respective age and temperament, one low, one high. A crumhorn and a penny whistle.

Every day they do this, as unchanging as the bird-calls that announce the dawn, nor do their other functions of the day seem less routine. From light through dark they labour at their work or else they labour harder in avoiding it. Such conversation as they manage is repeated daily, phrase for phrase. I do not doubt the thoughts they have today are much the same ones they had yesterday and will have served again, re-boiled, upon the morrow. Willingly they entertain this vile monotony. One might, if unfamiliar with our situation, easily assume that it were they hung on a spike, not I.

My father, penned within his grounds and left to nurse his three-fold madness; Catesby, Fawkes, the rest of them, all caught up in their diverse fervours, in the circles of their habit and their reason; we are all of us thus hoisted on our own petard. Each of us has his sticking place, and to each man his nail.

Of late, Gilbert and John have (when they speak of me at all) begun to call me ‘Charlie-Up-There’. ‘Francis’, a more upright-sounding name, is obviously not so suited to the slouching rhythms of their speech as 'Charlie': 'Which way blows the wind, young John? You take a look at Charlie up there and take note of where what bit of hair he has flies out to!' Once I had such lovely tresses, now a weather-vane for idiots.

Still, in all it pleases me to think that I have yet some function and some purpose to my being, slight and mean though it may be. Not only weather-cock am I but also trysting place, an easy landmark where young lovers may arrange to meet. Their brief and oft hilarious couplings against the bird-streaked wall below awake in me a phantom pang, much like the pang induced on hearing Gilbert's loud, torrential micturitions every morn. Though my equipment to accomplish such be gone, I too would like to poke a wench or piss against a wall from time to time. In truth, I cannot say which of these satisfactions' passing is the most lamented, though I wish that I had taken more time to appreciate the both of them while I was yet in life. Ah, well.

Besides my use as totem to the fumblings of young men, so also am I able to provide my services as target for the missiles of their infant siblings. Usually they fly wide of the mark, although on coming to my senses at this last occasion, I discovered that one of the more accomplished little hell-hounds had contrived to lodge a piece of coal big as a knuckle in the socket on the left. I must confess I am quite taken with it, fancying it lends my mask a roguish and yet gallant lack of symmetry as might a monocle, opaque and lensed with jet.

Upon reflection, a great while has passed since last I was Aunt Sally to the children's stones. No doubt they are away about some new, more seasonal diversion now. If I were not a mask then I would call them back.

It seems to me that this has always been my stumbling block, that I may not speak out for whatsoever I myself desire, yet only turn to people the compliant face they wish to see. If truth be told, my father's Catholic vision was not mine, yet when he put the proposition to me all I did was nod in puppet acquiescence. Nor did I do differently with Fawkes and Winter and the rest, unfolding their phantasmagoric insurrections in the gate-house there at Ashby. While they ranted, all I did was make mild protest at the heedless optimism of their course, and never once said 'No'. While rotting in the Tower, afflicted with a dreadful rising of the lights, each day I would politely thank my gaolers when they brought the slops I could not eat, and in this manner put a face on things. Putting a face on things was thus the principal endeavour of my mortal span, whereafter, justly, am I made a face that others put on things. Beware, ye that are loath to make commotion! Shudder, ye who would not bring attention on thyself, and see what shyness brought me, with even my gizzard now become a public spectacle. Behold, ye meek: this prong of iron is all the Earth ye shall inherit.

Testing my remaining senses: it would seem whatever curds of brain are crusted round this bone-bowl's rim have fallen further into disrepair, so that I am more sluggish in my thoughts and doze more now; brief intervals of sleep shot through with bright and foolish dreams.

I do not dream about the life I had. In all my dreams I am as I am now, hung fixed and without sight. In one, I hang outside an older town than this, although in some queer way the feeling of it is the same. I am in company with other body-scraps hung there to dry, but to my disappointment they are only torsos, mine the sole head set amongst them. In that comic style things have in dreams, I learn the headless, limbless relics are still capable of speech, but through their lower parts. I strike up a companionship with one of them, a woman's trunk whose talk is filled with plans and tricks and cunning, although insufficient, it would seem, to spare her from her grisly end. We hatch a plan between us to combine our best resources, with my head to be somehow set up atop her ragged neck. She tells me, grumbling through her loins, that she has heard of legs and feet that may elect to join with our conspiracy. Alas, the dream is over ere we can pursue this charming notion of completion and escape.

Another dream is simpler: I am set upon a low, flat rock, still warm from daylight's heat although the night breeze swirls about me, howling over endless distances and heavy with the scent of desert. I am wrapped around with chanting voices, circling through the darknesses without, as if of slow, gruff men that walk about me widdershins. There is the whispered crunch of trodden sand; the creak of armoured joint. The words they moan are foreign to me, strange and barbarous names that I may not recall upon awakening to the roar of Gilbert's dawn deluge.

'Tis pity. I had hoped the dreams we know in death might have more sense about them than those borne in life. These night-starts have no meaning that I may make plain, though I would note that all of them seem sprung from distant times, no doubt the Tuesday or the Wednesday that came after Father's surely hectic Monday of Origination.

Thus I doze, and dream, and dangle, and decay.

The hour is later now, and I have company.

I was disturbed some while ago by something heavy, scraped against the stonework just below me in a clumsy fashion. An accompaniment of John and Gilbert's gruntings from beneath allowed me to conclude at last that they were struggling to erect a ladder by which means they might climb up to join me here upon my lofty perch. At first this gross intrusion woke a panic in me, for I feared that they were come to take me down, where I would be subjected to some fresh indignity. After a time, however, their thick-accented exchanges made it plain that this was not to be the case.

' Set 'im aside old Charlie up there, so they'll make a pair.' This was from Gilbert, down upon the ground and no doubt holding fast the ladder's base while trusting the ascent to the more nimble John. The youth's response was come from closer by, his winded panting almost at my ear. There was a puzzling scent of rancid cheese which I at first supposed to be upon his breath.

' I'm trying to, but this one's fresher than what Charlie were, and not as easy in the puttin' on. You 'old me steady now, I nearly fell.'

This went on for a while until at last the youth called down to Gilbert with report of his success.

' Well done, John. Now you 'ang that pouch of 'is about 'is neck, else nobody'll know the bastard otherwise.'

Cursing beneath his breath, John evidently did as he was told, for not long after I could hear the rungs groan as he went back down, where followed further scrapings when the ladder was at last removed. At this, the gate-men both repaired inside. I noticed that the smell of cheese remained.

A silence next, and then a sound like grinded teeth, a tortured gurgling giving way to gasps, and sobs, and finally to words.

' By God! By God, where is the Captain now, and what is this stale putrefaction set beside him? Are his thousand men now fled that rallied once for Pouch and his just cause?'

Scarce had I realized that I was myself what he referred to as the putrefaction set beside him, when his ravings were renewed: 'Fear not, lads! Pouch fights on, and though they have your Captain bound they shall not still his mighty heart! For Pouch! For Pouch and Justice!'

I had longed to find companionship and here it was, presented to me, though perhaps more volubly than I might otherwise have wished.

'See how your Captain has been handled, with his bowels at Oundle and his arse in Thrapston! Take him home, boys! Take him home by Barford Bridge to Newton-in-the-Willows! Weep for Pouch amidst the weeping trees! Have I not told you, in the Captain's bag there is sufficient matter to defend against all comers? We'll yet have the day, if we stand firm and do not flinch, nor lose our heads!'

Clearing my throat of all but that iron shaft thrust up it, I addressed him. 'Your advice, Sir, welcome though it be, comes rather late. I fear that horse is long since bolted.'

An astonished pause ensued, the only sound being the subtle grating of my comrade as he made attempt to shuffle round his head upon the prong, the better to regard me.

At some length, he spoke again. 'By Jesu's Blood, Sir! Never did Pouch think to see a man reduced to your estate that yet had sensibility and speech.'

A further pause, in which he may have thought to include hearing in the list of my remaining skills and thus to reconsider his brash opening remarks.

When he resumed it was in milder tones. 'Sir, for whatever insults have been heaped like coals upon your . . .' Here he faltered, and then lamely stumbled on. 'That is to say, upon you. For whatever slurs and slanders you've endured, accept the Captain's full apology.'

I rattled vaguely on my peg, as close to a forgiving shrug as I could muster.

Ill at ease, the Captain made a further effort to engender conversation. 'Have you been here long?'

For all the world, to hear him speak you would have thought that we were waiting for a carriage.

`That depends upon the date,' I answered after some deliberation.

He informed me that it was, as near as he was able to determine having lost a day or so himself, the last week of October in the year Sixteen Hundred and Seven. This would seem to indicate that I have been suspended here for almost two years now. While I was struggling to absorb this notion, Captain Pouch (such is his name) continued with his prattle.

`Did you know, Sir, there is something in your eye?'

`Yes, I did. Unless I am mistaken, it's a lump of coal.'

`What an encumbrance. You have the Captain's sympathies. Pray, what of these pale, bony spikes that thrust up from your skull? Were you afflicted with these monstrous growths in life?'

`No. That is birdshit.'

Made disheartened by this cataloguing of my mortal ruin, I attempted to direct the conversation elsewhere, asking my companion how he came to find himself moored in such dismal straits.

With bile and indignation rising in his voice, he launched into a grim tirade upon the world and its injustice. `Aye, now there's a question! How does Pouch come to be here, that did no wrong save stand up for his birthright as an Englishman? Tyranny, sir! Cruel tyranny and the designs of despots laid the Captain low, as they would lay low all who strike for Justice!'

Here I made encouraging remarks, revealing that I, too, had fallen foul of an oppressor in my stand for liberty. This newfound kinship seemed to warm his heart (wherever that affair might be; in Thrapston or in Oundle) and he went on with fresh vigour.

`Then in faith, Sir, you are Captain Pouch's brother in adversity! He was a simple man, Sir, once, that lived by Newton-in-the-Willows, near to Geddington, where is the cross of blessed Eleanor.'

`I know the place. Go on.'

`Pouch had another name then, Sir, and was contented with his lot, but it would not be so for long. There was a serpent nestled in the Captain's Eden, poised to strike.'

`The tyrants that you spoke of earlier?'

`The same. A family of skulking thieves that had with their ill-gotten wealth seized land so that the good folk thereabout were left with only scrub on which to grow their food! Worse, while those same good people huddled on their scraps of grass, the scoundrels saw fit to erect a great, vainglorious edifice, the sight of which would surely tread those good folk's spirits further down into the mire!'

I knew a sudden sense of great foreboding as to where this narrative was headed. As I'd told him, I knew Newton-in-the-Willows well, and not without good reason.

Timidly, I made an interjection. 'This great edifice you mention: would it be a dovecote?'

'Then you know the massive, ugly thing? Aye, a gigantic dovecote! Did you ever hear such vanity? As if it were not bad enough they had already seized our village church, St Faith's, and claimed it as their private chapel! One day, when this insult could no longer be endured, the Captain rallied to his side one thousand men and swore they would tear down the hedges raised about the family's enclosures.'

'This would be the Tresham family?'

'Aye! You have heard of them?'

'Remotely.'

Every Sunday prior to my father's house-arrest we'd gone by coach to Newton-in-the-Willows. Each time, as we crossed the Barford Bridge, my father would recount the story of a ghostly monk said to reside there by the River Ise who, in the dead of night, would ride with travellers part of their way only to vanish further down the road. Each week I'd shudder at my father's tale as if I heard it fresh.

Kneeling there in the strange pale marble-coloured light that fell down through the windows of St Faith's, I'd bow my head and pray. As I remember, in the main I would entreat Almighty God that as we rode back over Barford Bridge we should not find we shared our carriage with the disappearing monk. On more than one occasion it occurred to me that my prayers and my presence in St Faith's served no good purpose save averting supernatural danger brought upon me solely by the route that I must take to church each week. It seemed to me that if I simply did not go to church then both myself and the Almighty might be saved considerable time and effort. I would struggle to suppress such thoughts for fear God would reward this blasphemy with, if not yet a visit from the monk, then something worse. However, though this sacrilegious notion would persist I was not, as it turned out, struck down by the awful supernatural punishment I feared.

Mind you, with hindsight . . .

After church, if there was time before our dinner was prepared, I'd go with Father to the dovecote that to me seemed big as heaven, filled with crooning, fluttering angel white. When I was young, I did not make the nice distinction that there is between the commonplace dove and its Pentecostal counterpart, believing at the time my father kept a flock of Holy Ghosts.

Perhaps he did. Perhaps that is the reason I have not been brushed by that celestial wing. Perhaps there are no more outside captivity.

Beside me, cutting through my reverie, the head of Captain Pouch continued with its diatribe against the monstrous Tresham family, recounting how he had inspired his thousand followers by telling them that what he carried in the pouch about his neck (from which he drew his name) would be sufficient to repel all enemies. Thus reassured he'd led them, whooping to the hedgerow barricades where they had wreaked some little havoc for a while before the local gentry and their mounted followers, incensed, arrived upon the scene to trample and disperse the rabble.

It would seem as if beyond that point the Captain's memories were vague. The hour when he was led out to the gallows was still clear to him, though mercifully he recalled but little of the hanging or the quartering that evidently followed.

I asked him if he knew how fared the family he so despised, to which he answered with some glee that early in the year my father, Thomas Tresham, had been taken sick to bed and soon thereafter passed away.

So. Dead, then. That great granite boulder of his head rocked forward for the last time. Finally released from the frustrated pacing of his grounds that had become his prison and set free into the company of other martyrs. Now, no doubt, he knew the date of the Creation to the very hour. No doubt by now he understood the Lord's bewildering passion for the number three and was ecstatically employed correcting angles for the angels as they laboured on some annexe of their own tri-cornered paradise.

Done with his tale at last, Pouch seemed to think that it would only be good manners to enquire as to my own, though this was clearly only by way of politeness and not any interest that was genuine. The Captain did not truthfully have room in him for any grand, heroic story save his own. That said, he was persistent in demanding my account so he might not be thought a bore.

'Come, let the Captain hear now of the noble struggle you yourself endured that led you to this sorry place. What is your name, Sir?'

After but a moment's hesitation, I responded. 'Charlie.'

'And your crime?'

'I cried 'Down with the King' while in a public place.'

Throughout my life, I'd learned the ease with which I might slip skilfully behind that bland evasive mask that would avoid unpleasantness. Now there was nothing left of me but mask, this talent had become more simple yet in its accomplishment.

Time passed. Before the sunset, which I know by its faint promise of impending chill, there was some nastiness.

I'd heard the birds land, two or three of them with heavy thuds, and had the time to wonder briefly at their presence after they had failed to pay a visit for so long, when Pouch began to scream, thus answering my queries.

Mercifully, I was not made to bear this miserable cacophony for long, since at approach of dark the carrion flew home to roost. The Captain had fared well as these things go, with but an eye and one lip gone, although to hear him moan and whimper you would think the sky had fallen in. In fairness, I suppose I have had longer to grow reconciled to our condition.

Other than the utterance of an infrequent sob, he did not speak again 'til halfway through the night when, in a trembling voice, he started to describe the stars that he could see through his remaining eye; their number and their cold, indifferent majesty.

I squinted round my lump of coal, and yet saw nothing.

'Is this Hell?' he whispered. 'Are there stars in that place? Is this

Hell for Pouch?'

I have considered more than once what manner of theology might be applicable to where we find ourselves. It seems to me that, in accordance with my father's strange numeric scheme of things, there are three possibilities: firstly, it may be that this is Hell after all, but on some other sphere and not beneath the ground as one might readily suppose. My second notion is that in my own case, it may be I am regarded as a traitor by the Gods of Protestant and Catholic faith alike and, being caught between two camps, am simply left to moulder here by both. The third and, given due consideration, the most probable of all my theorems, is that life is ordered by the principles of some religion so peculiar and obscure it has no followers, and none may fathom it, nor know the rituals by which to court its favour.

At dawn the birds (crows by the sound they made) came back and took the rest of Captain Pouch, since when I fear the fellow is sunk deep within some horror-stricken trance. He has not voiced a word.

I hear the children singing, somewhere far below, and hope that they might hurl another rock of coal to furnish me a second bright black eye, but they are set on other matters. As the words of their refrain float up to me, I know the work they are about and, in my sudden comprehension, am become almost as moribund as Pouch.

'Remember, remember,' they sing; they command. 'Remember, remember . . .'

We'd meet to drink, there in my father's triangular lodge. Bob Catesby, Guido Fawkes, Tom Winter and the others, talking young men's talk and vowing we would see the day when Catholics would bend no more beneath the yoke of Protestant oppressor. Once we hiked upon a pilgrimage to Fotheringay Castle, north of Oundle (where, if he might be believed, the Captain's bowels are currently interred). We saw where Good Queen Mary kneeled before the block and rendered up her soul to God, her head hacked off with nothing less than three ungainly blows, whereon her little dog ran out from underneath her skirts and would not leave her side.

Though I do not recall who first proposed the scheme, I fear it was myself, though inadvertently, who set the whole disaster into motion. Drinking in the lodge, I had commenced a passionate account of all the slanders and injustice that had robbed my father of his freedom;

almost bragging in a curious, underhanded way, as if the glamour of the elder Tresham's dire misfortune might thus be transferred to me. Alas, I was too eloquent, and had not finished my account before my drunken comrades were up on their feet and swearing that this monstrous calumny should not go unavenged.

I thought that it would be forgot once we were sober, but the notion of some great revenge for Father and the Catholic masses as a whole had somehow stuck. Fuelled by hot Sack and righteous fervour, soon my comrades had decided that we must not only strike a blow of protest: we must undertake to do no less than sound a clarion call that would awaken all who placed their faith in Rome to glorious insurrection. We ourselves would bring about the great deliverance of our faith!

Having witnessed all that had befallen Father for much lesser sins against the Realm, I had by this time grown afraid, and counselled them that this mad plot might mean the ruin and not the rescue of this island's faithful, but my counsel lacked conviction, as the counsel of a mask will ever do. When they began to speak of causing conflagrations at the seat of Parliament itself, I knew I did not have the courage to keep faith with them, yet by my very nature nor was I equipped to openly refuse and seem a coward. What was I to do? My face became in time opaque and still, where nothing could be read.

The night has come once more. Pouch was mistaken in his estimation of the date. It is November. From across the fields beyond the town a scent of woodsmoke taints the air, and in the relic of my wits I have a picture of the red sparks rising up to crowd the stars. What is it fans the flames of passion in a man? What promise was it that led Fawkes and Catesby on, or that inspired the thousand men of Captain Pouch?

Here, I recall the Captain's words as to the matter kept there in that pouch draped by young John about his neck, which would repel all foes. It seems to me as if that hidden talisman must surely hold the secret kindling of all noble causes or rebellions and, despite his current woeful state, yet can I not restrain my curiosity.

`Pouch? Captain Pouch?' I hiss. `Wake up, Sir. I've a question I must ask of you.'

He moans and swivels slightly; tilts from side to side. When he replies, his voice is soft and dazed. He seems to know not where he is.

`I am John Reynolds. My name is John Reynolds and I cannot see.'

I have not patience left to entertain such ramblings, and my entreaties grow more urgent. `Tell me, Pouch, what is it that you keep there in that bag about your neck? What is the source of power that hurls a thousand men unheeding 'neath the horses of their foes?'

His speech is slurred and bubbling. `The pouch?'

`Aye, Sir. The pouch. What is within the pouch?'

Some moments pass, and now he speaks: `A small piece of green cheese.'

`And that is all?'

He does not venture a response, and no more can I draw a solitary word from out his shredded lips. Well, then. There is my answer. There's the grail men leave their sweethearts for and follow even in the jaws, the smoking throat of War: a small piece of green cheese. How bitter, then, when first we catch the rancid scent of what we fought for.

On that sour November night two years ago, when Catesby rushed into the Ashby gate-house pale and breathless while we sat in wait for news, it was already plain the plot had been betrayed. Fawkes had been seized from ambush, whereon Catesby and four others had come back from London running relay on their steaming horses to announce the dreadful news.

Some of us thought, in desperation, to head off to Wales and there was even wretched, hollow talk of firing up Welsh Catholics to make our mis-timed revolution a success, though in our hearts we knew we were all as dead men. The rest of them went West, eventually killed in flight or captured and then put to death by hanging, quartering and burning. For my own part, I sat weeping with my father there at Rushton Hall and waited for the King's men to arrive and take me to the Tower. They knew where I would be. I'd told them in the letter that I wrote my brother-in-law, Lord Monteagle, just the week before.

At least in payment for my treachery they spared me public execution, leaving me instead to die after a lingering eight-week illness in the Tower. While I was thus incarcerated, gaolers would delight in giving me each detail of my friends' demise. A story of this nature stays with me: one of the luckless crew — not Catesby, Fawkes or Winter; one I did not know so well — was taken to his place of execution and beheaded, then cut into four. Lifting the head to wave it at the mob, the axe-man cried, `Behold! A traitor's head!'

At which the head replied, `Thou liest.'

I have since wished that I might share a basket with a head that had such spirit, or yet rest beside him on some ossuary shelf, but it is better it should never be. With nothing else save face to show, I could not face him.

Somewhere in my dark, the children sing above the roar and crackle of the flames. Before they sang for us or raised their bonfires to support our effigies, they'd burn a doll to signify His Holiness the Pope, and prior to that no doubt some earlier sacrifice back unto that primordial Monday, that first fire.

The burning and the song are one. If I gaze hard with the black jewel that is my only eye, I see the spit and flare of it, away there in the centre of that cold, wet coal where is my night. It was my friends they set alight, not I. I was denied that last deliverance, to be consumed within that timeless bright that is in truth one single blaze decanted down across the aeons.

The tongues of heat and brilliance surge and leap and cast their shivering light within the sockets of the mask, so that the shadows quake and seem to give the face expression where, in truth, there is no such expression, nor was ever one.

ANGEL LANGUAGE
AD 1618

I carry in my coat a snuff-box, though I'm not much in the habit now. Inside its lid there is a painting, done in miniature, of Greek or Roman ladies at their baths. They sit with thigh and buttock flat against wet tile and lean one on the other, nipple grazing shoulder, cheek to belly. Steam-secreted pearls are beaded on their spines, the hairs about each quim curled into little nooses by the damp.

I think, perhaps, too oft on women for my years. The maddening petticoated presence of them, every sweep and swish a brush-stroke on the sweltering canvas of my thoughts. Their sag and swell. Their damp and occult hinges where they open up like wicked, rose-silk Bibles, or their smocks, rime-marbled underneath the arms. Their ins and outs. Their backs. Their forths. Warm underhangs and shrew-skin purses, dewed with bitter gold. Imagined, they burn fierce and sputtering, singing, incandescent in my prick, my centre. I may close the lid upon this snuff-box filled with nymphs, yet in my dreams its clasp is broke; its contents not so quickly shut away.

Once, I believed that when I'd grown into a man and married, I'd be plagued no more by the incessant posturings and partyings of my bordello mind. I would no longer suffer the relentless elbow-cramping visitations of these succubi, that mapped the foam-splashed shorelines of my passion; penned their snail cartographies upon my sheets and clouded my good sense with humid, feverish distractions.

So I hoped, but it was not to be. Though wed with an obliging wife whose cosy hole was made a velvet-curtained stage where to play out my lewdest skits, the tide of jiggling shadow-pictures did not ebb, but only boomed the louder in those bed-wrapped, warm-lapped latitudes upon the shores of sleep above the snore of spouse and cot-bug's measured tick. Denied thus any hope of swift reprieve from satyriasis, I sought to slake my thirst for carnal novelty with whores and serving-maids. When this did little more than whet an appetite already swollen, I drew consolation from the thought that soon I should be old, the imprecations of John Thomas surely grown more faint and hopeless, easily ignored.

Alas, with snow upon the thatch, there is yet wildfire in the cellar, stoked with willow limbs and jutting trunks. So much for good intentions. Often now it seems that my desire is worse than ever, with nought but the flimsiest of hints required to set my meditations on their soil-strewn and indecent path.

The lurching of this coach along the pitted Kendal road is all too readily become the pitch of marriage-couch, the pelvises of all aboard rocked back and forth in unison so that the fancy comes to me that but for some few feet I might be rocking to and fro inside the young wife sat there with her daughter on the seat opposing mine. When her pond-coloured eyes (what glistening secret tableaux have they seen?) glance up to catch my own, their frog-spawn pupils seem to widen, dark and open; querying. Lest any of my musings may be glimpsed in miniature upon my gaze, I look away to where the Lakeland hills are sprawled beyond the carriage window, a titanic slate-skinned harem, all asleep with wet grass slick and tufted on their tilted mounds, or tracking in a spidery Jacob's Ladder up each pregnant slope, to nipple cairns.

It has been some few weeks since I set out from Faxton for my tour of the judicial circuit, going first by way of Northampton itself, where to confirm my various schedules and appointments, then by coach out through the town's North gate, off on my yearly rounds. The gate was hung about with heads like blackberries upon an iron thorn-bush, ripe and heavy, these the dire fruits of sedition. Though the heads of Catholic plotters hung here many years ago have long since come unglued and toppled down to shard and dust, the sharp saltpetre tang of insurrection lingers in the town's stale air. The faces of the men seem all the time suffused with red like blisters on a firebrand's fingers, that may yet result in blood.

Things are the same throughout the land. I have presided at assizes ranged from Nottingham to Crewe, to judge such ruffians as are brought before me: poor men who are thin and poor men who yet manage to be fat. The swaggering young, the cringing old, the crutch-bound and the incomplete. In all their eyes there is a kinship, though their skin be pale as oatmeal, pink as dawn or tan as saddles. Green eyes, blue or brown, it matters not. Their eyes have all one hue, which is the colour of their great resentment, flecked with spark and promises of flame.

The women are another matter. Though with bitterness aplenty of their own they carry out their timeless work and seem to all intents as if they dwell apart from our hot world and tread the byways of some other, female land; one unaffected by the thrust and surge of man's enthusiasms, Empires or revolts. They bake the bread. They clean the clothes and bring forth babies they may smack and kiss. Between our wars we go to them and suckle at their fond indifference, their abiding constancy, these mothers; mothers once or mothers yet to be. These sauce-splashed deities.

Thus made divine, their desecration is at once made sweeter to the thoughts, and to man's private sensibilities.

Skirting some rut or fissure in the road, the coital lurching of the carriage is now made more urgent and erratic, groaning like a harlot's headboard as it bucks and jolts towards its shuddering conclusion, some fantastic spend of horseflesh, wood and iron. Amidst this jostling, the girl-child sat across from me has fetched her knee a clout upon the carriage door, so that her mother is now called upon to comfort her.

She does so in a strange, soft pigeon-murmur where what sense the words may have is not so soothing as her lapping, ebb-tide voice itself: `Ooh, there, what have you done now? Hurt your knee? Ooh, my poor darling, where? Let's see now . . . Ooh. Ooh, never mind, the skin's not broke although you'll have a fine old bruise there, won't you? Ooh, yes. Yes you will. A fine old bruise.'

These old, placatory rhythms lull the child, each dovecote `Ooh' a drop of balm; a jig of oil to smooth the creased and choppy waters of her brow, where it is visible below the black rim of her little bonnet. Soon, the road beneath the coach becomes more even and the child falls back into the fitful doze with which she has elected to pass by the time that yet remains before we come to Kendal.

Though its bound-up majesty may not be glimpsed beneath the solemn, rigorously fastened hat, I know her hair is chestnut red and long, so that it falls about her waist when it is not wound tight and crucified by bodkins. She's named Eleanor, although her mother for the most part seems to call her Nell, which is to my mind not so pretty. Both of them are come from further North, near by Dundee, to lodge with some old dame who has a room for rent outside of Kendal. Last night, when I first met with the pair there at the coach-inn where we each had paused upon our different journeys to a common destination, I was made acquainted with the facts of their predicament.

Her husband only recently passed on, young Widow Deene (such is the mother's name) has come with Eleanor down to the Lakelands where a lady-friend of hers had vouched that she may find employment as a seamstress. Having spent such meagre savings as she had upon the journey here with but a little over for her first week's rent, the luckless, lovely little thing has gambled much upon her friend's advice and frets, now that it is too late, upon the wisdom of her chosen course. Thus it would seem we both hope to have business waiting for us when we reach our destination, whether shirts to stitch or men to hang.

The widow's bosom falls and rises, falls again, with its imagined whiteness hid neath buttoned black only to shine more dazzling and more livid in my thoughts. A scree of freckles, there across the steep ridge of her nose. Her pale, worn hands rest in her lap and cup her secret warmth.

It was the daughter that I met with first, and in a manner such as to occasion quite a start in me. I came upon her half-way up the coach-house stairs, stood with a narrow, westward-facing window at her back, afire with sunset all about her rim; less like a child than like some spirit of eclipse. I saw her and I stopped and gasped, so much did she remind me of another child, upon another stair, one that I had not seen but only heard of, years before.

Francis, the sole fruit of my union with Lady Nicholls, had regrettably become involved in dealings with John Dee, the famous charlatan who lived at Mortlake, near to Richmond. Called upon to visit Dee's house overnight, he saw some few things it were better that he had not seen, yet nothing he had witnessed would come to perplex him half so much as having happened on a small girl standing half-way up the stairway of that dreadful doctor's house, a western window spilling ruby light behind her. Later, having learned there were no children in the house save for Dee's full-grown daughter, Francis came to be convinced that he had seen no mortal infant, but instead some spectral waif lost on her way to Paradise. His voice and hands both shook to tell me of it and so vivid was the picture he described it was as if I had myself met with the little wraith-girl, standing dark against her sunset. Thus last night, when I encountered Eleanor, lit just the same upon the coach-house landing, I was for a moment seized by fear of things I had thought put away with childhood, and I gawped at her with what must have appeared a fearful countenance until she spoke.

'Oh, Sir,' she said, 'I do hope you are kind. I've played outside and left my mother in the room we have together for the night, and now I can't find which it was. It's dark soon, and she'll think me lost if I'm not back.'

Although the child was reassured to find someone who might assist her in her plight, she was not yet so reassured as I, to learn that she had mortal voice, and kin, and flesh and blood. In my relief, I promised I would help her find her mother's room, at which she beamed and took my dry, age-spotted hand into the warm pink shell-curl of her own, then led me up the narrow stairs.

It soon became apparent that the child, returning from her play, had looked upon the first floor for the room she and her mother shared, when all the while their billet lay just one floor higher, leading from the coach-inn's topmost landing. Tapping hesitantly on the door, I was soon answered by a quite bewitching jade-eyed woman of perhaps some five and twenty years, her great relief at having found her child soon giving way to an effusive gratitude bestowed upon myself, her benefactor. Though I'd spent but moments with the girl and done no more than walk upstairs with her it was, to hear her mother talk, as if I'd single-handed snatched the infant from the slobbering jaws of wolves.

'Oh, Sir, you've brought her back. I looked from out my window and the sky had come so dark. I had no notion where she'd gone and was that worried I was at me wit's end. Nelly, now, you thank the gentleman for all he's done.'

Her daughter here performed a brief, embarrassed curtsy, mumbling her thanks, gazing the while towards the warped boards of what little floor their narrow room possessed. I saw she had her mother's ocean eyes; the same fine-bladed cheeks with their impressive line calling to mind the urgent frailty of Italic script. Two years at most would make a splendid bed-full of her.

While I smiled down at her child with what she no doubt took to be paternal fondness, Nelly's mother did not cease professing her indebtedness and admiration, head tipped back, lifting her lashes like the lids of jewel chests deep with emeralds to gaze up at me.

`To think a gentleman as grand as you would stoop to help the likes of me and Eleanor, why, Sir, it fairly takes the breath from out of me. Look at the handsome clothes you've got upon you! You must be a great physician, else a lord to dress so gay.'

I told her, in a modest and good-humoured way that should not seem too vain, that I was neither of these things, being instead a judge. I will confess the taking of a certain pleasure from her indrawn breath and widened eyes, having upon occasions in the past had cause to note that women will become enthusiastic, even wanton, in the presence of authority such as my station lends me. With one hand raised to her breast as if physically to suppress its palpitations, she now took a small step back from me, perhaps to reappraise my scale as one might do with mountains or some other scenic feature. Where she'd thought me small and near to hand she found me massive and remote. I saw myself reflected as a god in twin green mirrors and at her excitement was myself aroused in some small measure.

`Oh, what must you think of us, turned out so poorly? Never seen a judge, nor thought I should, and here I am with one that close as I could reach and touch him. You'll have come here on important business, I'll be bound.'

I told her that I had a case to try in Kendal, whereupon her ardour doubled.

`Kendal! Why, that's no more than the place where little Eleanor and I are headed with the morning's coach. Nell? Do you hear? We are to ride to Kendal with a judge.'

Though she could have but little comprehension of my office or that power it represented, Eleanor now looked at me for all the world as if she had been promised she'd be carried to her destination on the shoulders of Saint Christopher himself. She took her mother's hand, seeming afraid lest one of them might suddenly ascend to Heaven from the sheer occasion of it all. The Widow Deene, as she would shortly introduce herself, was meanwhile fired by morbid speculation with regard to the impending trial at which I should preside. Although throughout her tone was one of fascinated horror, I have more than once observed that in the fairer sex preoccupations with the charnel often mask an equal inclination to the carnal side of life's affairs. Whenever some rough sort is made to swing, one measures in the filthy-fingered gropings of the crowd the lewd abandon that this glimpse of their mortality awakes in them. The women, later, will perform an imitation of the hanged man's final dance, writhing beneath their husbands' lunging weight, so that I wonder if we were not most of us conceived to an accompaniment of creaking ropes and flailing, blackened tongues? Such a conception surely might account for our obsession, later on in life, with all the sudden, hurtful ways there are to leave it, such as Nelly's mother now evinced.

'It is a murder, Sir, you are to try? Please God that there are not such things in Kendal, not if me and Nelly are to make our living there.'

I reassured her that the fellow up before me was no cut-throat, but instead a sheep-thief of no great account, although this did not much relieve her curiosity.

'And shall he hang, Sir? What a thing it must be, saying if men are to live or die.' A colour had arisen in her cheek, so that I smiled a little, knowing her to be already taken by the glamour of my robe and gavel.

In response I held her eye and spoke in tones of great severity. 'If he is guilty, Madame, and I have no doubt that such he be, then shall he dance a Tyburn jig, or else he has a friend to swing upon his legs and speed him to a hastier demise.'

Here, Eleanor grew pale and clutched her mother's skirts. Cast on the ceiling by a low-set lantern, both their shadows merged to one; a dark thing with too many limbs. Noticing that her daughter had become afraid, the widow turned towards the girl and scolded her perhaps too harshly, no doubt hoping she should make a good impression on a judge were she to play the martinet.

'Now don't you make a fuss, my girl! You know what I have told you. We should thank the stars that we are being spoken to at all by such a noble gentleman as . . .' Here her words trailed off and, glancing from her child, she offered me a querying look, at which I understood that she was still in ignorance as to my name.

I introduced myself, to spare her further puzzlement. 'I am His Worship Judge Augustus Nicholls, come from Faxton in Northamptonshire, upon the circuit. Now you have me at a disadvantage, Madame. Who, I wonder, might you be?'

Seeming a little flustered, she announced herself as Mrs. Mary Deene, late of Dundee, if it should please me, whereupon I let my gaze drop for an instant from her face to the more softly angled contours there below and told her that it pleased me very much. At this we both laughed, she a little nervously, while Eleanor looked first to one of us then to the other, half-aware that meanings darted underneath the surface of our talk like pretty minnows, yet unable quite to grasp them ere they vanished in a twist of silver.

We exchanged some few words more, stood at the threshold of her stoop-backed attic room, yet more than words were passed between us: certain measurements of breath were evident. Some phrases had a tilt to them, some silences an eloquence, or so it seemed to me. We both avowed we should be glad to have the other's company upon the morrow's ride to Kendal, and expressed the hope we might have cause to meet while we were in that place. At this, content that my preliminary work with Widow Deene would be sufficient to its task, I took my leave amidst much curtsying and scraping.

In my larger chamber on the floor below I punched my feather bolster till it had a shape more suitable for entertaining sleep. Settling back, I closed my eyelids, where the darkness rose behind like a theatre's drapes as Widow Deene and Eleanor, both of them nude and with their autumn hair untied, danced with each other in a feverish arietta to high-pitched French fiddles, pale and twirling on that secret stage.

Out through the carriage window the November fields are made to dazzling mirror-flats by flood, where up above the clouds hang grey and heavy as cathedrals. Two drowned heifers floating swollen in a ditch; their staring eyes catch mine in passing, black glass bulbs now fogged, steamed white by death.

Besides a trade of pleasantries when first we climbed aboard the coach this morning, and of several lingering glances since, little of note has passed between the widow and myself today. Since I imagine we shall shortly reach the skirts of Kendal where the Deenes are to be lodged, then it were better I should soon promote the notion of an assignation, lest I miss my chance. If child and mother disembark a half-mile down the road from here and are not seen again for these three days I am in Kendal, why, what then? Then I must sleep alone, else pay some drab to warm my bed unless I would return to wife and Faxton without dalliance to keep me warm in mind and memory throughout the winter months.

Our carriage rolls along its track by open land with, in the distance, mountains steeped in cloud, or clouds that look alike to mountains. Some way off, across the fallow, ploughed-in fields, I spy a great black farm dog bounding at a furious pace across the ruts and frost-baked furrows, seeming easily to match its stride with our fast-moving carriage as it lopes along in parallel to us. I make attempt to estimate its distance from the coach, which is, perhaps, much further than I first assumed. Why, then, the hound must be of monstrous size to seem so large at such a great remove.

No. No, I see it now, the truth of it, and am embarrassed at my foolishness: the beast is not a dog at all, but rather is a horse. A clump of trees obscures its racing shadow-form from sight before I can confirm this logical surmise, while at the same time Widow Deene speaks from behind me so that my attention is diverted from the creature utterly to other, less ambiguous concerns.

'We shall be getting off soon, shan't we Nelly?' This, though spoken to the child, seems largely for my benefit. Unless I miss my guess, with this announcement of her imminent departure Widow Deene hopes to provoke me to a suitable response. Not wishing that so radiant a being should be made to suffer disappointment, I turn from the window of the carriage now to speak with her, and lift my straggling eyebrows up towards their centre in a great display of something like bereavement.

'My good woman, can it be that you and your dear child alike are to be taken from me in such haste? It really is too bad! In all my lonely weeks upon these roads at last I meet with true companionship only to have it plucked from me while it is new. I'd hoped that while in Kendal we might meet, the three of us, and thus continue our acquaintanceship, but now . . .' I let my words trail off and spread my hands here, miserably, as if I hold a world of woe between them like some dismal Atlas.

Little Eleanor, awoken now, at least is moved to sympathy by my performance. Turning on her seat to face her mother, she takes up the older woman's hands within her smaller ones and wears a look upon her pointed fox-cub face that is the very soul of earnestness.

'Mama, shall we not see the gentleman again? He was so kind, I should not like him to be gone.'

Her mother looks now from the girl to me, and once more, though it is the child to whom she speaks, her words are meant for older and more knowing ears. 'You hush now, girl. Why, think how all the Kendal folk should look upon the judge if he were seen there with the likes of us! With me not long a widow they've enough to whet their tongues upon, without us bringing shame upon His Honour in the bargain.'

Here I shake my head in pained denial, as though such considerations could not be more distant from my thoughts, although in truth there is much sense in what she says. It is not meet nor seemly that I should be seen abroad with persons of their type, and in my years I've learned that England is a smaller land than many would suppose. Sometimes it seems I cannot put a hand inside the undergarment of a Yorkshire lass without it happen that she's daughter to the second cousin of my wife's best-trusted friend.

Though Kendal be remote from Faxton, I am having second thoughts concerning the advisability of a liaison with the Widow Deene, though now her child pipes up again, with fresh suggestion: 'Could he not then come to visit with us, in the nice old lady's house where we're to stay? You said it was outside the town, so folks should have no cause to pay it mind where he was gone if he come calling. Do say that he might.'

The mother lifts her eyes once more to mine, and seems to hesitate. It strikes me that the girl's proposal is ideally suited to my purposes, and I am taken by the furtive, secret bond that it already weaves between us; the suggestion of a mutual confidence that might be taken further. Widow Deene is watching me intently, waiting for some sign of my response to Eleanor's idea before she dares to venture an opinion of her own. The moment has arrived to stamp my seal upon our tryst, and leaning forward in the rocking coach I set one hand upon the infant's knee as might an uncle, chuckling the while.

Beneath her skirt's thin dark the sinew of her leg is spare and taut, much like a bird's.

'Why, what a clever mite you are, to think of such a thing! Though for my own part I care not a whit if I am seen in company with two such lovely ladies, it would never do if in this manner I should compromise your mother's reputation in the town where she's to work. Yet thanks to you, dear girl, we have the answer! I would be delighted to come calling at your residence and break the bread with both of you at your convenience, if it should be your mother gives assent.'

It seems I've learned the trick of speaking through the child, just as her mother does. The way to do it is to talk to one while gazing at the other. When the object of one's gaze has such bewitching sea-spray eyes and lips plucked from a rose bay willow herb, this is not an unpleasant task. The widow, who returns my look, now seems to colour in her cheeks. Glancing away towards the worn boards of the carriage floor and with a tiny, private smile, she stammers her acceptance. The suppressed delight upon her countenance invokes a similar elation in myself, though in a different quarter of my person.

'Oh, Sir, I . . . why, of course I gives assent. You've no need to ask my permission. Not for anything.'

Her eyes dart up now from the floor's bare planks that have unravelling slivers of the Kendal road between their lengths. She reads my face to see if I have understood her last remark, its gauze-veiled invitation. Satisfied her imprecations have not fallen upon stony ground, she looks away once more before continuing. The tremor in her voice, so faint as to be scarcely evident, is thrilling yet to me.

'You'll see the house where we're to be set down. It is not far from here, and no more than a mile's walk out of Kendal. Better you should come by dark, though, people being ready to think ill of others as they are.'

I readily agree to this, and promise I shall call upon her this tomorrow night, before I am to sit at my assizes on the morn. A fuck will no doubt much improve my disposition and, in modest measure, may alleviate the dreary circumstances that attend to the condemning of a man. It comes to me that since she is a widow without funds and of uncertain character, it may be that a shilling would procure the services of little Nelly in with us as well. I think about the bathers in my snuff-box, how they plait each other's lank and wringing hair; a foam of women risen from their spa's warm depths.

The child is speaking to her mother now, pleased by the news that I'm to visit, clutching at the widow's sleeve excitedly. ' Oh, Mother, it will be so nice to have a gentleman attend to us. I've missed it so while Father is away from us in . . .'

Mrs Deene here shoots the child a sharp, forbidding look, so that the words die on her daughter's lips. Clearly, the pangs of widowhood are yet sharp in this woman's breast so that she will not suffer Eleanor to speak of her late sire. Nevertheless, there's something in the rueful face the child makes at this silent reprimand that stirs my pity, so that I am moved now to complete her speech in hope that I may smooth across her error and return her to her mother's favour.

' While your father is away from you in Heaven with Our Lord. Of course: it is but natural that you should miss his presence, and more natural still that you should long to know man's company. In that, you are alike with all your sex.'

Here, Nell looks puzzled, but a smile of such relief and gratitude lights up her mother's face that I am given courage to continue. ' Fear not, for tomorrow night I shall come visiting, and though I may not hope to cut as good a leg as would your dear departed father, I am confident of my ability to substitute in what were, surely, his least onerous responsibilities. To whit, attending to his child, and to his wife.'

Before this last I leave the merest pause, in which I raise my stare from off the child and let it fall upon the dame instead. A look of such intensity and understanding is transferred between us that we cannot either of us bear it long and after moments must avert our eyes. A pleasant, gravid silence next descends. I fancy we're each speculating heatedly as to the nature of the other's heated speculations.

Smiling to myself, I turn once more to watch from out the carriage window, but the dog or foal that I saw earlier is not anywhere in sight. The bare, black trees fly past, clumped like the bristles on an old boar's spine.

The silence lasts until we are arrived at some low cottage, all dun-coloured stone and mouse-brown thatch, set back a little from the road that winds on up the hill to Kendal. Here the Deenes must disembark. Anxious to show that I have strength despite my years, I help to lift what little baggage they possess from off the coach, which, it transpires, includes naught but a single satchel made of threadbare canvas. As I pass it down to her my fingers brush, almost as if by accident, against the widow's own gloved hand.

A slovenly and heavy-bodied girl about fifteen is come from out the cottage, with her tangled hair the same dull colour as its thatch. Her features are impassive. Eyes that seem dull-witted and perhaps too far apart surmount a flat nose, more plan than relief. Her mouth is wide with lips too full, yet might lay claim in certain lights to its own ugly sensuality. She pauses with one lard-white hand upon the cottage gatepost and regards the coach without expression. When I look behind her to the front stoop of the house itself I see a fat and age-creased drudge who's shuffled from indoors supported by a stick. She comes no further than the door, but stands unmoving with its pitch-stained frame about her in repugnant portrait. Her chins and jowls are like one rippled mass, this merging with the single massive contour of her dugs and belly. Tiny eyes a sticky black, like plum-stones pressed in suet, she stands leaning on her stick and, like the half-wit girl propped by the gate (who may, I fancy, be her daughter), gazes at the coach with neither word nor any look that may be read.

The Widow Deene smiles up at me and mouths, `Tomorrow, then,' before she turns and moves towards the cottage with her child in tow. The string-haired girl slouched up against the post now silently draws back the gate, admitting Nelly and her mother to what shall be their new home. As I pull shut the carriage door and settle back into my seat both Eleanor and Mrs Deene turn round to wave at me just as the driver spurs his horses into life and I am hauled away and on to Kendal. Smiling fondly, I wave back as they recede from view. Tomorrow night, then.

Several minutes pass in fruitless scanning of the fields about for some sight of the beast spied earlier, and then the narrow, twisting jetties of the Lakeland town spring up about us and I am arrived. The courthouse, where I am to lodge in upstairs rooms built wholly for that purpose, is a low but dignified affair of brick and timber, near to Kendal's centre. Having quit the coach and paced a while upon the cobbles of the court's rear yard to bring some circulation to my legs, I summon an attendant from within to haul my bags up foot-smoothed stairs of stone, thence to my bed-chamber.

I mount the steps ahead, while he, a man of middle years, trudges behind me, wheezing and complaining in my wake. There is a landing half-way up, where is a window facing West. I have arrived at Kendal late on in the day, so that the sky beyond the glass is red and I am struck by that uneasy sense of having seen before. As I approach the landing I experience a mad dread that young Nelly will be stood there with her hair aflame, though I have left her back along the Kendal road. Why this idea should wake such fright in me I cannot say, and when I reach the landing it is empty. We continue up the stairs.

My room is chill but comfortable. The attendant promises he will alert the various Officers of Court to my arrival and that I may meet with both these Officers and the accused upon the morrow. Setting down my baggage just inside the door, he takes his leave of me and I remain sat on my cot in sudden still and silence, foreign to me after all the pitch and clatter of the road. After a while I rise and, crossing to my window, close its bug-drilled shutters on encroaching night. For want of any better pass-time, I prepare for bed.

These empty rooms, upon the circuit: sometimes I believe that all my frenzied copulations are but efforts to drown out the wretched spectres of these tombs; these absences.

Undressing now, my thoughts turn to my son, to Francis, back in Faxton. What a cloud there is about the lad (though, being close to fifty, I must own that he is lad no more). A foul miasma of the spirit seems to have quite overtaken him that neither wife nor his sweet daughter Mary, my own grandchild, can dispel. He mopes and stares. He only sometimes reads and seems without all motive in his days.

Dee was the cause of it, else I am not a judge. It is some five and twenty years since Francis suffered his regrettable enthusiasm for things thaumaturgical and first sought out the charlatan's advice, going to Mortlake where he made the doctor promise of one hundred pounds if Dee should teach him how to fix and tine the moon, along with other dark things of this type. While Queen Bess was in life, Dee had her ear and was much sought after in matters sorcerous, for such dire practices were then respectable, however difficult it may be to accredit this behaviour now.

Almost a year from his first visit to Dee's house, something occurred which marked the change in Francis that persists and worsens to this day. Its details were not made entirely clear to me, but from what fragments I am able to assemble it would seem that Francis had occasion to peruse some documents pertaining to the doctor's past experiments and rituals, performed while Dee had in his servitude one Edward Kelly, an unconscionable rogue who died in gaol.

Although in later years I'd oft beseech that he reveal the content of those documents, my son insisted it were better for my soul that I remain in ignorance. To judge from how he starts and frights whene'er a window bangs and has always a wan, hag-ridden look about him, it may be that he was right enough in this. Such morsels as he did reveal were more than adequate to fire the most macabre imaginings, relating to the conjuring of awful presences, whereafter to transcribe their stark yet puzzling announcements. Dee, it seemed, had at some length compiled a grammar of the spirit language, that these `angels' as he called them might commune with him and he might in his turn make plain their utterances. These aetheric dealings were that aspect of the doctor's work which most concerned my son and later came to trouble him, but for my own part I found more to entertain me in the hints that Francis would let slip as to Dee's earthier transactions.

Of the papers shewn my son that cold March night in fifteen ninety-four were some describing ritual acts of a repellent carnal nature, while still other documents pertained to an arrangement, ordered by the spirits, that the doctor and his servant Kelly should both keep their wives in common. Whether Francis felt that with these revelations Dee was subtly proposing that my son should bring his own wife into some comparable arrangement, I know not. All I am sure of is that Francis made his outrage plain, at which a pang of anger passed between the doctor and my son, who stormed from out Dee's study in a bate and made his way upstairs to where a bed was set aside for him.

It was thus while he mounted to his room with naught but furious words unspoken in his head that Francis happened on the child. Stood with her face in shadow and the bloody evening red behind her through the western window, she raised up her arms with palms turned flat towards my son as if to bar his way. Haloed in flame, she spoke to

Francis in a foreign tongue, all aspirated vowels with scarce a consonant between that sounded much like `Bah—zoh—deh—leh—teh—oh—ah' and on and on; a string of heathen nonsense.

Francis was upon the point of asking who the girl might be and what her business was with him when of a sudden she stepped from before the window to the landing's shadows and the full light of the setting sun, now unimpeded by her presence, shone into his eyes so as to dazzle him and make him squint and glance away. When next he looked upon the stairway she was gone, nor was there trace of her remaining save a scent he said reminded him of myrrh.

Despite their quarrel and the fright that he had suffered, Francis could not seem to keep away from Mortlake. With the troubles between him and Dee soon mended, he made frequent visits to the doctor's house across the next six years, on more than one occasion forcing my grand-daughter Mary to accompany him, against my best advice.

Dee, at this juncture of his life, relied upon one Bartholomew Hickman as he'd once relied on Edward Kelly, needing, it would seem, someone to scry the aethers for him with a glass and tell him of the messages his `angels' would convey. All this came to an end around the turning of the century when, if my son may be believed, this Hickman was discovered as a fraud, or at the least a seer who had communed with naught but false, deceptive spirits. Near a decade's work was thus undone, and in the late September of that year my son and grand-daughter alike attended bitter and defeated ceremonies there at Mortlake where the documents accrued from Hickman's traffic with the spirit world were ignominiously rendered down to ash.

I will admit I thought it splendid that a faker should be thus exposed, but Francis would not be consoled. My son considered the affair to be a vast catastrophe whose true dimension I might never sound. Even my grandchild Mary seemed to have a pall about her, and would sometimes offer me a frightened look, as if she of a sudden knew me in another light. They neither of them went again to Mortlake after that, nor had they dealings with John Dee. It was not long before King James, a Godly Sovereign, ascended to the throne, whereafter the Magician found that he had fallen out from grace and so began his great decline. Not many years were passed before Dee had descended into penury and then, soon after, passed away at Mortlake tended only by his daughter, from which one assumes there were no spirits present in that instance to assist with his demise.

Pulling my night-gown on I mount the guest-room's wooden-boxed commode to make my stool, this being hard and painful in its passing. With my labours thus accomplished I snuff out the candle that I have undressed by and leap straight into my bed, the blankets dragged up covering my ears, without which muffling presence, ever since I was a child, I may not sleep.

I am annoyed to find that still my thoughts are turned to Doctor Dee, for there is something puzzling in him that I cannot leave alone. There seems a great predicament in how one measures such a man, that was too well-accomplished in the sciences material and politic to be discounted as a fool, and yet believed he spoke with angels. Can so fine a mind have found diversion for so many years in copying pointless syllables on to his endless tables, charts and journals? If this be not so; if by some fluke of reason all the messages that Dee transcribed were real, then what are we to make of a Heaven populous with incoherent angels, spouting nonsense credos in the speech of babes? I saw the `angel language' once, copied laboriously by my son into a journal that he kept. It was a grid of what appeared to me at least a thousand squares, each with some symbol or notation written in so that it seemed in sum a veritable map of lunacy; that mist-bound continent whence few return to tell what they have seen.

I shall concern myself no more this night with thoughts of wizards nor astrologers. The skull-capped and white-bearded vision of the doctor as my son described him to me dances irritatingly behind my eyelids until, with an effort of the will, I am enabled to dispel it and put in its place some several pictures of the Widow Deene in various shaming postures, these soon supplemented by a memory of the slab-thighed servant-girl that stood there by the cottage gate and stared at me with empty, stupid eyes.

My steam of thought condenses, beading into dreams against the coolness of my pillow, and a mumbling cloud descends. A crack is opened in the night to let me enter in, and slide, and sink, and sleep . . .

I wake before the sun with the attendant who assisted with my baggage tapping at the chamber door to tell me that a breakfast is prepared for me down in the dining room below. I thank him with a grunt and rise to dress as well as I am able in the dark. Whilst buckling my shoes I am reminded of a dream that was upon me in the night, wherein I was at Mortlake with my son and Doctor Dee, save in the dream his name was Dr Deene. He held a yellowed parchment up to us and said, ' Here is a map of lunacy', and yet when Francis and I leaned in close to study it we saw it was instead a map of our own shire, which is to say Northampton. More, it seemed to me as if the map were not drawn on to paper but tattooed upon a substance very much like human skin. I thought to look for Faxton but could find it nowhere on the chart, which filled me with a sudden formless dread. Here Dr Dee or Deene was moved to reassure me that all would be well if he and I were but to have our wives in common, though he may have said not wives but lives. At this, and for no reason, I began to weep and afterwards remember nothing more until my waking.

Properly attired now and removed unto the dining room, above a meal of scaith cooked in an oatmeal crust I'm introduced to my chief bailiff for tomorrow's trial, a doughty chap named Callow with a strawberry nose and great side-whiskers that surround his crab-pink face in white. As I pluck fishbones from my cheek to set as on some tiny ossuary shelf beside my plate, he reacquaints me with the details of the case I am to hear. A local man of no account called Deery stands accused of taking from their rightful owner both a ewe and ram, the last of which he sold, whereafter salted portions of the former were discovered on his property, so that his guilt is plainer than a wart.

Chief Bailiff Callow tells me that with breakfast done we both may walk to Kendal gaol and view the miscreant there in his cell, along with those less serious offenders I am also called upon to judge once Deery has been sentenced: drunks and whores; a shopkeeper accused of giving out dishonest measure; several brawlers and a bugger.

Out of doors, with fish and oatmeal resting heavy on my gut and breath like smoke upon the frozen air, I walk beside the bailiff neath a gauze of shadow down the steep lanes slippery with frost. The sky is ribboned water-blue and gold along its eastern edge, where West of that there are yet stars and from the fields outside of Kendal comes a gradual fugue of birdsong, each voice lucid and distinct.

The gaol, built out of rough grey stones, is in the very middle of the town where it squats like a monstrous toad that has been petrified by its own ugliness. Its walls have gaping chinks and fissures so that it is no more warm inside than out, consisting only of a cramped space where the turn-keys sit and whittle aimlessly at sticks, with several narrow cells crammed in beyond.

Sat in the first of these, a girl about thirteen with pale, untidy hair is suckling her babe, a ghastly, mottled little thing no bigger than a rat and by the look of it not long for life. Each time she makes attempt to tease her sallow, cone-shaped breast between the creature's lips it turns its grey and shrivelled face away to whine. The mother looks up briefly at me without interest, then turns her dull gaze back towards her child. The bailiff tells me that she is arraigned for brawling, and we pass on down the row.

Deery is in the next cell we approach. He sits upon his bunk and stares without expression at the wall, not even looking up at us when we elect to question him directly. Still a young man, Deery has the look of one once handsome and well-built now run to fat, the strong bones of his boyhood face yet visible, embedded in a bland expanse of dough. He sits there, feet apart, his forearms resting on his thighs with wrists as thick as infants' waists and ham-hock fists, the fingers intertwined into a hawser-knot at rest between his knees. His stillness is unsettling and complete.

I ask him if he knows I am to judge him on the morrow, whereupon he merely shrugs and still does not elect to look at me directly. When I ask him if he is aware that hanging is the punishment for theft of livestock he seems only bored, and after some few moments hawks a quid of startlingly yellow phlegm into the corner of his cell. It is clear that conversation is impossible between the two of us, and after but a cursory examination of the lock-up's other inmates, Bailiff Callow and I step from the rank miasma of the gaol once more into the biting Kendal air. The skies are light now and the town is properly awakened. A wood-merchant's cart with images of Saints and martyrs painted on its side rolls past drawn by a threadbare horse. Small boys climb on the baker's roof to drink the warmth and savour from his oven-vents and down the lane there walks a stooped old man all hung about with wooden cages wherein bantams make complaint.

With little useful to be done before tomorrow's trials I take the bailiff's leave and pass the morning by inspecting Kendal, stopping in a hostelry at noon to dine on mutton pie and swede. Thus fortified, I spend the afternoon in pleasurable meander through the nearby countryside. Some short while prior to heading back towards my lodgings where I may prepare for this tonight's encounter with the Widow Deene, it comes to me that I am in a mood of tense expectancy that is not all connected with that lady or her charms. I realize at length that part of me is half anticipating further glimpses of the animal that I saw yesterday as it raced there beside our coach, and laugh aloud at my own foolishness. This is not even near the place where I first spied the beast, that being on the other side of town. Besides, of what concern to me is some stray hound, or pony, or whatever else the creature may have been?

Returning to my rooms I change into a finer set of clothes and put fresh powder on my wig. Waiting until the Heavens' nightly silent battle in the western sky has run its bloody course, I sidle out into the first mauve fogs of dusk, taking much care that I should not be seen by anyone associated with the Court and holding underneath one arm my iron-knobbed cane for fear of cut-purses.

A doleful blue which all too quickly cools to grey descends upon the Lakeland hills with twilight, and across the flooded fields a loon is driven mad by grief. I am soon come upon the outskirts of the town, whence I continue on the Kendal road towards the cottage where the widow and her child are billeted. The mustard-coloured mud that now adorns my polished boots seems but a little forfeit weighed against the great rewards I hope may be in store for me. A widow who has much experience with married life and yet is eager to resume its carnal aspect makes for a more satisfying ride than any whey-skinned maid in service, and I dare suppose that the authority my office lends me may do much in making her receptive to my whims, peculiar though they be.

To each side of the darkening road the ditches pour and gurgle like a man run through the heart and all about an icy mist is rising so that I grow anxious for my first sight of the cottage lights upon the track ahead of me. When last I crossed this ground it was by coach and not so gloomy, yet I wonder if I have not made some error. Can the cottage really be this far outside of Kendal, or have I passed by it in the dusk so that it lies behind me now? Resolved that if I am not come upon the fat old woman's habitation soon then I shall turn back for my lodgings though it mean I must forgo the widow's company, I am afforded much relief to round a bend and sight at last the wan and jaundiced glow of lamplight seen through curtains, some way further down the lane.

With images of Widow Deene as I should soonest like to see her filling all my thoughts, save for those thoughts pertaining to the darling Eleanor, my pace is made more quick so that before I know it I am by the cottage gate. A flurry of emotion now descends upon me; a peculiar nervousness that I have known before when in such situations: partly it is lust, partly anxiety lest I have made too much of things and shall be disappointed. This time there is something else besides, an undertow of qualm I may not place, but all such trepidations must be put away. If I'm to hang a man upon the morrow, then I would this night impale a woman first, and so march briskly up a mollusc-skated path to rap the tar-streaked door.

A Pater Noster-while goes by until at last the door's unlatched and I'm confronted by the half-wit girl that I saw loitering by the gate when we arrived here yesterday. Encountering her now, I am less certain if she be indeed half-witted, or instead has cultivated a tremendous slowness, as a form of insolence. She stares at me in silence an inordinate amount of time before she deigns to speak, and when she does a lewd and knowing grin is smeared, much like a riotous slogan, on the flat wall of her face.

'You'll be they judge, then?'

Voice as thick and slippery as waterweed, her lazy slur has a suggestiveness about it that I soon discover to be constant and habitual. When I reply that yes, I am indeed His Honour Judge Augustus Nicholls and enquire as to her own name, she returns a smile that is at once flirtatious and amused, and holds my eye for some few humid moments before answering.

'I'm Emmy. You'll be wantin' Mary, though. You'd best come in.'

She ushers me into a lamplit passageway so narrow that, as she manoeuvres past me to pull shut the front door in my wake, we are both for a moment pressed together, face to face, there in that closely bounded vestibule. Her heavy bust is pressed against my coat-front, flattened so it seems to disappear in much the same way as the blade of a stage dagger. This sublime compression lasts for but a moment, then she's by me. As I turn and walk towards the lit room at the passage's far end I hear her close the door and draw a bolt across.

Another doorway, partly open, leads off from the hall upon my right, and as we pass it by I glance inside. Though it is lit by nothing save such light as filters from the passage where we walk, I can make out a vast array of painted plates and figures made from porcelain arranged upon a huge old dresser just inside the room, which seems immaculately kept and has a richly patterned rug upon its floor. In company with the dresser I can also see an ornate footstool and a quaint low table made of polished cherry-wood. Though I may not view all this front room whilst in passing, I am given the impression of a small, neat space so filled with heirlooms proudly on display as to allow no room for one to enter in. It has a pristine and unused appearance quite at odds with the dilapidated façade of the house, but I move on towards the light there at the hall's far end, and think no more upon it. Emmy walks behind me, and I hear her flat, bare feet upon the boards. I hear her breath.

The passage leads me to a room so different from the one I have just passed that they might be on separate continents, divided not by some few feet of hall, but by an ocean. From my contemplation of the neat front room so filled with beautiful possessions, I am plunged into a squalid hovel where the gnarled grain of the walls is choked by soot and there is everywhere a smell compounded out of mildew, broiling offal, and that odour that old women have, like tripes and piss. I understand that this is how the poor must choose to live, with all they have of beauty, worth or value hoarded in a room kept just for show, which they themselves may enter not, save that it be to dust or clean. Their true lives are played out behind these cluttered shrines in cheerless middens such as this, where I stand on the threshold now.

A hearth-cum-stove of iron and slate set in the end wall warms the room, but in a stifling way. Beside this, on a bow-legged stool that has her walking-cane propped up against it, sits the wrinkled and obese old dame that I spied yesterday, her eyes like coals in curds fixed fast upon me as I step inside with head bent to avoid the low oak beams. Seen closer to, I note she is afflicted with a moisture on the lungs, so that she wheezes, with her monstrous bosom heaving like the tide beneath her apron and a quiver rippling through her puddled flesh, across her jowls and goitered neck at every breath.

Set out there in the middle of this noisome chamber is a table far too massive for so cramped a place, that looks as if the cottage were built up about it, being far too broad to fit the door and very old besides, its surface scarred by carving-knives long snapped in hands long dead. Five chairs are set about the table, two of them already occupied by Eleanor and her enchanting mother, both of whom look up and smile upon my entry. I had quite forgot how green their eyes were, and decide that I might bear these miserable surrounds if they should be illuminated by such pulchritude.

'Judge Nicholls! You have come just as you said.' It is the Widow Deene who speaks, and the excitement and anticipation in her voice elicits in me smug assurance that all shall be well between us. Scraping back her chair across the rough stone tiles, she rises from her seat and steps across the room to greet me, placing one weak hand upon my elbow as she steers me to my setting, opposite her own. Stood leaning up against the passage door-jamb, Emmy smirks at the assembly. While attempting to ignore the girl, I make small conversation with the widow and with Eleanor until the bloated crone sat by the hearth ceases her wheezing for a moment to address us all.

'We'll get the dinner up now. Emmy, you stop gawpin' at the gentleman and pull us up so's I can dish it out.' Her voice, dragged up through a great surfeit of congestions, bubbles like a marsh.

Emmy, with an expressive sigh, quits her position by the door and crosses to the fireplace where she helps the swollen baggage labour up from off her stool. The two of them, who I am now convinced are child and mother, next proceed to ladle forth great bowls of hotpot from a vessel taken out the stove, these being set before us. Emmy takes her seat, next to my own, with many crafty sidelong leers, while the old lady, with some difficulty, sinks her gasping bulk on to the chair placed at the table's head.

With breath sufficiently recovered, she intones a grace: 'Dear Lord, bless this the meal we have prepared our guest, and may we have success in all our doin's.'

Although rude and unconventional, the blessing is not inappropriate.

Tonight, if luck is with me, I'll be doing Widow Deene, and hope to have no small success in this endeavour. Murmuring, then, an `Amen' that is heartfelt, I lift up my fork and start to eat, smiling across the table at the widow and receiving her smile in return. I fancy there is something secret in it, meant perhaps for but the two of us. Encouraged thus, with added relish I attack the mound of beef and vegetable heaped before me, pleasantly surprised by how agreeable its flavour seems.

Whilst picking at their food, the gathered females watch attentively as I wolf down my own, no doubt with apprehension lest such plain, rough fare does not meet with my cultivated expectations. Wishing to allay their fears, I heap great forks-full past my chin and, in between my mastications, comment on the dinner's excellence, for in all truth it is delicious. Highly spiced and peppered, every swallowing promotes a film of perspiration on my brow and upper lip; a stinging in my palate by which means my mouth is made a smouldering, infernal cave of molar stalactites with every jot of my awareness centred there. With fellows of my stamp, who have a taste for fire and pepper in their food, the rigours of enduring such a meal are part of its attraction. Panicked by the blazings of the tongue, it is as if the other instruments of sensibility are similarly plunged into a new condition: eyes may water or the ears may ring, with everywhere throughout the body's flesh a sympathetic tingling. I have often thought that such a state must be alike with that described by mystics, where all other bodily concerns are swept away by the intensity of a divine experience.

I think of Francis, hollow-eyed and stammering, filled with dread since the abrupt cessation of his work with Dee; with the demeanour of a man who has been sentenced, yet who must endure a long, excruciating wait until the gallows have been built. I cannot help but think he might have limited his own experiments with the sublime to the enjoyment of a simple dish such as I have before me now, my plate already half wiped clean, so hearty is my appetite.

Whilst I am lost within this culinary reverie, the women sat about me eat in silence save the chime of knife on crockery, with many glances made to me or to each other. Eleanor, who may have been provided with a smaller portion than we grown-ups, has already emptied out her dish and, turning, holds it out towards the gross and liver-fluked old woman seated at the table's head, there on the infant's right.

'Grandmother? May I have some more?'

At this, the aged mountain made of fat swivels her head around towards the child in an unsettling fashion, with her neck so swollen that it does not seem to move, but only that her features have by some means swum across that doughy head to face another way.

Her voice is sharp and harsh, so that the small girl flinches and draws back, afraid. 'I'm not your grandmother, you wicked girl!'

At the severity of this reproach an awkward silence falls upon the gathering, skilfully breached by Widow Deene who, smiling in a nervous way, attempts now to excuse her child. 'Of course she's not, is she, my lamb? It's just that with her having been so kind to us, that's how you've come to think of her. Now, Nelly, is that not the way of things?'

Here Eleanor, still pale and shaken from the scolding, nods her head and stares into her empty dish, which seems to mollify the wheezing dragon to her left. This withered old Leviathan now turns to speak with Emmy, sat here next to me, instructing the young girl to rise and serve a second helping for such mouths as may require it.

For my own part, I reluctantly decline the offer with a shaking of the head. A heaviness is come upon me, so that I become afraid lest I have rather ate too much already. If this well-stuffed lethargy should not abate, I fear for my performance with the widow later on. I shall not have the strength to mount her, having barely strength enough to raise another mouthful to my lips. Upon my mute refusal of a further serving, Emmy tilts her head upon one side and gazes down towards me quizzically, with ladle in one hand and oven-pot wrapped in a cloth beneath her arm. Those wide, plump lips crease now in a lascivious smile before she speaks.

'I think the judge has had enough already. Look how thick the sweat stands on his brow, as if this room's too hot for him.'

Setting the pot and ladle down upon the table-top she next stoops down a little, smiling all the while, so that her face is close to mine. The other three about the table seem to watch intently, all with rapt and yet unreadable expressions, much like birds. My fingertips seem numb. I hear a distant clattering that I think must be my dinner fork, now fallen to the floor. Near to, I see that Emmy has a spoiled complexion; yellow-heads in dense encampments, sheltering at the corners of her nose. Her voice is slow and thick as treacle pouring.

'Don't you fret about the warm, now, Judge. My mother says as we are all to take our clothes off for you later on. Then we'll be glad the fire's banked up so high.'

What is she saying? From across the table, Widow Deene speaks now in a reproachful tone I have not heard her use before. 'You mind now, Emmy. He might not be quite so underneath-the-weather as he looks.'

The adolescent seems to take no heed of this, but only cocks her head to scrutinize me closely, as if making up her mind before she speaks. 'Oh, no. I think he's had it, right enough. Besides, I know a way we shall soon see.'

She straightens up away from me. Without abandoning her smile she lifts her weighty arms to curl behind her neck where lie the fastenings of her smock, which she commences to unbutton. No one speaks. The room is silent save the fat old woman's ragged breath. My mind is swimming, and it comes to me belatedly that there is something very much awry here in this sweltering chamber.

Emmy has by now undone herself enough to work both shoulders from her dress, followed by one arm then the other. Finally, with a triumphant smile, she yanks the whole affair down to her hips so that above the waist she is quite naked. Do I dream this? Emmy's breasts are large and dense, that now she lifts her hands to cup and weigh. Flat aureolae, brown and violet, surmount each bub, the purpled nipples thrusting out like baby's thumbs. She steps towards me, cradling one teat in either palm and, with a vague anxiety that seems remote and distant to me, I discover that I can no longer move. The singing in my ears is louder, though I still hear Emmy as she speaks beside my ear.

'There, now. What do you think of them? Aren't they a lovely set of things? Why, I would wager that you'd like to suck upon them if you could. That's what gents like to do, I hear.'

Now she inclines her body closer to me so the musky scent of her is overwhelming. Lifting up one breast she tilts the nipple to my slack and gaping mouth, wiping it slowly back and forth across my lower lip, so that it folds, and bends, then springs again erect against my teeth. I try to close them on the slippery bud, and yet cannot.

'Now stop it, Emmy!' It is Widow Deene who speaks. 'I'll put up with this family's ways so long as I am married into it, but not all of us wants to see your lechery both day and night.'

In answer, Emmy lewdly rocks her body back and forth so that her breast pumps in and out between my numb, unmoving lips. It seems that the old lady seated at the table's end finds this so comic an effect that she begins to cackle, deep in her polluted, rattling lungs. Hilarity being contagious, little Eleanor next starts to smirk while darting cautious glances at her taut-faced mother, Widow Deene, as if to ask if it is yet permissible to laugh. At length she can contain herself no longer, and her mirth is given vent in snivelling noises down her nose, whereon the widow may not any more maintain her scowling and affronted disposition, starting in to snigger too, so that the four of them are laughing now.

The merriment endures a while and then is died away as Emmy takes her breast from out my mouth, a solitary pearl of spittle hung by a saliva thread there at its gallows tip. She takes a step back so as better to regard me and her smile is scornful now, filled with contempt.

'He won't be long now. We could make a start on divvying him up, once we've our clothes off so they shan't be marked.'

Now the old woman speaks from somewhere to my right. My head hangs slack against the back-rest of my chair and I have not the strength to turn it, so must listen only to the phlegm-harp of her voice.

'Don't be so daft, girl. See the way his eyes move back and forth! There's yet vitality in him and if we cut him now it would fly everywhere. We'll bide our time until he's gone. When blood no longer moves, the mess is not so great.'

I am afraid, despite the numbing fog that seems to hang about me. Did they say I should be cut? I make attempt at protest yet can utter nothing save a hollow moan. What has become of me?

Across the table, Eleanor now joins with the discussion, turning to the matriarch sat at the table's end. 'Is it all right to call you Grandma now?' The woman coughs her gruff assent and Eleanor continues. 'Grandma, it's so very hot in here. Can I take off my things like Auntie Em? You said that we would do it later.'

Here her mother, Mrs Deene, makes hurried interjection. 'Never mind what Auntie Emmy does. I won't have you grow up behavin' like your father's family.'

Now Emmy's mother, leaning in upon my field of vision, tips her great bulk forward in her chair to plant her elbows on the table-top and glare with hard resentment at the Widow Deene. 'Your Nelly's in this with the rest of us. That's what we said, and that's how it shall be. The reason it is being done at all is for her father, and your husband. Emmy's brother, and my son. You've wed into this family now, young Mary Deene-as-was, and you're a Deery. Deerys stick together.'

There is pause wherein the younger woman seems to wither under that indomitable gaze. Her eyes fall to her lap and she is cowed, at which the harridan continues, speaking now once more to Eleanor.

'If you've a mind to take your clothes off as we all agreed then so you shall, that they might not be splashed and stained when we commence the bloody-work. Indeed, we might as well all of us be about undressin'. He'll be gone before I'm out my underskirts, you'll see.'

It is an effort now even to breathe and waves of crashing blackness break within me, rattling as they drag their foaming tendrils back across the shingle of my thoughts, churn buried notions up into the glistening light. I think of Francis, and I understand the way he starts at every creaking of a door. I think of Dee. I think of Faxton, but I cannot bring a picture of it to my mind. All I can see is empty streets that wind past pitiable ruins before even these are gone and in their stead there is a great forgetfulness of grass, unmarked by spire or fence or gutter.

All about me now the women take their garments off amidst much whispering and laughter. Eleanor skips by, her skirtless, hairless body seeming almost without gender, to assist her grandmother in the prolonged unveiling of that huge, white form; the belly hung in folds above the almost bare pudenda where such few hairs that remain are yellow-grey, like spilled and dirty candle-fat. Propped naked up against the table's other edge is Emmy, with her buttocks white upon the dark, scarred wood as she helps Mrs Deene comb out her auburn hair. Was Deene her name? Or was it Dee? Or Deery? I cannot recall.

She sits and faces me across the table, wearing not a stitch, and keeps her eyes upon my face as Emmy starts to plait her chestnut locks for her. The room is like a furnace and I watch a crystal globe of sweat traverse the seated woman's collarbone to vanish in the smear of light between her breasts. The scene reminds me very much of something I have seen before, damp women tending to each other's hair, but fog-bound as I am I cannot place it.

To my right, Nell's grandmother steps shamelessly from out the tangle of her underskirts there pooled about her feet. Helped by the cherub Eleanor, she next retrieves a box of cutlery from somewhere up above the stove. Selecting carving knives from out the tray, she and the girl proceed to sharpen them against a hearth-brick that I cannot see, but only hear the measured slinth of iron on stone. There is a fierce pain in my belly that yet feels somehow remote from me, as if it were occurring to someone else. The waves of light and shadow that seem in my eyes to roll across the crowded room come faster now, like ripples.

Bored with waiting for my strangled breath to cease, the naked women next ignore me. Sat about their table, they make conversation over little things as if I were not dying here amongst them. They discuss their ailments, and the price of grain, and what they'll do once John is out of gaol. Without their clothes they seem not human but more like some cadre of weird sisters; Fates or Gorgons stepped from legend. All about them is a vaporous radiance that seems to boil away to subtle colours at its edge. The smallest gesture leaves its traces in the air behind, with a descending arm become instead like shimmering pinions, fanned and splendid. They are talking, but I can no longer tell the sense of what they say.

Their words are from a glossary of light, lips moving silently as if beyond the scrying glass and in my ears the singing has achieved a perfect clarity, the rounds and phrases of it now resolved. Above the roaring of the altitudes each foreign syllable is bright and resonant, is achingly familiar in its alien profundity, a layered murmur echoing in everything. I know this song.

I know it.

PARTNERS IN KNITTING
AD 1705

Inside the heads of owls and weasels there are jewels that will effect a cure for ague, for colic. Lightning is the spend of God that strikes an ash tree, where His seeds grow up, with rounded heads and slender tails, between the roots. A woman or a man may take these spendings in their mouth, and after have the Sight, so that they may put all their thoughts into a fire, to travel with its smoke towards the sky. Here they will meet with stork or heron that will bear them up until the Great Cathedral may be apprehended, with its perfect vaulted ceilings formed from naught but Law and Number. I have swallowed my own piss, and I have seen these things.

Not yet an hour since, Mr Danks, the Minister of All Saints came with Book and bailiffs to the cell I share with Mary, after which they brought us out and hung us from a gallows at the town's North gate until we were near dead, our gizzards all but crushed. Cut down, we were next tethered here. Wearing our rope-burns now like glorious chains of office, we are sat half-conscious and resplendent on our kindling throne.

Tied here beside me, Mary's small, warm hand is in my own. She is no more afraid than I, soothed by a breeze come from the terraces invisible, made tranquil in that mauve light fogging their night pastures. Even were our throats not so constricted by our lynching to deny us speech, no word need pass between the two of us that we may know these things. It is the same Realm, the same thought of Realm, where thought of Realm is Realm itself. They're going to burn me, and I'm not yet twenty-five.

Across the cold March fields the birds are building something delicate and terrible from strings of sound, from play of echo. We two are the last that shall be murdered thus by fire in England. This we have been told by Imps and things of colour that abide in higher towns where all the days are one, where are no yesterdays nor yet tomorrows. After this, no more of human tallow round a wick of petticoat. No more the fair cheek rouged by blister.

Now I slowly raise my weighted lids until both eyes are open, just as in that instant Mary does the same beside me. Seeing this, the gathered herd beyond our pyre make loud gasps of amazement and step back, their sty-born faces ill with terror. Widow Peak, who said she'd heard us talk of killing Mrs Wise, now draws a cross upon her withered tit and spits, while Parson Danks commences reading loudly from his moth-worn book, his words like smuts of ash wiped on the morning.

If you only knew, you barn-apes, what it was you burned here. It is not for me I say this, but for Mary, who is beautiful where I am plain. If you might see the corners of her eyes when she is saying something comical then you would know her. If you knew the strong taste in her cunt when she has not yet woken of a morning, you would look away in shame and quench your torches. Captured in her ladyhair, my dribble turned to jewels and each one had a water-painted mansion of homunculi tiny and bright within it. When she walks up stairs it is like song, and at the time of each month's blood she may speak in the tongue of cats, but then, what of it? It is all of this as nothing. Put a light to it, render it all to cinder, her red hair, the drawings that she makes.

I will admit that we have had the conversation of those nine Dukes ruling Hell. Having now seen that place it holds no fear for me, for it is beautiful, and at its mouth are precious stones. It is but Heaven's face when looked upon by the deceived and fearful, and in all my trade with its Ambassadors I have discovered them to be as gentlemen, both grand and fair of manner. Belial is like a toad of wondrous glass with many eyes ringed on his brow. He is profound and yet unknowable, while Asmoday is more like an exquisite web of pattern that surrounds the head: wry, fierce, and skilled in the mathematic arts. Despite their wrath and their caprice they are not bad so much as other to us, and are more than pretty in their fashion, that you should be envious of those who look upon such marvellous affairs of Nature.

Now a thick-browed man I do not know steps forward with his torch and touches it to knotted rags and straw there at the kindling's edge. We close our eyes and sigh. Not long, my love. Not far to go. The unseen balconies are not so high above us now.

We met each other when I was fourteen and came from Cotterstock to Oundle up the road because my parents wanted quit of me. Mary was just the same age, pale and freckled, with big legs and arms. She let me hide out in her dad's back yard those first cold months, and some nights in her room, if it should pass her sister and her brother were not there. We'd go about the town and play such games. With evening drawing in we'd dare each other into standing there beneath the Talbot Hotel's cobbled passage, leading to the dark yard at the rear. We'd swear we heard the ghost of old Queen Mary that had slept there on the night before they took her head, walking the upstairs landing with it tucked beneath her arm. Squeal. Hug ourselves there in the gloom.

Sometimes we'd venture out across the piss-and-ale-washed flagging of the yard and through to Drummingwell Lane, at the Talbot's rear. We'd stand and listen at the Drumming Well itself, that made a sound much like a drum the night before King Charles died and at other times beside, as with the death of Cromwell. We would cock our ears and hold our breath, though no sound ever came.

We'd run out in the fields to hide amongst the wild laburnum, and in fancy would be savage, blue-arsed men come from the Africas, that crawled half-naked with ferocious, droll expressions there between the drowsing, nodding stems. We stuck our fingers up each other and would laugh at first, become thereafter hot and grave. We found a dead shrew, stiff and with a gloss as though its death were but a coat of varnish, and one afternoon I watched her piddle in the cowslips, closed my eyes upon the wavering skewer of plaited gold that bored a sopping hole there in the soil beneath her, but heard still its pittering music and saw yet its braided stream within my thoughts.

Now comes the first kiss of the smoke, a husband's loving peck upon the nose, and just as with a husband we both keep our eyes shut while it's going on. Time soon enough for him to shove his sour and choking tongue half down our gullets. Raw and smouldering nettle-bite curls there behind our cringing nostrils, and I hope the faggots are not green and damp, or likewise slow to burn, for when our covenant was made, the Black-Faced Man said that we should not know the fires of punishment. A whistling silence foams up in my ears, as if at some unfathomable approach, but swiftly dies away, subdued amidst the papery crackling that is all about us now. Hush,

Mary Phillips, and be not afraid, for we were made a promise, you and I.

We found a livelihood that suited me, and also found a little room in Benefield where I might lodge those next ten years, though hardly did a day go by we were not in each other's company. As we grew up, the great adventure that there was between us seemed almost our coracle, that carried us away in time from that laburnum country, full of ghosts and secret games, to cast us up amongst the sulking islands that are men.

We wallowed in them, men, those next few years, didn't we, Mary? Although I confess I did more wallowing than you, you did not go without your share. Ditch-diggers, sextons, publicans, and slaughtermen still with the stink of killing on their hands. They bought us small beer in the front bar of the Talbot; took us up against the jetty wall just as they'd take a piss while on their stumble-footed journey back to wife and hearth. Because of this, I did not often sleep with them, but when I did I was surprised: if they are not awake, they are much softer to the touch, and more like women. What a pity, then, that they should ever stir.

Yet stir they did. They'd rise before me, gone before my eyes were open properly, and when I'd see them walking of a Sunday with their families only the wives would look at me, their faces hard. If these should glimpse me later in the market, gathered in their twos and threes, they'd call out after me, `There goes a whore', or else they'd teach their little ones to taunt me, crying, `Shaw the whore' and `Strumpet Nell' wherever I should walk. How is it that the pleasant, simple thing of knobs in notches might provoke such scorn, and shame, and misery? Why must we take our being's sweetest part and make it yet another flint on which to gouge ourselves?

Now comes a curious thing. Shifting against my bonds, I once again have cause to open up my eyes, whereon I find that everything is stopped. The world, the smoke, the clouds, the crowds and leaping flames, all of it still and without motion. Stopped.

How strange and charming is this realm with movement fled, how perfectly correct. The dragon frills of frozen smoke, upon inspection, have a beauty that is lost to normal sight, with smaller frills identical in shape that blossom, fern-like, from the twisting mother coil. To think that I had never noticed.

Looking down, I feel only a mild surprise to note that we are burning, me and Mary both alike. Why, these drab skirts of ours have never looked so fine as they do now, awash with fire and light and colour; ruby-hung with flames that do not move. There is no hurt, nor even warmth, although I see one of my feet to be scorched black. Instead of pain there is a passing sadness, for I have believed my feet to be the prettiest part of me, though Mary says she likes my shoulders and my neck. When we have been undressed of form we shall walk truly naked from our ashes, and there shall be not a part of us that is not beautiful.

Though she is strangled far beyond the point of speech, I can hear Mary's voice inside me saying Elinor, oh Elinor, and bidding me look deep inside the flames that have in some way without any seeming movement risen to my bosom like ferocious heraldry.

I stare at these inverted icicles of gold and light, and in each one there is a moment, tiny and complete, trapped in the shimmering amber. Here's my father, leathering my mother as she stoops across the kitchen table howling, this seen as if through an open door. Here is the dream I had when I was little, of an endless house filled with more books than there are in the world. Here's when I cut my shoulder open on a nail and here the dead shrew, waxed and chill.

Beneath the base of every flame there is a still, clear absence; a mysterious gap between the death of substance and the birth of light, with time itself suspended in this void of transformation, this strange pause between two elements. I understand it now, that there has only ever been one fire, that blazed before the world began and shall not be put out until the world is done. I see my fellows in the flame, the unborn and the dead. I see the gash-necked little boy. I see the ragged man that sits within a skull of blazing iron. I almost know them, almost have a sense of what they mean, like letters in a barbarous alphabet.

It was all for a joke at first, the picture drawn with pig-blood and the candle. We did not suppose that it would come to anything, nor be accomplished with such fearful ease. Some names were said aloud, and in the finish there were answers come as from an obscure place; from out a lively fog descended in our thoughts. This was in February of last year, when all the ponds were cauled and frozen.

Shivering bare, we squatted in my pinched up room and listened to the novel words we heard inside ourselves, this hearing being of a kind that cannot be accomplished with the ears, that is sometimes more like a drift of mood or vision than it is like speech. It told us many things.

We are all, each of us, the stinging, bloody fragments of a God that was torn into pieces by the birth-wail of Eternity. When all the days are done, She who is Bride and Mother unto all of us shall gather every scrap of scattered being up into one place, where we shall know again what we knew at the start of things, before that dreadful sundering. All being is divided between that which is, or else that which is not. Of these the last is greater, and has more importance. To know thought is to be in another country. Everything is actual. Everything.

At first naught but a voice within, the Black-Faced Man became apparent in small measures. First we had a sense of someone sitting in the empty chair that stood up in one corner of my room, but when we looked there would be no one there. At length we could both make him out by looking from the corners of our eyes, though if we gazed on him directly he'd be gone.

He was both tall and terrible, with hair and whiskers like a beast, his eyes a bright and pale goat-yellow in the painted lamp-black of his face. A dark and purple light hung all about him, and it seemed as if his flesh was everywhere embroidered with tattoo, in coiling lines like serpents or a new calligraphy. Things that were either branch or antler sprouted from his head upon each side, and when he spoke inside our thoughts his voice was deep enough to make the air grow cold. He told us that we must stretch out our hands, but only I dare do it, Mary being too afraid.

I stood there for some moments with my hand thrust out, and at the start felt nothing save for foolish. Presently, however, I could feel the faintest touch of something much like fingers wrapped about my own, and very cold into the bargain. When he spoke, it was to me alone, for when Mary and I discussed things later she confessed to hearing nothing at this point.

He said, ʻElinor Shaw, be not afraid of me, for I am one of the Creation, as are you yourselves.ʼ

He next said something that I did not understand, and asked that he might borrow something from us for a year and two months. It was not a solid thing that he desired, but rather something immaterial, so that at first I grew afraid, believing that he asked me for my Soul. He reassured me, telling me he asked for nothing save the mere Idea of me, for which he had some use I could not fathom, and this only for a little time. Even on this, my death day, I am yet unable to make out how the Idea of me might be of value, or to whom.

He promised in return that he would tell us how to call up Imps and have their conversation and obedience. Further to this, he promised that we should not feel the flames of Hell or punishment.

I am not certain how the piece of parchment was obtained whereon we made our marks in blood to seal the bargain. For a time I thought our visitor himself produced it, though from where I cannot think since he was naked. Now it seems to me as if it may have been there in my room a while before he came, forgotten until on that night we chanced upon it. He insisted that we sign in blood, saying that every human function and its fluid are possessed of awesome power, attractive to those spirits who do not themselves possess a body and thus find such substance novel. Going on from this, he said that we might let such Imps as we should summon suckle on the juices of our sex, which would placate them, causing them to favour us. He said this without any wickedness, as if to him there was no shame in such an act, although I blushed, as did my Mary when I told it to her.

What it was that happened next I cannot say. In my confession I have said the Black-Faced Man came with us both to bed, and had his way with us, and this is very like what did occur, but in another sense of things from that we are accustomed to. I am not sure that he was ever there in bed with us as we ourselves were there, in flesh, or that the things we thought he did with us we did not, after all, do to each other. Yet both of us felt him there with us in that delirious shift and tangle, that intensity of presence nothing like a man which pushed inside us, ice-cold yet exciting.

We were outside of time with him. Our bed was every bed where man or woman ever birthed or fucked or died. When Mary licked my bottom she could see a curious flower of light spread out from it so that we laughed, but in our thoughts his voice said to us, ` See this Rose of Power. There is one set beside each of the body's gates,' whereupon we became more sober.

When we reached our Joy there was a moment unlike anything where all the world was gone, nor ever had been there, but instead only the most perfect whiteness, and we were the whiteness, and we were each other made sublime, and we were nothing. Afterwards, if there could truly be an afterwards of such a thing, we slept until the morning when we woke to find ourselves alone with a dead candle and a bloodied parchment.

Now my arms and shoulders are aflame. Beside me, under Mary's skirts, I hear the hiss and sizzle of her scorching love-hair; secret, holy animal badge of our kind. How glorious it must look now, feathered with splendid fires and like a vision. I would rub my face upon it, drench my chin with sparks instead of spittle. I would worship it. I would adore it. Still there is no pain.

The things we were accused of, that we did, in scarce more than a year, kill fifteen children, eight men and six women with our diabolic art; that in like manner did we also rid the world of forty pigs, a hundred sheep and thirty cows, which by my reckoning suggests that we bewitched three beasts a week. Also, there were some eighteen horses that I had forgot. All about Oundle, and as far as Benefield and Southwick, not an ant was stepped upon without it being held that we were by some means responsible for the poor mite's demise. When they had quite run out of murders to accuse us of, they took to listing our more minor sins, establishing that we were bedfellows and also ' partners in knitting', which gave us much cause for merriment.

What was it that we knitted with our wax and clay, our little pins? If I am honest, most of it was little else but selfish entertainment, though as we came to know more of the Superior Realm it touched us, that we were both made more reverent. Yet still we giggled, bent above our knitting, and we cast off curse and charm in endless rows, and purled word into wonder.

Would that we might tell the half of it, the Imps we called and many higher creatures of that kind beside. As I have said before, the ease of it is frightful, if one is but shown. We had four kinds of Imp bound to our call, all of a different usefulness and colour. Some of them were intricate and red, and these had knowledge of both Art and diverse other matters. Some were dun, and shaped like decorated eels, or else like torsos that had tails, and though they did not seem so clever as the others, in their swim and flicker we could hear each other's thoughts, and on their ripples send our dreams across the world.

Some Imps were black, with shiny skin wherein was All of things reflected, as within a mirror. These were shaped like men, though smaller by a measure, and were used for prophecy, or seeing from afar. Gleaming upon their brow we saw the dark time gone before, and knew the days of falling fire to come writ on their ebon bellies.

The white Imps were like ferrets, or perhaps like slender cats with tiny hands like those of aged men, and something of an old man's face about their features also. These had no purpose save for harm. We did not use them. Not that often, anyroad.

The thing with Imps is that they must be given work to do at all times, lest they should grow bored with mortal company and take their leave. It is moreover only right they be rewarded for each task, which bounty me and Mary would dispense flat on our backs there in the chalk ring with our frocks up and our knees apart. After we'd done it, we were always tired. We could not see them as they lapped between our thighs, but only sometimes feel them, sucking on our little buttons.

(On that miserable night when Billy Boss and Jacky Southwel, Constables the pair of them, were sent for us, we were examined. All the men there present looked upon those little buttons, where we said our Imps had suckled us, and seemed very amazed, as if they had not seen such things before. Describing them, they said they were like teats or pieces of red flesh there in our privy parts. I pity their poor wives, if wives they have.)

Apart from Imps, we called up creatures of a great peculiarity, that are like monstrous dogs, sometimes called Shagfoals. They have burning eyes, and some are very old. They live near crossroads, or at bridges, where things have a choice to them and where the veil between what is and what is not grows worn and threadbare, rending easily.

These have a kind of pup, much smaller and more hideous to behold, being both black and blind, with long and questing tongues. Their presence puts an air of fear about things, but this thickens into an exquisite, shocking pleasure if they should be touched. We sent a pair of them to Bessy Evans when she said she had no fun in life, and look at all the thanks we got.

I still remember it, that morning stood in her front yard with Mary, Bessy going on about her John and how he hadn't touched her for a year, and slept off in a different room away from her. We said she was a fool to live so wretchedly, at which she asked us if we would send something to her that would do her good. We swore to do our best, and that next morning when we met with her she seemed a different woman, telling us how in the night she dreamed two things like moles had come into her bed and suckled at her lower parts, both front and back, which she informed us was both somewhat frightening, and yet at once agreeable. Later, when she gave evidence against us, she swore that these nightly visits made her so afraid she had to send for Mr Danks the Minister, who came up to her room on several evenings, where they prayed together that the creatures might be banished.

Four nights! By her own admission, that's how long the thankless cow took pleasure with our subtle pups before she thought to call a Minister, and only then because we would not send them any more and she desired a man up in her room to take their place. Four nights!

I'll tell you this, though mostly I like men the least, there's times I care for women not at all. When I think of the things we did for them in sympathy because they shared our sex, and how they all rushed to accuse us once the chopper fell. When they had muffins in their ovens and were yet unwed, or if they thought their man was bedding with another, then it was a different story. Then it was all `Nell, get rid of it for me', or `Mary, make her fatter than a pig and bring him back'. We cured their babies of the croup and charmed warts into being on the cocks of faithless men. We sent blue gems of light to ease their cramps when they were bad and gave them scripts to ward off those who rape and rob. We raved and prophesied and read the future in their turds.

But did we kill?

I think we did. Old Mother Wise at least and, yes, perhaps the Ireland boy. I cannot say we did not mean to, for we surely did when we called our enchantments down, but for my own part I regret it now. Anger, resentment, spite and all such common worldly moods are dangerous luxuries that one who works the Art cannot afford. They will return to you, like starving dogs. They will eat everything.

With Mrs Wise, it was because she would not sell us buttermilk, though there was more to it than that. For one thing, she kept company with all the rat-jawed village wives that called us whore, and shared in that opinion with them, this because Bob Wise, her husband, put his hand inside my bosom and was kissing me when he got drunk the Plough Day before last.

It is funny now I think of it: he was dressed up for Plough Day in the costume of the Witch Man, as somebody always does each year. His face was painted black, and he had twigs and branches tied about his head like horns, for such is the tradition. I asked him if he was wearing horns because his wife was in the hay with someone else, to which he answered that he did not care where she might be so long as he had me instead, and after kissed me on the mouth and grabbed my tit a little while. Though he was stout and coarse and nowhere near so tall, why did I not think of Bob Wise's fancy dress when first we fetched the Black-Faced Man? What is the meaning of this similarity, and why have I not thought upon it until now?

No matter. When his wife refused to give us buttermilk she called me all the harlots underneath the sun into the bargain, so that I grew angry and remembered all the times I'd walked between the stalls at Oundle Market with their shrieks and jibes still ringing in my burning ears and me too scared and full of rage to answer back. I stormed home, coming into Mary's room to wake her like hundred of bricks in high wind, and I was so cross that for a time she could not make out anything I said. When I was made a little calmer, I prepared an effigy of wax that was stuck full with pins, and Mary called a white Imp like a stoat with baby's hands that answered to the name of Suck-My-Thumb, or sometimes, when it fancied, Jelerasta. This appeared, talking at times in English but more often in a tongue we thought was Greek. It supped the nectar from the Rose of Light at Mary's loins and next was charged with the delivery of those hurts bound into my tallow mannequin, pierced like a martyr, almost lost from sight inside a hedge-pig ball of nail and bodkin. This was in the afternoon.

That evening, Widow Peak came by to visit. Though her husband's name was Pearce she is called Widow Peak because her hair has gone back at the sides just as it does with men in later life, to make a point in front. She had come in to ask if we might give her luck with men in the New Year, this being New Year's Eve, but though we wrote a charm for her she would not leave, and was still sitting with us when our door blew open as the church clock chimed for midnight. Suck-My-Thumb came in, returned from where he had been sent, and slid across the floor to leap in Mary's lap, where he enjoyed the warmth and scent.

The widow gazed in fascinated terror at the Imp and then would look away as if she was not sure just what it was that she could see, or even if she could see anything at all. It made us smile to see her so discomfited, since she had long outstopped her welcome, and I think that Mary hoped to frighten her off altogether when she said, pointing to me, ' See there, the witch that's killed old Mother Wise by making first a doll of wax, then sticking it with pins!' Widow Peak left soon after this, and we both laughed at it, and did not think that there were far more prudent things we might have said.

We learned next day that after taking leave of us the widow had gone straight across to Mother Wise's house, first-footing, where she found the woman to be in great pain, so that she very shortly after midnight died of it, God rest her mean and disappointed soul. I do not feel so bad for her as I feel over little Charlie Ireland, who I think we killed the week before.

The two deaths were not unconnected. In the case of Mrs. Wise, Mary made use of Suck-My-Thumb when my wax doll and pins would no doubt have made short work of the job alone. She did this, and indeed was glad to do it so that she might find work for the Imp and keep him happy, for it is a fact that Imps will stray or become snappish if they are not ever in employ, which exercise appears to make them stronger. Being stronger they demand more work, and so on. Once you've called them up, it is a difficulty knowing what to set them to, week after week.

Mary had first called Suck-My-Thumb a little prior to Christmas, when like me with Mrs. Wise she was caught in a fit of temper. This had been brought on by Charlie Ireland who, with other lads his age, would hang about in Southwick village, where we often walked. Mary had gone to Southwick looking for a ham that we might boil up for our dinner, and on coming out the butcher's was surrounded by a gang of boys, with Charlie Ireland at the head of them. Urged by his fellows, he called her an old witch and a whore and asked if she would gobble on his winkle for a farthing.

I have never seen her in a mood so bloody as when she got home that night. She did not speak a word, but went into her room where first, after a silence, I could hear her making noises as if she were frigging off, and then could hear her talking in a low voice, though to what I did not know. Some time went by before she would open the door, at which she was revealed stood naked with the sleek white weasel creature whispering in French as it coiled there about her heels, before next darting from the room and thence the house, gone from our sight.

We did not see the Imp again that night, and Mary told me that she had instructed it to journey up the dark and empty lanes and find the Irelands' house in Southwick, where it was to worry at the boy's insides, afflicting them with gripes and pains. The thought of his discomfort took the edge from off her wrath, and both of us believed that was the last of it until the evening after, when the baby-fingered creature came once more to us.

It paced and chattered in a multitude of tongues before our hearth, and seemed at first to sulk and then become enraged when we did not set work for it to do. It glared at us with hateful eyes or tugged our skirts with hot, soft little hands and would not leave despite our pleas and our commands that it should do so. Next it started up to rail at us in English, when it told us that we must now call it Jelerasta, and that it would not permit us sleep until we found a task in keeping with its nature.

In the small hours of the morning, with my spirit at its lowest, I begged Mary to contrive an errand for the beast lest I go mad and, weakening to see my weakness, she consented. Suck-My-Thumb (or Jelerasta) was once more sent out to nibble on the bowels of the unlucky child and, as we later heard, cause him to utter noises like a dog. When on the next night following the creature came to visit us again it was more big and more persistent, leaving us no choice but to direct it once again to Southwick and the Ireland home.

This time it came back almost straight away, within the hour, and seemed both furious and vexed. It told us, sometimes falling into other languages out of exasperation, that the parents of the child, no doubt advised by interfering busybodies, had filled up a stone jar with the boy's pee into which they had dropped pins and needles made of iron before they buried it beneath their fire-hearth. Suck-My-Thumb, for reasons that the Imp could not explain, was stopped from going in the house by this protection, and had so returned to us to keep us up all night with horrid tweaks and tugs and foreign phrases of complaint.

Next day, we both went bleary and contrite to see the mother of the boy, where we confessed our crime and begged her dig the bottle up and give us it which, foolishly, once we had promised that her son would afterwards be left uninjured, she agreed to do. That night the white Imp Jelerasta killed Charles Ireland in his bed while we slept sound as newborn babes. We used the pins and needles that we'd found inside the jar of piss to see to Mother Wise that following week, whereafter Suck-My-Thumb seemed satisfied, so that we have not seen him since that time.

Those were our murders. Those I will lay claim to, but no more. We did not kill the Gorham child, nor strike the Widow Broughton lame because she had denied us peasecods. No more did we strike down John Webb's carthorse when he said that we were witches, for his horse died long before we first met with the Black-Faced-Man. We were not witches then, nor were we called as such, but only whores. Aside from that the horse was old and rotting where it stood. Who would exhaust themselves by using Sorcery to kill it, when a strong wind would as well suffice?

Mind you, when Boss and Southwel came to call on us we readily confessed to all these things, as if we had a choice in it. They shoved us both about and made us cry and told us that if we did not confess we should be killed, whereas if we would own to 'Lizbeth Gorham's murder and some others we should be set free. Though we did not believe the last part of their promise, we believed the first and so made full account of all our deeds, both real and otherwise.

In time there was a sort of Trial, though so great was the bad opinion raised against us, with Bob Wise and Charlie Ireland's mother wailing from the gallery, its outcome was made plain before it had begun, whereafter matters were concluded with an undue haste and we were taken to Northampton Gaol there to await our burning.

By that time, we had not any reason to pretend, nor call our Power to rein, and while we were locked up we cursed and laughed both day and night, and brought about the most alarming scenes.

There was an afternoon when visitors were let into the gaol to see the sights; to thrill and shudder at the inmates in their wretchedness. A man called Laxon and his wife had come especially to view the famous witches who were to be burned. Both of them stood some time outside our cell and, though the husband had not much to say, his wife was full of good advice. She made some very pious talk about the error of our ways, and told us that our situation proved the Devil had deserted us as he did all who followed him.

It may be easily imagined that I soon was tired with Mrs Laxon's counsel, and so had recourse to mutter certain names and abjurations in the Angel Tongue, so that with but a minute or so passed the woman's skirts and smock began to rise into the air, though both she and her husband made loud cries and tried to stop them floating upwards in this manner, until all her clothing was turned inside out above her head and she was shown in all her nakedness. Both me and Mary laughed to see this, and I told the woman that I'd proved she was a liar.

Some days after, we were still in fits about the look on Mr Laxon's face, and kicked up such a noise it brought the Keeper of the Prison to our cell, who threatened us with irons. We said the Gorgo and the Mormo at him, after which he was compelled to tear off all his clothing and dance naked in the prison yard an hour or more until he fell exhausted with the foam dried white upon his lips.

We had our fun, and at the end of it they fetched us out and burned us both to dust. They had a stronger Magic. Though their books and words were lifeless, drear and not so pretty as our own, they had a greater heaviness, and so at last they dragged us down. Our Art concerns all that may change or move in life, but with their endless writ they seek to make life still, that soon it shall be suffocated, crushed beneath their manuscripts. For my part, I would sooner have the Fire. At least it dances. Passion is not strange to it.

I look about and see that it is later, and the sky is dark now, when not long ago it was the morning. Where have all the crowd departed to? Mary and I are almost gone; a sullen, powdered glower amongst the cooling ash. Tomorrow, little girls will dance between our ribs, the bowed bones charred and heaped like pared-off nails from dirty giants. They will sing, and kick up grey and suffocating clouds of us, and if the wind should blow our fragments into someone's eye, why, then there may be tears.

The embers wink out, one by one. Soon, they are gone. Soon, only the Idea of us remains. Ten years ago in the laburnum field we look into each other's eyes and hold our breath. A beetle ticks, down in the grass. We're waiting.

THE SUN LOOKS PALE UPON THE WALL
AD 1841

Novr 17 Wednesday — Awoke in mine and Pattys house at Northborough felt very fearful yet cannot say why or what about — I call it house for it is not a home to me & cant be called one — in the morning wrote a letter off to Mr Reid in Alloa & asked if he would loan me some of his Scotch Papers — having never had perusal of a Newspaper for some years I'd be very grateful for some entertaining incidents or literary News but if he will be good enough to send it me I do not know — in with my letter to him I enclosed a Song that is intended for Child Harold but I think it is not much of one and I may leave it out weather is very bad — all ˋvapour clouds and storms' that puts a melancholly light on things so I must make a struggle & buck up if I am not to feel as abject as when I was held at Matthew Allens Prison in the Forest — went a walk down by the old Brook in the afternoon and thought of Mary for in Truth I think of no one else although my new wife Patty Turner & our children are all kind to me — I am a lucky man that has two wives but I confess that I am worried not to hear from Mary for so long — I have not seen her for about a twelvemonth nor did she reply since last I wrote to her when I arrived in Northborough last July after my bold escape & walk of what they tell me is near 80 miles — I fear she has forgot me while I was in High Beech and was sad to come upon our secret Place there by the Stream where first we sat when we were young and in the Spring of Life some 30 years ago — the Hawthorn bush we played beneath is overgrown now so that I could not see which it was & yet I had a fancy that my First Wife might have lost some token when loves rapture thrilled us under its dark canopy those many years before — a Lace or Buckle I might chance upon if I but pulled aside the tangled branch & twig to look yet when I tried all that I did was step up to my knee in cold wet bog and poked my eye upon a thorn so that it wept and made me nearly blind — the Light was poor beside so that the Sun was silver through the smoke from off the Fields & looked more like the Moon — I limped back to the cottage with my boot soaked through and some pain in my foot where I am still quite lame since I wore that bad Shoe with half the sole hung off while on my Walk from Essex — Patty had been out about her cleaning work & being tired had little Sympathy for me when she came back — I told her I had looked for Marys buckle in the Hawthorn by the Brook & hurt my eye but she was cross & woud have none of it & started on her old tales about how She was my only Wife with me and my sweet Mary never wed at all to hear Her tell it — She said that she did not want to hear about the brook nor what Mary & I had done there & if I had hurt my eye it was my own fault poking in the hedgerow while I might be out and earning wages when we were so poor — I grew indignant telling her that I had written some time back to Matthew Allen asking what has happend to the yearly sallary my daughter Queen Victoria had promised me for I was told that the first quarter had commenced before last haytime else I dreamed it so — here Patty wept and became vexed without a reason much as Women do & said a hateful thing of Mary I shall not write in these pages — next She said that she would not live like this for much longer & that come this Friday we must ride into Northampton Town to see a place she thought would suit me better than my time in Essex at which mention I coud feel a heavy stone of anguish sink inside me — would have asked her more but in a fierce & stormy temper she stamped off to bed so that I am left here alone to write these words by weak and yellow Lamplight spilling down from off the shelf above the table — so I am to be put back in an asylum for there is no other place within Northampton they would think me suited to — Well that is it then & it cant be helpd yet I am sorry when I think of all the walking that I did on my escape from High Beech only to discover still another prison here at home — I can recall the Sunday in July when I was freed from my incarceration for a little while to walk in Epping forest where I fell in with some travelling folk who I took to be gypseys such as I once livd with in my youth but these were of another type that dressed in reeking fur & cowskin with their hair unshawn and with barbaric paint marks on their faces — it seems strange now when I think of it yet did not seem so then — I got on readily enough with this rough company & they confided in me that they had but lately been bereaved laying to rest a travelling woman of their order in a Grave between the trees — they told me that she had been troubled by a bad foot & looked at me very queerly when they said these words so that I felt afraid but not for any reason I can say — after a time they pointed out to me a sallow & unhappy idiot boy that skulked at the far edges of their camp where other travelling childern cruelly made to drive him off with stones He wept and made a piteous yelp each time they caught him on his shin & my companions told me that this was the halfwit son of she they had so lately put beneath the soil who coud not keep himself nor work towards the common good & so was banished now he had no Mother to look out for him – I knew a great pang in my heart towards the boy but soon he ran from sight between the spreading summer oaks & was thereafter never spoken of according to the harsh & brutal code by which such people live though I confess we in our Towns and Villages are not so very different nor less keen to make an outcast of a man – one of the Gypseys seemed to take a shine to me and offered to assist in my escape from out the mad house hideing me there in his camp – this seemed to me a good enough idea so that I was decided but informed him that although I had no money I woud get him fifty pounds if he woud help me get away before next Saturday to which he readily agreed – I am not properly decided on what happened next – sometimes it seems to me as if all of my meetings with the Gypsey took place upon that single Sunday afternoon while other times I can recall a whole week passing with me going back there on the Friday where I found my new friend seeming less than eager to pursue our plan so that I did not speak much of it & went back there two days later when I found their camp deserted and they were all gone – whether these things occurred throughout a week or on a solitary afternoon I do not know but either way it was agen a Sunday when I stood between the sighing trees and only had a burnt & blackened circle on the grass to say my Gypsey friends had ever been there save an old wide awake hat and a straw bonnet of what they call the plumb pudding sort – I put the hat into my pocket thinking that it might prove usefull for another oppertunity which with God's Will it so turned out to be – the hour is late & I am tired with all this writing – Patty is surely asleep by now and if I take care I do not disturb her getting into Bed then we shall have no quarrels – She is good to me despite her wicked tongue yet when I lie beside her I wish it were Mary Clare instead, who once was Mary Joyce I am a fool & so to bed

Novr 18 – Thursday – Did nothing

Novr 19 — Friday — Last night I had a dream where I returned to Northborough and found it empty with my cottage all deserted and my first wife Mary gone — Next in the dream I was married agen and living in the rushes by a river with my new Wife Patty Clare who once was Patty Turner & our childern although in the queer style that things have in dreams it was as if my second wife & childern all were ducks with dark eyes and green feathers until in my sleep I cried out loud and startled them so that they flew away from me across the fens & when I woke my face was wet with tears — went in a carriage to Northampton with my Second Wife & our Son John who at but fifteen years is quite the little man   dressed very smart & with a grave expression — I was proud of him & yet it tickled me to see him take his Mothers arm when we climed down from out the carriage for he played the Husbands part far better than did I myself — there was a bitter drizzle all about the town that hung suspended like an old grey sheet above its meadows yet I loved it still — There is a call this County has and when I was away from here in Mr Allens prison then I knew it well & heard its sweet voice that sang out to me across the fields & miles between us and my Heart was stirrd — though I have lived in Essex and have visited in London on no less than four occasions still my home is here & I do not forsee that I shall ever have the Strength to leave agen nor yet the will to do so — the Town is much changed since I last came here and is not so like the fond imaginings of it I had in my confinement with the Norman Castle little more now than a pile of stones and much of the surrounding common land fenced & enclosed — the fine old Churches though are well but many of the fanciful grotesques about the stonework of St. Peters are destroyed — I wanted to walk up to Sheep Street there to see its wonderful round church but Patty became tired & so made do with sitting on the steps between the pillars at All Saints instead at last went to an Inn to have some bread & cheese & half a pint of Ale I do not now recall its name but it sat at the top end of a lane where Bears were kept and was not far off from the round Church of the Holy Sepulcher — there was much boisterous talk around the Tavern of a folly built nearby in Kings Thorp where the road goes out to Boughton and a Mine was drilled into the Earth with hope of finding coal — it seems the Engineer was something of a rogue & had left bits of Coal about the Pit for men to find so that he might then sell his shares at better Profit — I am not surprised at this for Men of Trade are ever Cheats & Liars such as Edward Drury come from Stamford and the Publisher John Taylor who between them owe me close to fifty pounds that I have not forgot for all they say my wits are ailing — in the afternoon when I might no more put it off we went a walk to the Asylum on the Road to Billing & I must confess that it looks well enough for such a Place with old walls of brown stone that have a rustic look & that the trees beyond have overgrown though in the rain it had a dismal air — we met a Mr Knight who was in my opinion a most serious fellow showing me much sympathy for all the questions I was asked — he seemd most interested in my First Wife & asked when I had last seen Her to which I replied that we had been together but a year ago in Glinton whereupon he said Now come that cannot be when you have been four Years in High Beech at which I became confused and muddled in my Thoughs & so he let me Be he talked with Patty for a Time alone while John & I walked in the Grounds — we Stood together & we held each other by the hand and both said Nothing looking over the asylum land down to the silverd ribbon of the Nene and all the Villages Beyond — after a short time Patty joined Us saying that it was arranged & that there woud be found a place for me within a month whereat I was Dismayd yet made to seem that I were pleasd for Pattys Sake and for the Boy — they say that I may go out walking when I Like & that I shall not be a prisoner such as they made me there in Essex so perhaps it may not be so Bad though we shall see and in the mean time put as Brave a face on things as Fortune will allow — as we rode back to Northborough we did not speak of much and so I sat and gazed out from the carriage window on the darkning fields where I heard come the brief sore throated screaming of a Jay somewhere above the blackend stubble — we passed by an Inn where Men were Singing a lewd ballad & though Patty made a fuss and scolded little John for listening it made me smile — When I made my escape from High Beech on that Tuesday in July I took the route suggested by my friend the Gypsey though I soon went wrong and missed the lane to Enfield town and so found myself on the Enfield highway where I came upon an Inn much like the one that mine and Pattys carriage passed tonight save that the Public House there on the Enfield highway was more silent and more queer in its appearance — when I saw it first I took it for an empty Ruin with its roof caved in but on approach I soon saw that it was a Tavern good as any in the land its name upon the hanging sign was The Labour in Vain which seemd peculiar to my ear and those I have since asked of it say they have never heard of such a Place – as I passed by A person that I knew was comeing out the door this being the young Idiot boy I had seen driven from the Gypsey camp – he had an ugly Wound upon one knee that looked as though it had turned bad & so thick was his speech I coud not understand the half of it but when I asked what Way it was to Enfield he would point and gesture so that I shoud know his meaning and I walked on filled with cheer and confidence – so came at last by the York Road to Stevenage before the fall of dark – I climed a paddock gate & then some paleings to a yard where was a Hovel with trussed clover piled up for my Bed – I lay myself down with my head towards the North so that I might not lose my bearings when I woke yet slept but fitfully and had uneasy dreams – I thought My first wife lay there at my side her head at rest on my left arm and then it seemed that in the night she was took from me so that I awoke in much distress to find her gone yet as I woke I heard someone say `Mary' though I searched and there was nobody about and so I thanked God for his providence in finding me a bed if not a meal & once more struck out to the North it was a short while after seven when we got home to the cottage & so very dark and young John went straight up to bed beside his brother and it was not long before Patty & I had fallen to another quarrel over Mary – I think none the less of Her for what she says for I well know that she is tired and at her Wits End from my Antics but her words are nonsense to me – she Says John will You not see you never married her but only knew her when she was a girl and then it is Why do you Say she is your Wife when you have none but me & so forth & so forth until my poor head is fair spinning and once more she takes herself away to bed without me and Im left with nought save yellow light and yellowd pages for my solace but there is none – there is none

Novr 20 – Saturday – very morose all day & so did little save to look once more upon the song I Sent to Mr Reid which now seems better to me than when last it was reviewd

I think of thee at early day
& wonder where my love can be

& when the evening shadows grey
O how I think of thee
Along the meadow banks I rove
& down the flaggy fen
& hope my first & early love
To meet thee once agen

there is more to it but I am most pleasd about the openning — I must
press on and see Child Harold is compleat before I am confined for
I know not how else it shall be finished — in the afternoon I went
agen a walk across the common and down by the Brook for all I knew
that it woud make me melancholly & thought more upon the great
unfairness that there is in life where Men are frownd on for their lowly
station yet are more reviled if they shoud seek to rise above it — when
I was in Helpstone it was Johnny Head up in The Clouds & when I
thought myself superior to the common hord by virtue of a true Poetic
nature they would laugh at Me for what they said was my pretense
— and yet when I become more popular and would be calld to Read
before Gentility then being done I woud be sent to eat down in the
Servants hall so that it seems I may not be at peace in any one rank
of Society and thus I am nowhere at home — even my Marys parents
set agenst me & it seems to me they thought that I was too low born
to walk out with their daughter being of the better off variety — they
made pretense to other reasons why I should not meet Her & made
out as if I had done something wrong but I think now it was no more
than spitefull Pride that made them swear she would not see me and
thereafter keep the two of us Apart never agen to meet but then when
were we wed I cannot tell — my Memory is bad & I am muddled often
in my wits I will not think about it now — when I woke up that Second
morning of my journey and continued north I had gone but a little
way before there on the left side of the road I saw a hollow underneath
the bank much like a cave where were a man and Boy coiled up asleep
there as though inside an open grave — I hailed them at which they
awoke like Lazarus and for a time I thought the boy to be the HalfWit
driven from the Gypsey camp that I had last seen at the Labour
In Vain for in truth they both looked very much alike and yet the

more I looked the more I was not sure and so said nothing — man was older with an unkempt look and when I asked my way he spoke with something of an accent such as people have in Derbyshire telling me that the village to the North of there was Baldeck whereupon I thanked them and so hurried on — it seemed to me there was a smell of burning hung about the pair as if their clothes were full of smoke but this was more than like my fancy & I did not meet the two of them agen — I walked on for a while & some where on the London side I found a Public house they called the Plough where I was thrown a penny by a man in a Slop frock on horseback that I might buy half a pint of beer — I was not so lucky later on when I passed by two drovers who were saucy and unkind — one of them had a great pot belly with both of them very threatning in their manner so that I resolvd I woud not beg a Penny more from any one that I might chance upon — I travelled on through Jacks Hill which is nothing but a beer shop and some houses on a hill appearing newly built & saw a milestone saying I was more than Thirty miles from london — milestones passed by quickly early in the day but as the night drew on they seemed to be stretched far asunder & so I went on through many Villages I can not now recall although in Potton I met with a country man who walked with me until I had to stop and rest upon a flint heap near the roadside — I was hopping with a crippled foot where gravel had got in my shoe from one of which I had now nearly lost the Sole — here my companion had a coach to meet and soon made his farewells then walked on passing out of sight — after a time I followed weak and hungry hoping that I soon might find a place to sleep but it was not to be & I walked lonely past the lighted houses that were in the dark and saw the cheery scenes inside that near to made me weep as I passed by them starved and friendless — soon I did not know if I was walking North or south so that a hopelessness came over me & I was half convinced I headed back to High Beech and my gaolers until through the wayside trees I glimpsed a light bright as the moon that when I neared turned out to be a lamp hung on the Tollgate there at Temsford where a man who had a candle came outside and eyed me narrowly he told me that when I was through the Gate I shoud be headed north and so it was that I continued in more cheer and even some of my old strength about me while I hummed the air of Highland Mary — not long after I came to an odd house all alone and near a wood — it had a sign I could not read that stood oddly enough inside a kind of trough or spout & yet the house itself seemd stranger being more a monstrous hut of clay and reeds the like of which I have not seen before — there was a kind of porch over the door that being weary I crept in and glad enough I was to find I could lye with my legs straight — the inmates were gone to roost for I could hear them turning over in their beds as I lay at full length upon the stones there in the porch & slept sound until daylight when I woke up most refreshed & blessd the Queen for my Good Fortune as I must do now I am in Northborough with Patty and my childern though the one I Long for is not Here

I think of thee at dewy morn
& at the sunny noon
& walks with thee — now left forlorn
Beneath the silent moon

I think of thee I think of all
How blest we both have been —
The sun looks pale upon the wall
& autumn shuts the scene

Novr 21 — Sunday — Did Nothing

Novr 22 — Monday — Resolvd today I woud walk to Northampton by myself to find how easy it might be to visit with my Second Wife and family while I am held in the asylum there — I did not think it woud provide much of an obstacle to one such as myself whos walked so far & I was right enough although I had not counted on this lameness in my leg that made me some what slow — I set out with the dawn before Patty was risen or the children and struck out across the fields that are now bare and frozen hard and so not bad for walking though the look of them is dark & bleak — I passed among the villages and thrilled to see their simple life as it first woke to be about the day with schoolboys running in the lanes & gaunt young Greyhounds out to course for Hare there in the woodgrass coverts — in the pastures to my Left I saw some Gypseys though they did not seem the type that I had met in Epping forest nor the kind that I met after That upon the Highway when I woke that Thursday morning outside Temsford I stood up and walked a few yards off from the stone porch where I had made my bed the night before yet when I turned to look back at the strange house made of rush and clay where I had shelterd it was nowhere to be seen nor was its sign that I had Struggled so to read although I found an old trough with a hole which had a sapling grown up through it & concluded that I may perhaps have seen it as a signpost in the gloom puzzling over this I went on past St. Neots where I rested half an hour or more upon a Flint heap when I saw a tall young Gypsey woman come out from the Lodge Gate up the road and next make her way down to where I sat — she was a youngish woman with an honest countenance and seemd most handsome & about her neck she had a string of old blue beads made from a worn and cloudy kind of Glass I asked her a few questions which she answered readily and with good humour though after a Time I came to think there some thing crafty in her manner as if there were that about her that she must conceal — never the less I walked on with her to the next town having always had a fondness for the company of handsome women and as we were on our way she told me I had best prop up my wide awake hats crown with something and said in a lower voice that Id be noticed which agen made me believe that there was some thing sly and secretive about her so I took no notice & made no reply   at length she pointed to a small church tower which she called Shefford Church and said that I should go with Her along a footway that she knew which was a short cut that might spare a Journey of some fifteen miles — I had by now become afraid she meant to do Away with me if I should follow her from off my path though no doubt this was just my foolish Fancy so I thanked her and said that I feared that I shoud lose my way and not find the North road agen & that I had best keep upon the road at which she bade me a good day and went into a house or shop there on the left hand side   I travelled on and was so faint I have no recollection of the places that I passed save that the road seemed very near as stupid as myself in parts & often I woud lift my head up with A start to find that I was walking in My sleep — the day & Night became as one to me for I coud no more tell the difference twixt one & the other — I was lost to Time so that it often seemd that I was in Another place entire nor hardly knew my own name or yet knew what Year it was — I thought of this as I walked to Northampton now in the November cold — stopped only once to sit upon a stone wall by a Mill and eat some Bread & Cheese I had brought in my pocket to sustain me — with the passing of the day the weather was improved so that the grey clouds broke apart and let the Suns light through to fall upon the field whereat I was made Happy for a time until I found Her name upon my lips,

I cant expect to meet thee now
The winters floods begin
The wind sighs through the naked bough
Sad as my heart within

I think of thee the seasons through
In spring when flowers I see
In winters lorn & naked view
I think of only thee

enough of that I got up most refreshed and headed on towards the town though with my Foot still causing me some pain — it was not difficult to spot Northampton when it came in view ahead for all the smoke hung out like flags on the stiff autumn breeze — I stopped and had a drink at Becketts Well for there Thomas the Martyr that was tried and Sentenced here paused also but with more call for complaint than I and next I went on through the Dern gate into Town — we are all sentenced in our Fashion yet with most of us there is no Trial and we are Judged by measures that we do not know... how can they hail a Man one minute for his Verse and then the next they drop him like a burning coal when he has had his day in favour — Its a puzzle past my wits & it woud take a better Man by far than I to give its answer on the third or forth day of my walk from Essex I do not know which I was so Starvd I ate the grass that grew beside the road to satisfy my hunger which it did & tasted very much like Bread so that it seemed to do me good and I went on in better Spirits than before — after A time I reccollected that I had tobacco but my box of lucifers being exhausted

I had not the means to light my pipe so chewed the stuff instead & swallowed up the quids when they were done after which time I was not hungry — I went on through Bugden and then Stilton where I was so lame I lay me down upon a gravel causeway and went near to sleep & as I did I could hear voices that I took for Angels since at first I did not understand their tongue — One of them that seemed a young woman said poor creature then another one more elderly said O he shams but added next O no he dont As I stood up and limped upon my way — I heard the voices but did not look back & saw no one they came from and so on I went in way of Peterborough and my Home beyond across the summer meadows — I am sat once more about this Journal neath the portico of All Saints on the steps here and I can see down the hill of Gold street where the money lenders have their place & past the Mare fair & Saint Peters spire to where the castle's piteous ruin stands down near the bridge such as it stands at all — after I came to Town by the Dern Gate a little after noon I walked about a while & finding it to be a Market day resolvd to make a visit to that place not far up Drum Lane from the church where I now sit & scribble   in the sunlight all the traders made a cheerful scene with many varied stripes and colours in their awnings and the fruits and bales of bright new linen on display & I wish now I might recall the half of all the things they cried — the shops and houses that are built around the Market square are for the most part new & raised up since the great fire that they Had here when the square was ringed with flame & all the townsfolk made escape by going through the front door of the Welsh house where they pay the drovers come from Wales then got to safety out the back — there is a fine old coach Inn stood upon the square three hundred years now where black tongues of soot may still be seen that lick across the old rubbd stone & I thank God for his great Providence in saving all who were not burnt that day — after a while when I grew weary of the markets bustle I came to the graveyard at the back side of this church and walked amongst the stones a time — I found a marker for Mat Seyzinger the famous coachman on the Nottingham Times who I saw once & who in his day had a great following — there are not people such as once there were neither do folk now have the humour or the depth of character that they had then — Jem Welby overturned his coach before this very church and when asked to explain he said that He had tipped his passengers out in the road to count them No doubt now hed be thought Mad & put away as I myself shall be — Got up to the asylum on the Billing road not long before I heard the Bells chime three o clock where I am sat now by the gate — On my Way here my thoughts were Mary this & Mary that & nothing else but Mary In my fancy I have scolded her for having been so long apart from me & then have begged her to be kind and to forgive me so confused am I in all my feelings — are they right that say we were not Wed — it can not be for I remember on that day we walked down by the brook did She & I and there was all made right & we were married before God — I kneeled with her beneath the Hawthorns canopy where came a very greenish light & said There now this is our Church — why do they try to keep me from Her and tell me such Stories that it is small wonder if I am made Mad O Mary mary why will you not see me for now I am no where unless in Despair — when I walked here from Essex lame & dizzy in the head for want of food through Peterborough I came next to Walton & then Werrington and was upon the highway with my First Wife's home not far ahead so that my heart was light & when I saw a cart that came towards me with a man a woman & a boy in it I thought nought of it yet when it drew close to me it stopped — at this the woman jumps down from the cart & tries to get me into it with her saying O John john dont you know me But I did not know her and so thought her drunk or mad as I — but then the man sat with her says Why john this is your wife & so I looked agen and it was Patty and our son young Charles beside her — though it frightend me I had not known her I was filled with Joy to think I had one Wife with me agen and so might soon have two & thus I bade them take me on to Northborough that I should be by Marys side — we were soon in the sight of Glinton church but Mary was not there neither coud I get any information about her further than the old story of her being dead six years ago but I woud take no notice of this blarney for was it not one year since the broadsheets said that I myself were dead and lying in my grave   or were they right & this is Hell — I beat upon her neighbors doors & said I thought that She was here at which they said Well you thought wrong like Hobs Hog & and they shut me out — I sat upon the step of Marys cott in Northborough & cried while Patty & our son looked on and Said come away John cant you see shes not here — I picked a pebble up from off the path that once perhaps her tender foot had brushed & set it in my mouth & all was lost and Patty got me to the cart — On the way to our house that is called Poets Cottage by the people thereabout Patty sat by me in my weeping and was near in tears herself to see me so undone & all the time was saying Why john what is it that makes you say she was your wife You knew her when you were fourteen years old and she was ten and never saw her after that why do you say it why why why and I dont know and I cant say — I sit here now by the asylum gate and watch the sun grow long upon the tired brown stone whereover slump the boughs as heavy as my Heart — all of it vanishes like dust upon the Wind & nothing is made safe — I rue the dwindling hedgerow and the closed off Land & am made desolate to see the meadows heaped with brick — yet in the Market and the Town the aprons & the awnings hung above the shops are very much like flowers of a different kind & so too will be gone — time shall unravel all of us & now the shadows move on the asylum wall so quick their movement may be seen — I sat beneath the Hawthorn with her afterwards and said There we are married now & made her promis she woud not Tell any one what we had done — I turn and squint to where the light floods from the West like fire & for a moment see that Sweet child stood against it like An angel but it is a sack cloth caught upon the madhouse paleings & I never shall be free agen

While life breaths on this earthly ball
What e'er my lot may be
Wether in freedom or in thrall
Mary I think of thee

I TRAVEL IN SUSPENDERS
AD 1931

I travel in suspenders. Selling 'em, that is, not wearing 'em. That always gets a laugh. You'll often find a laugh will kick things off better than anything, whether you're talking to a client, or young lady. Or for that matter a constable. Do you know, very often in the motor that carries me back and forth from Angel Lane to the assizes I'll make some remark, you know. Just kidding them along, like, as you do. The other day we passed by this young woman in the street and honestly, the face on her, I've never seen one like it. I pointed her out to the young chap that I was handcuffed to. I said, `Ah well, there's no sense looking at the mantel when the fire wants poking.' As you might suppose, that raised a smile. They're human just like everybody else.

I've noticed on the corner just across the street from the assizes there's a Women's WC that backs on to the big church in the middle there, All Saints. It's down some steps and you can only see the staircase curving down and round away from you, with white tiles halfway up the wall. I'd like to know what goes on down there, I can tell you. Just imagine, eh, if you could have a look? I close my eyes and I can see it, with them pulling up their pants across their great big bums. I had dreams once, you know, when I was little, about being in the Ladies' toilets. I was quite a cheeky little monkey even then, you can imagine. There'd be that green muck growing between the tiles and Heaven only knows how it would smell. Like every fanny in the world at once, I'll bet. Now there's a thought. I'll bet you couldn't find a man who hadn't entertained it once or twice if he were honest.

There's a lot of women come to court sat in the gallery. You'd be surprised, some of the looks I get. I shouldn't say myself but I've got quite a following as if I were a blooming Picture Idol, not that I'm bad-looking in the natural way of things. Of course, I mustn't do much to encourage them with Lillian sitting there before the dock each day and mooning up at me. It wouldn't look good, would it, if I were to be seen making eyes at some lass in the back row with my own wife looking on? Not after that commotion with the papers printing what

I said to the police, about how my harem keeps me away from home.

My lawyer Mr Finnemore reckons I put my foot in it with that one, but then he's not what you'd call a worldly man. To my mind, for the greater part the general public have a soft spot for a dashing rogue, and secretly admire a great philanderer. If they'd had half the fun that I've had they'd be glad. Still, it won't do for Lily to seem too much of a martyr so I must take care and not be caught out, flirting from the dock. There's a brunette girl, busty little thing, that sometimes comes in on her dinner break and stands there up one corner looking at me. I should like it if she had suspenders on made by the firm I represent, and since they're not far off in Leicester there's a good chance that she does. You think about it one way, I'm as good as up her skirt already. How about that?

Lillian's already had a lot of sympathy and has been given work down at a shop in Bridge Street here so she can keep herself while she attends the trial. The station where I'm kept in Angel Lane runs right off Bridge Street so we drive up past the shop each morning on my way to court. A little sweetshop as it happens, so it's just the place for a sweet girl like her. Head over heels for me she is and always has been. Never likes to sit upon my knee, which is my favourite way to hold a woman, but in all particulars apart from that she's the best wife I've got.

If I should think, I'll have her bring me up a quarter pound of Menthol Eucalyptus sweets to see if they can ease my throat a bit. All of this giving evidence is making it play up. If I'm not careful I shall have no voice at all before they're done with me, and then where should I be? There's a great many people think me quite the best amateur baritone to sing down at the Friern Barnet Social Club in Finchley, where my 'Trumpeter What Are You Sounding Now' always goes down a treat. I've got a very decent set of pipes on me and shouldn't want a thing like this to muck them up. I know that men in general often take against a chap who has the lighter type of voice, but ladies by and large seem to prefer it. Wouldn't do to talk myself hoarse in the dock and spoil all that now, would it?

He was thrashing like a mackerel, banging on the windshield of my Morris. Not at all a pleasant thing to look at I can tell you, and the noise. You talk about a scalded cat. You'd think he'd be out cold and not know anything about it, but it was the fire. It woke him up. I'll be quite honest, I can hear it now. It wasn't even any words you'd take for English it was such an awful racket. Once he kicked the side door open and I thought, ' Well, that's it, Alf. You've been and gone and done it now.' Only by then of course the smoke and flames were down him and he'd had his lot. He fell down forward over the front seat with one leg out the car, and that was it. Of course, Joe Soap here stood downwind and didn't have the sense to move until my eyes were streaming. What a sight we must have been, the pair of us.

I saw the picture of my Morris Minor that they printed in the Daily Sketch and could have wept. Baby saloon it was, and not that old. I had the thing insured for one hundred and fifty pounds but don't expect to see a big return from it, things being what they are. Judging from what it looked like in the photograph there wasn't much left of the blessed thing. The mud-guards were all thrown about like ribs and you could see where all the rubber had poured off the wheels to leave the rims bare. If I ever catch them chaps that stole it, but then no, hang on, that wasn't true, was it? I made that up. It's such a job sometimes, just keeping track of everything.

That was the worst thing about keeping up two wives at once, apart from all the cost involved. It was a strain remembering my story sometimes, I can tell you. All the fiddling little details. Which one I'd told what. With Lillian it wasn't quite so bad because she's rather vague by nature and not so inclined to notice if I should slip up, but Ivy now, well. That's a different matter. It's not six months since I married her and she's already quick to pounce upon the smallest thing.

I married Lil November 1914, so that's more than sixteen year back now. In all that time, if she's had a suspicious thought she's kept it to herself. Even when evidence was put in front of her, such as when I brought her mine and little Helen's baby to look after — not the one that died, the second one, our little Arthur — even then she took it quieter than a mouse and said that she'd forgive me when I hadn't even asked her to. Young Arthur's nearly six now and I'll say this for our Lillian, she's brought him up as if he were her own. She's never shown him any side, not to my knowledge. Like I say, head over heels for me, she is. No questions asked. Hard to believe it's sixteen years. I missed our anniversary this last November what with all the set-to that we had. I'll have one of the coppers pop and get her something, if I happen to remember. Better late than never, that's what I say.

As for Ivy, I don't know if it will last for sixteen months, let alone sixteen years. It seemed a good idea when we were wed in June at Gellygaer, though when I say a good idea I mean that she was four months up the spout by then and showing large already, as the skinny ones so often do. God, though, the tits they get on them. It's almost worth it, having one more mouth to feed so long as you get lovely tits like that to stuff in yours. There now, you see? Another laugh. It's like I say with laughter, it's the best thing that there is to break the ice. Everyone feels that much more comfortable.

But to be serious, with Ivy something told me I was making a mistake from the word go. Not that there's anything about her I don't like, but just that you could tell somehow there'd be a lot of fuss involved. You take the last time that I saw her, when I went across to Wales that night directly after my `funny five minutes' out at Hardingstone. Now, as you might imagine, I was in a dreadful tizzy, having lost the car. I'd come out of Hardingstone Lane and stood faffing about there by the end and peering back along the path to watch the two men who had seen me leave the field. I couldn't spot them in the dark, although my Morris was still blazing, out across the hedgerows.

You know how it is at times like that. You feel that everything you do must look suspicious, although half the time you'll find nobody notices. I went and stood beside the London Road up near the old stone cross they've got there, where Queen Eleanor was set down on her funeral procession back to London, and it wasn't long before I'd thumbed a lorry down, on its way to that very place. I spun a yarn about a lift I'd missed from some well-off old chum who drove a Bentley, and the lorry driver was soon taken in. He drove me to Tally Ho Corner on the Barnet Road and we arrived there about six as it was getting light.

I told a fellow at the Transport Office there that my own car had been pinched from outside a coffee stall because to tell the truth by then I was quite dozy and forgot that rot I'd said about the Bentley. Still, I've got a way with people, there's a lot of folk have said it, and this bloke was no exception. Put me on a coach, the nine-fifteen for

Cardiff, so that I arrived there in the afternoon and caught another bus to Penybryn. I could walk from there to Ivy's house at Gellygaer and got in about eight that night.

Well, as I say, there's always fuss with Ivy. Not that it's her fault, it's just there always is, and that night was no different. First of all I had her father, old man Jenkins, buttonhole me in the passageway and ask why it had taken me so long to get there with his Ivy at death's door with illness and my baby on the way. You know how Taffy Welshman likes his bit of melodrama now and then, and he had Ivy sounding more like Little Nell than anything before he'd done with me. I told him how I'd had my car pinched in Northampton which I dare say I believed myself by then, I'd had to reel it out that often. It's a funny thing, but on my oath, stood in his passage at that moment I'd forgotten everything about that other poor chap and the fire.

After I'd gotten past the dad I had the daughter to contend with. Ivy was propped up on pillows in her room and she looked very bad. The baby was due almost any time. No sooner had I sat down on the bed than she was asking when we should move into our new house in Surrey. To be frank, it caught me off-guard and I looked at her gone out. I'd quite forgotten all the business about Kingston-on-Thames that I'd told her and her dad when I was tipsy at our wedding do. Before I could come up with something good she was in floods of tears and telling me I didn't love her, and how she was sure that I was seeing someone else. Why was I spending all these nights away and so on. You can guess the greater part of it.

They don't consider what you might have gone through, do they? Buy me this and buy me that and let's live somewhere else. Five hundred pounds a year I'm earning now from Leicester Brace & Garter and you might think I'd be well-to-do, but not a bit of it. All of it's gone on kids or women long before I see a penny of it. It's the same old story.

As it stood, although I hadn't mentioned it to Lillian, I'd planned to sell the house and furniture we had at Buxted Road in Finchley so that I could use the cash to get set up with Ivy and the nipper when it came. Now, you can call me what you like, but I've always been softer than I should be when it comes to kids. I'd make a settlement to Lily and young Arthur, naturally.

Of course, I couldn't say all this to Ivy without having her fall wise to Lily and my Finchley set-up, so I acted all offended and made quite a fuss about having my car pinched from outside the coffee shop so that it took me eighteen hours to get to Gellygaer. I find it often works if someone gets upset to act as if you're more upset than they are in return. When you're a smart chap like myself it never fails, and Ivy was soon telling me that she was sorry that she'd had a go at me, and it was just her nerves, what with the baby due and her so poorly. I said, `There now, Climbing Ivy, you can cling to me,' and when she did I put my hand inside her nighty-top and had a feel. Her tit was hard and heavy with the end part stood out like a football stud. I slept in their spare room that night and I was on the bone just thinking of it, even after all the upset I had during supper, with that neighbour and her bloody paper.

If I'm truthful it's my biggest fault, the sex. I'll tell you, half the time I think of nothing else, and when you're on your own a lot like me, driving from place to place, it makes it worse. You spend a lot of time with daydreams when you're up and down the road. Sometimes I'll have to pull in at a lay-by for a fiddle just so I can think of something else but fanny for an hour or two. I've got a catalogue I carry with me in the car with photographs of models in the company range. They're only little pictures with four of them to a page, and you can only see the women from their tummies to the top part of their legs. You'll think I'm crackers but to me they've all got different characters, and things about the way they stand so you can tell what sort of girls they are. Some of them, they're the type you know that you'd get on with, and that they'd have decent personalities.

There's one that I call Monica. If you look close up at the photograph you can see a light sort of fuzz upon her legs, so I imagine her as blonde. The sort of girl you might find working at the counter in a Post Office, wearing her hair the way they have it now, all straight on top and curled up round the back. She'd look nice in light blue. Her belly button is the kind that's more upright than wide, so that it's like a little keyhole in a peach. She's got one of the newer long-line corsets on that seem to flatter women with more slender hips, which to my mind seems a wise choice and shows she's more the thoughtful type who takes a lot of care about her clothes. You can tell just by looking at her skin that she can't be much more than twenty.

That's the age, I'll tell you, when they're fagged out and fed up with younger lads and start to see the older fellow as romantic. If I could have Monica just hear me do 'The Cobbler's Song' from Chu Chin Chow then I could have her drawers down quick as that. Of all my harem, do you know that sometimes I think I like Monica the best? She doesn't cost me anything or get me into trouble. I just shoot off in my hanky, close the catalogue and drive away.

I wasn't always like this, with the women. Ask my Lily and she'll tell you: when she knew me back before the War it was as much as I could bring myself to do to give a kiss goodnight, I was that shy. It wasn't until I'd enlisted in the 24th Queen's Territorials I had the nerve to go up to a girl and ask her out. The uniform, you see. It made a difference, you can laugh now, but it's true. I've heard women go on and on about how terrible it is the way men fight, but once they see the boots and buttons they're all over you. They wave you off then stay at home and send white feathers to the conshies. Half the fellows in those trenches wouldn't be there if not for the way their girlfriends look at them when they're dressed up for war. Deny it if you can.

To be quite honest, Lily was the first girl I'd been out with, although I was getting on for twenty. When she first got me to bed I was that green I lay on top of her with my legs open for a time before I realized what I should be doing. In all honesty it wasn't that successful. Well, I couldn't get it in and ended up feeling that sick about myself, and when Lil said it didn't matter that was worse. We never did it right until about a week after we wed. I mean, we'd rubbed each other off and kissed, but that was all, and when we did finally manage it, it was all over in a flash, though that got better as time passed. All told, though I was no great shakes in bed, I think we were happier then, me and my Lillian. It was a shame that we were never blessed with kids, although I've made up for it since.

Four months together, me and Lily had, and by the end of it the How's-Your-Father, it was smashing. We were that in love, and then, come March in 1915, I was bundled off to France. My God, that was a terror. You don't know until you've been in one. You live in mud and all around there's lads no older than yourself with half their jaw blown off, and you give up on everything bar doing what you're told. I've seen a horse that had no legs lie shuddering in the muckpit like a bloody seal. I've seen men burn.

I'd only been in France two months before I caught the shrapnel at Givenchy. Head and leg. The head was worst, apparently, though Muggins here can't bring to mind a blessed thing about it. Not the moment that it happened or the morning that I'd had before, and not much after. Gone. Clean as a whistle. First thing I knew afterwards was being halfway through a plate of dinner at the hospital. I lifted up a spoon of stringy mash and looked at it, and I remembered that I was Alf Rouse. It was the most peculiar sensation, I can tell you.

I don't have the education to explain it but the world seemed different to me after that. I don't mean that the War had opened up my eyes, like I've heard other fellows say. I mean the world seemed different, like as if it was a different world, a stand-in for the real one. How can I explain it? Everything looked wrong. Not wrong, but put together in a hurry as though it could fall apart at any time. The best way I can say it is like when you're doing art in school, and Miss gives you a sheet of paper first where you can try things out and make a mess, because it's not the proper picture and it doesn't matter. When I woke up in that hospital it was like waking up inside the practice scribble, not the picture. Nothing mattered. You could rub it out and start all over. When I think about it, I suppose I've pretty much felt that way ever since, though now I'm used to it.

That was the point where I first got my `thing' about the weaker sex. Of course, for one thing there was opportunity, what with the nurses they had over there. You wouldn't think to look at some of them, but there was more of that went on than you'd suppose. You see, to all intents and purposes they were the only women over there and they could have their pick. You wouldn't think they'd feel much like it what with seeing chaps half blown to bits all day, but I could tell a tale or two, believe me. Well, of course, I had a twinge of guilt from time to time regarding Lillian, but nothing that would bowl me over. Like I say, by then things had all sort of flattened out, and nothing that I thought or did seemed to amount to very much. I mean, I know there's right and wrong, but you come to a point where, honestly, you're not much bothered.

Once I had this chubby little RSN who sucked me off while there was some poor fellow with no hands lay raving off his chump in the cot next to mine. I played along, but frankly wasn't very struck upon it, if you can believe that. There was something funny with this nurse that put me off, the way she acted. Gone a bit mad, by the look of her. You got a lot like that.

When I was pensioned out the following year and came back home, it didn't ease up on the female front one bit. If anything, it just made matters worse. That was the wound, you see, did that. That's what attracted them. My injury. What I just said, about girls being daft for chaps in uniform, well, that was nothing to the way they were if you were hurt or wore a bandage. Even when the bandages were off, if you just talked about how you were wounded to 'em, that would do the trick. I'd pull my hair to one side so that they could see the scar up by my parting, and I'd let 'em touch it if they wanted to. I'll tell you, ten minutes of that and I was up 'em. They were gasping for it. They're some funny wonders, women. I can't make them out, not after all the ones I've had. It must be getting on for seventy or eighty of them that I've done it with since I took up commercial travelling when I came out the army, but they're still a mystery to me. I expect they always will be, now.

I won't say little Helen was the first girl that I took to bed while on my travels. After all, I'd had five year of it by then, but it was Helen who I came to care about the most. I wanted to look after her. She was a child, when all was said and done, and so she needed looking after. Anyone would do the same, that had a heart.

A little Scottish girl, was Helen. Little servant girl. I used to have her in the back seat of the Morris. There were lots of memories in that back seat. I'm sorry that it's gone. I suppose that when you think about it, she was on the young side, Helen. Only fourteen, but you know the girls these days. Very mature and well developed. If they're old enough to bleed, they're old enough to butcher, that's what I say. Good one, eh? I heard that first when I was in the services, and thought that it was proper comical.

I got her pregnant, but it died soon after it was born, which was an upset at the time. It's like I say, I'm very fond of children. Anyway, I kept on seeing her and two years later, by the time she was sixteen, she'd fallen with another one. Now, Helen, she was only young, but she could be insistent, and this time she put her foot down. Said we must be married for the kiddie's sake, and there wasn't much that I could say to that. I'd told her me and Lily were divorced, you see, so couldn't use the fact I was already wed to get me out of it. It was a pickle, I can tell you.

As it turned out, what I did was go through a sham wedding with her, just to keep her happy, then I set her and baby up at this nice flat in Islington where we could live as man and wife. I told her I'd be on the road a lot away from home. Of course, I'd told Lily the same thing back in Finchley, so it all worked out quite nicely for a time. Still, she wasn't daft, and in the end she got suspicious I was having an affair outside of marriage. What she didn't know of course is that I was and she was it.

It all came out eventually, and my God, but you should have heard the uproar. I don't know quite where I should have been if Lily hadn't been so understanding. She's said all along it's not my fault, me being a sex maniac, and that it's only happened since the War. They both agreed to meet, did her and Helen, after things calmed down, and sorted it all out across the French sponge at a Joe Lyons' corner house. They both thought it was best if Helen's baby, little Arthur, should have somewhere decent to grow up, so me and Lily took him in to live with us at Buxted Road. You can say what you like, there's not a lot of women as would do that for their chap, now is there? Take another woman's baby in and feed it?

She's one in a million, is my Lily. I remember that last night before this all blew up, the last time I saw Buxted Road. We'd sat there in our front room with the lights out, me and Lillian and little Arthur, watching all the rockets and the Roman candles going off just up the road, it being Bonfire Night. I'd told her I'd got business up in Leicester with the braces and suspenders people, so she didn't mind when I set out just after seven to head up the Great North Road towards the Midlands. I let her have one of my extra special kisses by way of farewell, since I was feeling bad about the way things were between us and I meant to leave her.

Pulling out of Buxted Road; I went straight round to Nellie Tucker's. I'm ashamed to say I'd not been round there since she'd had the baby just the week before, so you could say that I was overdue. I can't remember, did I mention Nellie? I took up with her in 1925, during the troubled patch with Helen and our Lily. I was under a great deal of pressure at the time, as you might well imagine, and I turned to Nellie so that I'd have someone I could talk about it to, as much as anything. Naturally, one thing leading to another how it does, it wasn't long before we'd got a baby. Lily would have killed me, so I kept it quiet and paid five pounds to Nelly every month for maintenance. That was all right until she fell again, this last time. Had it the end of October, on the 29th as I remember.

I went round to see her after leaving Lil that night and got round there a little after seven. Both the eldest and the baby were in bed by then, so we could have a quick one on the couch. I felt a bit blue afterwards, the way you sometimes do, and started pouring out my troubles to her, telling her about all of the debt that I was in. She's a good listener is Nellie. Always has been.

How it is with me, I suppose it's like that film A Girl in Every Port. Victor McLaglan. Do you know that one? That was a smasher. Went last year to see it with our Lily, and the women that were in it, well, what a selection. Myrna Loy, she's nice. And Louise Brooks, although to be quite honest I'm not half so keen on her, her hair like that. It looks too lesbian, if you know what I mean. The real star, though, to my mind, it was Sally Rand. You must know Sally Rand. 'The Bubbles Girl'? She danced with fans and these big bubbles, and I have to say that there's a lot of art in what she does. She doesn't wear a stitch beneath those bubbles, yet you never see a thing. Her song was 'I'm Forever Blowing Bubbles', naturally enough. A lovely girl.

I stayed at Nellie's for about an hour and left just after eight. I should have had a pee before I left but anyway I didn't, and so by the time I got past Enfield, heading out St Alban's way, I was near bursting. I saw this pub just set back from the road a bit and thought, 'Well, I've got time for one to brace me for the journey.' Also, I could use their Gents. It's funny, I've been out that way before and though I know most of the pubs up there, this one was new to me. I think it's how you come upon it, round a bend. The first sight that I had of it was when my headlights swung across and caught it, and at first it looked half derelict. They ought to do it up a bit, in my opinion. It'd be money well spent, because set back there from the road I'll bet that most folk overlook it. Had a funny name, as I recall, although I can't think what at present. It'll come to me, I'm sure.

I parked the wagon round the back and went inside, and it was first stop Gentlemen's. God, talk about Relief of Mafeking. It was one of those where the stream seems to go on for hours. Well, I'm exaggerating, but you get the gist. I came out of the W.C. into the bar, and there was hardly anybody in at all. Dead as a doornail.

Labour In Vain. There, what did I just say? I knew it had a funny name. Propped up against the bar was this old tinker with a funny stand-up hat. Quite honestly, he looked half-sharp, so I steered clear of him. I got the girl behind the bar to serve me with a brandy, then I looked about to find a place where I could sit. Up in one corner was a scruffy looking chap, sat talking to this little lad of ten or so. I thought it was his son at first, but then the boy said something to the man and left the bar. He didn't come back, so perhaps he didn't know this other bloke at all; just happened to be sitting with him when I looked. I fancied chatting with another chap to pass five minutes after having women rabbit on at me all day, so when the little lad got up and left I went and sat at the next table to the scruffy item.

We struck up a conversation before long, and I could see he was impressed when I showed him my business card. It turned out he was heading north as well. He'd come from Derbyshire originally, he said, which wasn't a surprise given how thick his accent was. He told me how he'd had a job up at the pits there, but he'd thought that he might make a go of it in London, as so many do, and headed south. You won't be shocked to hear it hadn't worked out how he'd planned, so now he was on his way back to Derby, hoping for his old work at the pit.

They've asked me why I offered him a lift, as if I had some motive for it, and they won't believe me when I say that back then at the start I'd no idea what I was going to do. I said I'd take him up as far as Leicester because I felt genuinely sorry for the chap, and that's the long and short of it. He made a fuss about getting me in another drink before we left, by way of gratitude, and he had one himself which, to be frank, was one too many. From the state of him, he'd had a few before I'd got there, and once we were in the car I didn't get a lot of sense from him. Most of the time he was asleep and snoring.

It might have been a different story if I'd had a bit of conversation like I wanted, just to take my mind off my troubles. As it was, the only company I had was far too sloshed for conversation, so I'd nothing else to do but drive along and brood on things, with him behind me rasping like a saw-mill. I got madder with him as we went along. I mean, there I was in the midst of all my troubles, Nellie's baby born a week before and Ivy's nearly due, and meanwhile there was him snoring like a carthorse, slobbering on my upholstery. I'm not saying that I feel any animosity towards him now, of course not, but it's how I felt about it then.

We drove on up the Roman road towards Northamptonshire, which we came in by way of Towcester. It's a funny thing, what you remember, but I can recall what I was thinking when we passed Greens Norton church spire on our left. I don't know why, but I was thinking back to when I was a little lad and we lived on Herne Hill, just up the road there from the Half Moon Inn. When I was younger I was that inquisitive, how children are. I wanted to know everything. One day, I couldn't have been more than seven, I remember asking Mam about Herne Hill and why they called it that. She said she didn't know, but if I was that bothered I could look it up in Pear's Encyclopaedia, so I did.

I don't know if you ever opened up a book, back when you were a nipper, and you saw a picture that was just so frightening you slammed the book and never dared to look at it again? Well, that was how it was with me. I opened the encyclopaedia to the page I wanted, under H, and there was this old line engraving of this bloke, and he had antlers like a deer growing out from his head. I know it doesn't sound much now but I was terrified. I'd never seen a picture in my life until that point that had upset me half so much, I can't say why.

I shut the book and went and hid it underneath the wardrobe in my parents' room, beneath some copies of Reveille that had ended up there. I wanted to bury it, you see, I was that scared of it. Why I should think of that chap with antlers as I passed Greens Norton church I've no idea, but there you are. The mind's a funny thing. You don't know why you do things half the time, or at least I don't.

You take what I said that evening when I got to Ivy's house in Wales, just after I'd been in her room and touched her up. Her parents had been kind enough to offer me a nice bit of boiled bacon and potato for my supper which I was halfway through eating when there came a knock upon the door. The Jenkins had a neighbour three doors down who seemed to know all of their business, which included me and Ivy, and it turned out it was her stood on their doorstep with a copy of the local paper. Had we seen, she said, the picture of a car found in Northampton? Now, that's how it is in villages, you see, with everybody knowing everybody else's business. I'd not been in Gellygaer more than an hour or two, and here was somebody had heard already what I'd said to Ivy's dad about my motor getting pinched. As it turned out, I still had worse to come.

They asked her in and let her show this paper round to everyone, and when I saw it I was in the middle of a mouthful of boiled ham. I'll tell you, it's a wonder that I didn't choke. There was a picture of my Morris Minor standing burned out in the field at Hardingstone. There was a paragraph beside it said a human body had been found inside the wreckage. Well, it's like I said, you don't know why you do or say things half the time, but when I looked at that I blurted straight out, without thinking twice, `That's not my car.' I followed that by mumbling something about how I'd not thought there'd be such a fuss made in the papers over things.

It was a bloody stupid thing to say, I think now looking back on it. I mean, it was my car, there wasn't any doubt about it. You could read the licence plate, MU 1468, as plain as anything. It was about the only bit that wasn't burned away. All I did by making out it wasn't mine was make myself look fishy and get everyone's suspicions up. I got out of it best I could by claiming I was tired and making off to bed in the spare room, where I thought about Ivy's tits and had a quick one off the wrist to take me mind off things.

Now usually, no sooner have I brought myself off than I'm fast asleep, but not that night. Oh no. I didn't sleep a wink except for bits where I'd doze off and have these horrid little dreams that woke me up almost before they'd started. They were vivid at the time, but now I can't remember anything about them, only that they put the wind up me so that I lay awake until the first light crept across the lily-patterned paper on the end wall.

By the time I was up, the morning paper had arrived. It was the Daily Sketch. They'd printed the same photo of my burned-out Morris, only this time they gave out my name as well, which I thought was a blessed cheek. Of course, that really tore it with regards to Ivy's parents. All that I could think to say is that there must have been a dreadful mix-up somewhere and that I was going back to London until it was sorted out. The Jenkins had another neighbour, name of Brownhill, ran a little motor business down in Cardiff. He piped up and volunteered to run me back there on his way to work so I could get a coach to Hammersmith. I couldn't very well say no, so I made my goodbyes to Ivy and said what she wanted me to say about how we should both soon live together in Kingston-on-Thames. Her father shook my hand, though not without some prompting on the part of Ivy's mam, and then we drove away.

It was a long drive down to Cardiff and I don't know if it played upon my nerves, but for one reason or another I found that I couldn't for the life of me stop talking. I kept on and on about my car and how it had been stolen from outside a coffee shop, and this chap Brownhill just kept staring at the road in front of him and every now and then he'd say, 'Oh yes?' or 'Is that right?' but other than that it was blood out of a stone to get a word from him. When we arrived in Cardiff he insisted on accompanying me down to the station, where he saw me on the coach for Hammersmith.

Of course, I've been told since that what he did was get straight on to the police as soon as he'd made sure that I was on the coach. He told them I was on my way and that some things I'd said to him had been suspicious. If you ask me, he just wanted to be in on the excitement. It's the same with all them village types, there's nothing they love better than a bit of scandal. Still, I've wondered if it might be Ivy's father put him up to it, arranging me a lift to Cardiff with that very thing in mind. It isn't very nice, to think he'd do that, but I wouldn't put it past him. Never has been very fond of me, has Ivy's dad. He took the attitude she'd given up a good career in nursing for a chap he thought beneath her station, as though anyone in Gellygaer ever earned five hundred pounds a year.

I suppose if I'm completely candid with myself, it was the nurse's uniform as much as anything attracted me to Ivy in the first place. It's a 'kink' I've got, and once more I can only think that it might be connected to the War in some way. Hospitals and that. Sometimes, even the smell of Germolene or of surgical spirit, it will get me going quicker than a good rude book. She looked a little cracker, Ivy did, what with that little hat and those black woollen stockings. It's a pity, but she's not been able to get into her nurse's outfit since she passed the five months mark, and that was quite some time back now.

I'll tell you what, it's very cold in here for January, don't you think so? Angel Lane. I'll tell you this, I've not seen many angels around here this last two months, only a load of bobbies all with faces like the rear end of a bus. Not that I'd know an angel if I saw one. Naked women, that's what I imagine angels are. Now that'd be a thing to have fluttering round you when you kick off, wouldn't it? A lot of nudes? That's how I'd like to go. There's ways a good sight worse than that, believe you me.

He was still fast asleep when I saw the first sign for Hardingstone, the chap whatever-his-name-was I'd picked up in the pub outside St Albans. Bill. I think he said his name was Bill. He was still snoring, and for my part half of me was in a panic over how I'd cope with all these bills and wives and children while the other half kept thinking of that fellow with the reindeer antlers in the Pear's Encyclopaedia. No idea why. It's like I say, the mind can be a curiosity at times.

Somewhere amongst all this, I first hit on the notion I should take the turn along the lane to Hardingstone when it arrived. What happened after that I'm in a muddle over still. I've told so many stories I can't tell myself which ones are true and which ones I've invented. Do you ever get that? No?

I made a statement about everything that happened to the gentlemen from Hammersmith police station who'd been there waiting for my coach when it arrived from Cardiff, thanks to Mr Brownhill sticking in his oar. To tell the truth, I made a proper Charly of myself when I got off the bus and found them waiting for me, three of them. I'd not expected it, I suppose I should have, but I'd not. I was so taken back, I said the first thing that came into my head. I said I was glad it was all over, and I told them that I'd not had any sleep. I said that I was on my way to Scotland Yard that instant. That's all fair enough, but before I could stop myself I went and said I was responsible. I didn't say for what, but all the same they gave me quite a look. I could have kicked myself, the trouble that I've had about it since.

I don't know if I told you, but they tried to trip me up on that in Court today, except I was too clever for them. There's a saying, back in Finchley, that you have to get up early of a morning to catch Alfie Rouse. The prosecuting counsel, Mr Birkett, he was asking me why it had taken nearly two days for me to report what had gone on to the police, which threw me for a minute, but I soon recovered.

'Well,' I said, 'I've very little faith in village constables such as you'll find at the more local, smaller station, so I thought I'd go straight to the top. Didn't I say that I was on my way to Scotland Yard when I got stopped in Hammersmith?'

He didn't like that, I could tell, the way I wouldn't let him pin me down, so what he says next is, 'Oh yuss? Didn't you also say you were responsible? What did you mean by that, my good man?' How they talk, you know.

Now, I was feeling pretty cocky by that time, so I came back smart as a whip and said, 'Well, in the eyes of the police, I thought the owner was responsible for anything that happened in his car. Correct me if I'm wrong.'

I raised one eyebrow when I said that last bit, that 'Correct me if I'm wrong', so that the jury and the girls up in the public gallery could see that I was playing with him, and I thought I heard a couple of them chuckle unless it was my imagination. They're on my side, you can tell. A fair proportion of the jury's women, so I'm bound to be all right. I've caught the eye of one or two of them, and I've a good idea which ones have got a thing for me. If I just stick to what I've said, there'll be no upsets.

When they met me off the coach at Hammersmith Bridge Road, they took me to the local station where I told them what had happened early on that morning of the sixth, as best I could. I said I'd picked the chap up on the Great North Road, outside St Albans, which was true enough, and that as we'd got close to Hardingstone I'd thought I saw his hand upon my sample case, which I keep in the back seat of the car where he was sitting. Later on, I started to nod at the wheel a bit, and later still I heard the engine spluttering and playing up like I was running low on petrol, so I thought I'd pull into a field just off the main road there and down the lane a bit. Also, I needed to relieve myself, it having been a long drive from St Albans.

He woke up as I pulled in the field, and I told him that I was going to refresh myself. I said that if he wanted to be useful he could take the petrol can from the back seat and top the tank up, since it seemed that we were running low. I lifted up the bonnet and I showed him where to put it, then he asked me if I'd got a fag that he could cadge. I'd given him quite a few already so I said I hadn't, and then walked off from the car a stretch so that I could relieve myself in private. I'd gone some way from the road and had my trousers down when I heard this big noise and saw the firelight coming from behind me. I pulled up my trousers and I ran towards the car but I was too late. I could see him there inside, but there was nothing I could do. The silly bugger must have lit his cigarette while sitting with the petrol can. The things some people do.

They saw I'd got my case with me and asked if I'd gone back to get it out the burning car, but I was ready for that one. I'd seen his hand upon the case and had an idea he might steal it, so I took it with me when I left the motor. I told them I went into a panic when I saw the car go up, as well you might, and ran towards the road where those two young roughs saw me coming through the hedge. I said that I'd been at my wits' end ever since, and not known what to do, which was no more than the unvarnished truth.

Later, policemen from Northamptonshire arrived in Hammersmith to talk to me, then brought me back with them to Angel Lane here. I asked if I could see Lillian, and when they said that I could see her a bit later I'm ashamed to say I rather let my feelings run away with me, what with being so tired, and told them what a woman Lily was, and how she was too good for me and always made a fuss of me and everything. I mentioned how she wouldn't sit upon my knee, but how apart from that one drawback she was all a man might wish for.

If I'd stopped there I'd have been all right, but I was in the mood for showing off and anxious to impress, so I went on to tell them how I had a lot of ladyfriends around the country, and how my harem took me to several places so that I was seldom home. Somehow that got back to the papers, though as I've remarked, I feel it will work for me rather than against, despite what Mr Finnemore might think. He's just a barrister. He doesn't know the first thing about women.

That poor chap. I can see him as we pulled into that field, sat in the back seat fast asleep. All I could think about was bills and babies and how everything was coming down around me. I got out of the car as quietly as I could and went round to the boot to see if I could find the mallet that I've kept there ever since me and Lil went to Devon camping several years back. I suppose I keep it with me for protection: when you're on the road a lot like I am you can meet some funny people. I was rummaging about back there and I suppose I must have made a bit of clatter, which is probably what woke him.

Anyroad, the next thing that I know I hear the car door open at the back there and him getting out. I lean around the open boot to look and there he is stood with his back to me, trying to get his trousers undone by the look of things, so he could have a Jimmy Riddle up against my tyre. I thought about Lil and the boy in Finchley, how they'd take it when I sold the house and furniture, and Nellie with another baby now to feed, and Ivy and Kingston-on-bloody-Thames and how my life was like a nightmare, worse than any picture in a book. I wished it had been something in a book, then I could slam it shut and never have to think about it any more. At some point while all this was running through my mind I must have finally laid hands upon the mallet.

Actually, they look quite nice, the fields out there in Hardingstone. I didn't see too much of them that night, what with it being dark, but from the photo in the Sketch they looked like proper country fields such as they used to have round London when our dad was little. Sort of wild and overgrown a bit around the edges, not like parks at all. With parks, it's all a lot of borders, forms and flower beds. There's no adventure to it and to my mind it's effeminate. Now what a lad wants is to go off crawling in the bushes like an Indian, or find a little den or something in the reeds where he could just sit by himself and not come out 'til he was called.

He turned towards me just as I was bringing down the mallet so that rather than just tap his head there at the back as I'd intended, I caught him above the ear and he went sideways like a pole-axed cow. He fell against the Morris and slid down it until he was face first on the grass. He made a noise, just one sound on its own he spoke into the mud, but didn't move. I stood there staring down at him I don't know how long, breathing like you do when you've just had one.

I'd not really thought about what I was going to do, up to that point. I mean, the idea hadn't come to me at all before we got to Towcester. I looked down at him, pegged out there in what light there was coming from inside the car, the little over-head, and knew I'd better think of something quick.

Now, as a salesman, or commercial traveller as I prefer to call myself, I'm at a great advantage in the thinking stakes. My line of work requires a man who's used to thinking on his feet. I'll give you an example. There's a firm up north I visit once a quarter where I've known the buyer years, a nice old chap who's partial to the younger woman and has cash enough to spend upon a string of girlfriends. I've buttered him up, across the years, by bringing him some of the racier suspenders now and then that have a lot of frills, just as a present he can pass on to his favourite young lady. Anyway, I get there one day, march into his office with a handful of the cheekiest suspenders that you ever saw, as if I'd done the tidying at a brothel.

What I didn't know was he'd been sacked a month after I saw him last for fiddling the till, and sat there in his place was this old baggage with a face like vinegar who'd not see fifty-five again, with tits like two pigs in a hammock. I stopped dead and looked at her, then at the bunch of scanties in my hand. Quick as a flash, it came to me. I looked her in the eye, then made a big display of dumping ten bob's worth of best suspenders in the office paper basket with the torn-up envelopes and such. She looked at me like I'd gone mad. I put my best voice on and told her, `Madam, I apologize. I'd heard a lady was in charge of this department and I'd thought to gratify myself to her by offering her garments that might make her more alluring, but I see now that this would be quite unnecessary.'

I might just as well have said that I could see this would be quite impossible, but kept a civil tongue about me and it paid off as I knew it would. One of my better clients after that, she was. The point I'm trying to make is that it's all a part of life for a commercial traveller, coming up with ideas at a moment's notice.

I bent down and reached beneath his belly so that I could pick him up, and tried to get him round towards the front end of the car. My idea was, you see, to get him in the driver's seat or thereabouts. I didn't fancy trying to manoeuvre him in past the steering wheel and so I hauled him all around the car's front to the other door, which meant I pulled him through the headlights that were still switched on. By God he looked a sight, dragged through the beams like that. He had blood coming out of one ear by now, and from the look of it I'd smashed his cheekbone where I'd caught him with the mallet. I'll be honest with you, I thought he was dead.

You'd think I'd know the difference between somebody alive and someone dead, but how things are for younger chaps, it's not the same as when you've fought a war. It all gets rather blurred in my opinion, the distinction between live and dead. You see a fellow face down in the muck with only half an arm, and yes, I suppose he might well be alive, but if he's not dead then he will be in an hour or two, so, really, what's the point? It sounds harsh, but like a good many things, it's something you get used to. I did. I was a War Hero, I was. Had a medal and a scar, up near my parting. Did I show you?

Had to put the blighter down so I could reach across inside the car and open up the passenger-side door which, being worried about car thieves, I keep locked up as a rule. Having done this I went back round and shunted him about again until I'd got him face down in the front seat, although he looked very awkward, with one leg all squashed up under him. I thought to take my sample case out of the car from where it was down by the driver's seat. It had the catalogue inside, you see. I'd not want Monica to end up in a bad way.

Next I fumbled in the back seat for the petrol can I keep there and began to splash it round inside the car, with quite a lot of it falling upon the thing there in the front. I was just doing this and wondering what had happened to the mallet, which I couldn't think where I'd put down, when suddenly he made a noise. He seemed to mutter something, but it wasn't any language that I've ever heard. It gave me goosebumps, I can tell you. I shut all the doors after running a petrol trail back from the car, and then I thought to have a shufty underneath the bonnet so that I could loosen up the petrol union joint and take the top from off the carburettor. I know cars, you see, my line of work and all. A clever little touch, was that, so that it might look as if it had been an accident.

I looked around a bit but couldn't find the mallet, so I went back where I'd left the petrol can to mark the ending of my trail, then struck a match. The flames ran off across the grass like little ants that march in file, and then there was that noise like a great sigh and they were everywhere across the car. My little Morris Minor.

That's about the time that he woke up and started screaming and twitching about until he kicked the car door open, but by then, as I said earlier, he'd had his chips. I'll tell you what was bad: he had one leg stuck out of the car and I don't know how long I must have stood there staring, but it burned right through. It just fell off and lay there on the grass, this burning leg. To be quite frank I've never seen a picture like it.

In the strictest confidence, the thing that everybody thinks is cleverest about the operation was a thing I hadn't even thought of for myself until the deed was done. To hear the papers talk, the idea is I did it all on Guy Fawkes' Night so that the fire would be sure not to draw attention, which I must admit is very smart indeed. I wish I'd thought of it before the fact. The truth is, that's just when the idea came upon me, on that night, there in that field. Came to me in a flash, from out of nowhere. That's just how it happens sometimes, I suppose. It wasn't until later as I stared into the flames I thought about it being Bonfire Night. I thought, ` Well, that's appropriate.'

After I'd stood there quite a while and made my eyes run with the smoke, it came to me I'd best be moving on. I walked across the fields to where a gap cut through the hedge led out on to the Hardingstone Lane. As luck had it, just as I came out on to the path I ran straight into these two chaps, both sozzled from the look of them, and coming home from some Guy Fawkes' to-do down at the local Palais. The Salon de Danse, I think I've heard it called. As I approached, I realized that they could both see the car on fire across the field, and thought I heard them mention it.

I thought it best to put on a bold face and bluff it out, and so I said, ` Looks like somebody's had a bonfire' or some words to that effect, the Guy Fawkes notion having come to me by now. They both stared at me and said nothing, so I hurried on towards the main road up ahead.

It was a clear night. Proper crisp. The moon was out and showed up very bright upon the dead Queen's cross there by the London Road. Everything smelled exciting, frightening, full of smoke and gunpowder and like a war. My scar was itching so I stood there scratching at my head as if I was somebody gone out. I had a suitcase of unmentionables in one hand and a box of England's Glory matches in the other. I was someone else, with their whole life in front of them, and I was scared to death but it felt grand.

I can't wait to get out of here. I'm going to celebrate. I'm going to fill the world with babies, songs and lovely underthings. I'll treat my Lily to a hat and go to bed with plain girls to be kind. I'm not a bad sort underneath, and I believe the jury know that. Oh, a rascal sometimes, to be sure, sharp as you like with no flies on him, but a character, a man with a romantic heart that leads him into trouble. I look down at them from out the dock and know I've one foot in the door already with them, how they look at me. It's just an instinct. You can always tell, you know, when they look hesitant.

They're buying it.

PHIPPS' FIRE ESCAPE
AD 1995

They're buying it.

The last words of the previous chapter, written in grey light, stand there upon the monitor's dark stage, beneath the Help menu that's lettered up on the proscenium arch. The cursor winks, a visible slow handclap in the black, deserted auditorium.

The final act: no more impersonations. No more sleight-of-voice or period costume. The abandoned wigs and furs and frocks are swept away. Discarded masks and death-husk faces are returned to Property and hanging on their pegs. The grub-chewed skull of Francis Tresham dangles next to the wax imprint of John Clare, moon-browed and lantern-jawed. A cast of Nelly Shaw, the lips drawn back across her teeth in burning agony, bumps up against the papier mâché cheek of Alfie Rouse, an unintended kiss.

On stage, although the set remains the same, the scenery is somewhat modified. Some of the buildings on the painted nineteen-thirties backdrop have been whited out and new ones added; Caligari hulks against the slate November sky. It's 1995. The lights go down. The empty rows wait for the final monologue.

Pull back now from the screen, the text, the cursor and its mesmerizing trancebeat pulse. Become aware of sore eyes, overflowing desk. The hollow ashtray fashioned like a yawning frog, a gross cascade of cigarette end and sour pumice spilling from its china throat. The index finger of the right hand, poised above the keys. The author types the words ` the author types the words'.

Stand, and feel the energy that crowds the room, a current siphoned back through time from all those future readings, all those other people and the varying degrees of their absorption, their awareness half-submerged within the text and half-detached from moment, from continuum, and therefore reachable. Draw in a massive breath of it, its scorch and crackle. Everything feels right and powerful. Everything is happening correctly.

All around, the reference books relating to the town are heaped up into towers; become a small-scale reproduction of the town itself. *There's Witchcraft in Northamptonshire – Six rare and curious tracts dating from 1612*, and the selected poems of John Clare. The Coritani, the crusaders, the compendiums of murder and the lives of saints in a topography of history made solid, cliffs of word some forty centuries deep that must be navigated to attain the door, the stairs beyond, uncarpeted and thunderous. Move down them like an over-medicated avalanche towards the living room; the television and the couch.

History is a heat, oppressive and exhausting. Fall rather than sit upon the at-risk heirloom sofa and attempt to locate the remote control by touch alone, groping among the permafrost of magazine and empty teacup that conceals the carpet, for its own good. It would be much simpler just to look, admittedly, but more depressing. Fingers close on the device, a fruit and nut bar as imagined by a silicone-based life-form, and locate the necessary stud. A vague southerly flail ignites the news on Channel Four. History is a heat. Zeinab Badawi nightly holds aloft the blackened crucible for our inspection.

Balkan ceasefire conference chopped up into seven-second mouthfuls by a motherly and helpful camera, to reduce the risk of choking. Both sides' representatives appear embarrassed, blanching at the flashbulbs. Playground brawlers called out to the front, made to apologize and shake hands with an after-school resentment already apparent in the eyes and voice. Let's not have any more talk about rape camps or genetic cleansing. Go back to your desks.

Forthcoming visits to the North of Ireland by President Clinton are expected to focus attention on a peace process that's rapidly becoming an embalming process. Clinton, Kennedyesque if one measures things in hair and blowjobs, has announced that he won't come to Ireland just to switch on Christmas lights, although if Congress has the White House phones cut off by then and the electric disconnected, he may think again. Two families of Irish Clintons, one from each side of the border, are contending for the honour of the presidential issue sprayed against their family tree, but hopefully it won't erupt into sectarian violence.

An analysis of last night's budget, which concludes the likeliest effect is that the wealthiest ten per cent will now be better off, the poorest better off dead. The Nigerian government has lynched Ken Saro Wiwa for protesting against the environmental sodomy inflicted on a homeland traumatized by petrochemical adventurism; Shell-shocked. Momentary whiteness under the lagoons of Mururoa.

Old editions of the local *Mercury & Herald* from the sixteen-hundreds list Northamptonshire's then recent deaths from causes long since rendered utterly unfathomable: Rising Lights, the Purples. One man listed here as 'Planet Struck'. Sat slack-jawed in the cathode aura of this photogenic Armageddon, the phrase seems overdue for a revival. The relentless onslaught of this stupefying imagery that pounds our inner landscapes flat, a carpet-bombing of the mind. The language of the world, that overwhelms us. Nothing is conveyed save for an underlying sense of landscape at its most unstable, pliable as sweaty gelignite. History is a heat, a slow fire with the planet just now coming to the boil, our culture passing from a fluid to a vaporous state amid the violent and chaotic seethings of the phase transition. Here, in the rising steam, a process moves towards its point of crisis, interrupted only by a break for the commercials.

Startlingly, amidst the beautifully modulated list of global thrills, spills and extinctions, comes a near-unprecedented mention of Northampton: council tenants in the Pembroke Road whose gardens back on to the railway line attempt to call attention to a new leukaemia cluster. You can hear the spectral squeal and mutter of the night freight on the other side of town when there's a west wind. Brother Mike, who's prettier, sometimes funnier, but frankly nowhere near as charismatic, lives just off the Pembroke Road with his wife Carol and their kids. They want to move, but showing their prospective buyers round the premises in Haz-Chem suits and helmets isn't going to make things any easier.

To be quite fair, the whole spread of estates from Spencer to King's Heath has had a post-nuclear appearance since the sixties. Just a decade earlier, King's Heath had won awards for its design, seen as the perfect model for a future England which, unluckily, it proved to be. By 1970 even the sweetshop had steel shutters, and neglected dogs banded together into terrifying medieval hunting packs. The local nightspot seemed to have been decorated by a schizophrenic window-dresser who'd last visited the cinema for *Barbarella*, or perhaps *Repulsion*, with gaunt female mannequins emerging anorexic and concussed from wall and pillar into an emetic light show. King's Heath youth struck matches on the plaster nipples, passing round ten Sovereign, and drank themselves into amnesia or animosity beneath the swirling biriani-coloured radiance of a faulty gel-wheel, later for the most part either knocked or banged up in accordance with their gender. The town shrugs, in timeworn response to its own physical decline: it's not as if it was expecting something better.

Switch the television off, momentarily defeated. Partly concealed by three weeks of unread *New Scientist* and empty biscuit wrappings, is a draft of the preceding chapter. Still not sure whether the shop in Bridge Street that offered a job to Lily Rouse was a confectioner's or not, but in the end decide to let it stand in deference to the processes of fiction rather than the less substantial processes of history. Lily remains between the sugar-cataracted jars; proclaims her husband's innocence with wince-inducing loyalty while weighing out the Rainbow Drops. They drive him out to Bedford Prison, Bunyan's second home, and he goes to the gallows, ultimate suspender, with her name upon his lips, no minor feat of memory when one considers all the wives and co-parents he might have thought to mention. What's it all about, Alfie?

Bunyan: first to chart the land of spirit and imagination lying under middle England, mapping actual journeys undertaken in the solid realm on to his allegorical terrain. Likewise, it seems that the intention of his work was to awake the apprehension of a visionary landscape from beneath the subjugated streets and fields; fire an incendiary dream to make the dull and heavy matter of the shires and townships burn with new significance, and be transformed. September 1681 saw a new charter brought down by the Earl of Peterborough in Northampton, with these scenes reprised in Bunyan's *Holy War* the following year, but relocated to the allegoric town of Mansoul. In this alias, the sense of mythic weight and moment wielded by the place and its inhabitants is underscored, the town's huge and invisible centrality confirmed.

One great advantage that *The Pilgrim's Progress* as a narrative enjoys over the current work is in its structure, with the pilgrimage progressing to a necessary ending in redemption. Here, however, there is no such tidy resolution within reach. The territory is the same, but here we have no single pilgrim save perhaps the author, or the reader, and only uncertain progress. While redemption's not out of the question, it's an outside chance at best. It's hardly been a major theme thus far.

This final chapter is the thing. Committed to a present-day first-person narrative, there seems no other option save a personal appearance, which in turn demands a strictly documentary approach: it wouldn't do to simply make things up. This is a fiction, not a lie.

Of course, that tends to place the burden of responsibility for finishing the novel on the town itself. If all its themes, motifs and speculations are to be resolved, then they will be resolved in actual brick and flesh. Trust in the fictive process, in the occult interweaving of text and event must be unwavering and absolute. This is the magic place, the mad place at the spark gap between word and world. All of the subtle energies pass through here on their journey into form. If properly directed, they'll provide the closures that the narrative demands: the terrible black dogs shall come. There shall be fires, and severed heads, and angel language. An unlikely harmony of incident and artifice is called for, that may take some tracking down. There's nothing for it but to take a walk.

Outside, the rain falls hard upon Phipps' Fire Escape, a constant amber static through the Lucozade glow of the sodium lamps. This whole estate was raised by brewer and industrialist Pickering Phipps around the turn of the century as a last-ditch attempt at spiritual salvation. Long odds, from the look of things.

He placed a foundry up on Hunsbury Hill to overlook the town and gouged away at the remains of the adjacent Iron Age settlement in search of ore to build the railway. Most of what he paid his labourers would be returned to him across the bar-tops of his taverns on the Friday night he doled it out. Northampton had a lot of pubs back then. You could start at the top of Bridge Street and with only half a pint of bitter at each stop along the way never reach the Plough Hotel down at the bottom end, by then receded to Infinity.

Phipps reasoned that his drinking dens might be perceived as having set temptation on the straight path of the righteous and that taking a dim view of all this, the Almighty would be certain to condemn him to the flames. His only chance, the way he saw it, was to curry the Creator's favour by constructing an estate that had four churches but no public houses. By slipping this modest bribe to God, seen as Northampton Borough representative writ large, the brewer thought to thus avoid a furnace deemed more hideous than that which he'd erected up on Hunsbury Hill. Though designated ` Phippsville' in official documents, native consensus soon re-christened it Phipps' Fire Escape. Home of ten years now, at one house or other.

There seems to be a local predilection for expressing contours of the spirit world in terms of stone and mortar, matter in its densest, most enduring form. Phipps builds a dry and austere maze, its terraced streets become the rungs of his ascent to Paradise. Simon de Senlis builds his round church as a Templar glyph to mark the martyrdom and resurrection. Thomas Tresham codes the outlawed Holy Trinity into his lunatic three-sided lodge. These testaments of brick are weighty paragraphs writ on the world itself and therefore only legible to God. The rest of us who do not build express our secret arcane souls in scripts more fleeting, more immediate to our human instant: wasting spells or salesman's patter. The betraying letter. Prose, or violence.

Squinting through the dark and drizzle, turn from Cedar Road to Collingwood, the downpour now a steady sizzle of dull platinum on the uneven paving slabs. Pass by the small, uncertain row of shops with a sub-post office so often blagged that it's established a cult following among the audience of Crimewatch, most of whom are criminals who tune in for industry news and gossip. Walking on, past alley mouths that open on the long and lightless gullets of back-entries, puddles rippling in the sumps and sinkages of century-old cobble, iridescent moss accrued between the blunt grey stones. Rapes here, and strangled schoolboys, yet these miserable and poignant corridors don't even get a walk on in the local A-Z. Our real, most trenchant streetplans are mapped solely in the memory and the imagination.

A right turn, into Abington Avenue, the cold slap of its crosswind and the driven rain. Across the street stands the United Reform Church, one of the four pillars upon which rests Phipps' blind swing at redemption. Francis Crick came here to Sunday school back in the 1920s, evidently so impressed by Bible stories of a seven-day Creation that he went on to discover DNA. The dual helical flow of human interchange spirals around the recently refurbished building: brawls at closing time, and copulations. Love and birth and murder in their normal vortex.

Kettering Road, and the backwater junk emporiums that have collected in the tributaries of the town, an algae of grandfather clock and gas-mask. The abandoned Laser-Hunter-Killer Palace with the soaped up windows where the future closed down early for lack of local enthusiasm. Further down, stranded amidst the traffic flow of Abington Square on the brink of the town centre, stands Charles Bradlaugh's statue, finger raised and resolutely pointing west towards the fields beyond the urban sprawl, assisting Sunday shoppers who've forgotten how to get to Toys'Я'Us.

Charles Bradlaugh was Northampton's first Independent MP and the first atheist allowed to enter parliament, though not without debate. The night that his admission to the Commons was decided saw a demonstration in the Market Square with riot policemen sent in to administer the smack of a firm government. No stranger to controversy, he was sentenced to prison with Theosophist and Match-Girl agitator Annie Besant for the distribution of an `obscene publication', being contraceptive information of a kind thought generally unsuitable for wives or servants. Amongst local politicians he has little competition save perhaps for Spencer Perceval, British Prime Minister unique for being, firstly, from Northamptonshire, and, secondly, assassinated. Bradlaugh stands upon the grassy knoll and points accusingly at Abington Street, at the shopping precincts, at the fag-end of the twentieth century.

Abington Street, pedestrianized some years ago, has flower baskets dangling from the gibbets of the reproduction Dickens-effect streetlamps, with a creeping sub-Docklands aesthetic gradually becoming evident in its façades. It's as if when Democracy and Revolution came at last to Trumpton, the corrupt former regime of Mayor and Council were airlifted out with CIA assistance and resettled here, to brutally impose the values of their Toytown junta on this formerly alluring thoroughfare.

Some fifty years ago this was the Bunny Run, the sexual chakra of the town, where giggling factory girls would squeal and totter through a well-intentioned gauntlet of the neighbourhood testosterone. Now, in 1995, the cheerful lust has curdled into harm and frequent bruisings, violence manifested in the architecture of the street itself, inevitably percolating down to find its outlet on a human scale. The sumptuous and majestic New Theatre was demolished first in 1959. Faint echoes of George Robey, Gracie Fields and Anna Neagle pining from the sorry rubble. Next went Notre Dame, a red-brick convent school, Gothic receptacle for ninety years of schoolboy longing, and then finally the yellowed art deco arcade of the Co-Operative Society: a beautiful, faintly Egyptian relic with a central avenue sloping down as if designed to roll the final stone that would wall up alive those slaves caught browsing in the Homecare Centre.

Here, unmasked, a process that distinguishes this place as incarnated in industrial times. The only constant features in the local-interest photograph collections are the mounds of bricks; the cranes against the sky. A peckish Saturn fresh run out of young, the town devours itself. Everything grand we had, we tore to bits. Our castles, our emporiums, our witches and our glorious poets. Smash it up, set fire to it and stick it in the fucking madhouse. Jesus Christ.

At the street's lower end a ghostly and deserted Market Square rises upon the right, while All Saint's elderly patrician bulk looms underlit upon the left. A rank of Hackney cabs shelters against the church's flank, hunched in the rain and glistening, like crows. The shop-fronts opposite on Mercer's Row invite another reading of the town: only the ground floors have been modernized, as if the present moment were a heat-haze of tumultuous event that ended fifteen feet above street level, with the higher storeys in the lease of earlier centuries. Go upstairs at the butcher's, Sergeants, and the Geisha Café would be open still, with spectral waitresses gliding between the murmuring, empty tables bearing sandwiches, triangular and numinous. Bram Stoker sharing tea for two with Errol Flynn between the Repertory Theatre matinées.

Splash on, rounding the front of All Saint's with its sheltering portico. A plaque here to the memory of John Bailles, a button-maker of the sixteenth, seventeenth and eighteenth centuries, the county's best attempt to date at a robust, no-nonsense immortality. Near six score years and ten: a long time to spend making buttons. Only zips and Velcro killed him.

The church stares with blank Anglican disdain down Gold Street's narrow fissure; stone-faced Protestant resentment is directed at any Semitic shades remaining in this former haunt of money-lenders. In the thirteenth century it was from here that local Jews were taken out and stoned to death, accused of sacrificing Christian babies in the course of arcane, cabbalistic rites. This was among the earliest incidents of violent European anti-Semitism that were recognizable as such, the town as eager and precocious in its pogroms as it was reluctant to stop burning witches.

During World War II a bomber crashed up at the street's top end, a great tin angel with a sucking chest wound fallen from the Final Judgement. It was drawn down inexorably by tractor beams of sympathetic magic emanating from the subterranean speakeasy that's under Adam's Bakery behind the church, a marvellous forgotten space designed to reproduce the shape and seating of a buried aeroplane. Imagined engine-drone above the cold flint jetstreams, the clay strato-cumulus, like calling unto like, dragging the bomber overhead into a helpless and enraptured nosedive. One lone cyclist with a broken arm after the impact knocked him from his saddle, otherwise no casualties. These streets again show their surprising and capricious mercy. One by one the townsfolk file out through the Welsh House from the burning Market Square. The cyclist rises dazed and injured from the wreckage and stares dumbstruck at Jane Russell, pouting, painted on the ruined fuselage.

From Gold Street over the dual carriageway of Horsemarket, more horse-power stampeding there now than ever, where a left turn would lead down towards the Fritz Lang horror of the Carlsberg Brewery. It was in the Copenhagen branch of this establishment that physicist Niels Bohr first formulated his axiom that all our observations of the universe can only be seen, in the last analysis, as observations of ourselves and our own processes. A haunting notion, hard to write off as the product of one Special Brew too many, and as true concerning observations of a town as when relating to the cosmos, or the hidden quanta.

Cross Horsemarket into Marefair with the unforgiving mausoleum of the Barclaycard credit control headquarters on our right. Poker-faced, its gaze concealed behind opaque black windows, it gives nothing away. Northampton, once the centre of the boot and shoe trade, that grew fat on war and saw John Clare's long desperate hike as one more pair sold, is now the seat of Barclaycard and Carlsberg, perfect icons of the Thatcher years reflecting our new export lines: the lager lout, the credit casualty. Here we go, here we go. Here we go.

Across the street are council offices where Cromwell is reputed to have slept and dreamed the night in 1645 before he rode to Naseby and midwifed the gory breach birth of our current parliamentary democracy, the adult form still clearly warped and traumatized by this unspeakable nativity. They marched the Royalist prisoners out to Ecton afterwards and herded them into a paddock by the Globe Inn for the night before the march to London, trial, imprisonment or execution. Many of the wounded died there in the field behind the Inn. A century later William Hogarth, a recurring patron, offered to design and paint a new sign for the Globe, and changed its name to the World's End with a depiction of the planet bursting into flames. The pub signs of the county are a secret Tarot deck, with this card the most ominous, the local theme of fire asserted in its final, terrifying aspect.

Walking on, St Peter's church stands floodlit, golden in the last few shakes of rain, a Saxon edifice rebuilt after the Norman conquest. A funeral service was held here for Uncle Chick, a wide boy in more ways than one: black marketeer of the family, he lost a leg in later life but not his splendidly unpleasant sense of humour, nor the knowing leer of a supernal toad with diamonds in his brow. The vicar eulogized him as a decent, law-abiding man, respectable in every way. Dad and Aunt Lou kept looking at each other in bewilderment throughout the service, having no idea who he was on about.

Here too the half-wit's vision and the beggar woman, crippled by the gate. The bones of Ragener, unearthed in an unearthly light. The brother Saints, Ragener and Edmund; their remote November graves and separate miracles.

When they found Edmund's severed head it was protected by a fierce black dog that would not let them near. The frilled pink gums, curled back across pale yellow teeth; the murdered saint with fly-specked gaze, a mouthful of dead leaves, his hair, alive with ants: these are the icons of a secret local heraldry, the cryptic suits that mark

Northampton's deck: Flames, Churches, Heads, and Dogs.

Down Black Lion Hill, still on the path suggested by Charles Bradlaugh's finger, to the crossroads and the bridge beyond, the ancient heart of the community, where everything began. The Shagfoals, as described by local folklore, are believed to favour crossroads or a river-bridge, sites where the fabric is stretched thinnest between our world and the hidden place beneath. The town, of course, has crystallized around these very features; and so gets no more than it deserves.

St Peter's Way curves south from here, and to the north extends St Andrew's Road, childhood address and western boundary of the Boroughs, this town's oldest, strangest quarter, sprung up where the neolithic track of the Jurassic Way that stretched from Glastonbury to Lincoln crossed the River Nene. Simon de Senlis' castle stood here once beside the bridge, where Becket came to trial and was condemned, the castle itself suffering a similar fate not long after. Now Castle Station stands here, with the relocated postern gate a sole remaining fragment of the former structure like a dead man's ear saved by his murderer as a memento.

On the corner sits the Railway Club, this evening's destination. Since Mum's death four months ago it has become the venue for a weekly meeting with the brother; point of contact now that the maternal Sunday dinner table is no more. Beyond the double airlock doors that grant admission from the street there is a single large, low-ceilinged hall that's lit as though for neuro-surgery. A low stage at the far end where sometimes the bingo caller sits, charged with the arcane glamour and authority of his profession, audience hanging breathless on each syllable as on the utterance of a divine, or numerologist.

Other than children, it's unusual to discover anybody here that's under fifty. The collective ambience is overcast, abruptly lit by static discharge from a kippered laugh. This atmosphere is stable, soothing and familiar. These are people who have always been here, by the vanished castle, by the bridge. The words have changed but not the voice, nor yet the greater part of their complaint.

The brother's here already, at the usual table with his son Jake, six years old, already either self-possessed or just possessed. The drinks are ordered and the conversation, easy as old shoes, turns to the week's events. Mike, after five years, has discovered where Dad's ashes ended up; where Mum's will follow. Not that nobody's been looking during all that time, of course. Simply that no one at the crematorium appeared to have the first idea of how to find Rose Garden B; had recently declared albeit wrongly that Rose Garden B did not exist. This had given rise to a brief flurry of unsettling suspicions: Soylent Green is people. Luckily, the matter was resolved and the parental plaque discovered quite by chance among the lanes of roses, ranks of men and women wondrously transformed to petal, scent and thorn.

Having concluded his account the brother sips, wiping antipodean surf from upper lip before he speaks again. ' So what have you been doing?'

' Just the book.'

' That's the Northampton book?'

Nod of assent, followed by a cursory description of the work, before professional imperatives assert themselves and the inevitable panning for material begins; the strip mining of every conversation for a word, a stolen fact or phrase. Mike is subjected to a wearying rag-picker's litany: how old, now, is the Railway Club? Who built it? Any anecdotes? Any old murders, old celebrities, old iron? One eye on his eldest son, across the club's far side and busy organizing other children into cadres of Power Ranger-Jugend, he considers.

' Uncle Chick once had a crate of ale away from out the keg room where it opens on to Andrew's Road. Dragged it along St Peter's Way to Nan's house up in Green Street. This was Christmas night. Snow everywhere. If he'd not been so pissed he would have thought. The coppers only had to follow back the trail to his front door. That was the only time they ever had the law down Green Street over Chick. He was more careful after that.'

The reference to Green Street strums a tripwire of association. Home of the paternal grandmother, the Nan, her house that smelled of damp and human age and withered apples. Mum's side started out there, too, before the council shifted them to Andrew's Road. The green sloped down behind St Peter's church towards the bounding terrace at the bottom, a barricade against the industry and asphalt that encroached beyond. The houses are all gone now. Nothing stands between the dwindling, naked patch of grass and the encroaching office blocks that quietly and politely shuffle ever closer, buzzards on their very best behaviour.

Thirty years ago, Jeremy Seabrook wrote his influential work on poverty in Britain, called The Unprivileged, and focused sensibly on nothing more than an articulation of what Green Street was and what it meant: that aggregate of lives and incidents and want. Green Street was made the emblem of a disenfranchised class; of an impassioned plea that street and people both should be restored. The answer, demolition in both instances.

It would be near impossible even to formulate that plea today, the emblems and the archetypes long since worn down to cliché and self-parody. How shall we speak, straight-faced, about the local whore who turned a trick so Nan could buy a jar of Marmite for the kids? Maudlin Northampton shite, all tarts with hearts and we-were-so-poor-rickets-was-a-luxury. And yet a girl whose name has not survived would take a stranger up her in a back yard for her neighbour's children, and how is it we no longer have a language to contain such things?

Back in the Railway Club, the conversation settles in a holding pattern orbiting the Jupiterian mass of Uncle Chick, a gravity that lack of corporate substance has not diminished. Mike recalls the first drink that he had with Chick after the leg was off. They'd been with Dad and Uncle Gord up to the Silver Cornet, stopping on the way back for a Sunday paper at the newsagent's. Mike stayed there in the car with Chick, uncomfortably wondering how to broach the subject of his uncle's missing leg, the stump propped up beside the gear-stick.

While they waited there in silence, they became aware of a lone figure that approached them with a painful slowness from the street's far end, resolving as it neared into a wretched, downcast man afflicted both by a club foot and by a prominent hunched back. Chick watched the man limp past, eyes narrowed in the underdone puff-pastry of their sockets, finally dispensing with his silence to address the brother: ' 'Ere, Mick. Goo an' ask that cunt there if 'e wants a fight.'

Laugh. Get another round in. In the end the talk makes a complete lap of the circuit and ploughs back into the starting post.

' So what's this book about, then?'

It's about the vital message that the stiff lips of decapitated men still shape; the testament of black and spectral dogs written in piss across our bad dreams. It's about raising the dead to tell us what they know.

It is a bridge, a crossing-point, a worn spot in the curtain between our world and the underworld, between the mortar and the myth, fact and fiction, a threadbare gauze no thicker than a page. It's about the powerful glossolalia of witches and their magical revision of the texts we live in. None of this is speakable.

Instead, deliberate and gecko-eyed evasion: ' Well, it's difficult to say until it's finished.'

Sup up. Jake stands grave and still while helped on with his winter coat, the robing of a midget cardinal. Outside, walking towards the station forecourt for a cab, he pauses by the repositioned postern gate, insists the placard there is read aloud. According to his dad, he shows worryingly early signs of a familial obsession with location and its antecedents. Town as a hereditary virus. Cancelled streets and ancient courtyards have become implicit in the blood.

A cab ride down St Andrew's Road to the girlfriend's. The Boroughs rise from here up to the Mayorhold, a triangular enclosure where the locals once held a yearly mock election and appointed some local drunk or Tom-of-Bedlam as the neighbourhood's own mayor, an annual gesture of contempt directed at a civic process which excluded them. The Mayorhold now a stark and ugly traffic junction; the mayoral position has been vacant for some years, its tin-lid chain of office long since lost, forgotten. Only find it, and an older, truer town aflame with meaning would rise from these embers, from these lame parades.

Dropped off in Semilong, a kind of index to the Boroughs, compiled later. Rushed farewells to Mike and Jake before the cab continues with them to King's Heath. The hill of Baker Street runs down towards the intermittent buzz of Andrew's Road, to Paddy's Meadow and the Nene, the freight yards ranged beyond. The meadow takes its name from Paddy Moore, ex-Army Irish lifeguard at the bathing place there in the slow faun river. Children, watersnakes and sometimes otters from upstream, he overlooked them all. Gave swimming lessons to the crowds of naked boys, who were no doubt encouraged by the swagger-stick kept tucked beneath his arm and his occasional displays of corporal violence to the last chap out the water. When they closed the baths and made him sweep the lanes instead it broke his heart and killed him. These enclosures are a patiently accreted coral of such days and lives.

Over the road down at the bottom of the street, is the spot where a remote acquaintance bled to death last year on someone's doorstep, following a stabbing. Fiery Fred, who knew the victim better, was down here doing a loft conversion for the girlfriend and got pulled in by the Murder Squad, all anxious understudies for the next Lynda LaPlante production. Asked him if he was 'The Amsterdam Connection'. Double Dutch to him: he'd just been somewhere near the killing ground the day it happened. Live here for long enough, you'll end up round the corner from atrocity.

Here, at the furthest point inland, the navel of the nation, all the bad blood gathers, with eruptions not infrequent and more violent crime per capita than cities of far greater notoriety. These bloody sunspots of activity seem to be motivated only by the fluctuations of the town's magnetic field: a sexual tourist fresh from Milton Keynes, his throat cut by a pair of rentboys. They drove him round for hours on the pretext of looking for a hospital while his identity leaked out on to the rear upholstery. The motive, robbery, according to the courts: a Ronson lighter, three pounds forty pence. A child found mutilated, burned and partly eaten in a garage, fifteen years ago. A retarded boy kept in a back shed, treated like a dog by his embarrassed mother till he killed her with a breadknife.

Darkness concealed behind net curtains. Madness. Harm. On even the most casual inspection of Northampton's canvas, these hues dominate. Wonder and melancholy and a mordant humour are present, undeniably, but it is the blood that captures the attention. Why here? Why so much? Is there some primal episode lost in the county's prehistoric past, a template for all such events to follow? 'Murder Mecca of the Midlands', Dave J calls it, Godfather of Goth living up by the town's north gate among the heads of traitors and the ashes of burned women.

Meanwhile, back in Baker Street, the girlfriend is at home. Melinda Gebbie, underground cartoonist late of Sausalito, California; former bondage model recently turned quarkweight boxer. Like so many others, sucked in by this urban black hole, utterly invisible to television, only made apparent as an absence by the way the light of media bends around it; by the devastation out at its perimeter. She strayed too close to this event horizon, where the lines of the A45 converge, and was absorbed. Though her perception of the world remains frenetic, to observers situated at a hypothetical location outside town, she would appear to be unmoving, frozen for all time upon the brink of this devouring singularity. Nothing gets out of here that is not pulled back in. The sheer escape velocity required is near impossible, a contravention of the special laws of relativity to which this place is subject.

It is a gravity to which Americans seem more than usually prone, perhaps responding to the atavistic tug of this, their birthmud. Washington and Franklin's families were émigrés from Sulgrave and from the world's end of Ecton, possibly escaping from the aftermath of Civil War. The Sulgrave village crest of bar and mullet, stripe and star, is resurrected in the banner of the upstart colonies. This link provokes the ominous mirage of vast glass-sided skyscrapers rising up above the sleeping hamlets, yellow taxis jostling for position in the cobbled lanes. This landscape is the lost placenta of America, discarded but still dark and slick with nutrients. Attracted by ancestral spoor, the county's prodigals are called back in, leaping upstream through the Atlantic billows to their spawning ground.

After some moments shivering on the doorsteps of Semilong, the knock is answered. Asked in, to a Fauvist pocket universe of colour, art materials, an insane proliferation of peculiar souvenirs, ornaments and a spectromatic range of pencils that defies imagination, some are only visible to dogs or bees. Upstairs, a pornographic tableau of transsexual Action Men and wayward Barbies, surgically augmented by imaginative use of Fymo. Brother Mike called round here once to water plants; was badly startled by a lifesize cardboard cut-out figurine of Mrs Doubtfire and a seemingly stuffed dog in the front bedroom; hasn't been back since.

Sit, a hallucinating Gulliver among the Lilliputian robots, trolls and mutants. Feel immediately relaxed; at home. Drink tea and fill her living room with smoke. Say hateful, frightening things to her pet cat when she's not in the room. Forget the novel for a moment, though no more than that.

She tells me she's been having dreams of dogs: a bald, blind Shagfoal puppy taken to her bed in one; another with the huge skull of a spectral dog unearthed, identifiable by gaping, monstrous sockets. In the mind they take their exercise and need no wider yard to mark out with their scent. Although subjected to endless and tedious recountings of each work in progress, this is all Melinda dreams of, the giant black hounds that only bark in dream and manifest about the margins of this fiction, portents yet to be resolved.

Stay for an hour or two then cab back home. Climb up the ladder to the attic bedroom, ocean green rag-veined with gold. There is an altar set into the glazed brick recess of the chimney, crammed with statuettes of toads and foreign deities; an image of the beautiful late Roman snake god that is currently adored. The reek of myrrh. A greenish light infects the serried spines of books on Shamanism and Qabalah, Spare and Crowley, Dr Dee and the Enochian Host, keys to the crucial world of the Unreal. Five years ago, this narrative began in tales of antlered local witchmen, with no intimation of the personal involvement in that occupation yet to come. The text, predictably, melts into the event. The neolithic boy, his mother lately dead. The crematorium and its elusive rose-yards all within a half-mile of the Bronze Age burning-fields. Wake with a loose tooth fallen out and resting on the tongue.

Although at times unnerving, this was always the intention, this erasing of a line dividing the incontrovertible from the invented. History, unendingly revised and reinterpreted, is seen upon examination as merely a different class of fiction; becomes hazardous if viewed as having any innate truth beyond this. Still, it is a fiction that we must inhabit. Lacking any territory that is not subjective, we can only live upon the map. All that remains in question is whose map we choose, whether we live within the world's insistent texts or else replace them with a stronger language of our own.

The task is not unthinkable. There are those weak points on the borderlines of fact and fabrication, crossings where the veil between what is and what is not rends easily. Go to the crossroads, and draw up the necessary lines. Make evocations and recite barbaric names; the Gorgo and the Mormo. Call the dogs, the spirit animals, and light imaginary fires. Walk through the walls into the landscape of the words, become one more first-person character within the narrative's bizarre procession. Make the real a story and the story real, the portrait struggling to devour its sitter.

Obviously, this is a course of action not without its dangers, this attempted wedding of the language and the life; this ju-ju shit. Always the risk of a surprise twist ending with the ticket to St Andrew's Mental Hospital; a painful, slow decline in company with the forsaken shadow of John Clare.

The Clare association hits a nerve. There is a public house in town, a former centre for the area's artists, its bohemians, its chemically bewildered, recently remodelled and refurbished as the Wig & Pen in hope of pulling in a passing trade of briefs and magistrates that somehow never quite materialized. The owner of the bar commissioned a Sistine-type ceiling decoration with selected local figures interposed between the barristers and judges. The resultant work depicts the current author in an upper corner, deep in conversation with John Clare. What advice is he offering? ` Don't go too heavy on the working class thing' possibly? More probably it's ` Find another job.'

The bed is comfortable and the attic room serene, another Fiery Fred conversion. Big John Weston did the pointing on the brickwork, overcome with hubris to the point of signing his creation with a chisel in the bottom right, above the skirting board. Weston, a former junky and, more recently, a former biped, is a hazardous anomaly put on this planet only to fuck up the fossil record: epileptic roofer; one-time skylight burglar. They told him it would end in tears. He broke both legs when he went through a warehouse ceiling and the door downstairs was unlocked all the time. On the occasion when he dived head-first from a third-storey roof while in a seizure he was lucky and his skull was there to break the fall.

The bad one was the leg, that first time. Veins collapse, shrinking before the needle, and the circulation fails. The limb ballooned into an agonizing comedy inflatable, drew substance from the body as it did so until Weston was a giant angel-skeleton trying to fight its way out of a brown paper bag. The visits to the hospital were harrowing. His tolerance to opiates meant that it was impossible to find a dosage strong enough to touch the pain that would not also kill him outright. Somehow he survived with a full complement of limbs intact and took the cure. Stayed clean a month or two, then offered to safeguard a pharmaceutics cabinet belonging to a friend. The first his wife Rene knew about his tumble from the wagon was when he went on the nod there at the dinner table, face down, bubbles rising through the mash. Said he'd been feeling a bit tired just lately.

When his circulation failed again early this year they couldn't save the leg. He's been through detox and rehab again since then, kicking while there's still something left to kick with, and the signs look promising. He hopes one day to surf the Internet. Hang five.

The curious proliferation of both injured and completely missing legs within the current text emerged unbidden, much like the preoccupation with November, from the histories themselves. The crippled nun, Alfgiva, and the lame crusader, Simon; Clare's bad foot on the trek from Essex and the burned-through leg outside Alf Rouse's car. After a while, one notices the wide array of signs and murals in this boot-and-shoe town that depict a leg or foot outside the context of the body. We may read these lost or damaged limbs as warning hieroglyphics on the place's parchment, coded tramp-marks denoting the difficulties and dangers of the trail.

The severed heads are harder to resolve; a starker, more insistent motif and reiterated with a greater frequency. The minted head of Diocletian or the more substantial one of Mary, Queen of Scots. Poor Francis Tresham, Captain Pouch, and the mysterious head revered by the Knights Templar. Ragener, and Edmund with a black and snarling Cerberus to carry him by one ear to the underworld. Heads are the soft and staring eggs from which the fledgling skull hatches. They are the bloody emblems of an information, final and chthonic, that exacts a price. When Odin asked for wisdom from the head of Mimir, he paid with an eye: this knowledge carries with it a curtailment of perception, or at least a narrowing. The depth-vision is forfeit.

Time passes, jumpy interrupted continuity in life and manuscript. The eldest, shortest daughter comes down on the train from Liverpool for Christmas, in a state of mixed intoxication by the time she reaches Castle Station. Ringpulls now in eyebrow, ears, nose, lower lip, as if her large shaved head were full of hidden pockets. Leah. Everybody thought it was a lovely name. Means ` cow' in Hebrew. In a day or so her taller, younger sister Amber will be following, a fourteen-year-old, fifty-foot-tall Goth whose biggest influences are Morticia Adams and the World Trade Center. Walked out from her school six months ago and stared down various education/welfare representatives until they buckled to her hideous will and let her go to night class. Such a privilege, this company of gorgeous and alarming women.

Caught up in the seance-trance of this last chapter and in search of a denouement, a way out, a fire escape, it seems a final expedition is inevitable, necessary. Fiery Fred is roped in as chauffeur; Leah in tow. Depart late afternoon for Hunsbury Hill with snow upon the ground, in Fred's most recent surge of optimism. Graduated from a halal school of motoring, all of his previous cars he butchered personally, by the book. Tattooed and ear-ringed, with eyes like Broadmoor buttons beneath the panto-demon ginger brow, he is a horrid dream invented by the middle class to terrify their children. Laugh like Pig Bodine, out of *Gravity's Rainbow*: Hyeugh-hyeugh-hyeugh. He has the courage and the fines of his convictions, both outstanding.

Fred was handling the door the night that Iain Sinclair and his mesmerizing golem Brian Catling did their reading at the round church of the Holy Sepulchre. Asking for trouble, really, the deliberate conjunction of two charged, shamanic presences with this still-unexploded site. Halfway through Catling's reading of *The Stumbling Block* there came an interruption, an outburst from a sometimes homicidal medicine-head of local notoriety. Poetry hooligan. Evicted swiftly, he was led off to a nearby bar by Fred and offered a placating drink. Next, explosion. Broken glass. A foam-jawed lunge across the table at Fred's jugular. Two teeth knocked out, blood everywhere. Thrown from the bar-room in the wake of his attacker, to the street outside, Fred found himself staring into the quivering muzzle of a gun and hoping that he wouldn't die there, in between the Labour Exchange and the Inland Revenue, a victim of that local speciality, the stroll-by shooting. Somehow extricated himself. Slept downstairs with a sword that night, unconsciously sucked into the crusader aura of the church and the event.

These sudden violent surges, tidal movements in Northampton's undermind, that blossom into gory actuality at the least provocation, hidden forces that exist beneath the surface, underneath the paved veneer of waking thought and rationality. The town is like a mind expressed in concrete, its subconcious buried deep in lower reaches where the fears and dreams accumulate. This underworld is literal, though occult: webs of tunnels lace the earth below the settlement, burrows that wind back to its earliest days. The major churches are believed to be connected in this way, with rumours of a passage running underneath the river to the abbey out at Delapré.

Though glimpsed in living memory, with bricked off entrances in childhood cellars, this pellucid subterranean domain is now consigned to legend, with the council issuing denials that such catacombs exist. Once more, the slippage between fact and folklore: a vital, hidden strata of the county's psyche is suppressed, refused.

The eagerness of the authorities to edit out this secret subtext from the county's narrative is suspect, and unduly purposeful: the crypt beneath De Senlis' round church of the Holy Sepulchre that represents the tomb of Jesus at Gethsemane is known to exist, yet has no entrance and has not been seen since the foundation, centuries ago. When labourers in nearby Church Street broke through their trench wall into a draughty space beyond, it was beyond doubt that they'd chanced on the forgotten crypt. The rector, feverishly excited by this prospect, hurried down to Church Street the next morning to discover that a council work gang had been called out overnight to concrete off the opening.

The undertown is out of bounds. The sacred space has been co-opted by Civil Defence contingencies: the bunkers of nuclear-exempted bureaucrats, the dressing rooms where they will underwrite the Apocalypse. No more may we peel back the flagstones to reveal the cadavers of murdered saints, bones marrowed with appalling light. Cold certainty replaces visionary speculation. Thus displaced, the landscape's secret soul moves elsewhere, a fallback position that can be successfully defended. The mystery retreats behind its oldest bulwarks; seeks the highest ground.

In the Briar Hill estate just down from Hunsbury Hill, Neolithic remains were discovered, predating the leavings of the Bronze and Iron Age found further up slope. Fred's vaguely suspect vehicle crawls through the narrow, winding roads between the housing blocks; avoiding areas where the yellow Neighbourhood Watch stickers are the thickest, he parks in a silent close.

On foot through the estate and up towards the relic Iron Age camp, with Leah striding through the snow ahead, face rattling and chiming, mournful music in the gloom. She talks about a dream she had some weeks ago in which she found her bedroom occupied by a colossal coal-black dog, its horse-sized form slumping across a bed too small for it, wheezing and straining in the throes of labour yet too enervated to give birth. She had to reach inside and pull the monstrous Shagfoal puppies out into the light, at which the dream mutated and she was in hospital, having just given birth herself to these blind horrors and yet filled with a maternal pride and overwhelming love for her repulsive children. She showed them off to visitors, who looked up from the cradle speechless with distress. Cot death. Her newborn blackdog babies all lay stiff and chill. She woke up racked by helpless tears of loss.

The black dogs sniff around the book's periphery, nose through the nightmares of those closest to the author as the text and its phantasmal hounds alike draw closer to the brink of actuality. Shagfoals are seldom seen these days outside of dream. A solitary sighting in the 1970s: a motorist on the A45 found a massive shadow-dog big as a pony keeping pace with his fast-moving vehicle as it raced through the fields beside the road. Since then, though, not a glimpse. Half-real perhaps, or only solid intermittently, a creature out of Borges' bestiary that pads through the shifting wastelands at the edge of form, perpetual firelight in its flaring eye.

The Briar Hill houses are a labyrinth in the descending dusk, made unfamiliar by their powdering of snow. At last the huge white circle of the strip-mined camp presents itself, ringed round by ditch and looming ash tree, stark against the failing light. An eerie silence. Nothing stirring in the clustered homes beyond the treeline. Maybe everybody's gone.

Why did its Iron Age inhabitants abandon this place with such haste that all their brand-new corn querns were left behind? Not fire. Not plague, nor flood, nor the attack of wild beasts. Not the Romans. Something happened here. A settlement of sixty or so people tumbled out of history and into myth, more victims of the worryingly flimsy border-territories separating those two states.

Off in the twilight, men are laughing. Something runs down from the rim of the raised ditch and sits down in the snow, there in the empty campsite.

Peer myopically, then turn to Fred. `What's that?'

He frowns, trying to focus through the half-light, red brows knit.
`A dog.'

`What colour?'

Further scrutiny of the still-seated and unmoving form, that neither barks nor growls.

`Black, by the look of it.'

Two men burst from the cover of the trees, run laughing down the slope to where the shape waits motionless. One of them picks it up and slings the limp, inert weight of the animal across his shoulder, like a sack. The pair then race off chuckling across the frozen site, engulfed by shadows on the far side, gone from view. Was that a dog? If not, how did it run downhill and thirty feet across the field? Some time, thing change and come like other thing. Here, in this gloaming no man's land dividing dark from day, the chasm yawns between what happened and what never was. The certainties of history fall in, are swallowed whole. Only the anecdote, only the tale remains.

At length, we file out from the site bewildered. Past the trees, a classic view of the recumbent town, seen from the spot at which the earliest line engravings of the place were executed, although with the subject much changed between sittings. Then, church spires ruled a small cluster of low buildings. Now, a field of Pernod-coloured stars, a luckless constellation grounded by inclement weather.

Eastward is the shimmer of the new developments that have doubled Northampton's size and population over fifteen years. Blackthorn and Maidencastle, named nostalgically after whatever natural feature was paved over to create them. Bellinge. Rectory Farm and Ecton Brook. A former Eastern Bloc now simmering with malice: crack, and guns, and flamed-out cars.

Towards the west, the jaundiced earthglow of Northampton's epicentre, of the splashpoint from which the great slow rings of brick and mortar rippled out. Everything is visible from here. Lift up both hands before your face to either side and you can hold the town, its lights strung in a cat's-cradle between the outstretched fingers. Pubs and terraces. Neglected cinemas, adapted and transformed. The traffic moves, a constant toxin, through the over-burdened arteries. The cold and bright heart falters, clots of neon accumulated in the valves, but carries on, the coronary averted for the moment, a postponement only.

Drive home. Settle down to write here on Phipps' Fire Escape. It's been five years since the book was started. That was when the Galileo probe set out for Jupiter, the earliest broadcast images just now arriving on our screens: hereto unseen phenomena of gas in thrall to monstrous gravity. Beguiling comet scars. The long-anticipated landscape is at last revealed.

Some chapters back, the notion of a shaman with the town tattooed upon his skin, its boundaries and snaking river-coils become a part of him so that he might in turn become the town, a magic of association with the object bound up in the lines that represent it: lines of dye or lines of text, it makes no difference. The impulse is identical, to bind the site in word or symbol. Dog and fire and world's end, men and women lamed or headless, monument and mound. This is our lexicon, a lurid alphabet to frame the incantation; conjure the world lost and populace invisible. Reset the fractured skeleton of legend, desperate necromancy raising up the rotted buildings to parade and speak, filled with the voices of the resurrected dead. Our myths are pale and ill. This is a saucer, full of blood, set down to nourish them.

The Dreamtime of each town or city is an essence that precedes the form. The web of joke, remembrance and story is a vital infrastructure on which the solid and material plane is standing. A town of pure idea, erected only in the mind's eye of the population, yet this is our only true foundation. Let the vision fade or starve or fall into decay and the real bricks and mortar crumble swiftly after, this the cold abiding lesson of these fifteen years; the Iron Virgin's legacy. Only restore the songline and the fabric of the world shall mend about it.

Unconcerned, the site turns up its collar at the first breeze of the next millennium, attempts to play down its anxieties. The population swells, spills over into cardboard box and piss-streaked doorway. The surveillance cameras on every corner are a hard, objective record of the town's reality, admissible as evidence. If we are to refute this brutal and reducing continuity, a fiercer, more compelling fiction is required, wrung from the dead who knew this place and left their fingerprints upon its stone.

John Merrick, sitting painting by the lake at Fawsley, monstrous angel-foetus head in silhouette against the silvered waters dazzling beyond. Hawksmoor at Eastern Neston, stooped and squinting lines of ink through his theodolite; aligns the whole thing with Greens Norton church spire although nobody is certain why. Charles Wright, the Boy o' Bell Barn, moving everyone to tears with recitation at the Mutual Improvement Hall. The thieves, the whores and ditch-damp victims. Witchman, alderman and madman, magistrate and saint. We teem from the demolished slipper factories and arcades to gather in the streets of Faxton, of the villages that simply disappeared. We stand and speak our piece in our own moment, and about us fires of time and change fan out unchecked. Our words ignite upon our lips, no sooner spoken than made ash.

It is the last night of November, with the month a cold expanse of smoke and cordite and celestial signs, behind us now. The time has come to end and seal this working; to complete the story-path with absolute immersion of the teller, a commitment and a sacrifice. The moment for concluding ritual arrives, announcing itself in a change of mood and light, a sense of shapeless possibility. Up in the hazy marine dapple of the attic space, a ring of ceremonial tallow is now set to glare and slobber. In this stuttering of shine and shadow, the fixed edges of location are become ambiguous, a further loosening of the world. The information in this flickering light is that of any century.

The rite is simple, of its kind, intended only as a point of focus, a conceptual platform on which to stand amid the swirl and shift of this delusory terrain: imaginary serpents are placed at the compass points to guard against the mental snares those cardinal directions symbolize, while at the same time an appeal is made to equally symbolic virtues. Idea is the only currency in this domain, and all ideas are real ideas. A heavy language is engendered and employed to fix these images as marker buoys within the mind. This incantation and the novel both progress towards the pregnant, hanging silence of their culmination. This is how we do things here, and always have done.

Wine and passionflower and other substances of earth. Shapes painted with contorted fingers on to empty space. Deranged, of course, but then derangement is the point. Speak the desire in terms both lucid and transparent. Write it down lest it should be forgotten when the spasm hits. Deep in the stomach now the tingling approach of horrid ecstasies. A naming and a calling, and then silence. Failure. Nothing happening, and then the rush of other. Sudden heat loss and convulsion. Hurried, white-faced navigation of a loft-ladder become an Escher staircase, only managing to reach the strip-lit ultra-violet of the bathroom as the venom surges up to spill into the yawning porcelain.

Shivering and hallucinating, with an opalescent glamour now descended even on the trailing threads of sepia bile. Pale snakes of light swim through the tangled hair. Beard jewelled with vomit, and the flickering eyes rolled back. A need to spit, to drink and wash the scalding acids from the punished throat.

Downstairs, there is a curdling of the atmosphere, a thickening of presence as the evocation's final paragraphs approach. These words, as yet unwritten, are incipient in the loaded air. The television's on. Drifting across the luminous, insistent window of the screen, an image of the new Crown Court, on Campbell Square behind De Senlis' round church, penetrates the shimmer and delirium. The outcome of a murder trial, the crime occurring months back with a resident of Corby fatally assaulted in his home, all details previously withheld. The fine hairs at the nape rise up. The room grows cooler as the veil begins to tear. There's something coming through.

Shots of the relatives, grieving and haunted as they leave the court. Something about the victim's head: they couldn't find it at the crime scene. Lost for weeks until discovered underneath a hedge. Found by a black dog. Dragged across the grass and pavement, through the purpling twilight of the Corby streets, the dark jaws clenched upon a pallid, waxen tuck of cheek. The imagery is risen, chill and glittering, like a dew. One of the trophy's eyes is limp, half-closed, the grey hair caked with mud. Labrador breath, a hot and urgent whisper in the cold, deaf ear. Black jackal lips peel back, impart the snarling knowledge of Anubis, travel information for the lately dead. The head bumps through the guttered litter, nods in solemn affirmation of this grim intelligence, and knows what saints know. Round and bloody, a full stop penned in a larger hand.

A static ocean swells up, roaring in the mind. Hands raised, alarmed, into the field of vision. Gaze at incoherent characters and words that seem to crawl across the naked skin, an epidermal poetry. The lampglow is obscure and scumbled, as if filtering through smoke. There is a want of air.

Reel through the kitchen to the back door and the yard beyond, staggering out into the weed and starlight, gradually becoming calmer in the clean night breeze, beneath the slow and distant wheels of constellation. All the old, same lights. Their perfect, sombre continuity. Stand swaying here upon Phipps' Fire Escape, the promised sanctuary of the century to come, a creaking and uncertain balcony, that is not now so far above. Through roiling clouds the landings of the vanished years below, these lower floors all lost in spark or panic and devoured already. Overhead, long rags of cirrus snag upon the arc of night, an interrupted glimpse of grace through veils of fume and soot.

These are the times we dread and hunger for. The mutter of our furnace past grows louder at our backs, with cadence more distinct. Almost intelligible now, its syllables reveal themselves. Our world ignites. The song wells up, from a consuming light.

ᴺᴱᵂPERSPECTIVES

Listen to
VOICE OF THE FIRE
by Alan Moore

New Perspectives marks the 25th anniversary of Voice of the Fire with an epic new audiobook. A stunning cast narrate all twelve chapters transporting listeners to the heart of Alan Moore's Northampton.

Narrated by Mark Gatiss, Toby Jones, Aisling Loftus, Alan Moore, Pamela Nomvete, Maxine Peake and more
Directed by Jack McNamara
Composed by Adam P. McCready
Produced by New Perspectives

Available on audiobook platforms now

New Perspectives are the leading touring theatre company for the East Midlands region, creating thought-provoking dramatic work on live, digital and hybrid platforms.
www.newperspectives.co.uk

Supported using public funding by
ARTS COUNCIL ENGLAND